# THE VANISHING
# MERCENARY

TONY DALBY

DEDICATION

Thank you to my family for their patience.

*The Vanishing Mercenary* is the first of the Jamie Nelson Investigates series

Other titles are:

*The Missing Director*

*The French Artist*

All available via Amazon

# THE VANISHING MERCENARY


Tony Dalby


1


Heavy feet thumped up the wooden stairs and then materialized as a bouncer. Or someone built like one. The man growled at me, 'You the detective?'

I couldn't decide whether he was angry at something I had done, or because he'd had to climb up to my tiny office. He stood in the doorway wheezing and swaying. A bouncer with asthma. He wore a black open-neck shirt, black trousers, black shoes and had squeezed himself into a black three-quarter-length coat. He could have been an undertaker for deceased mobsters. Though the Blues Brothers wraparound shades hardly seemed respectful – even for gangsters.

'You deaf? I said are you the detective?'

'That's what it says on the panel downstairs.'

He came into the office with a bunched fist. 'I ain't got time for funny business. Are you Nelson?'

'I am,' I said, wondering why a short-tempered hood from the Bronx had washed up in southeast

England. I reached for a pen and said, 'And you are...?'

'No writing!'

I had a bad feeling about the man and the trouble he might bring but, in the circumstances, I couldn't afford to be choosy. In the three weeks my agency had been in existence, I'd only received two potential jobs: the first was a request to find a missing cat (which I turned down on account of me being allergic to them). The second was to intervene in a domestic row where both the parties had a history of alcohol-fuelled violence. As I'm a coward, I turned that down as well. Now I only had two days left before I had to get out of my cousin's office - together with my sleeping bag and other worldly possessions - because he was due to return from a "financial conference" in Marbella and didn't want me hanging around. The problem was, I'd blown all of my severance pay on setting up the agency and keeping myself alive. With my bank balance heading for a fat zero, I was desperate for any job. Even if it involved cats.

The bouncer peered over his right shoulder. I followed his gaze to my cousin's tree fern, which I remembered I should have watered. The bouncer sniffed and said, 'Anyone else here?'

Considering that (a) the office was little more than a broom cupboard; (b) even a stick insect would be obvious amongst the wilting tree fern; and (c) I didn't think the bouncer expected me to be a psychic medium, I said, 'No, there's just us.'

'Good.' He shoved a stubby paw into his inside pocket. I watch too many movies because I thought he was reaching for a gun but all he drew out was a fat white envelope. He pushed the sunglasses onto his shaved head and squinted at the writing on the envelope. He looked up and said, 'You're James Munroe Nelson?'

I nodded and tried not to look worried. Because none of my advertising had used my full name. He wasn't a tax inspector because I hadn't filed anything yet. I hadn't taken out any loans, so he wasn't a bailiff. That left the possibility that he was an enforcer for a local gang who intended to shake me down for protection money. The bouncer dangled the fat envelope in front of my face and said something rather cheering, 'Job for yer.'

In my head, birds trilled and I heard a J.S. Bach fanfare, from one of his sunnier days. Until that soundtrack scrunched to a stop when I realized that any job for this bruiser would hardly be ethical. 'What is it?' I said, trying to sound professional.

He sniffed and said, 'I was told you don't have no other cases.'

'Even so...' I was annoyed that someone had investigated me.

'Surveillance,' he said and waggled the bulky envelope again. 'Everything's inside.'

'What sort of surveillance?'

'Does it matter?'

'Yes.'

He shrugged. 'Old man. Watch where he goes, who he contacts, what he says. End of each day, you email a report to the client.'

At least that bit about the bouncer not being my client was encouraging. I said, 'Who is the client?'

'He stays out the picture.'

'Why did he pick me?'

'How the friggin' hell do I know, Nelson? Stop wasting my time. You want the job or not?'

'I need to know more.'

He struggled to control his temper. Then he said, 'The client - who stays anonymous - has rented a flat for you. For a month. He'll pay you two fifty pounds sterling a week, cash, and will reimburse reasonable, receipted expenses.' It was a memorized speech. Then he tapped the envelope and said, 'First week's here. Used notes. Untraceable.'

I was tempted. Two hundred and fifty quid would pay off my bar bill at the Rose and Crown Hotel, and still leave me some working capital. And if I span the job out, I might even earn enough to put a deposit on a flat. A small flat, admittedly. Nevertheless, the elephant still hovered above the tree fern. Namely, why had the heavies chosen me to keep tabs on an old man? So I asked him.

He growled, 'Quit stalling Nelson, I ain't got all friggin' day.' The bouncer reset the shades over his watery eyes as if to end the conversation.

I reached for the envelope but he lifted it out the way. 'Come on, Nelson, you want the job or not?'

'I'm not sure.'

The bouncer growled some more and tossed the envelope across the desk and scattered my carefully arranged pens. 'It's all in there,' he said. 'Open it and read.'

As I reached for the envelope, he put his paw over my hand, and squeezed until my finger joints popped. It hurt like hell, but I wasn't going to give him any satisfaction by yelping. He pushed his fat face close to mine. In the mirror finish of his shades, I was silhouetted against the glare of the office window. 'You try any funny business, Nelson, and I'll break your scrawny neck and dump your body where no one'll find it. We know everything about you. Understand? Everything.' He crushed my hand some more until I nodded. Then he leaned back, spat at the tree fern, powered out the office, and then thundered down the stairs.

I rubbed blood into my hand and knew that taking any job for a client who "knew everything about me" and who employed a gorilla as courier, was not the wisest career move. Not that I had much choice. I went to the window, rattled up the sash, and looked down. The bouncer was swaggering down the High Street towards Tonbridge railway station, scattering people who were out for a gossip in the September sunshine. It annoyed me that he had brought his hard-man ways to my quiet market town. Well, temporarily my town. I leaned out to watch him power over the Medway bridge. Then he was gone. Across at the Rose and Crown Hotel, the Hungarian barman was lugging out his A board announcing Lunch-Time Specials. I turned to stare at the fat envelope on the desk, wondering if I had chosen the wrong line of work after all. I went over and picked it up, half intending to mail it back to the mystery client but the only writing on it was my name. To find a return address, I would have to open the damn thing. I decided to put off making the decision and stuffed the envelope in my pocket. Then I headed for the Rose and Crown to plead with the barman to put one final lunch on my tab.

The main reason I was reluctant to take the bouncer's job was because my life had developed into a bit of a disaster area. Mainly self-inflicted, I must admit. A month previously I had been working relatively contentedly as a political analyst at the Strategic Intelligence Unit – a sort of hush, hush British government agency. Three weeks before the bouncer's visit, the SIU had sacked me. It hadn't come as a complete surprise because I had just submitted a report that was critical of the British arms dealing trade. My wife... my ex-wife, that is... always said that my downfall would come because of my "naïve honesty". My usual reply was that I preferred to sleep nights rather than worrying about what lies to tell to which people. The last time we had that conversation she'd said, "Fine, Mister Perfect. Collect your stuff and get out. This is my house and you will agree to a divorce." Ever the gentleman, I did as she asked. To be honest, it was a big relief for both of us. Initially we had reasons to marry but they had not been enduring.

Anyway, my dear ex-spouse was 100% right viz-a-viz my career. Not that I would ever admit it to her. The SIU told me they had to "let me go with immediate effect". Human Resources stripped me of my pass, my keys, my laptop, my membership of the City Gym (which I only used for coffee and the shower) and, finally, my dignity. I became a plague carrier, so I did a swift exit from the office to save embarrassment. I vowed that I would never again get involved with spooks, government agencies, or unsuitable women.

When I had emerged from my subsequent bender, I decided to set up a detective agency - using the craft MI5 and SIU had taught me. I believe it's what the HR types call Transferrable Skills. I would use my Golden Handshake from SIU to let me Right Wrongs, Reunite Lost Souls, and Champion Underdogs. Assuming it earned more than claiming government Benefit. If I was even eligible for it these days. So I set up Nelson Discreet Investigations and for a week I was full of excitement and ready for any adventure. Unfortunately, it had proved as popular as trying to sell sand to a Sheik.

.

2

Apart from the cash in the client's envelope, there was a letter telling me I was to stay at an address in the small town of Chertsey, northwest Surrey. I was to go to the florist shop half way along Guildford Street where, on the right of the shop, there would be a blue door, on the frame of which would be two buzzers marked Flat 1 and Flat 2. I was to press Flat 1 button. It was so, and I did so.

The door was wrenched open by a pot-bellied, unevenly shaven man who glared at me. When I explained who I was, he demanded identification, so I showed him the instruction letter from my client. He grunted, 'Follow', and then turned to climb the steep stairs. In dog-terms, I suppose you could say he was a bullmastiff. A few steps up he realized I wasn't following. 'Come in, Meester Nelson, shut door, and follow me to flat.' He had an East European accent and, as he plodded up, he told me he was the landlord; that he lived on the floor below my flat; and that he never went out. It didn't sound like an invitation to pop down for a cup of tea. I counted three small CCTV cameras as I went up the stairs. When we got to the top landing, there was an industrial sized one with an infrared lamp pointing directly at Flat 2 door. When I had worked in MI5, my latent paranoia was a useful asset. Now it was working overtime, telling me this case was definitely not just about surveillance. Not that I would get any info from the landlord, because he would be in the pay of my client.

When the bullmastiff opened the door, foul odors hit me. The place looked as if it had last been decorated when Margaret Thatcher was in power. Had I been paying the rent, I would have said adios and gone back down the stairs. Except I wasn't paying; I had nowhere else to stay; and I had very little cash until the client's second payment arrived. So I had to make the best of things.

From the landing, I followed the landlord into the tiny lounge where a single window looked down onto Guildford Street. Then on through to the back of the flat, where a narrow kitchen was growing fungi. Beyond, there was a tiny bathroom artistically speckled with black mildew. Between that and the lounge, a single bedroom reeked of BO and stale cigarette smoke. I threw my grip and sleeping bag on the bed and the shock made the divan part company with the headboard. The landlord either didn't notice, or didn't care. Nor did I care, because I had decided I would get fewer bites from bedbugs if I slept on the couch.

When I followed the bullmastiff back to the scruffy lounge, I saw several things that didn't fit. In the corner sat a curved 42" HD TV with sound bar, next to which was an audio dock and snazzy media center and the sort of laptop that reviewers call "top end". 'Whose are those?' I asked.

'Come with flat. OK?'

'OK.'

'Wi-Fi included. No need for password.'

After the landlord had gone, I searched every room for cameras or microphones. After seeing the CCTV cameras outside, I had a hunch the client would like to keep tabs on what I got up to inside. But I found nothing. Of course, I had been out of the Secret Service for six years and in that time technology would have evolved.

There were plenty of windows facing the flat, both front and back, but I saw no movement in any of them. It didn't reassure me. Professional watchers know how to make themselves invisible. The flat had no rear exit, so I spent time planning how to get from the kitchen window onto an extension roof and then down into a back alley - in case I had to leave in a hurry.

I used Blutack to display all the contents of my envelope on the kitchen wall. The client called himself Mr. Brown. My only contact was to send him the daily email report. The target was a George Fraser of Victory Road, Chertsey. There was a local newspaper clipping about him and the accompanying photo showed an emaciated 67 year old, with a white goatee beard and a bald head. The article said that Fraser had appealed to the Chertsey Member of Parliament to get him the military pension he had been denied. A second clipping was from the paper's editorial of the same date. In the archaic style of some local rags, it said that Fraser's case was, "symptomatic of the moral dishonesty abroad in government," and hoped that, "the forthcoming change of Prime Minister would herald a new era of caring democracy. Especially towards military personnel who had bravely taken up arms against our enemies."

Did that mean I was tailing Fraser because of his protest? That suggested Brown was working for the Social Services Fraud Office, or the Army, or MI5, or someone in government. Perhaps all of them, if someone had finally cracked how to do Joined Up Working. Nevertheless it was odd that, in the current economic climate, any of them had spare cash to hire a private investigator on such a minor protest, in sleepy northwest Surrey. Of course it was feasible that, because Fraser had involved the local MP and had complained to the local paper, Fraser was in danger of opening some Pandora's Box of ancient iniquities. But as far as I could see, Fraser had done nothing illegal. The government would have endless rules and regulations surrounding pension eligibility which would make Fraser's claim clear-cut. So I discounted the government angle. I didn't think the army would put pressure on Fraser - they were too busy fighting insurgents in foreign lands, and budget cuts at home. Which left MI5 or Social Security. MI5 was so stretched trying to keep up with potential terrorists that I reluctantly concluded it must be a Social Security operation. Which meant saying goodbye to my quixotic dream of championing underdogs.

The fourth sheet I tacked up was on headed notepaper of the *Chertsey and District Volunteer Driver Bureau.* They thanked me for agreeing to be a driver and listed dates and times when I was to pick Fraser up and taxi him to and from the hospital or shops. There was also an official NHS Volunteer badge with my name and photo. The client's attention to detail was very thorough. Worryingly so, because the photo was a copy of one I had recently sent to the Passport Office. I checked the date on the volunteer bureau letter: three days after the SIU had sacked me. Coincidence, or what? The final item was a contract from a local car rental firm, hiring me a vehicle for a month. It seemed too good to be true. And far too comprehensive for a simple fraud investigation.

Before I made contact with Fraser, I decided to find out something about the town so I pocketed the rental papers and left. Chertsey is an odd place. Once, it must have been an important hub for the surrounding villages. But with the advent of the motorways; the collapse of farming; and the rise of out-of-town retail parks it had been left high and dry. For some reason, it hadn't become gentrified like elsewhere in northwest Surrey. So it snoozed in a post war, working class, bubble. The main street was a narrow canyon of charity shops, cafés, and small independent retailers – there was even a bookshop. Though cars were parked nose to tail down one side of the street, the flagstone pavements were empty. I had a great deal of empathy with the abandoned feel of the place.

Along the main street, there were three dimly-lit pubs. The sort where the drinkers stopped what they were doing or saying as you entered, and glared at you until you retreated. In the end, I adopted the Crown Hotel in Windsor Street. It was a red brick, mock Tudor place that had a big, dusty bar room with lead lights, and a mahogany color scheme. There was real ale on the pumps, a dartboard, decent toilets, a swanky restaurant out the back that was way over my budget and, via hotel reception, a useful escape route to the rear service yard. Farther along Windsor Street was Chertsey Museum where the receptionist gave me a résumé of the area. Just inside the entrance of the building, there was a drinks machine and tables where I would be able to type up my reports. Oh, and there was a toilet. Such things are important when you are on the road. At the public library on the other side of town, the librarian was frosty until I told her I had just moved in to the area and wanted to join. I didn't let on it was only to use their broadband. The laptop in the flat was terrific, and the Wi-Fi convenient, but I knew they would have eavesdroppers. And, so that I wasn't tracked by anyone, I switched off my cellphone.

From a charity shop that was about to close, I bought a well-read Terry Pratchett paperback called *Thief of Time,* and a road map of northwest Surrey. I bought supplies in a minimarket, dumped the stuff in my flat, collected the hire car, and parked it in a street with unrestricted parking for when I would need it. Then I walked to Victory Road to get something to put in my first report.

Away from Chertsey town center, and the incongruous glass and steel office blocks near the station, most of the buildings were small, semi-detached, two-story houses. Most were Victorian redbrick with some pebble-dashed ones from the nineteen thirties. A few brash modern houses had been shoehorned in and these flaunted giant *cordyline australis* palms that waved over black and chrome Chelsea Tractors squatting on immaculate block-paving drives. Fraser's house was next to the sleepy Victory pub, on the corner of Victory Road and Station Road. On the opposite side of the road were small industrial units: a print works, a joinery, a metal dealer, that sort of thing. Behind them, a three-coach electric train clattered along the tracks towards Addlestone and Weybridge. Only the flaking paint on Fraser's windows seemed to be holding the frames together. The thick net curtains were brown with age and stained by condensation. The once-white front door was battered and grimy. Between that and the low brick wall by the pavement was a weedy no man's land. The place was shouting, "Help", though no one seemed to be listening. It wasn't the only cry for help in the street.

Outside the pub a chalkboard said faintly, "Happy Hour, 4pm to 6pm". However, I decided not to go in. If Fraser was inside, he could get twitchy when I called for him in my official capacity. Instead, I walked round the block and then stood by the joinery entrance as if waiting for a lift. I had reached chapter three of the *Thief of Time* before Fraser shuffled out of his house. He was carrying an empty beer glass and went straight to the Victory. He was inside for three minutes fifty seconds. Then he walked back home, holding a glass of Guinness before him like a holy sacrament. A bag of crisps was jammed under one arm. When the light went out in his hall, I guessed he was in for the night, so I ambled to Chertsey station to check train times and the layout, in case I needed another way out of town. A throwback from the Service training manual: "When first on assignment, examine your environment thoroughly." Then I went back to the Crown for a bar meal before returning to the flat to compose my first report, using the wonderful laptop and the Wi-Fi. After all, I didn't have anything to hide. Yet. After that, surprisingly, I slept the sleep of the innocent.

Next morning I was up early because I had to take Fraser to a mobility shop in Staines. Or Staines-on-Thames as they want people to call it now. I was about to leave, when someone pounded on the flat door. I expected the landlord but it was the bouncer. 'Client says your report was...' he screwed up his face to search his brain for the word the client wanted him to use. He came up with, '...unacceptable.' He was so proud of it, he repeated it.

'How so?' I said.

'He don't need no geography lesson, and he don't need no social comment. Says he's paying you for information he don't have, not creative friggin' writing.'

'So what doesn't he have?'

'I just deliver messages.'

'You must have some idea what he wants.'

'Squeeze him hard. Something'll pop out.'

'And how do you suggest I do that?'

'You was the one in MI5! Find out who his friends are. What his neighbors think of him. What newspaper he reads. Who he owes money to. What he moans about. What he's frightened of. Why he thinks he's owed a pension...' Each time he made a point he pulled down one of his stubby fingers. When he was still left with spare fingers he frowned. 'Oh, and find out what he intends doing if he don't get his way. Hell, I told him you were no good for this.'

'So why didn't Mr Brown take your advice?' No answer. Though it gave me something to ponder on. And something to worry about: that even the bouncer knew I had worked for MI5. The muscled messenger, after a period of inactivity, pointed a nicotine-stained finger at me, bunched his fist and then jabbed it at me. He turned and swayed away down the stairs.

I arrived in Fraser's street fifteen minutes early, though I wasted ten minutes of that going round and round the streets trying to find a parking space. When I walked back to Fraser's, the old man took ages coming to the front door, and then only opened it a crack. He looked more ancient than in his photo. And it hadn't shown his magnificent hooked nose, or the pale scar that ran down his right cheek.

He snapped, 'What you want?'

I showed him my fake ID and told him why I was there.

'Where is Michael?'

Fraser had a Balkans accent. I told him that Michael had been moved to another job. Fraser was not happy. When he discovered I had parked the car a couple of blocks away, he went crazy. Said the reason he needed transport was because he couldn't walk. I should have double-park outside, like Michael. I suppressed my irritation by reminding myself I wasn't there to champion Respect for Volunteer Workers. So I apologized and fetched the car.

Fraser didn't speak when he got in. Nor for a long time after. He wore a scabby brown leather jacket that might have been new in the seventies, jeans, and a dark peasant cap - the sort French farmers used to wear. When we were motoring along the dual carriageway to Staines I said, 'Lived in Chertsey long, Mr Fraser?'

'Yes.'

I tried again. 'I recently moved here.'

Silence.

After another mile I said, 'Didn't I see your picture in the local paper?'

Fraser turned to examine me. Then he said, 'You a reporter?'

'No.'

'Secret Police?'

I laughed, 'No. I got the sack from my London job. I'm volunteering until something turns up.'

He grunted. 'Sack? From what?'

'Oh, research. Boring stuff on Europe.' Another lengthy silence. I still had nothing to put into my report. When we got to the roundabout near Staines Bridge, I decided I might as well be direct. 'So, Mr Fraser, why won't they give you a pension?'

He thumped the car door. 'Bastard politicians. Same, whatever country.'

'But you were in the army?'

After a pause he nodded.

'Then why shouldn't you get an army pension?'

Fraser looked at me again, and then sighed. 'Not so simple.'

'How come?'

'I fought for British, but not in... proper army.'

'Oh?' I kept my questions light to suggest I was just whiling away a tedious journey. Time, though, was running out. We had crossed the Thames and were entering Staines' shopping district. Luckily, the lights outside Debenhams turned red and, as we waited, Fraser swiveled to face me. 'You keep secret?'

I shrugged, 'Sure.'

'I was mercenary. For British Army.'

We were getting somewhere at last. 'To fight?'

'Of course, to fight. What you think mercenaries do? All time my wife was alive we had plenty money. Plenty. Then she... passed over.' His eyes

16

moistened and he gulped. 'So benefits disappeared... pouf!' He waved his hand as if to clear smoke. 'Then I thought, I have British passport, I fought for British, I should have British Army pension.'

'But they turned you down?'

'Said I do not qualify. Bastards. I sure qualified to do their dirty work.'

I wanted to ask what sort of dirty work but I thought it might frighten him off, so I waited, hoping he would tell me more. The lights changed. Fraser said, 'I went to see local MP. People told me he was good man. He listened and said he thought I should get pension. Said he would raise my case with right department.'

'And?'

'Nothing. So I went back to see him. This time he said, "I have been advised by the Secretary of State that you have no case." Exactly those words. Said if I tried to claim what I am not entitled to, they would put me in prison.'

'Did he say why you had no case?'

'I had not been "a regular serving member of Her Majesties armed forces".'

'Even though he knew you were a mercenary for the British?'

'Yes.'

'When were you a mercenary?'

'Long time ago.'

'How long?'

He got angry, 'Mister, you not here to ask questions, you here to drive. There is the place, on the left. Drop me and come back in one hour.' I turned into a side street, pulled up on the double yellow lines in front of the mobility center and, when he had gone in, I went into town to find somewhere to park. I grabbed a takeaway sandwich and a coffee and took them to a grassy area by the Thames. A cold wind shuddered up the river from the east and rippled the brown water. It was obvious that someone in the government had told the MP to distance himself from Fraser. I wondered who would have that authority. And why would they put that pressure on.

On the journey back Fraser would say nothing so, after dropping him at his house, I went to the library to read up on British Army policy towards mercenaries. There wasn't much. A 1989 addition to the Geneva Convention had banned their use, though few states had actually ratified the protocol. A British Green Paper of 2002 had attempted to regulate what it euphemistically called "Private Military Companies". There was a lot of verbiage about their historical significance and how useful they might be in helping to react swiftly to future international crises if the standing army had to be further reduced due to budget constraints. In evidence to the Select Committee on Foreign Affairs, the Foreign and Commonwealth Office were vague about PMCs but never went so far as to request a ban. The military seemed to keep very quiet. Possibly because they were already using them. The Green Paper came to nothing. There was no follow up, so things remained a fuzzy status quo.

Thirty minutes prior to when Fraser had walked to the Victory the previous night, I was sitting in a corner of its bar room. Technically, Happy Hour. A small TV near the ceiling gabbled news of a massacre in a part of the world the news anchor couldn't pronounce. The substantial bar woman leaned on the counter, reading a Metro newspaper

18

open at the entertainment pages. In another corner of the bar room two morose workers sipped pints of lager and divided their time between scowling at the TV and at me. I eked out my Guinness and immersed myself in the curious deeds of Pratchett's History Monks.

Twenty-five minutes later Fraser entered, bearing his empty glass. I got up and offered to buy him a pint. At first, he didn't know who I was, and then he was suspicious. I said my flat was close and I was trying out the local boozers. He let me pay for his beer and crisps, and then he reluctantly joined me at my table. I nattered; he wouldn't respond. I bought him a second pint, and he began to moan about the bastards in government. Followed by the bastards in the British army. Oh, and the bastard way the British system treated ordinary people. Suddenly his eyes narrowed, 'You sure you not reporter?'

I shook my head, 'I have never worked for the media.'

He shut his eyes and sighed. 'Listen, mister, I make this bloody protest because I got nothing to lose. I tell bastard MP: if government refuse to give me army pension, then I talk. I know things, from my time as mercenary with British Army. Things they frightened will come out. I make such a stink that...' He stopped when he realized what he was saying. He got up, and then left without finishing his beer or taking his crisps.

When the door stopped rattling the bar lady said, 'Don't bother trying to be friendly with that one.' She wiped the spotless counter either side of her newspaper. 'Like most people round here, he keeps hisself to hisself.' I took that to be my first Oral Warning. I raised my glass to show I understood. I read twenty more minutes of Pratchett - in case she (and the two workmen who had hardly touched their drinks) got the impression I was only there to see Fraser. Then I left. I posted Fraser's packet of crisps through his letterbox, returned to the flat and padded out the meagre scraps I had gained for my second report. Though I omitted the bit about someone, possibly in the government, being frightened if Fraser made a stink. Because I intended to find out some more about that first.

Next morning, there was no bouncer on the landing, so presumably the client had learnt something from my report, or thought I was asking the right questions. Possibly the slow-drinking "workmen" in the Victory were not workmen at all, but on Mr Brown's payroll, to check how proactive I was being. Anyway, the day's task was to take Fraser to the local general hospital for an eleven a.m. appointment at the Outpatient clinic. I double-parked outside his house to put him in a good mood, but the plan failed because he remained silent the entire journey. When I dropped him at the front entrance of the hospital, all he grunted was, 'Be in reception. One hour and half. OK?'

I said OK. He left. I parked the car. None of which was any use for my next report.

In hospital reception, I killed time browsing the rack of second-hand paperbacks. I bought a dog-eared *Ascent of Man* by Jacob Bronowski mainly for its first paragraph: "Man is a singular creation. He has a set of gifts which make him unique among the animals; so that, unlike them, he is not a figure in the landscape - he is a shaper of the landscape." I was relieved the good Doctor thought I was that capable. Currently, I didn't share his confidence. I took the book to a vacant seat and read for a while, hoping he would offer more encouragement. He didn't, so I did a tour of the hospital to get my bearings. I finished at Outpatients and asked a stressed but attractive nurse how long Fraser would be. She estimated fifteen minutes. I went down to the café in reception. Around me, patients staggered in and out; medical staff marched along burdened with case files and problems; and cleaners followed their machines like zombies. The only things that didn't fit were the two security guards near the front doors. Not because they were security guards per se, but because they kept staring at me. It wasn't because of the car - I had paid their exorbitant parking fee and was well within the parking bay lines. I had shaved that morning, so they couldn't say I was a vagrant. I wasn't wearing a baseball cap or a hoody. I didn't think I looked a threat to anyone.

Coming down the escalator, I saw the blonde Outpatient nurse I had spoken to. Her hair was scragged back from her pale, sad face so I wouldn't say she was conventionally pretty. Nevertheless, she had a certain... sparkle. She wore no wedding ring, so I decided that if she came into the café, I would speak to her. It was time I reacquainted myself with women. Nothing serious. Divorce, and a recent unfortunate episode involving a Russian girl, had made me wary.

Nursey headed for the café and smiled as she passed my table. My heart flipped like a post-pubescent schoolboy's but I looked over my shoulder to make sure she hadn't been making eyes at a dishy doctor. When I saw the empty tables behind me, I felt stupid. I turned back, intending to say something light-hearted or vaguely intelligent but she had already gone to the servery. I was perfecting a chat-up line when I noticed that the security guards were heading straight for me.

The tall, thin one led. He had a chin like a chisel; cheekbones that tensioned his facial skin to snapping point; and eyes that would have won prizes for Prolonged Intimidating Staring. The short one trotting behind him had Asian roots, was developing a paunch and he was biting his lip. Which I took to be nerves. Why?

Chisel barked, 'Name?'

He irritated me, though I was more annoyed that he might ruin my chances with the nurse, so I just pointed to my volunteer's badge.

He read it. 'Mr Jamie Nelson. Just so. Come with us. Please. Sir.'

The "please" and "sir" were afterthoughts. As if someone had told him to be polite against his nature. I had no reason to go with him, so I didn't move.

The short one cleared his throat, 'It really won't take long, Mr Nelson. Our supervisor would like a very quick word with you.'

I still didn't move.

'You've done nothing wrong.'

'I'm waiting for a patient,' I said.

'This is about him,' said the short one. 'Mr Fraser? Mr George Fraser... of Victory Road?'

I frowned and looked at them again. Had the old boy croaked it? No, the nurse would have said something and she certainly wouldn't have smiled. Perhaps Fraser had lodged a complaint that I was harassing him. Or were these goons part of the investigation I was harnessed to? Frankly, I didn't give a damn. I had no wish to be involved with the mechanics of the operation. I intended to do the minimum necessary to claim my fee. Right now though, I needed to get a date with the nurse. 'Look, guys,' I said, 'I'm just a driver. I bring patients here, I wait, I take them home.'

'We appreciate that,' said the short one. 'However, it is... uh, vitally important that you come with us. We estimate Mr Fraser will finish at Outpatients in ten minutes. What our supervisor has to say to you will only take five.'

They knew what they were talking about. I checked them for ID. On their white shirt pockets was the word "Security" stitched in dark blue. They had radios in their belt holsters; they had black trousers and black shoes like every other security guard in the universe... but nothing told me who they were, or who they worked for. 'Mind telling me your names?' I said.

'You don't need to know,' snarled chisel. Then he did jaw exercises to show me how many muscles he possessed. More, probably, than the total number synapses in his brain. 'Come on, Nelson, you're wasting our time.'

And I was tired of being pushed around. The reason I became an investigator was so I could make my own decisions – run life my own way. I looked round for the nurse and saw her having change counted into her palm. 'Some other time,' I said. 'I'm busy.' I stood, intending to intercept the nurse, but Chisel grabbed my arm.

The Asian guy squeaked, 'Go easy Toby.'

'I will, if Nelson co-operates.'

As the nurse walked towards the escalator, she bit into a chocolate bar. 'Back to the grindstone,' she called to me with a lopsided, chocolaty grin.

I smiled back, despite the pain from Chisel's grip. I watched the smooth, confident way her body moved. Beneath the stretched uniform, I could see the impression of her bra straps and panties. 'See you soon,' I called.

'Not,' said Chisel/Toby, 'Until you've seen the boss.'

I laughed. It might have worked in *The Big Sleep* but not in a hospital in Surrey. I turned to face him. 'How plain do you need the message, "Toby"? Piss off. I've a life to re-organize.' I made to follow the nurse but the man jerked me back, gripped my other arm, and frogmarched me across the lobby to the white swing doors marked, "NO ENTRY. STAFF ONLY".

Chisel growled, 'Adam! Get the doors!'

Adam trotted ahead, opened one of the doors, and then held it as Chisel bundled me into the corridor. When Adam pulled the door shut, I struggled to get free. The man called Toby slammed me against the wall and drove his forearm up against my throat so I had to stand on tiptoes to breathe. The peppermint he had recently sucked failed to mask his bad breath. 'Don't push me Nelson. All you have to do, is walk down this corridor, and listen to what the man says. You got a problem with that, take it up with him, not out on me. OK?'

I didn't answer, so he bounced me against the wall to loosen my tongue. 'Understand?'

I gargled, 'Yes'. There was no reason to get hurt. The man was a professional. Of sorts. The Asian guy, Adam, used his shirtsleeve to wipe sweat from his forehead, and then he cleared his throat. 'This isn't the way we do things, Toby.' Chisel ignored him, pulled me upright, and then pushed me into a walk.

I wondered whom the "we" were, who didn't do things that way. I was certain they were not hospital security. And they seemed too melodramatic for the Department of Work and Pensions fraud section. Police, then? Special Branch and Serious Crime liked a bit of rough stuff. Although they tended to shout a lot, and at least one of them would have flashed their police ID. That left three other possibilities: undercover cops, organized criminals, or spooks. None of the options filled me with joy.

I tried again. 'Who wants to see me?'

No answer.

'Who do you work for?'

'Give it a rest Nelson. Just walk.'

Adam came alongside and said, 'You'll understand when we get there, Mr Nelson. Really, it won't take long.'

I decided not to push up my blood pressure. I would listen to their man and then tell him to get lost. I'd return to Outpatients, ask the nurse to have a drink with me when her shift finished, collect Fraser and go home to change.

The corridor we were walking down was clinically white, though with the usual behind-the-scenes scruffiness. The florescent tubes glared down on the medical equipment that had been stacked on battered trolleys lining one wall. At intervals, NHS notices were Sellotaped to the paint: "Do not leave equipment here"; "Switch off unnecessary lights"; and "Do Not Tolerate Abuse." Was that irony? Our jerky shadows marched along as if we were marionettes. Then Chisel pulled me to a stop outside door M141. Adam straightened his back and knocked.

'Enter!'

The voice from inside sounded old-school Civil Service. Imperious and irritated in equal measure. Adam opened the door and Toby shoved me so hard I stumbled into the room. "The boss" sat behind a battered steel desk. He wore a well-cut pinstriped suit, a new white shirt, and an old school/ regimental/ club tie. His thin brown hair was greased-back and receding. He had small, piggy eyes. He was resting his chin on his steepled hands and was pretending to read the documents that were spread across the desk in front of him. Behind me, I heard the door shut. Through the window, I saw traffic flow down the ramp to the hospital car park. Somewhere, far off, a phone rang incessantly.

The man breathed in deeply through his nose, and then let it out as a sigh. He looked up. 'So... James Nelson.' He pasted on a wintry smile. 'I asked you here, because I need your help in a little matter of, shall we say, national security.'

3

As soon as I saw the pinstriped Civil Servant, I knew we had met somewhere, though I couldn't remember when or where. Possibly at one of the endless meetings with government departments trying to discern what they actually wanted from the Service (and later SIU) rather than expecting us to guess. There again, I may have bumped into him at a London pub, and I only remembered his face because he owed me a drink. Whatever, now he wanted me to think he was Someone of Extreme Importance.

'Do, please, sit, Mr, uh, Nelson.' The man who used many commas waved his white hand at the paint-spattered, grey plastic chair on my side of the desk. I only did as he asked because I wanted to conclude the business swiftly. His smile continued to show, though it spread no further than his thin, bloodless lips.

I said, 'So, what's this all about?'

The man spread his hands. 'In the circumstances, I would rather not go into details.'

'What "circumstances"?'

'I am not at liberty to say.'

'Then perhaps you can tell me why your goons dragged me here?'

His lip-smile faded. 'Had you co-operated, there would have been no cause to "drag" you anywhere.'

'You still haven't said why I'm here.'

'Let us say, we need your help to speed up our operation.'

'What operation?' It didn't make sense until I twigged that the man in front of me was my anonymous client. 'Are you Brown?'

He raised his eyebrows and pursed his lips. 'Not very quick, Mr Nelson, knowing your background. Though I suppose you eventually reached the correct conclusion.'

Brown wouldn't be his real name. Even so, it was easier than calling him "The pompous twat in Room 141". I said, 'Why the interest in Fraser?'

'Forgive my bluntness, Nelson, but that is none of your business.' He so enjoyed playing the Big I Am.

'Then how about telling me what this "speeding up" involves?'

'Merely that, when you take Fraser home in a few minutes time, you will use this route.' He pushed an A4 sheet across the desk towards me. It was a roadmap of the local area. His carefully manicured fingernail followed a road highlighted in yellow. It went a longer way round than I had come. Presumably to keep the old man out the way while they searched his house. Or bug it. Or to plant "evidence" that would scupper his credibility and negate his pension claim. Presumably the house team had moved in as soon as I had driven Fraser away. But something had gone wrong, so Brown needed more time. Playing dumb I said, 'How can going the long way back speed things up?'

Brown took a slow inward breath before he spoke. 'Perhaps I should remind you, Nelson, that you are the hired hand, and I am the paying client? The accepted practice is that I give the orders, and you obey. No discussion. No delay. You are, after all, being paid above the market rate.'

'But why mess him about? He's just a harmless old guy.'

'Not quite as harmless as he would have you believe.'

'Care to tell me why?'

'No.'

'Then I'm sorry, Mr... Brown, I'm doing nothing underhand.'

'Come on Nelson. All we need...'

'I mean it. Find someone else.' I stood.

Brown raised his eyebrows. 'You are impersonating a volunteer driver. Is that not being underhanded?'

I sat. Brown was from the SIS or the Security Service. Or, rather, MI5, as he was obviously managing a team in the UK. Which meant the plan he was following would have been thrashed out by teams of experts in soundproofed meeting rooms. Carefully building in safeguards to prevent outcomes they didn't want. Such as me being difficult. I needed to be careful.

Brown said, 'If you need more incentive, how about this? A colleague recently had the good fortune to recover some technological goods. Items stolen from a dyspeptic High Court judge. You may have seen them? A fairly decent plasma screen, a laptop, that sort of thing. Usefully, they have your fingerprints on them.'

He meant the equipment in the flat. I had been stupid to fiddle with them.

Brown went on, 'Do as I ask, and the items will be cleaned before they are delivered to the local police station. If you fail to co-operate, CID will discover a fingerprint match.'

'I don't have a police record.'

'Au contraire. Our clever backroom boys have inserted a file in the national fingerprint recognition database. It will allow the police to link you to the death of a Russian national called Tatyana Olizarenko. I believe you knew her rather intimately?'

'Bastard,' I said.

Brown waved his hand as if a fly had invaded his airspace. 'I am not asking you to do anything illegal, Nelson. For a few minutes work you will get your full month's fee. You may consider our contract completed at...' he looked at his expensive wristwatch, '... shall we say one p.m. today?'

I decided to squeeze something more from him. 'And I keep the flat for the month?'

Brown frowned but said, 'If you must.'

'What about the car?'

'Don't push your luck, Nelson.'

'Before I agree, I need to know what Fraser has done.'

Brown considered this before he said, 'We are more concerned about what he might do.'

That suggested I was part of a damage limitation exercise to neutralize or - at the very least - hush Fraser. I'd had nothing to do with Tatyana's death but, because the Metropolitan Police Specialist Crimes Directorate were making no headway finding her killer, they had let me know they didn't believe my alibi. If I upset the Service too much, they could plant evidence that would send me to jail. Even so, I didn't intend going along with Brown's plan willingly. I said, 'Tell me more.'

'You know all you need. From the gentleman's own mouth.'

I was about to protest that he hadn't told me anything of substance. Then I realized the only way Brown knew that I knew, was because they had bugged the hire car. And probably the "workmen" in the Victory were MI5 agents.

Brown turned to look out the window. He drawled, 'The powers-that-be hoped the problem would go away if they kept Fraser at arm's length. As usual, they miscalculated. Fraser appears rather desperate, so he could become... rash. We have clearance to... remove the risk.'

'Risk to whom?'

'You know better than that, old boy.' Brown tapped the side of his nose. 'No names, no pack-drill. "Theirs not to reason why; theirs but to do and die".' He turned to face me again and switched on his lifeless smile. 'Come now... Jamie. Your reports say you can be intelligent. Use your brain.'

I remained silent.

So did he.

To break the stalemate I said, 'Why me?'

'The JISC gets edgy if we stray from authorized mission protocols. You used to be in the firm. SIU is virtually in the fold. You are kosher and now you are freelance. What's the big deal? All I need you to do is drive Fraser slowly along that route and then you can go to ground and blow your fee on booze. I believe that is what happened when you left SIU? Forget Fraser ever existed and leave it all to the grown-ups.'

At least I knew who Brown was now. JISC was the

Joint Intelligence and Security Committee - the cross-party government body that monitored and funded the secret services. Therefore, Brown was an MI5 controller who had been tasked to remove an inconvenient itch. If Brown thought I knew why Fraser was a problem, it meant someone important was worried about repercussions from that mercenary job. An assistant in the Parliamentary Office must have noticed the newspaper article, done some research, flagged it up, and the result was that MI5 had arrived mob-handed with the cleaners. I should have been more alert. There had been all the signs of a Service-led, covert operation: complicated set up; money no object; hyped-up operatives; and blind allegiance to the cause.

When I first joined the Service, I had reveled in such gung-ho, team-games crap. Then the repetition and the skewed reality got to me and I had to leave before my brain was permanently messed up. Now I was determined not to let them suck me in again. Apart from my golden handshake, the only positive thing about being sacked from SIU was that I could choose what I did. And who I did it with. That meant refusing to work with spooks. I was about to tell this one to go to hell, when a thought struck me. Had MI5 organized my dismissal? It would make sense of the date on the volunteer bureau letter, and the use of my passport photo. 'We've met before,' I said, studying his face. 'Where was it?'

'London,' he drawled, 'is a collection of villages. Eventually, you see familiar faces.'

He made it sound like a quote but I wasn't in the mood for literary quizzes. Of course, he didn't have to be Service. He could be from a hush-hush unit in the Executive or the Ministry of Defence. Not that it really mattered. At best, Fraser was on his way to protective custody at some remote army barracks. Behind me, I heard scratchy talk in an earpiece. Toby said, 'The target is leaving.'

Brown stood. 'Be realistic Nelson, there's a good chap. I am perfectly aware this is your only case. I also know you are not able to return to your cousin's office in Tonbridge. You have virtually no money, you have no friends, and nowhere to live. What sort of life is that?'

'It'll get better.'

'Only if I allow it, Mr Nelson.'

I closed my eyes, hoping it was all a bad dream.

'Come now,' said Brown, trying to placate me. 'You were with us once. All I ask is that you scratch our back. Then, we won't scratch out your eyes.'

Ho ho, very funny. Once the Service gets its hooks into you, you are doomed.

He went on, 'You really shouldn't let ethics get in the way of... what is it the costermongers say? "A nice little earner."?'

Poser. I hadn't heard the term "costermonger" since I had studied Victorian Novels at college. However, he was right about one thing - I did need the money. And somewhere to sleep. Would it be so bad to drive Fraser the long way to his house? It wasn't illegal. Or immoral. I wasn't responsible for what Fraser had done in in the past. Besides, it would give the old boy an outing in the countryside. I wasn't any good trying to rationalize it, though. The operation was seedy and it was disturbing a recently bereaved man who needed hospital treatment. So I still said nothing.

'For god's sake, Nelson, get off your stupid high horse before you fall.'

Chisel/Toby said, 'He's reached the top of the escalator.' That meant someone else was on location... maybe two.  See what I mean about money being no object?

As I approached the roundabout at the hospital perimeter, I positioned the car in the right-hand lane instead of the left and Fraser sat up.  'You going the wrong way.'

I said, 'Fancied a different road back.  It won't cost you any more.'  Not that Fraser was paying.

The old man looked at me, and then twisted round to see if anyone was laying in the back foot well.  There wasn't, because I had already checked.  And in the boot.   I took the first exit from the next roundabout signed "M25 and Weybridge".  That put me on Brown's yellow-marked road.  The speed was derestricted so I put my foot down and was soon doing seventy.  No reason to make Brown's job easy.  The traffic lights at the roundabout over the motorway changed to red, so I braked.  Fraser wound down the window and looked back.  When I checked the rear-view mirror, I could see nothing suspicious.  Just a line of cars and vans behaving themselves.  The lights turned green.  I took the exit for Chertsey and had just swapped to the left hand lane when a black 4x4 Audi with smoked rear windows raced past.  It swerved in front of me, and then braked hard.  At the same time, a mud-splashed, green Range Rover came alongside my right.  In the passenger seat was the bouncer.  He held up a sheet of paper on which was scrawled the words, 'PULL OVER'.

'Secret Police!' yelled Fraser.  'Go faster!'

I couldn't push the Audi out the way; there was no hard shoulder on the left; and the Range Rover blocked my right side.  Behind, traffic was tailgating me.  Our procession decelerated to fifteen miles an hour, then ten.  Cars hooted us.  The Audi put on its emergency flashers and slowed some more. I had two options: go along with the hijack; or find a way out. The Range Rover sped ahead of the Audi and the line of cars behind began to pass. I checked the rear-view mirror. On the roundabout, the lights must have changed because no more traffic was approaching. As the last car passed me, I stamped on the brake and clutch and Fraser nearly hit his head on the dash. Then I slammed the gearshift into second, rammed the accelerator pedal to the floor, and let the clutch up. The car bucked, my tires squealed and, before anyone could react, I screamed past the Audi and the Range Rover. I changed up to third, thumped the accelerator back down, and then went into top. I reached the cars that had overtaken me and I weaved between them to get in front. Then I caused more horns to blare when I cut in front of them at the next roundabout, to take the Chertsey exit. The Audi was catching up so I jumped a red light at the next junction and yanked the steering wheel left to take the left fork. When I heard a police siren, I searched for a residential road to hide in on the left.

The first was a dead end so I roared on to the next. I skidded into it, went halfway up, parked on someone's drive, and pushed Fraser down. The Audi sped along the main road towards the town center. Followed by two police cars. Despite my heart pounding as if it would give out, I chuckled. One up to the good guys. Fraser unfolded. He looked white and haunted. He said, 'I thought you were with them. The Secret Police.'

'No,' I said. 'Are they after you?'

Fraser snarled, 'You driver, not interrogator.'

'You've been interrogated?'

Fraser nodded.

'Why?'

He didn't reply. I heard another police siren so I reversed out the drive, and then drove slowly away from the main road. I turned right, and cruised past the Victory. A battered blue Volvo was parked outside Fraser's together with an anonymous white transit van. Now what? I decided to carry on to the station, park there, and consider my options. I may have kissed goodbye to seven hundred and fifty quid and the flat, but I felt oddly elated. At the end of the road, I turned left towards the station but that was my big mistake. A police car shot out of the station car park and blocked the road in front of the level crossing. An officer leapt out and, in B movie fashion, held up her hand to stop me. In my rear-view mirror, I saw another police car approaching from the town, its headlights flashing, and the blues on the roof pulsing.

'You better stop,' said Fraser. 'No way out.'

In the mirror, I saw the black Audi overtake the police car. There were rubbernecking pedestrians on both pavements, so I couldn't risk doing an *Italian Job* to escape. Nor could I get round the police in front because the level crossing barrier had come down.

Fraser said, 'Thank you for trying, Mr Nelson.' As he undid his seatbelt, he leaned towards me, cupped his hands round my ear, and whispered, 'If anything happens to me, feed my pigeons.'

'What?'

'Feed... my... pigeons.' Then he got out and walked to the police officer. The Audi came alongside me. Brown was driving and he levelled his first and second fingers at me and pulled an imaginary trigger. Then he edged his car forward and stopped next to Fraser. The Chisel jumped out, dragged Fraser out of my car, and bundled the old man into the back of the Audi. The uniformed police officer protested and

Brown produced some documentation. The officer was still not convinced. Brown got someone on his cellphone, and then handed it to the officer to listen. A train whined and clacked across the crossing. Then the officer nodded to whoever it was on the phone and handed the instrument back to Brown. The officer went to look into the Audi at Fraser and the bouncer, then she turned around and walked away. The level crossing opened; Brown returned to the driving seat of the Audi; and then revved the engine. The police car unblocked the crossing and Brown and Co. scarpered in a cloud of exhaust and tire smoke, heading for the motorway.

The incident had put the police in a foul mood and they dearly wanted to charge me with dangerous driving except it was evident they hated taking orders from spooks and decided I was not one. Even so, they took their time searching the hire car, and examining my documents. They also had their control run my name through their databases while they breathalysed me and took mouth swabs to test for drugs. When everything came back negative, they thought they might as well check my tires and lights. Thankfully, the care hire company had done a good job so, displaying a distinct lack of good grace, the police eventually let me go, with a warning to drive more carefully.

I returned to the flat in Guildford Street because I had nowhere else to go. Though the high tech gadgets had gone, the toaster and kettle were still in the kitchen, so I made myself tea and peanut butter on toast, and considered my next move. The police hadn't said anything about stolen goods, or murder enquiries, so I assumed Brown was keeping those threats as his insurance. Meaning that if I was a good boy and said nothing, I could keep my fee and live in the flat for a month. Trouble was, I didn't intend letting things lie. The spooks had abducted a frail old man, and they had dragged me into it. The least I could do was find out what was going on and, ideally, get the old boy released. But where would I start? By now, Fraser's house would have been stripped - or evidence "found". The bar woman at the pub had said he kept himself to himself so she wouldn't be much help. That left the hospital. There was an outside chance he may have let something slip to the outpatient nurse. I warmed to the idea. If I played my cards right, she might still agree to a date.

As spooks were involved, I took out my own insurance and bought a Pay As You Go phone in the name of Nicholas Apollinaris. It had been one of the MI5 covers I had never used and somehow I had forgotten to hand the paperwork in when I resigned. Hopefully, no one would still be around to twig it was me.

Outpatients was deserted but then it was after four. I hallooed into the corridor that said Staff Only, but no one replied. Before the person watching the hospital CCTV screens got suspicious, I marched into the staff area as if I had a right to be there. I had a vague plan that the patient records might give me a clue. If I could find them. The first room seemed to be an examination room. From that, a door led to a consulting room. I was about to open a desk drawer in there when I heard someone enter.

'What are you doing?'

It was my nurse. She had unbunched her hair so that it framed her face. On the fanciable register, she had gone up to an eight. When she recognized me, she frowned. 'I saw you earlier. You're not allowed in here. Clinic's over.'

I had to decide whether to lie or to involve her. I didn't want her to get hurt so I said, 'Mr Fraser thought he left his keys here.'

'If he did, they would be at reception in Lost Property. If you don't leave immediately, I'll call security.'

Then she remembered who she had seen me with in reception. 'Hang on. Do you work in security?' She got angry. 'You've been told before; medical areas are out of bounds unless there's a security issue.'

I held up my hand. 'I'm not hospital security. Though I am investigating Mr Fraser.'

'Show me your warrant card or whatever it is.'

'I'm a private investigator.'

She looked at me with a sour expression. 'Working for whom?'

I wish I knew. 'The government, indirectly. But, look, I am concerned about Fraser. Something happened to him... after we left the hospital.'

'What?'

I ignored the question. 'Can you tell me why he comes here?'

'Of course not,' she said. 'Haven't you heard of patient confidentiality?'

I nodded and started to leave. At the door, I turned and said, 'Sorry we met this way. Can I buy you a drink when you're off duty? To apologize?'

'No. Now go.'

Oh well. The best laid plans of mice and men etc. etc.

In the lobby of the hospital I used the payphone to ring my ex-boss, the SIU director, Sergey Salnikov. Luckily, he was still in his office. I said, 'It's me.'

'Who is "me"?'

'Jamie.'

'This… is not a good time.' He sounded wary.

'Sergey, I need a favor. Can you access N°·3 database to find out what it has on a George Fraser. White Caucasian, British Citizen, naturalized. Born in or near the Balkans. Age mid-sixties and about five five.' I told him the address.

He said, 'Why should I do that?'

'To pay me for all the unbilled hours I put in? Look, the old boy's in trouble. Gone missing. Our friends who live by the Thames might be involved.'

My ex-boss swore in Russian. Then he said, 'Which side of the river?'

'North. So I just want to...'

'Why you?'

'Uh?'

'Why are you involved?'

'It's a long story but, I promise, I'm doing nothing illegal. Can we meet? Then I'll...'

'I am about to leave for home. With regret, Jamie, I cannot help. Please do not contact me again.' He put his handset down.

I stood there for a while, thinking. Sergey had never been so abrupt, even when angry. Something was wrong. Before he defected, he had held a senior post in the KGB, so he could take plenty of stress. I also knew from experience that he wouldn't be pushed around. In the six years I had worked for SIU, I had never heard him be so negative. Of course, there had been plenty of time for MI5 to get to him. Unless he was just plain guilty that he had given me the push. I decided that we needed to meet face to face.

Sergey lived in a small house on the edge of Weybridge - a gift from the government of the day for all the Soviet intelligence he had delivered. I had been there a few times for heads of department drinkies. He had a youngish wife, a daughter at college, and a son at secondary school so I had to be careful I didn't get them into trouble. Salnikov commuted by train and always walked home down the hill from the station. His house faced open common land with heathland and woods nearby. If I used the trees for cover, I could check whether anyone was watching the house.

I parked the car at the Hand and Spear pub near Weybridge station, and worked my way down the hill through the heathland. Any moment, I expected a Surrey matron to appear, walking a Shih Tzu called Hermione, and demanding to know why I was skulking. My cover story was that I was a researcher at the University, monitoring endangered heathland Lepidoptera. Creative, though it would only work if no one asked me which specific butterflies were endangered. Or why I didn't have a net. I hoped Sergey had left the office when he had said, and hadn't stopped for a drink; otherwise, I was in for a long skulk. I told myself I was being professional. Making sure I didn't compromise the subject. It didn't help much. Every minute wasted meant Fraser was further away. And deeper into MI5's web.

When the trees thinned, I could get a good view of Salnikov's house and the grassy open space it faced across the road. I studied all the parked cars. Only one showed signs of life: the familiar beat-up, blue Volvo estate, in a small car park across the green. The driver was inside, resting the zoom lens of a DSLR camera on top of the steering wheel. The lens was pointing at Sergey's house. I looked there. No movement. I looked at the Volvo driver. Motionless. Waiting for Sergey. Or me. Or both.

I didn't think Sergey would have ratted to MI5, so that probably meant the government was still keeping him under surveillance. I backtracked up the hill, watching the road for Sergey, or more watchers. There were no parked cars, though, nor anyone loitering. When I reached the top of the hill, I sat in a bus shelter and waited for Sergey. After each train arrived, a platoon of commuters marched down the hill towards the town. After the fourth trainload and no Sergey, I began to worry. A bus turned up and the queue of commuters that had built up in the shelter seemed uncomfortable that I wouldn't get on. 'It is the only service, you know,' said a stressed middle-age gent in a sharp suit with red handkerchief, red braces, and red cheeks. I thanked him but said I was waiting for a lift. As he climbed aboard he growled, 'Then you shouldn't be waiting in a bus shelter.' Tsk tsk, I had broken another rule.

Eventually, I saw Sergey walk over the road bridge from the down platform. He had aged. The beard he was trying to grow made him look like a down-at-heel European aristocrat. I tried to work out if anyone was following him but, as most of the commuters walked at the same speed, in the same direction, and all had the same hangdog expression, I had no way of telling. I crossed the road and started to walk slowly down the hill, ahead of Sergey's platoon. The first clockwork soldier soon overtook me. When Sergey came alongside, I speeded up. 'There's someone watching your house,' I said. 'Blue Volvo'.

He jumped and glared at me over his steel-rimmed glasses.

'Don't look at me,' I said. 'Someone might be following.'

'I told you no contact,' he growled, though he did

look away.

'Did you tell MI5 I rang?'

'Of course not. What is all this?'

I didn't want a Q&A session so I said, 'MI5 hired me to do surveillance on an old man. Now they've abducted him.'

My ex-boss snorted.

I said, 'I want to find out who this George Fraser is. And where they have taken him.'

'So you can ride in like a Cossack and rescue him?'

'I just need to know what's going on.'

'Still searching for your mythical Truth?' said Sergey. 'I am surprised you did not learn your lesson with that arms report.'

I said, 'Did MI5 tell you to sack me?'

'I told you. The government cut our funding. Someone had to go.'

'Who suggested me?'

He didn't answer. Sergey had not slowed his pace, which meant we would soon be in view of the watcher in the Volvo.

I said, 'Why are you under surveillance?'

Eventually he said, 'They wish to remind me I am still a liability. Twice a year they send someone with a camera. They stay a few days, and then they vanish. Your intelligence services have never trusted me.'

Back when Sergey had defected, the government had been delirious at catching such a senior Soviet agent. Then they began to worry that he might defect again. Taking our juicy titbits with him. 'Look, Sergey, if Fraser's a sleeper, or a terrorist, I'll forget everything. But I have an idea it's because the old man is irritating a politician. I won't keep quiet about that. Didn't you leave the Soviet Union to get away from political corruption?'

'Only the secure can talk of principles, my friend.

Why not find a job in tourism, or sales? Forget all this.'

I could now see part of the green. 'Sergey, you owe me. They're throwing big money at this. Just see what you can find and I'll promise not to contact you again.'

'Where is the surveillance unit?'

I told him.

He nodded. 'Once I thought of taking them tea and sandwiches. Until I realized it would not be... playing cricket. It would make them suspicious. So now, as long as I keep everything routine, they do not worry. Please, Jamie, leave me in peace.'

'Will you look at the database?'

'If I can. Then you must stay away. I wish to retire to Cornwall.'

I thanked him and told him to email anything he found to the Crown Hotel, Chertsey, marked for the attention of Mr Apollinaris. But not from work. From the internet café near Farringdon station.

'As you wish. Now go.'

I stopped and someone bumped into me. A flustered young woman with music pumping into her earlobes. I apologized, then patted my pockets to make out I had left something on the train. I hurried towards the station and glanced at each commuter marching down the hill. I recognized no one. No one made eye contact. No one turned round and followed me. No one got out a phone. And no one had a transparent wire curling from an earpiece into the back of his or her collar. Not that any of that particularly reassured me.

.

4

The Crown was busy but there was a free table in the corner so I took my pint of Young's there and opened my tattered copy of the *New Yorker.* I can't remember where I bought it, but I keep it for those odd moments when I need something challenging to take my mind off a problem. The next article to tackle was something about modern interventionist warfare. After two mind-numbing paragraphs I still had no clue what the writer was going on about, so I sat back and looked around.

The lamps over the bar splashed warm light on the bottles, the hand pumps, and the faces of the clients. Behind me, on the road, evening traffic hummed sporadically. There was clubby chatter in the bar and no music apart from the slow, throaty tick of a pendulum clock. It was a good position because from there I could see the front door, the whole of the bar and the entrance to the hotel and restaurant. I ought to have felt comfortable. Spock would probably have said that my unease was illogical. But my Mother used to insist that I respect what she called "premonition".

The chili I had ordered arrived with sticky rice, no tacos and less civility. At least the food was hot. My spirits began to lift until the weasely face of Evan Evans pushed through the street door. Right again, Mother. Evans worked in SIU, but in the Business and Commercial section. We had been buddies until I found out he was using the information he wheedled out of me to claw his way up his section. He wasn't especially bright but he was tenacious and the master of Advanced Point Scoring. The last I heard, he lived in Lambeth. At least twenty miles away as a crow might fly, and a great deal further by road - so there was no way his arriving in the Crown was a coincidence. He slithered into the bar but failed to spot me. At the counter he ordered a half of lager.

Our 'friendship' had officially ended when I began dating Melissa from Accounts. She was a ditzy brunette who brightened up the grey office but, in the end, she proved a bit too off her head for me. Evans was convinced that I had stolen her from him. If they had ever been an item, it wasn't public knowledge. Certainly, Melissa had never mentioned him. Not that long-term relationships were her thing. After we'd had some fun, she dropped me to date a spook. Or so the gossip at the water dispenser had it. Some people have no taste.

I tried the *New Yorker* again, hoping the dense discussion would make Evans disappear. It didn't because he plonked himself in the chair opposite me. In doing so, he jogged the table and slopped a third of my Young's Special Ale over the article I was reading. He said, 'Well, well. Fancy meeting you here boyo.'

I looked up and made a supreme effort to give him a non-committal smile. His lips, under his bristly excuse for a ginger moustache, were set in the usual sneer. His ginger-eyelashed eyes stared. I shrugged and wiped beer off a darkening picture of Camp Bastion.

He said, 'Just like the old times.'

'Leave it out, Evans,' I said. 'Why are you here?'

'Free country. I can drink where I like.'

'Why Chertsey? Why this pub?'

He grinned. He loved making people feel uncomfortable. Mistook it for power. 'I fancied a country pub for a change.'

He had always irritated me and this time it was no different. 'Then why don't you push off and find a pub that is actually in the country. In case you missed it, this is a town.'

Evans laughed. 'Still moody then. Let me buy you another beer, as you seem to have spilled most of that.'

I was speechless. Mainly because Evans never, ever, buys anyone anything. Even so, I declined.

'Come on Jamie. Let's be civil. Melissa was a long time ago. Anyway, we did have a few good times. Remember when we...?'

I cut him off. 'Stop pissing about. Why are you here?'

He pouted as if I had spoiled his fun. He took a minute sip of his drink and then did a big, theatrical pause - like the presenters do in those TV elimination shows. 'A little bird told me you've been asking about a certain old soldier.'

I assumed he meant Fraser. But how had he found that out? The weasel was loving every moment and examined my face to extract every milliliter of satisfaction. I was tempted to walk out but I needed to find out why he had come. Or rather, who had sent him. A couple of guys came over to the dartboard nearby and threw some warm-up darts. I pushed my bowl of chili away and folded my damp magazine. 'OK Evans. Let's go out the back; it'll be quieter.'

Unfortunately, it turned out to be noisier. There was a function on in one of the rooms off reception, but at least the lounge was empty. Evans had brought his drink along and took another tiny sip before he spoke. 'Jamie, you never told me why you left MI5 to join SIU.'

I didn't intend telling him so I kept shtum. It didn't stop him, though. 'The Service must have been far more interesting than Salnikov's little sideshow.'

'Come on, Evans, cut the crap. What do you want?'

He ignored the question. 'Did I ever tell you I applied to MI5? Turned me down, they did. Said they didn't require any more economists. Especially, they implied, not ones from Cardiff University.' Then he beamed. 'But life has a funny way of coming right in the end, don't you find?' He raised his glass. He wanted me to think he was now employed by the Secret Services. I hoped their standards hadn't slipped that much. Though it struck me that he might have been working for them all along so they could keep tabs on Salnikov and on what SIU were up to.

He leaned forward and whispered, 'Did you know Melissa's pregnant?'

'What?'

He enjoyed my shock.

I did a quick calculation and knew it couldn't have been me. 'How is she?'

'You don't really care, do you? Not the way the great Jamie Nelson works, is it? Love them, dump them, and move on. Like that Russian girl you had. The one that was killed? You pretend to be nice but inside you're a heartless bastard.'

He was wrong on several counts. Melissa being one. In the geekish, monochrome world that spooks and their agencies operate, she refused to be intimidated by the rampant male egotism. For her, life was an adventure and round every corner there was sure to be a laugh. I knew she would fall eventually, but I still admired her determination to be different. And genuinely liked her. I said, 'Is the baby yours?'

Evans blushed and looked away. 'No. No she...'

'So Melissa isn't the reason you're here.'

He cleared his throat and looked at me again. 'True.' Pause. 'All right. I'm here to tell you not to ask any more questions. About George Fraser.'

Second Oral warning. The Service had sent a hamster to nibble my ankles.

'And if you don't stop,' he continued, 'someone will get hurt.'

Me? Fraser? Or did they mean Salnikov? 'Pray enlighten me, Evans.'

He sat back and grinned smugly.

I said, 'Who told you to give me the message?'

He took another sip of his lager. 'And you are to stop contacting Salnikov.'

They must have bugged Sergey's office phone. It would have given them time to brief Evans, organize a car, and get him down here.

Evans went on, 'He has been ordered to go on extended sick leave. Overwork, he'll say. Past it, if you ask me. A has-been. He may once have been a celebrity, but the Cold War's ancient history. It's not even on the school curriculum. Time someone younger took the helm of SIU. Someone brighter. A graduate.'

Oh God, they had promised Evans he could be in

charge. Presumably as long as he "kept the channels open". I had seen Salnikov less than a couple of hours earlier. He had looked tired but not particularly sick. And he hadn't mentioned anything about going on leave. But how did they know I would be in the Crown? To find out, I needed to play Evans along. 'I suppose I should congratulate you.'

'Uh?'

'MI5 letting you join them at last. Let me buy you a drink to celebrate.'

He almost said no, then downed his lager in one and then held out the empty glass. 'Same again.'

'Aren't you driving?'

He looked abashed. 'Uh... no.' So, a pool car had brought him. When I returned with his drink, Evans had stretched out. He was enjoying the situation. I was glad, because it would put him off his guard. I set the drink on the table in front of him and said, 'Do you know why Fraser had to vanish?'

I watched his eyes. The muscles beneath them twitched. Then he nodded.

'Why, then?'

He licked his lips and gulped. Perhaps weighing the might of the Official Secrets Act against his desire to show off. In the end, the OSA won. He said nothing and grabbed his drink to prevent me confiscating it.

I said, 'You're all piss and wind, Evans. You picked up some gossip and came along to annoy me.'

'No! Fraser has to be kept under wraps for a few weeks.'

'Why?'

'He's become a... liability.'

'Why?'

'Can't say. But when he's released, he'll be well looked after.'

'I want to visit him.'

50

'No visitors.' He looked over his shoulder before whispering, 'Look, I shouldn't have told you all that. My job was just to warn you off.'

'Who gave you the job?'

'I only know him as...' Then he looked horrified when he realized how much trouble he might be in. He stood. 'Gotta go. Remember, Nelson, you're not unbreakable. To be frank, I was glad they kicked you out of SIU. Got too... high and mighty. And don't think I made any of this up. Something pretty damn serious is going on. If you want my advice, you'll pack up your things and go home now. If you have one.'

At that moment, the outpatient nurse burst out of the function room, heading for the toilets. She was wearing a pinky-red top, a short, ruffled brown skirt, and red shoes. Around her neck hung a necklace made from a single flat shell on a leather thong. On her wrist was a slim silver watch. She wore only one ring: a daisy on the little finger of her left hand. I hadn't meant to gawp. When she saw me, she stopped and glared. Evans was staring at his empty glass. I didn't want him connecting the nurse to me in case he told Brown... to get his revenge for the Melissa thing. Nursey began to walk towards me so I had to do something quick. All I could think of in the spur of the moment was to stand and turn my back on her.

I felt rotten. More than anything in the world at that moment, I wanted to talk to her but the fates had dealt me bum timing. 'All right, Evans,' I said, 'I hear what you say. You have completed your mission. Return to base and report a success.' Behind me, I heard the red shoes stop. Then they clacked back across the tiles towards the toilets. If I made a habit of upsetting her, I would never get her on a date.

Evans didn't move, so I put a hand under his armpit, hauled him upright, and brushed his shoulders as if I was sending him off to high school. He flinched at the contact. So I patted his cheek to make him feel even more uncomfortable. 'If you're on probation, Evans, you'll know someone is monitoring you. And you wouldn't want your driver to clock up unnecessary overtime, would you? Bad economics. Be a black mark on your next assessment.'

He walked to the bar entrance but then turned. 'Why can't you play by the rules, Nelson? Like everyone else.'

'Perhaps I don't like the game?' Ha, ha, very funny. Should have been a comedy scriptwriter.

Evans was about to offer more advice so I had to do something to get him out the building fast. I balled my fist and ran at him. He skedaddled to the street door, wrenched it open, and then it banged shut after him. I felt a satisfied glow. I heard the hand dryer whoosh faintly from the ladies toilet but I stayed at the door to the bar in case Evans sneaked back. I needed to apologize to her - then buy her a drink to make up. Or should I offer dinner for two in the hotel's swanky restaurant?

She called out, 'Look, I had a long, tiring day and I was snappy but you don't have to rub it in.'

I turned to look at her. She looked terrific. And she had given me a last chance. I decided to ignore Evans and I walked towards her. As I did so, a tall black girl emerged from the function room. She had long, straight hair; a gold necklace; and a gold Lurex dress short enough to display most of her terrific legs. She slid her arm round my nurse's waist. 'This man a problem, Chloe?'

'No, Ursula. Thanks.'

The Ursula took her arm away and stepped

between Nurse Chloe and me. It was stupid of me, I know, but she frightened the bejasus out of me. In my defense, she was spookily like Grace Jones in that old Bond film. She leant down and growled in my ear, 'Be kind to her.'

'Of course,' I said. It felt as if the Head Girl had ticked me off.

'She don't need no more hurt. You get my meaning?'

Yo sister. I nodded and she backed towards the function room, watching me. Definitely Head Girl.

'Sorry about that,' said Chloe. 'Ursula decided to be my guardian angel.'

'I wouldn't like to meet her when she's not being angelic.' I thought that was a damn fine line in the circumstances, but it didn't even raise a smile. An awkward pause followed.

Chloe nodded towards the noisy function room, 'It's a birthday party. For one of the consultants.'

'Bully for him.'

'Ursula thought it would be fun for me to come.'

'Is it fun?'

'No.'

I opened my mouth and hoped something intelligent would pop out but before anything could, the hotel receptionist bustled into the lounge waving a piece of paper at me. 'Oh Mr Apollinaris. A message for you.'

It was handwritten and said, "I have to take a vacation. A complete rest, so no contact, please. S. Wicklow53.' I thanked the receptionist, folded the paper, and put it in my pocket. It was Salnikov, though I had no idea yet what the Wicklow bit meant. It could wait because I needed to concentrate on Chloe. Unfortunately, when I turned to speak to her, she had gone. I went to the entrance of the function room and looked into the mass of party people. Ursula came over and inserted herself between me and the action. 'What do you want now?' she said frostily.

'Look I'm sorry I'm late,' I said, 'but I got tied up in an operation. You know how it is.' It was not technically a lie. Just that the operation hadn't been a medical one.

'Name?'

'Nelson. James.'

'I haven't seen you at the hospital.'

'I'm based in Kent.' I saw my nurse so I slipped past Grace Jones aka Ursula. I weaved between guests juggling glasses, canapés, and polite conversation and stopped in front of Chloe. I said, 'You look beautiful.' All right it was cheesy, but it was also true. It didn't have the required effect.

She frowned. 'What are you playing at?'

'I'll tell you, out in the bar.'

'I can't, we're waiting for...'

My elbow was gripped by Ursula. I mean, really, really gripped. The woman was stronger than a wrestler. '*Doctor* Nelson? You're name is not on the list.'

'Really? This is the annual reunion of the North West Surrey Gynecologists?' Oh ha bloody ha.

Ursula blinked. She could grow on me, though it would take a hell of a long time because she was so far out of my league. 'No' she said, 'it isn't. This is...'

'I beg your pardon. I must have come to the wrong hotel. Or on the wrong day. Or something.' I told myself to stop babbling.

I put a hand on Chloe's back and guided her towards the bar. Surprisingly, she allowed me. Even better, Ursula didn't follow. Thankfully, Evan Evans had not returned. In the relative calm I said, 'We haven't been formally introduced. My name's Jamie. Jamie Nelson.'

'That's what it said on your volunteer's badge. So why did that receptionist call you Mr Apollinaris? And why did you tell Ursula you were a doctor?'

'Long story.'

'Then make it quick because, in three minutes, I'm going back to the party.'

OK, so it wasn't a fantastic start but at least it *was* a start. I said, 'The Apollinaris thing was to try to confuse my ex-employer who is being incredibly annoying. Obviously, the deception failed because they sent the ginger weasel you saw me with earlier. And I didn't tell Ursula I was a doctor - she assumed it. I kept quiet because it was the only way I could think of seeing you.'

After considering that she said, 'OK. So why were you snooping at the hospital?'

I told her. Well, more or less. I know, I know, I said I hadn't wanted to get her involved. But frankly, now I was up close, I didn't want to lose her and three minutes is incredibly short - especially when the someone who has made that particular rule keeps looking at their watch.

She was terrific. A tad obdurate perhaps, but she made me realize how much I had missed female company since Tatyana. After the three minutes were up, Chloe didn't leave. Though it took a monumental amount of persuading before she would agree to go back to the hospital to check Fraser's records. She said the only way she would agree, was if she didn't violate patient confidentiality. Meaning, she would be in total charge. The first thing she had to do was tell Ursula she was leaving. I caught her arm as she left. 'I have one condition,' I said.

'What?'

'Don't say anything... <u>anything</u>... when we get in the car.'

'Why not?'

'My employer has bugged it.'

She looked at me as if I was nuts. Perhaps I was.

It was still visiting time at the hospital, so we entered through the north entrance. No security. By the time we reached the escalator that rumbled down to the empty reception area, we saw only cleaning staff. We turned left into the deserted outpatient wing and our footsteps squished down the shiny corridor. I resisted the urge to check behind to see if anyone was following. There were enough CCTV cameras hanging from the ceiling to feed thirty screens in a security center somewhere, so we had to look as if we belonged. We reached the clinic where Fraser had been, and Chloe told me to sit in the waiting area. She took a long time to come back. Then she said, 'I don't understand it. His file's missing. I definitely put it in the cabinet.'

'Does it usually stay there?'

'Until it's collected to be entered in the database.'

'When do they normally get taken?'

'Next morning.'

'Might they have already put it on the system?'

She shrugged.

'Can you check?'

She almost said no but then turned and went back. This time she was gone ages. I resisted the urge to follow her. The evening wore on. Apart from a few distant snatches of conversation, occasional doors banging, and the lift intoning, "First floor, going down," nothing disturbed the meditative air. For something to do I fiddled with my phones and, just as I remembered you weren't supposed to use them in hospitals, a text pinged in on the old one from Mary, my ex. I felt immediately irritated. She said, "*Need to meet urgently*". We had been divorced, what? two years? How could anything be urgent now? I switched the phones off. When Chloe returned she said, 'I can't make it out. The system says there is no George Fraser. I checked everywhere. He's vanished.'

'You're certain he was on there?'

'Of course,' she said. 'I use the database at the beginning of every shift. It holds the appointments, a note of the referrals and the outcomes. Fraser's entry had been there ever since his first clinic.'

'And definitely today?'

'Yes. The only reason an entry disappears...' She stopped.

'Well?'

'TTD.'

'What's that?'

'Treated, Transferred, or Died. Even then, there's a trail you can click back on. But for Fraser there's absolutely nothing. As if he never existed.'

'Can you tell me what he came to the clinic for?'

Pause. 'No.'

I wondered whether to push her. I assumed she had already broken the rules by looking up the files off duty, so I decided against it. Wasn't fair. She could lose her job.

She said, 'All I can say is, he needs regular medication.'

'How regular?'

'Monthly.'

'What if he misses?'

'He mustn't miss. I can't tell you any more.'

If MI5 had taken his records, they would know what was necessary to treat him. They had the means but there was no guarantee they would give him the medication – unless he co-operated. 'OK,' I said, 'let's go.' As we walked towards the exit, I marveled at how swiftly MI5 had got their act together. Of course, the clean-up could have been ready for months. 'Did Fraser behave differently today?'

'No. He was never chatty. I assumed it was because he was poorly. They get that way sometimes. He didn't seem to have any friends or relatives. No one to live for since his wife died.'

'You sure there was nothing out the ordinary this time?'

She shook her head.

'OK, what exactly did he say to you?'

'Um, he complained about the waiting time – but then he always does. He wanted to know who the doctor was – he has a thing against one of them. And then... oh, yes, there was something odd.'

'What?'

'Silly really. He mentioned pigeons.'

I stopped walking and turned her to face me. 'What did he say about them?'

'He'd never said much before about his home life.'

'Chloe, what did he say?'

'Uh...' She frowned as she tried to recall it. 'He said, "If anything happens to me, will you feed my pigeons?" Just that. I assumed he meant when he died, so I came out with all the usual patter and said he had years left in him. In any case, Social Services deal with that sort of thing.'

Perhaps the old man had given us a lead after all. I said, 'He said exactly the same thing to me.'

'Curious.'

'Perhaps not. We need to see these birds he was so worried about. Now.'

'Now? I'm not dressed for it. And it's dark.'

'Don't worry, I'll hold your hand.'

She batted me round the ear. I yelped, mainly because it hurt.

5

To be honest, I had no plan. But then we were only checking on a bunch of pigeons. Weren't we? If the car was audio-bugged, I assumed it was GPS tagged as well. So to be on the safe side, I parked near the station and walked Chloe to Victory Road. I expected there would be someone outside Fraser's house logging visitors. As we approached the pub, I saw the nose of the blue Volvo in the yard opposite. The watcher had picked a good location. He or she could monitor all approaches to Fraser's house from there. I remembered, from my first visit, that the pub had a back yard imaginatively called The Beer Garden. It contained the toilet block, stacks of metal beer kegs, a few battered tables and chairs, a dog kennel, and a rubbish skip. The area was separated from Fraser's back garden by a high brick wall. I pulled Chloe to a stop before we reached the junction. 'See that Volvo to the right?'

'Yes.'

'There's someone in it doing surveillance. We're going to walk straight to the pub but make sure you look away from the car so the watcher can't see your face. Understand?'

'Yes, but...'

'Listen to me. We go into the pub, I'll buy a couple of drinks from the bar, and then hopefully there will be an empty table by the back wall under the TV. We will sit there and chat about nothing in particular and, after five minutes, I want you to go out to the toilets. They are in the back yard. I'll wait two more minutes and then I'll follow.'

'Now hang on! Why all the cloak and dagger? Mr Fraser just wanted us to...'

'Trust me. If we mess up, it might make Fraser's situation worse.'

She frowned. 'I want to know what I'm getting myself into.'

I closed my eyes and suppressed a sigh. What had that gentlemanly aim been? Not to get her involved?

She said, 'I'm waiting.'

'OK. The man in the Volvo is from MI5. Probably. Fraser's house is immediately to the left of the pub. It's in darkness at the moment, but a team will be arriving to search it. They will probably wait until morning - because neighbors don't fret so much if they see a crew come in daylight in something like a decorator's van - but I can't guarantee that. Until they arrive, their control will want to make sure no one muddies the patch. In other words, us.'

'You want us to go up against MI5?'

'Avoid, that's all. The Volvo driver can't see into the pub yard. So we'll get into Fraser's back garden by going over the yard wall.'

'You must be joking!'

I shook my head and pushed the pub door open. There were more people in the bar than on my previous visit but there was, indeed, an empty table near the exit. I didn't recognize anyone, or see anyone acting like a spook. Either the bar lady didn't remember me, or didn't want to. She practically threw my change at me and growled that the pub was closing in fifteen minutes. I almost suggested that closing at ten pm on a weekday when you had plenty of customers was a recipe for bankruptcy. But I didn't. Maybe it was only closing to the public and the local constabulary – which left friends to stage their own "private party". It didn't concern me so, like normal customers, we took our drinks to the table and talked about books and movies.

At nine fifty, I looked at my watch. Chloe played her part like a pro. At nine fifty two, I finished my beer and followed her. No one took any notice of us. It was cool outside. There was a ghostly white glow from the street lamps and high up a full moon shone. The light was useful to stop us breaking our necks but, if anyone was already in the house, they would easily see us go over the wall. I peeped round the corner of the evil-smelling toilet block and looked up and down the road. No one was loitering. No one was sitting in any of the parked cars either side of the road. The watcher was still in the Volvo because I saw him or her light up a smoke. I went to the back wall of the pub yard, shifted two empty beer barrels close to it, and climbed on top. I bobbed up to do a quick recce, then got off the barrels to consider my next move. I had seen an oblong of garden gone to seed; an empty greenhouse with broken glass; a shed; and a single concrete path that led from the back door to the pigeon loft at the bottom of the garden. The house was in darkness. In the next door property, someone was in because downstairs yellow light seeped between the drawn curtains.

I whispered to Chloe, 'Wait here, until I get back.'

'And get raped? Not on your life.'

'Go into the pub, then, and keep a lookout.'

'I'm sticking with you, buster. We're both in on this.'

I didn't like the idea, but it was clearly not the place to argue. I stacked more barrels to form a reasonably stable pyramid. Then I climbed up, went over the top of the wall, and dropped onto a bed of weeds. I heard Chloe scramble up, and saw her silhouette as she rolled over the top of the wall like a commando wearing a party dress. Perfect execution, rather marred by the noisy landing on her bum. 'Well thanks for catching me,' she said. I touched my hand to her mouth briefly, to tell her not to speak. Then I pointed towards the pigeon loft.

The door was fastened by a padlock but the screws on the hasp had given up trying to grip the rotten wood. I put my ear to a panel but I couldn't hear any pigeons snoring – or whatever they did at night. Using my trusty Swiss Army Knife, I eased off the padlock and laid it on the ground. I pulled door open. Of course, it creaked. Curiously, it didn't seem to have disturbed the pigeons. Even odder was the lack of smell. I snapped my on torch briefly. The reason for the silence and the lack of pong was that there were no pigeons. I pulled Chloe in and shut the door. It was warm and woody and smelled as if it hadn't been used for ages.

'Where are the pigeons?' whispered Chloe.

I flicked the torch on the cages. Empty. Even the floor was clean. No pigeon had lodged there for years. On the wall hung a clipboard. I riffled through its curling papers but they were only records of birds, their age, weight, when they had flown... that sort of thing. All old dates. So what had Fraser meant?

'He said *feed* my pigeons,' said Chloe. 'Perhaps he wanted us to look in the pigeon feed box?'

I was about to say there would hardly be food if there were no pigeons but Chloe picked up an old Huntley and Palmer biscuit tin, and shook it under my nose. It rattled. I shone the torch on it. The word FEED had been written onto a strip of masking tape. The tin opened easily - as if it had been used a lot more recently than the dates on the clipboard. It was three-quarter full of corn but something beneath glimmered. I fished out a sealed plastic bag that contained papers and an old audiocassette tape.

'What is it?' whispered Chloe over my shoulder. I slit the plastic bag and took out a sheet of typewritten paper headed, "This Is My Story." It looked disappointingly like a creative writing exercise. Except that, towards the bottom of the page, I clocked the word "mercenary". I pushed the paper back in the plastic and stuffed the lot into my pocket. This must have been what Fraser wanted us to find. I replaced the lid on the tin and put it back where Chloe had found it. Then I went to the door, opened it slightly, and looked at the house. Unfortunately we now had a problem. Because torchlight wavered in Fraser's kitchen. Though there was a thin curtain pulled across the frosted glass panel I could see more than one person moving around. We had to exit sharply, stage left. I showed Chloe and whispered that we had to go back over the wall. We left the shed, I closed the door and pushed the hasp screws back, but they wouldn't hold. I broke a twig from a shrub, snapped it into two short lengths, and shoved them into the holes. This time the screws held. I joined Chloe at the wall. She was making a huge amount of a noise searching for something to stand on. There wasn't anything, so I clasped my hands in front of me and whispered to her that she should stand on them. 'Meet me back at the car,' I said. Then I hefted her up. She grabbed the top of the wall, heaved herself over, and a second later I heard a monumental crash as the pyramid of barrels fell and careered across the beer garden.

Somewhere near, possibly in the pub, a dog barked. Then a key turned in Fraser's back door and, against the glass, I saw the dark shape of the person who was about to come out. I had no time to get over the wall so I ran across Fraser's garden and dived over a four-foot wooden fence into the next door's garden. I landed on something hard that turned out to be a fishing gnome. I worked my way towards the neighbor's side gate, made sure it opened, and then positioned myself behind a low hedge by their back door to see what would happen. Fraser's back door opened. Two men – Brown and the chisel-face called Toby – came into the garden and shone powerful torches around. They ignored the shed and the greenhouse and concentrated the light on the pigeon loft. Then they marched towards it. Chloe and I had said nothing in the car, so the only way they knew about the pigeon feed was because Fraser had told them. Willingly or not. Toby kicked the padlock off and they went inside.

I retreated through the neighbor's gate, walked out to the street and turned right, towards the main road. As if I was a careful pedestrian, I took a quick look over my shoulder before crossing the road. Upstairs at Fraser's house a light was on. They hadn't quite closed the curtains and I saw a man reach up to search the top of a wardrobe. The Volvo was still in the yard so I carried on walking away from the house. My hand hurt and, in the lamplight, I saw my palm was bleeding from a cut. The revenge of the gnomes.

Chloe fussed over the cut and insisted I clean it. She said she could do it best in her flat in the nurse's accommodation. I was sorely tempted. I had been on the go for hours and was desperate to rest. Or have sex if that was on the agenda. But to go to her's would signal a more than average involvement. And as I didn't know what we were getting into, I suggested we find an out-of-the-way pub.

The Otter was more eatery than a pub, and it wasn't that far from Chertsey, but at least it was busy. The tiny bar room had several empty booths, so I chose one with a view of the front door. 'I need to freshen up,' said Chloe.

When she got back, I went to the washroom. I cleaned my hands and face, then I begged a blue sticking plaster for my injury from the kitchen staff. I got some drinks and we spread the contents of Fraser's package on the table. There wasn't much. A creased black and white photo showed a man in a greatcoat, scarf, and dark trilby hat. A younger Fraser - about forty, I guessed - standing in front of

Corinthian columns. There was no scar on his face and he was smirking. A Local Man Makes Good sort of expression. No wedding ring. As for the background, there wasn't much to glean. It could have been a Greek or Roman temple, a museum, a bank, or even a Presbyterian church. There was one tiny clue. An out-of-focus sign said something like "HAPUR". 'What the hell is that?'

'Search me,' said Chloe.

'Were you wanting food?'

I jumped when the server hovered by the table.

'Only we really stopped taking orders fifteen minutes ago.'

I wasn't hungry but Chloe said she hadn't eaten, and needed something or her insulin levels would drop. The server said they had a spare fillet of crusted Sea Bass on a bed of crushed field-fresh minty peas with a side order of pommes frites. Posh fish and chips. I made do with a chicken baguette someone had refused.

When the server left, I examined Fraser's "Life". It had been typed on an old manual machine and it ran to a page and a half in English. There was no indication there was more. As he had gone to a lot of trouble to hide the package, and had given us the same clue, it suggested the package contained something important. The "Terrible Secret" he had alluded to perhaps. The tone of his account was bitter. He felt he had been let down. He asserted that he was honest and had always strived to uphold the honor of his family. His reason for leaving his testimony was to clear his name and his conscience. After some waffle about a soldier's duty to follow orders, he got down to facts.

*"When I left school, I joined infantry division of Albanian Army, defending our*

*borders. I was called "The Eagle," for the way I hunted down insurgents and deserters. In 1978, the Chinese stopped giving money to our country, so then us soldiers were not paid. But we were loyal to our country so, for a while, we stayed together. We stole food and drink from the villages to survive but I did not think this was right. I said we were in army to protect our people, not make their lives worse. They called me a Coward Dog and worse. So I deserted. I got job on a pig farm, but after they found out I had been in army, they asked me to leave. People were still very afraid of the authorities. I went to work for a fisherman near Shkodër. He was good man and found me somewhere to live. I cleaned his catch, mended his nets and boat, and guarded his property at night. A few months later, a man called Franz Schulenburg arrived in the village asking for me. He said he would pay me well to be mercenary soldier. I had nothing to lose, so I went with him to a training camp in mountains. Not Albania. Maybe Italy or the north of Yugoslavia. It felt as if I was being tested. I must have been OK because after maybe two weeks they sent me by train to Vienna."*

The account ended there. At least we now knew Fraser was Albanian; that he had been recruited as a mercenary; and had come to Europe. Schulenburg might be a lead, but I didn't hold out much hope. He could be Austrian, German, or Swiss. He could be

Jewish or American. It could also be a false name. I read the account again, then slid it over to Chloe. The only other item from the package was the plastic TDK audiocassette. There was no writing on the blank panel that usually carries the tape contents. If Chloe didn't have a tape player, I was sure I could find one in a charity shop.

'So what do we do now?' she said, pushing the typed sheets back.

'Bit more research, I guess.'

She said she wasn't on duty until the next afternoon, so I told her to meet me in Chertsey library at ten a.m. It was the sort of place people might bump into each other.

She said, 'You sure you don't want to come back to my flat? For a drink?'

I took in the way light sparkled in her hair as she moved her head. I looked at her wide eyes and knew I had to be careful. Precious cargo. I said, 'Best not. For now.' She paused, nodded, and then turned her head away. I smelled her perfume for the first time. I noticed the emerald earring and the mole on her neck underneath her left ear. It was one of those moments when your senses become heightened. I knew the signs. It had happened with Melissa and with Tanya. Damn.

The door to my flat was ajar so I knew something was wrong. Through the gap, I saw an upended chair. I listened but heard nothing. I went in, touching nothing. The lounge was a mess. Cushions had been ripped and scattered; the sofa dismembered. The bed had been stripped, the mattress pulled off, and my sleeping bag slashed. My travel bag had been emptied, drawers yawned open, and the bedroom carpet had been lifted around the edges.  It wasn't a burglary, because nothing was missing.  It wasn't vandals because they hadn't smashed things, left graffiti, or urinated. It wasn't druggies because there was a logic: the place had been systematically, if roughly, searched. Someone was in a hurry to get something and also wanted to send me a warning.

I heard a noise in the kitchen and went there. Brown was sitting at the table.  He was in his black overcoat, staring at a coffee in a take-away carton as if he was hoping to get a confession from it.  His face was strained and ashen.  I said, 'Did you do this?'

He waved a hand.  'You have something of ours, Nelson.'

'I don't know what you mean.'

'Oh come on.  It's late and I want to get home.'

I was surprised he had a home.  Of course, it could have been a euphemism for his office.  Maybe he was one of the undead who didn't need sleep.  I said, 'I have no idea what you are talking about.'

He stood and glared out the window.  The lamp in the rear alley threw a yellow wash on the brick wall but nothing moved except for a cat prowling for mice.  He said, 'What did Fraser tell you?'

I said, 'You bugged the car.  You know what he told me.'

'I heard your clumsy fishing trips.  I heard a bitter old fool who would traffic his daughter for cash.'

'Does he have a daughter?'

'That's not the point!'  Brown was angry but trying to control it.  His neck was flushed and, on the cheek I could see, there was a spot of unhealthy red. Blood pressure.

I watched his reflection in the glass.  He looked like a ghost and the image jangled a remote memory cell. We *had* met. Briefly, several years back. Not on a project, but during the time I was in the Service. One of the cold, lateral thinkers in Strategy Section? To a man (and they had all been men) they had been professional dreamers who had dropped out of the real world. They lived off caffeine and the heady mix of puzzles, paranoia, and adrenalin in their never-ending campaign to beat the Terror. Whichever particular Terror it was that month. I had also been in a room with Brown a second time, a couple of months before I left MI5. We had not been introduced, and he hadn't been called Brown then. I had the impression that people were afraid of him. Because of his connections, maybe, or his reputation. For me, he was just one of those shadow men who disappeared as soon as you focused on them. No wonder I had forgotten him.

Brown turned towards me. 'You never did like obeying orders. We should have kicked you out of the Service long before your probation was up.'

We? 'I wasn't kicked out, Brown, I left.'

'You should see someone about your delusions.' The old Brown was back. The uber-cool operator. The actor playing private school head. Though I decided he had probably been to a state comprehensive. Which would explain the Stonehenge-sized chip on his shoulder. He said, 'Why did you go to Weybridge Station?'

I shrugged. That meant the car did have a satellite transponder. I would have to switch models in the morning.

'And Chertsey station? And Ottershaw?'

I said, 'I wanted a walk, then I wanted something to eat in a country pub.'

'Don't play games, Nelson.'

'Aren't you playing games with me? You hired me for surveillance, not abduction.'

'I truly wish I had not bothered. Come on, Nelson, end this. Where is Fraser's stuff?'

I wondered if Brown had hired me because the Service wouldn't give him clearance for a big operation. So he'd tapped people who had once worked for the Service. Knew the boundaries and how to bend them. The downside of that was, if Brown was running a renegade operation, Fraser might not get medical attention in a Service safe house. However, I was pretty sure Adam was in MI5. He had said, "*we* don't do things that way". Perhaps, some aspects of the set-up were kosher but Brown had expanded his fiefdom. He would have erected a firewall between the different parts of the operation, and his MI5 control. I said, 'Where is Fraser now?'

'Safe.'

'You know he needs medication?'

'Ah. Information from your compliant nurse. Reassure her we have his complete medical notes. He will receive the appropriate care.'

'You are still keeping him against his will.'

Brown slammed his palms onto the kitchen table. His coffee container bounced off the tabletop and plopped onto the floor. A tidal wave of latte oozed from it. Brown was breathing fast and his lips were a thin line of anger. 'Don't get in my way, Nelson. Nothing would give me greater pleasure than inflicting serious and lasting damage on you.'

'Why?' I was pushing my luck, but I thought that if I made him lose his temper, he might let something useful slip.

'Because you...' Then he clammed up and reassumed his control. He swallowed and straightened up. Shoulders back, chin up, tummy in. It was a ritual. 'I wonder if you had noticed, even in your self-centered, humdrum world, that it takes very little to tip a life into chaos.'

It wasn't philosophy, but a threat. I waited for the punch line.

'I can destroy your life. Very quickly. Unless you assist me.'

I still said nothing.

Brown sighed and brushed his overcoat with the back of his hand. 'You are out of your league, Nelson, you know that.' I watched a downy pigeon feather float down to land in the puddle of spilt coffee. 'There are people less... principled than me, who would have no qualms about silencing you.'

'Who might they be?'

He closed his eyes briefly and then made an effort to change his tack. 'Please... Jamie. All I ask is for a little co-operation. And for you to forget you ever met Fraser. He means nothing to you. Agreed?'

I wanted to shake my head. Instead, I just stared at him. Brown glared back at me for what must have been a couple of minutes, then he marched out. I heard him take the stairs three at a time, heard the front door slam, heard an engine start and, after the clump of a door closing, his car roared off.

I stood there, feeling my heart pump. Why had Brown chosen me to do his dirty work? Especially as he seemed to hate me. Who were these "less principled" people pulling Brown's strings? No neat answers arrived so I decided to be a law-abiding Ordinary Citizen and report the break-in. Just in case the landlord accused me of destroying his flat with a wild, drug-fuelled party.

After a long time in a telephonic queue, the sleepy female voice at 101 thanked me for waiting in a broad Northumberland accent, and launched into a catalogue of statements and questions. Eventually she got round to asking why I had called. I told her.

'Anything stolen, sir?'

'Not so far as I can see. But the place has been trashed.'

I heard her fingers tapping a keyboard. In the background, I could hear the tinny chatter you get from busy call centers. 'Is the intruder still on the premises?'

'No.' There was a lot more I could have said, such as did you think I asked them to hang around while I call the police? But I decided to play it straight.

She said, 'Is there any obvious method of gaining entry?'

'The front door was open.'

'Did you leave the door open, sir, when you went out?'

I took a deep breath before I said, 'No.'

'Did you lock it?'

'Yes.'

More taps. 'Has the door been forced in any way, sir?'

'No.'

'Do you leave a key under the outside doormat? In a flowerpot? With a neighbor?'

It was beginning to get annoying. 'No. Look I...'

'Could it have been someone who has, or had, legal entry to the property, and used their key? A landlord or a previous tenant, perhaps?'

'Or a jilted lover who came back to wreak their revenge? Oh come on, officer! I'd appreciate a little sympathy here.'

'I am a police civilian, sir, and there is no need to shout. I should warn you that our conversation is being recorded and the police will take action against verbal abuse, swearing or racial insults against me.'

'Sorry.' It was late and I realized I was all in. 'Do I get a crime number?'

She read it out to me.

'Will anyone come by?'

'I'm sure you appreciate, sir, that in these difficult economic times, the police must conserve resources. As you tell me there has been no theft, no injury and no significant damage...' She left it hovering in the air. She meant, why the hell did you bother? Why add to their mountain of paperwork? 'Of course, if you insist on further action, sir, I can arrange for a uniformed officer to attend within...' More tapping, '...fourteen days.'

'Don't bother.'

'You have said you do not wish the police to attend?' She sounded hopeful.

'That is correct.'

Triumphant tapping. Inevitably she said, 'Is there anything else I can assist you with at this time?'

'There are some noisy drunks in Guildford Street having a football match with a waste bin.'

'Is there any criminal damage? Or actual bodily harm...'

'Oh forget it.'

'There's no need to adopt that tone. Sir.'

I hate it when people use "sir" as a kind of threat. I sighed. After all, she was only doing her job. 'I'm sorry. It's been a long day.'

There was a pause, this time unaccompanied by tapping. She said, 'Bit of a bummer eh? Hope you get it sorted, pet. Night.' She disconnected the line but I kept listening. There were no other clicks. But then, tapping technology has moved on since Ian Fleming's day. I wondered whether the 'break in' had been a cover to plant more sophisticated bugs. However I was too tired to look for them so I locked the door to the landing, and dragged the couch across it. Then I pulled the mattress onto the bed, laid on it fully clothed, and pulled my wrecked sleeping bag over me. At half time in the Guildford Street waste-bin match, I fell asleep.

Next morning, someone interrupted a brilliant dream. I was on a tropical island. Achingly blue sky. Palm trees waving above me. Waves lapping nearby on white sand - that sort of thing. A waiter had just brought a tray of colorful cocktails to me and there was a collection of semi-naked maidens around. I tried to hang on to the vision but some idiot kept hollering my name. I got up and went into the disaster area that had been the lounge. The landlord's red face was thrust through the gap of the doorway. 'What you done? You leave now! I not have orgies in my flat. You lose your deposit!'

Someone else trying to push me around. And the bastard had obviously tried to let himself in. I said, 'I'm paid to the end of the month. Anyway, it was a break-in. I reported it to the police.'

'Police?' he screamed. 'Waddayawannado that for!'

I pulled the couch away from the door and he came beetling in, checking things, and saying, 'Ohmygod,' frequently.

'I'll straighten it out,' I said, filling the kettle. 'Whoever got in, used a key. Besides you and me, who else has one?'

'Since when do you only need a key?' It was the voice of experience. Maybe Brown had something on him, too.

'It might help if you changed the lock.' I scooped a handful of cornflakes from the top of a golden mountain on the floor and then stuffed them in my mouth.

'Lock not broken. No need to change.' There was Ukrainian logic to that. As he left, he turned and pointed a nicotine-stained finger at me. 'End of month, you go. I want no trouble. From nobody, hear?''

'I hear.' It gave me three weeks to find a job and a new place. Well, two weeks –because I still intended finding the Eagle and understand why they had to silence him. I presumed it was tied up with what he had done as a mercenary... the famous "incident". I could think of only two reasons it would matter now. One, that he had been involved in something extraordinarily evil organized by the UK or, two, that he had been involved with something that could still embarrass a person or persons of influence in the UK. I hoped the audio tape would tell me which.

I checked my watch. An hour before I was due to meet Chloe. I washed, shaved, and put on my last clean shirt. I made sure Fraser's stuff was still with me, inserted it in the middle of the previous day's newspaper, and tucked it under my arm. Then I went down to the Ladybird Café at the top end of Guildford Street for breakfast.

It didn't look promising. It had net curtains half way up the plate glass windows, and looked gloomy. Inside, tables and chairs had been shoehorned into two small, shadowy rooms. The tabletops were covered in oilcloth of a red and white check pattern that reminded me of seaside cafés. The fake timber beams were overdone but the coffee smelt good, and the carbohydrates on other people's plates looked exactly what I needed.

A serving lass who ought to have been at school came to take my order. She brought me black coffee in a white mug and, as I sniffed the aroma, I gazed out the window and saw Adam. He was standing in the doorway of Barclays Bank opposite. I stood and beckoned to him. The poor sap must have been detailed to follow me. My scrambled eggs with bacon and toast arrived at the same time as Adam. The girl hovered for his order but Adam shook his head. He didn't want to sit but was embarrassed at the way people in the café looked at him. He was a lousy secret agent, but I liked him. I decided to let him play the scene out and forked a pile of egg into my mouth.

As the girl was still hovering, he asked for a cup of hot water and then he sat. I ate more eggs. The women on the next table were swapping graphic details about operations they had endured. They were as excited as if they had been talking about kayaking up the Amazon. Or an expenses-paid trip to Disney World. Adam's hot water came in a willow-pattern cup and saucer with a slice of lemon in it. Just proves you can never tell the quality of a café by its decor. When the girl returned to the counter, Adam cleared his throat. 'How are things?'

'Fine,' I said and ate some toast.

Eventually, he said, 'Fraser lost something.'

'Oh?'

'Something important. He's, uh, keen to get it back.'

'Fraser is keen, or Brown?'

He didn't answer.

'Why ask me, Adam?'

He bit his lip. He was definitely in the wrong line of work. 'We wondered... I wondered... if the old man had given you anything? For safe keeping? It would really sort things out if you handed it over.'

Fraser must have told them he had an insurance policy. I said, 'What sort of thing?'

'Oh, well, papers. You know the sort of thing.'

'No. Fraser left nothing with me.' Which was a hundred per cent true.

Adam nodded, though he didn't seem happy with the information. 'Brown thinks you're up to something. Be careful of him. He doesn't always act...'

'Ethically?'

Adam nodded again. 'He tries to pretend he's the perfect gentleman but...'

'He isn't?'

'No.'

'You and Brown are Service, aren't you? Does his control know he's using sub-contractors?'

'I can't comment.'

'How come he's getting away with hiring muscle? Toby, and the guy who looks like a bouncer.'

'I can't say.'

'What can you tell me?'

Adam pursed his lips and stood. He said, 'Sorry. I have to go. You sure you don't know anything?'

'I can't say anything.' He walked quickly to the door but turned when he reached it. 'Be careful, Mr Nelson.'

I nodded. 'You too.' I meant it.

His hand went for the door handle but he changed his mind and came back to the table. 'Why does Brown hate you?'

I shrugged. I didn't have a clue.

'Usually he's cold. Clinical. He runs his operations by the book and he insists everyone acts unemotionally. Except this one. When anyone mentions you...' He let the sentence hang. 'Did you cross him when you were both in the Service?'

'We never worked together.'

'Something happened, for sure.'

I shrugged again. The café bell tinkled as Adam opened the door and went out. He crossed the road and resumed his position in the bank doorway. I couldn't work out if the little drama had been on Adam's initiative, or part of Brown's master-plan. Either way, I had to watch my step. The Pigeon Feed information was obviously important. And, seemingly, exclusive.

The first charity shop didn't have a tape machine. The second had four... one in a bundle with ten Catherine Cookson audio tapes complete with headphones. I bought that and a second-hand Harrods carrier bag to put it all in. Adam stayed on the opposite side of the road, watching me. I couldn't go to the library with a tail, so I backtracked up the street and went into a chemist shop. I peered over a rack of depilatory products to see where Adam had got to. He was across the street, watching the front of the drug store, and biting his fingernails. By the tills, there was a rear exit. I waited until a gaggle of people came into the shop from Guildford Street, slipped out the rear door and walked smartly down the alley to the rear car park. I jogged across it and turned right along the ring road. When I was half way round I dodged in front of a parked transit and looked back. No Adam. I ran the rest of the way to the library and got there out of breath.

'You're not very fit,' said Chloe. 'You need a medical.'

'Only if you do it.'

'Oh ha, ha. Were you jogging for exercise, or running away from someone?'

'I was shaking off a tail.'

'The same people who were searching Fraser's last night?'

I nodded.

'Before I get too involved in all this, you owe me some explanations.'

I was thinking how I could do it without giving away any information when the front door of the library was unlocked and the librarian cried out in surprise to see two customers waiting. We went in and headed for a private study booth. I plugged in the tape machine and popped in Fraser's cassette. What came out was definitely Fraser's voice. Except that he was speaking an east European language I couldn't identify. Possibly Albanian. I gave the headphones to Chloe and she shrugged her shoulders. I switched the machine off. I said, 'I know someone in the University of Kent who'll do me a translation.'

'Meanwhile?'

'Meanwhile, we'll see if there is anything on the internet about Fraser.'

There wasn't. As Chloe was on duty at twelve, we decided to grab an early lunch. First she did some shopping while I went to the hire company to swap cars. They were sniffy about it until I said I would accept their smallest, oldest vehicle. Then I picked Chloe up and we went to the Kingfisher, by the Thames. While we waited for the food, we watched the pleasure boats float under the elegant stone arches of Chertsey Bridge. 'I've never been here before,' she said. 'Funny how you can live in a place and never get to know it.'

She said it to break the silence. I hadn't said much because I knew if I got involved with Chloe, I would put her in danger. I could handle Brown, and even the hired heavies at a push, but not if they got at me via her. Trouble was, I didn't want to dump her either. She was the best thing that had happened for ages. I said, 'This whole Fraser thing...'

'What?'

'Might be best if you didn't get tangled up in it.'

'I love crime stories.' she said.

'This isn't like NCIS. It could be... risky.' In a genteel Surrey pub, by a lazy river sparkling in the sun, it sounded as if I was exaggerating.

She said, 'We made a good team last night.'

'We did.'

'But now you're saying, back off.'

'Brown is unpredictable. I still have no idea what's behind all this but it's something big. And I was told they would get rough.' My old mobile rang. It was the phone company confirming my new contract was now live and that it came with a bonus of two hundred free minutes and two hundred free texts. Which was very generous of them. Especially as I hadn't requested any contract change. They could have made an error. However it was more likely to be the result of the Service applying a tap. I was glad I hadn't called the professor on it. I switched the phone off, even though they would already know my location. I sighed. Here we go again, I thought.

Chloe asked what was up, so I told her. She said I was being paranoid. I agreed. We ate the meal in relative silence and, when we had each paid half, she said she ought to get back to work. I gave her a lift and then used a payphone outside a school to call Frank Dunning at Kent Uni. He wasn't overjoyed at getting extra work but he owed me a favor because I had been the one who recommended him to the SIU.

At Chertsey station I bought a return rail ticket to Weybridge. Once there, I bought a single to London Waterloo. When I arrived I checked I had no tail, then I crossed over the footbridge to the Waterloo East station and used a ticket machine to get a day return to Canterbury. The journey through the Garden of England was pretty but seemed to last forever. I decided not to use a taxi when I got there so I huffed and puffed up the killer of a hill to the university campus. Chloe was right. About me needing to get fit.

The Department of East European Languages stood apart from the main buildings in a block of its own. Inside, I passed booth after booth of students staring at screens. They had earphones clamped to their heads and were muttering into microphones. They looked like slaves, stuck in an academic netherworld. I asked where I could find Dr Frank Dunning and they sent me upstairs.

When I breezed into his office he was sat at his desk opposite a pretty young brunette, who had a tight skirt half way up her thighs. She was making notes; he was watching. Dunning jumped when he saw me and his thick glasses made him look like a startled Bugs Bunny. When he realized who I was, he said 'I'm busy.'

'This shouldn't take long.'

He closed his eyes momentarily and sighed. 'Nevertheless, you will have to wait. I need to finish this.' I retreated to the stuffy corridor and tried not to breathe too much, in case I caught the meningitis virus that posters on the walls warned me about. I had never been studious. Oh, I'd gotten by. But it had seemed like a waste of time. I'd wanted to do real work. Hadn't done me many favors.

The brunette eventually came out and flashed me a shy smile while she tugged her skirt hem down. She assumed I was another lecturer rather than just a lecher. Perhaps Dunning's humdrum life had a silver lining after all. He leant out of his office, 'Mr, uh...?'

'Jamie Nelson.'

'Oh, of course. From the Strategic Intelligence Unit. Yes. Come in, and, uh, do close the door behind you.'

He was treating me like a student but I let it go because I needed him to co-operate without him asking too many questions. 'I've come by this tape,' I said, and placed it on his desk. 'It's very important I find out what's on it.'

He pushed the cassette around with the end of a pen, as if it might be contaminated. 'The label says Catherine Cookson? Surely you need the English department.'

'It's not Cookson inside.'

'What is inside?'

'A testimony I need to understand. In Albanian I think.'

'Surely the Foreign Office has its own translation department?'

'You know SIU isn't quite government, Frank.'

'Why me?'

'Because you're good and I know you can keep a secret.'

He nodded. Whether in agreement, or the realization that he was caught, I couldn't tell.

'You want a flavor, or a...' His voice dwindled to nothing.

'A flavor will do initially, then a word for word translation if it proves as important as I expect.'

Dunning looked crestfallen. 'The funding cutbacks here mean I have a monumentally heavy workload, Mr Nelson. I cannot guarantee quick results.'

'I wouldn't have asked you unless it was strategically imperative.'

'Quite. Though...'

There was a knock on the door and a curly-headed boy lounged in. 'Hi.' He threw himself into the only other chair as if his muscles wouldn't keep his bones upright any longer. Once in the chair, he summoned enough energy to pull out his phone which he started stroking.

Dunning and I stared at him for a while but the youth was unconcerned. Dunning said to me, 'As you see, I am busy. Tutorials.'

'This is important, Frank.'

He huffed and snorted and the tousle-headed youth sniggered, though he could have been reacting to something on Facebook. 'Very well,' said Dunning, 'I have a cancelled appointment in thirty minutes time. I will listen to the beginning of your tape to assess its scope.  Wait for me in the café next to the Gulbenkian.'

They talk like that in universities.  I wondered whether monks had behaved similarly in their monasteries.  Not that there would have been pretty females hanging around.  Or were there?

The café was noisy because every surface was hard and utilitarian – presumably so it could be wiped down with the disinfectant that had added a layer into the food smells.  Chairs were forever scraping the tiled floor and the students yakked so loud I found it difficult to think.  Dunning arrived ten minutes into the slot he had allocated me.  He took off his watch and set it between us to make the point that time was ticking.  He sat, and carefully positioned the tape cassette next to his watch.  Then he looked at me.  'It is Shqip...Albanian.  The speaker is a Geg, from the north of Albania or possibly Montenegro.'

I wanted to hurry him up, but this was his academic preface so I let it run.  'The Albanians are descended from Illyrians who were fabled for their storytelling, though the native style we have here derives from the nineteenth century revival by, uh, Jeronim de Rada.  In the preamble, the speaker calls himself George Fraser, though I doubt that is his real name.  The closest Albanian given name is Gjerj.  Frasheri is a relatively common patronymic.  He employs a surprisingly Ciceronian style which, I assume, was the result of schooling by a Roman Catholic priest.  They still operated in the north, you know, as a legacy of the Ottoman...'

'Professor,' I growled, 'what's on the tape?'

'Well obviously I only listened to a fragment.'  He paused, wiped his glasses on his jumper, and then went on. 'In the classic storytelling fashion, the opening sets the scene and...'

'What's it about!' I hadn't realized how stressed I was getting. My shout hushed the clattering hubbub in the café. When people saw who I was sitting with they laughed, as if they knew what I was going through. I apologized. He was a boring old fart but he also happened to be a very clever one, who could provide something I needed.

He picked up his watch to check the time. Then he leant forward and said in a low voice, 'The tape is a testimony, in the form of a narrative, about how he was recruited by the British as a mercenary. He says he will tell of his training and the operational unit he was sent to. He will tell of a covert operation that happened in a place called Zinder, in Africa. I heard no more, Mr Nelson, because I simply do not have the time. Government agencies such as yours may be interested in such... childish adventures... but I have students to push through a course which, frankly, I am aware they loath. Without my sustained, significant input, they will fail. This, the university cannot let happen. Or the funding agency will reduce our budget even more. Do you understand? Forgive me but I must return to my tutorials. That, after all, is what I am paid to do.'

For Dunning, it was quite a speech. I felt like clapping though I didn't, because I also felt sorry for the prune. He was as trapped as any of us. He pushed the cassette box across the patterned Formica. I left it where it was.

'Frank,' I said, 'I hear what you say. And I appreciate that I'm asking a hell of a lot, but it really is vital I know the details of what Fraser got up to. Find the time; we'll pay.'

'In cash?'

I was surprised he could be so worldly-wise. I nodded. I wrote my new phone number and Mr Apollinaris' email address on a page of my notebook, tore it out, and slipped it under the cassette case. Then I pushed it back across the table. 'You don't have to do it all in one go,' I said, trying to sooth him. 'I don't even want a verbatim translation. Email me a chunk of the sense of what you find whenever you are able. Will you do that?'

He stood, put on his watch, and then pocketed the tape with my note. He said, 'I will do my best. Make the payments via the usual arrangements.' He walked away. I had no idea what "usual arrangements" SIU used and it wouldn't do any good asking anyone there. Maybe, if I tracked down Sergey, he'd tell me. And he might also know why the incident at Zinder was such a hot potato.

6

So far, the only new information I had was the place called Zinder. I wandered into the Uni Library but every terminal was in use. None of the students looked as if they were going to move from the keyboards until sundown, so I resorted to uncool book research.

A world gazetteer told me that Zinder was a town in south central Niger. Apparently it had a fair amount of mining and commerce, and there were processing facilities for the surrounding agricultural products (peanuts, cassava, and millet). A black and white photo showed a dusty square with a mosque, square sub-Saharan houses painted white, and a few palm trees. There were also three people, a dog, and a battered car. There was one good road to the capital, Niamey, which had been built in 1980. Bully for them. No suggestion, though, why the British may have gone there on a covert operation.

My new phone rang. Chloe. I answered and a librarian ordered me to leave, so I talked to Chloe as I trotted down the stairs.

'I've been suspended,' she said.

'Why?'

'Because I searched medical records when I was off duty. When they checked the CCTV recordings, they saw you. They won't listen to anything I say.' Her voice was close to breaking up.

'Sorry.' Brown was spreading his net. I reluctantly admired his diligence.

'Maybe it's for the best,' she said. 'I'm not cut out to be a nurse.'

'Rubbish. You were brilliant with the patients.'

'That was crowd control. Anyway, the hospital won't let me back to work until they finish their investigation.' The silence that followed increased my feeling of guilt. Then she said, 'How are you getting on?'

'Not spectacularly. Look, I have to go and see another expert. I can't say who or why, in case some fancy algorithm latches on. But can we meet? At seven thirty. Where we ate last night.'

'Yes.'

'They will probably follow you.'

'Who?'

'The people who told your bosses to look at the CCTV.'

'You mean...'

'Don't say it!' I heard her breathing. Thinking it through. I said, 'Why don't you do some window shopping? You will probably spot the people who are following you. When they get bored, give them the slip. But try not to let them know you're onto them. OK?'

'I'll try.' She sounded worried.

I said, 'Your bosses can't do anything to you. Because you've done nothing wrong. If it helps, I'll tell them everything.'

Silence.

'Are you OK?'

After a pause, she said, 'I guess.'

'Be careful.'

She rang off.

I was tempted to drop everything and go to her, but I didn't think that would leave me enough time to get to Sandhurst before the military clocked off. At the train station, I bought a cheese and tomato baguette and a takeaway black coffee and caught the high-speed Javelin train back to London to save time.


The attendant at the small Sandhurst museum was an ex-RSM who hated civilians and everything to do with them. Especially, he hated museum customers. He wasn't even impressed when I asked for the Colonel by name.

'Well you can't see him willy-nilly. You need to book an appointment. Not today though: we close in five minutes.'

I fished out one of my SIU business cards, scribbled a note on the back, and passed it to the sergeant. 'Show him that,' I said.

He scrutinized it to see if there were any microchips or hidden explosives.

The RSM wanted to tell me that if I didn't get lost, I'd be on a charge but he clearly didn't want to upset his colonel, so he turned and marched off. I listened to the sound of his metal-heeled boots click away down the parquet flooring until he knocked on a distant door. After a pause, I heard it open and the sergeant barked something. Then the heels returned. 'He says he'll see you.' The sergeant was clearly surprised and annoyed.

The colonel looked older than I remembered. I told him I was researching old Africa campaigns, but I was lacking any information on the Zinder operation. His eyes glazed over. I heard his belt creak as he leaned back. I could smell the polish evaporating from his mahogany desk. Or was it from his moustache? Eventually he snapped upright and said, 'Made an error there, old boy. Never went to Zinder.'

'Are you sure?'

'Hundred percent. Odd name. Bound to remember.'

'Could you look on the MoD database?'

'If you wish, though...' He tapped his head to imply his memory was better than any machine. Nevertheless, he turned to use a keyboard and, after a few abortive searches, he shook his head. 'As I said. No action in or around Zinder. Not our patch. You could speak to the Frenchies if you have a month or so. Red tape, and all that.'

'What's the Army's position about using mercenaries?'

The colonel looked over the top rim of his steel-framed spectacles. 'You mean Local Advisors?'

'No. Mercenaries.'

'Been known. MoD calls them PMCs. We officially employ them on convoy escorts, protecting sensitive sites, mine clearance, routine stuff. But offensive combat?' He sucked air in through his teeth. 'Need to speak to Special Forces about that. Always risky using PMCs, though. Your average

Mercenary is a bit off the wall. Psychotic. Or delusional. Follow me? Impossible to assess strengths and weaknesses in them. Result: unreliable in combat. Oh, they can handle the hardware but they don't take kindly to discipline. Ergo, no teamwork. Too risky. Get my drift?'

'I do. But, hypothetically, could we have put a covert unit of mercenaries into French territory? A unit that, forever reason, couldn't be traced back to the British Army?'

He cleared his throat and then picked up my card and stared at it. 'Well you are quite aware of what those hush-hush units are capable of. But why bother? Eh? Sub-Sahara? Nothing there for us, old boy.'

Beneath his old soldier act, I sensed he was being evasive – or irritated that I might know more than him. I said, 'Just for the sake of argument, if MI6 and Special Forces organized it, would anything appear on your database?'

He pushed my card back across the desk. 'Probably not. Certainly not on open files. Officially, of course, nothing like that goes on.'

'But off the record?' My question dangled. Outside, on the square, I heard multiple boots crunch and a drill sergeant scream. A sparrow cheeped. A clock ticked. A million deals were closed on the world's stock markets. Somewhere it was sunrise. Somewhere the sun had just set. Babies were born. People died.

The colonel cleared his throat. 'I'm afraid I have been advised not to talk off the record.'

I got up and we shook hands. I said, 'If you find anything, can you ring me on my new phone? It's clean.'

'Clean?'

'Untraceable.'

He nodded. I wrote the number on the back of my SIU card and put it back on his desk.

He didn't touch the card. 'All I can do is ask in the mess tonight. Owe you something, for keeping my name quiet after our last... uh... contact. Appreciated.' He meant I had not credited him as a source in my arms dealing report. I hoped the colonel wouldn't think to enquire whether I was still in the SIU.

I said, 'We're like journalists. A matter of honor.'

'Capital,' he said, 'capital.' He stood and showed me to the door. Before he closed it he whispered, 'Be careful of the RSM. When he's hungry, he's apt to bite.'


Chloe was sitting in the same booth at the Otter pub. She looked tired and drawn, which made me feel extra guilty. I went to kiss her cheek but she flinched away and it didn't seem appropriate to shake hands. Maybe I was going too fast. We ordered, and when the waiter had left she said, 'Someone did follow me round the shops.'

'And?'

'I think I lost him. Little Asian guy.'

If Adam didn't buck his ideas up, HR would be sending him a P18B Written Warning. My new phone rang. The Colonel. In the background, I could hear men laughing and the clatter of cutlery on china. The Colonel cleared his throat. 'That, uh, matter we spoke of old boy.'

'Yes?'

'Can't be specific on the squawkbox, but something did take place along the lines you supposed. Political, rather than military.

Apparently, nipping something in the bud. Get my drift?'

'Yes. When?'

'Eighties.'

'Can you give me any more?'

'Details erased, old boy. Got it from someone who was told it by someone who's long dead. Person I got it from doesn't want to get involved. Advised me to beat a hasty retreat. Why don't you tap one of your ex-amigos in the, uh, place south of the river?' He meant MI6. His source must have given him a very strong warning. The noise around the Colonel escalated. 'Look, have to go. About to parade in the puddings. How's your old Russian, by the way?'

I had temporarily forgotten about Sergey. 'Been told to take a holiday.'

'Overwork?'

'No.'

'Ill?'

'No.'

'See what I mean? Dangerous waters. Always thought you're in an odd trade, dear boy. Never know who to trust and so forth. Look, must get back. Chaz Eversfield's leaving do. Knew him, did you?'

Old soldiers think you know all the movers and shakers in the army. 'No, sorry.'

'Salt of the bloody earth.' The wine was beginning to work. 'All the old boys going. New crew on the parade ground now. All we hear is staff cuts and bloody risk factors. Oh well, toodle-pip.'

Our drinks arrived, and then I brought Chloe up to date.

'Mr Fraser has terminal cancer,' she said. 'He needs a blood transfusion once a month and an injection fortnightly. You sure they can do that?'

'Yes. If he co-operates.'

'How can they be so callous?'

'They see it as their duty to protect the majority; by whatever means.'

'That's stupid.'

I shrugged. 'For all we know, Fraser is a sleeper for Al-Qaeda or Daish. Or perhaps he's just dangerous to someone on high because of what he might reveal about Zinder.'

'That was a long time ago.'

'Someone may still have a lot to lose.' Of course, I was only building theories on whispers and supposition. I needed facts. I couldn't wait around for the professor, so I would have to tap the brain of someone in SIS. Our starters arrived. Unfortunately they were delivered by Mr Brown.

He laid the plates carefully on the mats and then squeezed into the booth next to Chloe. 'Well,' he said, and switched on his wintry smile, 'here's a turn up for the books, and no mistake.' He must have put a double tail on Chloe, because I was sure no one had been near me all day. Brown picked a glazed pink crescent off Chloe's prawn cocktail and popped it in his mouth. 'How delightfully eighties. Do tell me this establishment offers Black Forest Gateaux for sweet? I didn't realize how reactionary these places are. Or is it called retro-chic? I confess I am rather out of touch with popular food fashions.'

I said, 'Cut the crap, Brown, what do you want?'

'No pleasant chit chat? No solicitous greeting. Oh dear. Well, I suppose it is getting rather late. You two meeting here wasn't coincidence, was it?'

Chloe frowned and looked at me but thankfully, she held her tongue. I didn't know how much Brown knew about us, so there was no reason to volunteer any information. 'You are the uninvited guest, Brown, why are you here?'

Brown used Chloe's napkin to wipe his lips and fingers. 'A surprisingly tasty shrimp ruined by a spectacularly inferior mayonnaise. And you can cut out the high and mighty tone, Nelson. I, unlike you, have a job to do.'

'Get to the point.'

'Very well. I shall use Sir Ernest Gowers' *Plain English*. No ifs, no buts. No taradiddle. Here it is: continue with your... "investigation", either of you, and I will personally ensure you are locked up for a very long time. Comprendez?'

The color drained from Chloe's face.

I said, 'OK. You win.'

'Bravo,' said Brown. 'Almost worth me risking the salmonella that is undoubtedly attached to the shrimp.'

I said, 'At least tell us what it's all about.'

Brown considered, or pretended to consider, but then shook his head. 'Can't be done. And not just because I hate your guts, Nelson. I took a look at your annual reports and they confirmed my opinion that you are totally unreliable. I rather warmed to a particular phrase an assessor used of you: "Constrain him, or he will pursue his own interests to the detriment of the department". You never were cut out to be a team player, were you Nelson?'

'And I thought it was because I came from the wrong school.'

'That too, I dare say.'

Chloe chipped in, 'Why have you taken Fraser?'

'Past sins my dear. They catch up with us all in the end.'

She said, 'He needs medication.'

'Please be reassured, nurse, he is receiving the best private healthcare available. I guarantee he will not suffer, medically. Remember, if you mention any of this to anyone, the next time you see me will be when I visit you in prison.'

'There are no grounds to arrest us,' I said.

'You know some will be found. Even if it is burglary in your case and gross professional misconduct in Miss Hall's case. However, I am certain we can find other things if the CPS needs convincing. He turned to face Chloe. 'Permit me to give you two pieces of advice, Miss Hall. I understand you have been a reliable employee. Please do the sensible thing and walk away from all this. In return, I promise you will be immediately reinstated with no record of the suspension.'

'And?' said Chloe who seemed to be more angry than cowed.

'Secondly, you need to know that Nelson here - however charming he may appear - is conniving, has no morals, and a zero respect for women. For your physical and emotional safety, I would strongly advise you to leave here immediately. Or, if he is paying for the meal, leave immediately after you have braved the Black Forest gateaux.' He laughed at his joke, stood, and did a slight bow towards Chloe. 'This really must be the end of your little game. Hear? Both of you.' Then he left.

For a long time neither of us spoke. The waiter took away the starters and brought the main course. My appetite had vanished but I ate mechanically. I paid and left without bothering to see if there was any gateaux. I did several loops around the area but no one was following, so I drove Chloe home. As I went down the access road to the staff accommodation, I looked back to the small public car park at the back of the MAU. The battered Volvo was there. I didn't tell Chloe. I parked in the square behind the flats, switched off the engine, and then doused the lights.

After a while she said, 'So where do we go from here?'

'We do what Brown says.' In the light from the lamps on the back of the flats, I saw her turn to look at me. I put a finger to her lips. I said, 'I'll walk you home.'

After the slightest pause she said, 'Very well.'

We got out the car. It felt cold enough for there to be a frost even though it was only September. We walked in silence towards the entrance. At the door, she turned. 'Well?'

'Lay low, wait for the NHS to clear you. If they get difficult, contact me, and I'll tell them everything. In fact, I'll do that anyway.'

'No. I'd rather you didn't. If Brown has done this, it will only make him angry.'

'Then take a holiday. Forget about me and all this.'

'What if they won't clear me?'

'Brown is a bastard but I think he'll stick to his agreement. Do as he said, and he will put everything right. You might even get compensation for wrongful suspension.'

'But it's not fair!' She thumped her fist on the doorframe. 'Mr Fraser is suffering because of all their... shenanigans.'

I felt a giggle bubble up at her quaint word choice but I stifled it. Not the moment. My phone vibrated but I let it carry on. I wanted to kiss

Chloe... run my fingers through her hair... that sort of thing. But my brain told me to back off.

She turned to me, 'What Brown said of you... are you like that?'

I considered the question carefully, decided I wasn't, and told her so.

She said, 'Will you stop looking for Fraser?'

'No.' It would take more than a puffed up toad like Brown to stop me. Though I knew he could execute his threat.

She said, 'In that case, I want to help.'

I put my hand on her arm. 'No Chloe. It's too dangerous. You'll get hurt.' In the washed-out light, I saw tears glisten in her eyes.

'But we can't let them do this to Fraser. It's not his fault. We have to fight them!'

Bravo, I thought, we'll wave our pitchforks, man the barricades, and sing that song from Les Miserables. The only thing I said was a pathetic, 'We'll see.' My mother-in-law had said that. At first, it had irritated me because it was so vague. In time, I realized it was her way of letting people down gently. I added, 'I'll ring you in the morning.'

'Promise?'

'Promise. But when we talk, say nothing specific. Unless you want to mislead the person who will be earwigging.'

'You mean they've bugged my phone?'

'By now, definitely. Assume everything is possible.'

She nodded and turned her cheek towards me to receive a chaste kiss. Not exactly what I'd had in mind but, hey ho, it was a start, so I dutifully gave her a peck. Her skin was soft and warm and smelled of apple blossom.

The text had been from the Professor. He said he had been able to spend very little time on the translation. However, he anticipated he would have enough to email something in the morning. He used correct spelling, capitalization, and punctuation in the text. But then, he was a doctor of languages.

7

The professor's email came in at seven the next morning. "The narrative," went the covering note, "is woefully ill-structured with frequent lapses into dialect." I groaned. I hadn't asked for a critique of the bloody thing. "How accurate it is I cannot, of course, say. Nor can I deduce how reliable the narrator is. As you probably know, there is a tradition in storytelling of the unreliable..."

I yelled and nearly threw the phone across the bedroom. When I calmed down, I opened the attachment.

> *With other recruits, I was taught basic French. That was to be the common language used by our intake of mercenaries. We went on operational training in Austria and in the mountains east of Trieste. Then Schulenburg had us*

*flown to a desert. It could have been Iran...
or Iraq, for all I knew. The soldiers in
charge of us were brutal and we were sent
on a live operation to destroy what we
were told was a missile base. Many soldiers
were stationed there, and they defended
fiercely. One of our team had his head
blown off by a mortar. When we got back,
several quit. However, I had been used to
fighting, I was fit, so I knew I could cope
with anything. A few of us were flown to
Vienna where Schulenburg interviewed us
one by one. He told me he could see I was a
professional, and he gave me a contract to
sign with his company. I saw none of my
intake again. I went to Angola to kill
insurgents. After that, I was sent to Nigeria
to assist the rebels. Schulenburg wired
most of the money I earned to my family in
Albania. In July 1980, I was pulled out of
Nigeria and sent to Morocco. Once there, I
was instructed to go to the Hotel Toubkal
to meet a man called Philips. Schulenburg
implied that he was a British agent but
Phillips refused to say who he represented.
He asked me many stupid questions. That
night, Schulenburg phoned me and told me
I had been sub-contracted to the British
Army but I must never divulge that I
worked for them nor say anything about
my time with them. He promised that,
during the contract, the British would pay
me extra and would look after me
whatever happened. I was taken to a
training camp in a desert somewhere in
Algeria. There were about thirty other*

*mercenary fighters and some regular soldiers from the British Army. They taught us some English, though they also spoke French. They trained us in tactics and use of the weaponry which was all Russian. Kalashnikov AKSU-74s mainly, and Tokarev TT-33 pistols. Then we rehearsed an attack on an installation. Three of the other mercenaries came from Schulenburg's company but none from my intake. We were forbidden to talk to each other about our previous lives or operations, so I found out little from the rest. They said if we were found talking, we would be sent home. In September that same year (1980), seven of us were flown south. I found out the place was called Babura, in northern Nigeria. We set up camp there and were told to clean our weapons but to stay inconspicuous until we received further orders.*

There the translation ended. Obviously the professor had tidied it up, but it was a promising start. Hopefully, the rest of the tape would produce facts I could check. So much for the Colonel saying the British didn't use mercenaries in the front line. Assuming, of course, Fraser was telling the truth. I tried to ring the Colonel, to ask if he could find out what had happened in Babura but his phone was on message service, so I left something vague.

Surprisingly, I slept like a log – until my new phone rang. I looked at my watch: 8:30 am. It was Chloe.
'I've been thinking.'

I stopped myself making any smart-arse comments. 'Oh?'

'I really can't let this drop.'

I did the mental equivalent of a sigh.

She went on, 'Why should he be allowed to push everyone around like this? We have to find out where Fras...'

'Hey! Be vague, remember?'

'Sorry.' Pause. 'We need to meet.'

'I have to go up to town today to...'

'We need to meet.'

There was a dangerous edge to her voice. One that suggested she might go and do her own thing so, however much I hated the idea, I had to lasso her to my cause. I could have done without a passenger but when needs must... I said, 'Be at the local museum exactly ten minutes after ten. Understand?'

'Yes.' Another pause. 'Thanks.' She hung up.

I switched on my old phone just in case there was a legitimate job for Nelson Discreet Investigations. There were two messages: one from someone telling me he could get generous compensation, on no win no fee terms, for my recent road traffic accident – which I hadn't had. The second was a ratty message from my ex: "*This is Mary. Remember me? Get in touch immediately. What the hell have you stirred up?*"

She sounded almost as worked up as the time she accused me of having an affair. Which had been entirely groundless as I didn't succumb until months (well, weeks) after our divorce. Anyway, I wasn't ready to phone Mary, Mary, Quite Contrary about anything. Even though I was intrigued. Something must have riled her to break her self-imposed purdah. Nevertheless, my immediate need was for a shave etc. Then I went for breakfast.

From habit, I locked the flat before going down the stairs. My lovely landlord was sitting on the bottom step, facing the open street door, smoking a black cigarette. 'I watch you, mister,' he said as I squeezed past. 'You get away with nothing, understand? Twenty three more days and out you go, no messing.'

I bade him a sweet good morning and stepped onto the pavement. On the opposite side of the road, a frozen Adam was hunched into a doorway against the wind. I went over. 'Morning.'

He scrabbled for his radio to switch it off. 'At least you didn't say, "good morning".'

I laughed and linked my arm in his. 'Come on you poor sod, I'll buy you a vegetarian breakfast at the Ladybird.'

'It's not allowed.'

'Look, I know you've been told to shadow me. If we're together, I can't disappear can I?'

'I suppose not. Though I'm not very comfortable with body contact.'

I let his arm go. For a while, we walked side by side in silence. I kept a look out for other watchers but saw none.

'To tell you the truth,' he said, 'I don't think I'm suited to this.'

'We all have to start somewhere, Adam. I did two years on surveillance. Hated every long hour. Better things'll come up...'

He sighed, 'I don't think I'll last a year.'

The Ladybird was busy but there was a table at the back near the till. I ordered and, when the food came, I said, 'Did you know Brown's having you followed?'

Adam dropped his knife and the café buzz stopped briefly. He gulped and said, 'How do you know?'

I didn't intend to elaborate. 'Believe me, I know. Be careful.'

'Brown is playing his own game.'

'Meaning?'

'He ordered me not to refer anything to Centre, unless he agrees.'

In the old days, when agents used their instincts in the field, control gave them their head - as long as the goal was achieved. But since all the bad publicity after the terror attacks everything had been tightened up. Now no one makes a move unless it is sanctioned from above. Which suggested that if Brown was running a maverick operation he was either crazy or had sanction from on high. I said, 'Why is he so worked up about this particular case?'

Adam shrugged and crammed a slice of buttered toast into his mouth. He reached for his tea and glugged it back. Then he stood. 'Thanks. But, really, it will only make things worse if we are seen together.' He grabbed the last piece of toast and headed for the door.

'Adam,' I called.

He looked round.

'Be careful, remember?'

He nodded and went out the door, switching his radio back on. The bell seemed to jangle a long time. Thinking back to my days on the Security Service, I decided there were probably two people watching Adam. Brown would expect me to find one, feel smug, and not bother looking further. There was obviously a good deal of budget being thrown at this. It wouldn't be long before the accountants got wise. Or did he have access to a private slush fund?

As I left the Ladybird, I leaned against the next-door shop pretending to read the *Daily Express* I had lifted from the rack. I located Chisel. He was making a bad job of hiding behind greenery at the edge of the parish church graveyard. He may have had his uses as muscle, but he was lacking in surveillance skills. You have to appear natural... merge into the context, that sort of crap. Chisel clearly had no honest reason to be doing what he was doing - especially with a DSLR camera with a zoom lens. However, he did present me with a problem. I had intended to pass the church to get to the museum. There was another way round, but I couldn't leave him where he might spot Chloe. So I made sure Chisel saw me, then I turned, and walked away from him down Guildford Street.

Surreptitiously, I searched for watcher number three. It was a fair bet he was beyond my flat. Not in a building, because he would need to be mobile. I didn't think they would use a parked car because of the lack of spaces and the evangelical zeal of the traffic warden. A shop then? Or on a roof? Beyond my florist was a narrow gap - the entrance to Gogmore Lane. I knew, from my reconnoiter on the first day, that it doglegged between small factories to join Windsor Street half way between the church and the museum. If I could locate the third watcher, and distract the others, I could use the lane for a disappearing act.

I went into the drug store and bought an Essential Travel Pack –in case I was going to be on the road a lot. Adam was nearby, positioned to check if I went up to the flat. We didn't acknowledge each other as I passed him. The poor guy would already get a bollocking for having had breakfast with the mark, so I didn't want to make things worse. I walked on down the road. Outside the florist, a huge Dutch lorry was unloading flower boxes. The vehicle totally blocked the one-way street and the drivers that had backed up behind were growing restless. I still couldn't see watcher number three.

I scanned all the roofs, all the shops, all the cars. When I did see him, I laughed out loud and made an old lady near me drop her string bag of onions. At the far end of Guildford Street, by the mini roundabout, the bouncer was perched on a mountain bike several sizes too small for him. He stared back at me belligerently and I waved. If the same cast list was being used it meant that Brown's budget wasn't limitless. Across the road, a traffic warden homed in on the flower lorry and told the driver to move on. I turned to look in the shop window behind me and focused on the reflection of the street. The Dutch driver went into the flower shop. Soon after, he came out with his delivery papers. He disappeared behind the far side of the lorry and I heard the doors there slam. Then the driver walked into the road to get to his cab. The engine started and the air brakes raspberried off.

As the lorry moved down Guildford Street, it blocked Bouncer's view of me. So I ran across the road in front of a white Transit that was following the lorry. I risked a quick look back at Adam but he was talking to the little old lady with the onions. Chisel was too far away to see what I was up to, but Bouncer would soon realize I was mobile. I was in Gogmore Lane before the flower lorry passed the Bouncer. I dashed to the T-junction, turned right, and then slowed to a fast walk so I didn't draw attention to myself. The Bouncer could soon catch me up on his bike, so I had to move fast. Along the lane, machinery in the old buildings chugged and hammered. Outside one, a man was smoking, and he watched me with a blank expression. Otherwise, the lane was deserted. Belatedly I checked whether they had put up a helicopter but, thankfully, the sky was empty apart from a socking great four-engine Emirates jet straining up from Heathrow. I stopped where the lane met Windsor Road and rang Chloe. It switched to her message service so I cut the call, then texted her to abandon the museum meeting and go instead to Addlestone railway station in an hour.

Once the watchers realized I had vanished, Adam would be sent to check the flat. The landlord would report that the cupboard was bare, and then they'd get Adam to watch my hire car. Chisel would set up shop at Chertsey railway station taxi rank, and Bouncer would cycle around town looking for me. They were all long shots, but it's all you can do in the circumstances.

I looked back at the church. Chisel had disappeared so I walked smartly down Windsor Street. I carried on past the museum and then crossed the road to Abbey Green. I continued walking along the pavement, and then went in to a small public open space in front of the Social Services offices. I sat on a bench and waited. I was hidden from the church but I could see the museum entrance and the road that came from Staines. Chloe hadn't replied to my text, so I needed to be there in case she turned up.

Five minutes before museum opening time, two ladies arrived, unlocked the iron gates of the redbrick Georgian building, and went in. Fifteen minutes later, Chloe appeared, walking from the Staines direction. As soon as she reached the museum, she turned into the entrance. No one followed her. Five minutes later, the bouncer cycled past at a speed that wasn't safe in a town. I waited another minute, then sprinted across the road and into the museum. The lady at reception was beside herself at having two customers so early in the morning. I said, 'I'm supposed to meet my sister here. Has she arrived?'

The lady smiled and pointed to the toilet. 'Why don't you wait in our conservatory? I've switched the drinks machine on.'

I thanked her and managed to work out how to produce black coffee. My second. I needed to ease up on the caffeine. Somewhere an ancient clock toyed with time in the way old clocks do: Tock ker tick; tock ker tick. The lady at reception kept an eye on me while she took a call. Chloe appeared and the receptionist pointed at me. I kissed Chloe on the cheek and told her she was temporarily my sister. She frowned as she sat. 'What was all that about in the text?'

'Why did you come if you got it!'

'I thought you were trying to put me off. I want to find Fraser too, remember?'

It irritated me that she hadn't done what I'd asked, but it wasn't the place for histrionics. So I told her it was getting too hot for her to stay involved. Before I had finished, she put her hand on my mouth. I tried to continue, but it is incredibly difficult to keep track of what you want to say when slender, perfumed fingers are resting on your lips.

She said, 'I need to tell you something. My husband died of cancer six months ago. I have no friends. I don't have a job. I need this.'

I mumbled something about being sorry about her loss, but her fingers stayed on my lips.

'To be honest,' she continued, 'I have more than once considered... ending it all. We were very much in love.' A tear ran down her cheek. She removed her fingers from my mouth and then used the back of her hand to wipe her face. 'My old friends helped me get back into nursing. But I couldn't stay where I was because there were so many memories. I moved here and got a single person's flat in the hostel. I had some stupid affairs that made me feel even lonelier. No one knows my background and I'm not going to tell them. They think I'm just a workaholic who had a troubled past. So I work... I worked... every shift. To fill the emptiness. Ursula... you've met Ursula...'

'Oh yes, I've met Ursula.'

'She realized what I was going through. She... released me. I was just beginning to feel normal again when this happened.'

'I'm sorry.'

'No, I didn't mean it that way. Going to Mr Fraser's house woke me up from a bad dream. At last I had something to strive for. Besides, I... enjoy being with you. And I don't want it to end.'

Everything I'd thought of saying was redundant now, so I kept quiet. It was a touching speech but I knew I would be better off without the extra baggage. But, hell, sometimes you have to go with the flow. At least we agreed on something: I, too, didn't want our friendship to end. Not that it was a justification to put Chloe in danger.

'Well,' she said, 'say something.'

I looked over my shoulder for inspiration and saw, reflected in the plate glass of the entrance lobby, the image of a bulky cyclist propping his bike against the metal gate. 'We have to hide,' I said, getting up. 'One of Brown's men is here, and he's not interested in finding out about local history.' I pulled Chloe towards the first museum room and as we passed the receptionist I said, 'My sister's ex-husband is coming in. Please don't tell him we're here. He can be violent.'

On cue, the glass door at the entrance opened and the receptionist gasped. By then we were in the old part of the building. Tan colored lino floors, polished wood banisters, prints of old Chertsey on the walls, that sort of place. I pushed Chloe up the creaking stairs to the first landing. It worried me that, when I had spoken to the receptionist, I could see her display of the CCTV feeds. If I had, so would the bouncer. I hoped the screens only showed the exhibition rooms, not the corridors or landings.

'Who is it?' whispered Chloe.

I put a finger to my lips and pulled her away from the balustrade. The bouncer hadn't met Chloe, as far as I knew, but they would have sent him an image. It would be a Code DQ: Detain for Questioning. Downstairs, I heard the bouncer's voice and then the receptionist's reply, but I couldn't make out what was being said. Soon after, there were heavy footsteps as the bouncer entered the old part of the museum.

I pulled Chloe into the first exhibition room. It was a dimly-lit display of ancient costumes. In the glass cases, dresses floated like headless ghosts. I whispered to Chloe to get on the floor behind the central display cabinet. I squeezed behind the open door. For all his bulging muscles, the bouncer wasn't that fit, because he was breathing hard by the time he reached the top of the stairs. Burned himself out doing speed cycling, maybe. He paused on the landing, listening. I held my breath and prayed that Chloe wouldn't move. Somewhere above, I heard a phone ring, then the sound of the second woman's voice. Bouncer moved. Not upstairs, but into our exhibit room.

Through the crack in the door I saw him look, sniff and then he went out. He crossed the landing to the doorway of the other exhibition room and looked in there. When I heard his feet thud up the stairs, I nipped round the doorway to see him go along the next landing. I fetched Chloe and, when I heard the bouncer go into the fourth display room, we tiptoed down the stairs hugging the wall. As we went past the receptionist, she pointed at the security screen. The bouncer was doing a rapid tour of the remaining display rooms. She said, 'Is that him?'

I nodded and pushed Chloe towards the exit. The receptionist called, 'He called me a liar. My dear, however did you get tied up with such a brute? My cousin Myrtle had an unsuitable boyfriend once... now what was his name...?'

I didn't wait for the rest of her story. I pulled Chloe across the road, and a lorry blared its horn at us. We ran into Colonels Lane, down the right-hand side of Abbey Green, and then hid behind a stand of trees at the far end. We worked our way along the cover until we could look back at the museum entrance. A display plaque, burnt and scored by vandals, informed us we were amongst the ruins of one of the most important abbeys in Britain: Chertsey Monastery. King Henry VIII had done a good job demolishing it because only a few footings were left, and they wouldn't have hidden a Chihuahua. I supposed it was irony that we were trying to find sanctuary there.

I knew from my earlier wanderings, that there were only three routes out: back across the green to the main road; to the right, across a footbridge onto the Thames-side marsh; or down a cutting on the left that eventually led to the churchyard. Each had its drawbacks, so I decided to wait and see what the Bouncer would do.

Chloe said, 'Tell me about yourself.'

'Uh?'

'I told you things about me. I want to know about you.'

Secret service agents, or subcontractors of same were pursuing us, and she wanted my family history? 'Not now,' I said. 'Keep watching the museum.'

'Why are men so... single-track? Look, you can see there's no one. While we wait, you can talk.'

My instinct was to keep the shutters drawn but, dammit, I fancied the woman so I didn't want to wreck the enterprise before it had properly started. Even though trading personal life-stories seemed perilously akin to commitment.

'For instance,' she said, still determined, 'are you married? You don't wear a wedding ring but at times you act... spoken for.'

'I'm no longer married.'

'Ah! Tell me about her.'

'I'd prefer not,' I said, remembering the phrase from an American short story I'd read years before. My past was my own. God knows, I had made plenty of mistakes but it was still my life.

'Is she alive?'

She wasn't going to give in, then. 'Yes.'

'Divorced?'

'Yes.'

'Who divorced who?'

'Chloe!'

A pause of five seconds. 'Just tell me that.'

'She divorced me.'

'Because you went with another woman?'

She said it with excitement, as if it was blurb on an airport lounge paperback.

'Not until after we separated.'

'Who was it?'

'Who was who?

'The woman you went with?'

'A crazy girl from the agency I worked with. Called Melissa. After that, a Russian secret agent called Tatyana. Both relationships were complete and utter disasters, so I'd rather not talk about them, OK?'

Pause of less than five seconds. 'Do you still see them?'

She sounded serious. Measuring me against her criteria of male acceptability. She repeated the question when I didn't answer. To end the interrogation I said, 'My wife, Mary, was... is... a career Civil Servant. We met when I was in MI5. Her father's a sort of squire in Buckinghamshire - farm, woods, stately home, and magistrate - that sort of thing. Mary's Mater and Pater had lined up some rich country bozo for her to marry, but she rebelled. Coincidentally, I wanted to prove to my middle-class parents that I wasn't the failure my father said I was. So, after six pints of beer, I proposed to Mary. She, having matched my alcohol units in double G and Ts, agreed. The wedding ceremony was a disaster. But we clung onto the hope that opposites can sometimes learn to get on. For a while, we did. We moved into a tiny house in Hounslow. Am I boring you?'

'No, no, go on.'

'After two months there, we knew we'd been stupid. Six months later, we hated each other's guts. So, we worked as much extra duty as we could, to avoid meeting in the house. We left post-it notes on the fridge if we needed to communicate. A successful week was when we never saw each other. I became a slob to annoy her. She reacted by becoming more refined. Couldn't last, of course. She fell for some dummy with Eton and Oxbridge pedigree. He and split his time between his London flat, a place in the Cotswolds, a villa in Tuscany, and a timeshare in California, for God's sake. She told me to leave because she wanted to sell the house. Her lawyers made a convincing case that I had tricked her into marriage, and that termination was necessary because of "cruelty resulting from the husband's social immaturity", or something equally bizarre. They won, of course. Money always wins.'

'And the others?'

'I was too boring for Melissa.'

'What about the Russian girl, Tatyana?'

'She... died.'

'I'm sorry.'

Curiously, I felt a huge feeling of relief that it was in the open. Even in my 2am musings, I had never condensed it so well. Mercifully, Chloe said no more. Just patted me on the arm as if she was a mother whose little boy had grazed his knee. Though it had hurt a damn sight more than a graze. And the pain hadn't yet gone away.

Two white-faced, emaciated youths sidled up. 'Ere, you're hiding ain't you?'

'No,' I said, 'we're studying the history of Chertsey Abbey.'

'Nah, you ain't. You nicked somefing. Give us money or we tell.'

Never let anyone tell you that the youth of today lacks initiative. When necessary, they have all the skills they need to survive.

'Scuzzers after yer?' He meant the police. The youths looked back to the road half wanting, half fearing the blue flashing light of a police car.

'No.'

'Who then?'

I was trying to work out how to turn the situation to our advantage when Chloe said, 'I've run away from my husband. He said he's going to kill me.'

The boys leered at me. 'This your bit on the side?'

'I am not,' Chloe said. 'Now push off.'

I was impressed at how confident she sounded. Though it made me wonder how true her life-story had been. Surely she wasn't in the pay of the Service too? Chloe extracted a five-pound note from her purse and gave it to the tallest boy. He held it to the sunlight that filtered through the trees to check its pedigree. 'Secret's safe with us, darling.' He said it with a smirk, though it may have been his attempt at empathy. Then, without another word being spoken, the boys ran diagonally across Abbey Field towards the museum.

I said, 'They're off to find your "husband", to squeeze more cash out of him. Even if they get nothing, they'll tell him we're here so they can watch the action. We have to move.' I walked smartly away, through the wrought iron gates in a tall wall.

'Wait!'

I let Chloe catch up then, hand in hand, we hurried along behind the wall that led back to Colonels Lane. We crossed that, and then turned left. A little further up we veered right and I urged Chloe into a run. I found the footpath between the houses that would return us to the High Street. It concerned me a bit when I saw a CCTV camera pointing down from the back of a warehouse but I didn't think Brown would have had time to cover all the territory. I pulled Chloe to a walk and motioned her to keep quiet. The path squeezed between a building and the iron railings that surrounded the churchyard. If Chisel had returned to his tree lookout, we were trapped. Luckily, all I could see were grey, leaning gravestones.

At the end of Church Walk, I looked for Brown's team. I couldn't see any of them so I put my arm round Clair's waist and maneuvered her left. We couldn't go down Guildford Street, in case Adam was still there. And we couldn't use the station. Assuming the bouncer was still in Windsor Street or Abbey Gardens, I led Chloe past the Crown Hotel, and headed out of town. When we lost sight of the junction, I called a local taxi firm to take us to Weybridge station. It was time I found out what my old boss was up to.

8

In the taxi, I talked non-stop about movies. It was a combination of nerves, and the fear that Chloe might say something the driver would remember when Brown interviewed him. The taxi dropped us at Weybridge station and we walked down the slope towards the booking office. When the taxi had left the station forecourt, I stopped Chloe to tell her we had to find out what was up with Salnikov. I had a feeling he was involved, and it would save me time and effort if he came clean. Assuming I wasn't too late. Brown was efficient so they may already have banged him up in prison somewhere. Always best to check the obvious first, though.

Down on the heath, the watcher was in the same blue Volvo, pointing the same camera at Salnikov's house, so we retreated up the road a little way. Coming down the hill, a woman was delivering glossy magazines, so I offered to take a batch of them from her to deliver to the houses as far as the pub. It would help in our research, I lied, for an article we were writing on letterboxes. I held out a ten-pound note. She shrugged, pocketed the money, and gave us thirty or so of the glossies. When she had gone up a side street, I described Salnikov and his house to Chloe, gave her the magazines, and told her to put one in every house down the hill. At each doorway, she had to find a reason to delay – a difficult letterbox, awkward gate, that sort of thing. On a sample, she was to ring the doorbell and ask the householder if they enjoyed the content of the magazine. When she got to Salnikov's, she was to ring the bell, and if he came to the door she was to say "Arklow53". Then tell him to go to the Ship Hotel, Weybridge, in one hour. 'Got all that?'

She said she had.

'Don't say anything else to him. If someone other than Sergey comes to the door, do the patter about magazine content. And don't let the person in the Volvo see your face. He or she will be taking photos of you. Carry on delivering to houses beyond Salnikov's, and ring a few more doorbells until you cross the road after the pub at the bottom: the British Volunteer. By then, you'll be out of sight of the Volvo.'

'Won't they follow Salnikov?'

'Probably. But he won't do anything rash. I expect they threatened him unless he co-operates.'

'They can't do that.'

'They can. Sergey is a special case. I'll tell you about him sometime. Now off you go. I have to get to the Ship without the watcher seeing me. Meet you there in... forty-five minutes.'

Chloe arrived in the reception lounge of the Ship holding a W H Smiths carrier bag. We met as if we were old friends. I led her to the bar and bought her a drink, then chose a seat by the front windows, and chatted about silly things. A party of three elderly people were reminiscing in a far corner. Otherwise, the bar was empty. From where I sat, I could see the approaches to the hotel. I could also see the lounge, the courtyard, and the doorway to the rear car park.

Ten minutes later, a taxi pulled up by the front entrance. The blue Volvo was following close behind but as there was nowhere for him to park, he hovered on a double yellow line. Salnikov got out of the taxi and the watcher took some shots of him walking to the front door of the hotel. When the Volvo driver saw a traffic warden heading towards him, he put the car in gear and sped round the corner towards the hotel car park. Salnikov took a long time to come into the bar. When he appeared, he strode directly to us and put a hotel key card on the table. 'Quickly. Take your drinks and go to room 12. I shall drink alone here, and read the magazine provided by your young lady. When my tail gets bored, I will go to the toilet in... twenty minutes? I'll come up briefly. Go now, before he appears.'

Room 12 was stuffy and hot. Time dragged. We sat in the two easy chairs listening to the dull rumble of traffic in Weybridge High Street. I had propped the door open so Salnikov wouldn't have to knock. He came after thirty minutes and shut the door behind him. 'Your young lady...'

'Can be trusted.'

He dipped his head at her and then turned back to me. 'This Fraser thing is coming from someone in government. High up. Powerful.'

'Who?'

He shrugged. 'I cannot find out. And Jamie, you were right about your arms report, they did want you punished. Perhaps this is connected? Though it does not explain why they want me out the way.'

'Are you ill?'

He shook his head. 'Someone I knew vaguely phoned to advise me I was suspended. Because of misuse of SIU budget, he said. When I asked my current handler in MI6 what was going on, she said I was to lay low and not get involved with Fraser's case – or with you. If I do meddle, they will revoke my British citizenship, cancel my pension and... distress my family.' His eyes watered. He had feared that happening all along. 'What have you stirred up, Jamie?'

I filled him in with all I knew.

Sergey listened in silence then shrugged, 'I regret I cannot help you.' He glanced at his watch, 'Now I have been absent long enough.'

'Can't you give me anything?'

'No. Use your own contacts in SIS.'

'Come on, Sergey. We used to be friends.'

He thought for a while, then wrote something on the pad by the telephone. 'This is the man who wanted you kicked out.' He opened the door, looked out, and then turned to say, 'Please do not contact me again. And do not leave this room for one hour. Udachi.' With that, he left.

I stood to one side of the window and looked round the curtain. After ten minutes, Salnikov left the hotel. He stood on the edge of the green near the Monument, waiting. Then the same taxi that had brought him drew into the slip road in front of the hotel. I smiled. The old KGB man had lost none of his fieldcraftiness. Sergey got in the taxi and, as it turned right into the High Street, the blue Volvo joined the stream of traffic, four cars behind the taxi. Like a scene from a movie.

'So who is he?' said Chloe. 'Apart from being your ex-boss?'

'He's a good man. He defected from the USSR towards the end of the Cold War. Brought some useful KGB stuff that speeded up Perestroika. For a while he was flavor of the month in MI6. When the thaw came, old enemies were forced to be friends, which meant Sergey became an embarrassment. Coincidentally, our government set up the Strategic Intelligence Unit to monitor economic or political threats from Johnny Foreigner unknown, and the Service put Salnikov in charge. I suppose they thought if he was kept busy, their worries would disappear.'

'Did they?'

I shrugged. 'Sergey did all the right things but they never trusted him. They fretted that as he'd swapped sides once, he could do it again. So they kept a tight rein on him. They let him buy a retirement house in St Ives, and he intends to move his family down there. My guess is that it was just a carrot to keep the donkey heading in the right direction.'

'Meaning they don't intend letting him go?'

I shrugged. 'Who knows?'

'Do you trust him?'

'Sergey? Yes. He is a Russian realist.'

'Why did he defect?'

I shrugged again. Sergey and I had talked about it, but the reason he gave for becoming a traitor often changed. 'All I know is that he still loves Russia, though not the way it was governed - or is run now. I love Britain, but that doesn't make me keep my mouth shut when I see wrongdoing. Especially by politicos.'

'So now what?'

I was in a hotel room with a beautiful woman I fancied and we had an hour to kill. I knew what I wanted to do. However, I had to stay focused. I went over to the telephone pad and tore off the top sheet. Sergey had printed a single word: "CONSTANTIN". It didn't mean anything to me. I put it in my pocket, removed the next three blank sheets, and put them in my other pocket - in case the pen had left indentations. Old habits die hard. To Chloe I said, 'We need to do some digging in London.'

I saw the excitement in her eyes. She was beginning to enjoy this too much. My new phone pinged. Professor Dunning. Thankfully, he didn't start with any academic waffle.

*A few days later, some British Army SAS soldiers arrived on foot. A major was in charge, but there was also a captain and two sergeants. Six more mercenaries arrived from the East. These all spoke Russian, wore Soviet uniforms, and carried Soviet weaponry. We had to learn some Russian phrases, which we were told to shout when we went into action. A group of African soldiers joined us but they set up a separate camp that was run by Sergeant Ryan. We trained hard for four weeks. One of the Russian-speaking soldiers, and two of the Africans, were badly injured and taken away but were not replaced. The Major told us we were on a top-secret mission to maintain world peace. If we were captured, we had to say we had been recruited by the*

*Soviets. We were not told the target, or the reason we were attacking. [I have obviously condensed and rephrased a good deal here. Fraser has a penchant for repetition and the recounting the minutia of camp life, which I assume, does not immediately interest you. I will, of course, include everything in my final report. Dunning.] At the end of training, we were split into two groups. The Major led one. I was allocated to the one led by the Captain. Each had a mix of Africans and whites though all the Russian-speakers came with us. We marched north and, after two hours, stopped for food and drink. Then the Major's platoon headed northwest. We never saw them again. We were allowed rest and then the Captain gave us another briefing. He told us there had been a change of plan. Instead of preventing the coup, we were to suppress it once it had started. We were authorized to kill all the rioters. For five hours we marched north, northeast and then camped at the border with Niger. The Captain said we had to wait there until he got final orders from London.*

Dunning's message ended there. 'Bugger.'

'What?'

'No names... apart from this Sergeant Ryan.'

After she had read it she said, 'Why were the British involved – rather than the French?'

'That's one of the things we need to find out.'

There had been no word from the Colonel, and his phone was still switching to voicemail. So I left another vague message asking him to contact me. Then I rang someone in SIS Central Facilities I had used a few times. In the usual MI6 cryptic-speak, all she said was, 'One thirty.' Had she said "one", it would have meant: "Meet in the National Gallery café at one pm". One thirty meant the Founders Arms on the south bank of the Thames, between

Blackfriars Bridge and the Globe. "Two" would have been sod off, I'm tied up. Time was short so I'd have to get a shuffle on. 'Come on,' I said to Chloe, 'We'll brainstorm on the way.'

'Didn't your boss tell you to wait for an hour?'

I wondered if she meant anything by that. I decided that, as a good nurse, she was only following instructions. I couldn't cope with the disappointment that might result from an alternative interpretation.

In London, I sent Chloe to the House of Commons Library to do some research while I marched along the Thames Path towards the Founders Arms. It was a curious design from the late sixties: modernist, one story, and hexagonal. Its attraction - apart from the beer - was the quiet Thames-side location. It had a stunning view across the river to St Paul's and the City of London. As it was a sunny lunchtime, the outside tables were filling quickly but I needed somewhere away from curious gazes. I grabbed a table inside, next to a riverside window, and a potted palm that screened me from most of the pub. I ordered food for myself because I knew the officer I hoped to meet wouldn't eat. She was a bit odd, but I had great respect for her professionalism.

The usual office types piled in to down a quick lunch, and made the pub noisy. When my steak and ale pie arrived, I divided the time between watching the ebb and flow of the crowd and the view out the window. I tried to pretend I was by the Grand Canal in Venice. It didn't work. Occasionally a tug soldiered against the tide, pulling a string of refuse barges linked two-by-two. On the waterbuses, tourists leant over the rails, snapping everything.

Seagulls balanced on the remains of wooden jetties and looked superior. I like London. Well, not all of it, but the bits I like, I love. It lets you be anonymous, yet you feel part of something alive. Buzzy.

Doreen Allard came through the entrance and looked around the bar for me. She was late fifties, built square, and her greying hair fizzed like wire wool. As she sat, she said, 'How's your love life, boy?' She leaned over the table and pinched my cheek. 'Looking peeky. Still not eating proper food?'

Mrs Allard demanded that everyone be ruddy-cheeked and full of vim. Ready to ride to hounds or dance naked in a fountain after knocking back a brace of double whiskey and sodas. Though she cultivated the image of being a country-set Grande Dame, I knew the only countryside she was comfortable in was Kew Gardens. She lived, fairly simply, in a block of Art Deco flats near the British Library. Nevertheless, we were comfortable in our roles, for life would be pretty dull if everything was literal. I said, 'Unrequited love, I'm afraid, Mrs Allard.'

'Tell Auntie Doreen everything.'

She didn't really want to know, although a good agent – in whatever department – is always ready to hoover up CX. I said, 'Some other time.'

'It's not that unsuitable Melissa person again.'

I was surprised she knew.

'Don't look so innocent. Everyone lapped up your escapades. We'd be a poor bloody spy outfit if we didn't know the tittle-tattle about our own community.'

Nevertheless, it irritated me that they had been so nosey. I thought I had put enough distance between me and 'their' community. 'No, it's not Melissa.'

'She's with child, did you know?'

'So a weasel told me.' A pause. 'It wasn't me.'

'Good. So,' she said, small talk over, 'why did you want to make contact?'

I described Brown.

She nodded. 'Know him. Slippery, two-faced tart. Why's he a problem to you?'

I told her. Well, most of it. I also described Adam, the bouncer and Chisel, who she didn't know.

'So what can Auntie do for you?'

I asked her to look in the Service databases to see if Brown's show was authorized; to find out who had requested the operation; and to establish where Fraser was being held. I also asked her to trawl the archives for anything about a covert British operation in the 1980's, in Nigeria or Niger. While I spoke, she looked either at the menu or out the window. She took no notes. Eventually she said, 'You don't want much.'

'Anything will be useful.'

'If they get wind I'm snooping...'

'Then don't take risks. Can I buy you lunch?'

She shook her head. 'On my way to a briefing by some lah-de-dah merchant banker. God, I hate industry briefings. Never understood why they insist on our section going. To be frank, young Jamie, the place is going to pot.'

'A drink, then?'

'New company policy: "refrain from alcohol whilst on duty unless operationally imperative". It's all Budget, Budget, Budget; Rules and Regulation; and risk-bloody-analyses. And the endless reports that have to go here, there and everywhere. Seen the job adverts for us they run in every unseemly rag? What would that nice Mr Cornwall have said?'

I let Doreen rant on about the drift downwards from the service's "good old days"; the relentless rise of the cyber world; the volatility of populist governments. It was my way to pay her for what she might do. After a while, she stopped and grinned. Then she reached over and gripped my arm, 'There's something you've not got off your chest, Jamie boy, I see it in your face. Either that or you are three days constipated.'

'Uh, well, I've kind of implicated someone innocent in all this. If it's possible, could you get her a false passport? In case Brown gets rough?' I slid over the photo I had taken of Chloe on my phone.

'Your new filly?'

'Not technically.'

'Wholesome looking. Good teeth. Make a fine mother. You have my permission to bed her.'

'I'm not sure she'll let it come to that.'

'Then you're slipping, boy. Why does she need a falsie?'

'She helped me on something that's got her suspended. Brown made threats so I might need her to disappear.'

'Have you any idea how difficult it is to get a falsie is these days? The authorization? The paper trail?'

'You used to say, "In HR anything is possible".'

She grunted and then said, 'Anything else?'

'Can you transfer funds into this account?' I gave her a slip of paper with Mr Apollinaris' bank details. 'All you can safely get away with.

'Jamie!' She gazed round the room to check everyone out. 'You left the Service a long time ago.'

'Something dirty's going on, Doreen. Possibly involving the Executive. They might have put people inside the Service... or even in your beloved Security.'

'And you think an ex-ex-employee can sort all that out? No, sorry, Jamie...'

'Doreen, please. I know I'm onto something, but first I have to protect Chloe. Help me, and I'll try and sort out this conspiracy.'

'Conspiracy? Tcha! You've been watching too many movies.' She looked out the window again. I followed her gaze. In the brown river I saw swirls of current as the ebb tide mixed with the river's flow. Doreen said, 'Are you in love with this gal?'

'No.'

'But you have hopes?'

I shrugged.

'So you play your old aunt for a sucker. Then you'll skip the country with this... Chloe... and set up as Mr and Mrs Apollinaris in Zagreb or somewhere equally anonymous. Am I right, or am I right?'

'Wrong. I have no intention of going to Zagreb.'

She laughed and stood. I reached out to hold onto her hand. 'Fraser was about to uncover something big, Doreen. With potential to inflict damage on someone important. I have to find out what went on, and who's behind Fraser's disappearance. And get Fraser released. But I can't do it without your help.'

She sat and sighed. 'I've always liked you Jamie, but I can't forget how you tricked me into giving false information.'

'It was necessary, I'm sorry. It worked out in the end.'

'The end does not always justify the means, even in our industry. Why did you really leave SIU?'

I supposed an exchange of info was only fair. 'Someone pushed me. Supposedly over one of my reports.'

Doreen guffawed. 'You mean that stinker you turned in about arms dealing? Surprised it took them so long to give you the Order of the Boot. All right, one more question. Why bother? Why not walk away from this conspiracy theory of yours, woo this Chloe with gusto, bed her, and then set up home in an arty two room flat in Hastings?'

To be honest, I didn't exactly know why. Curiosity? Revenge? A chance to prove I was a better agent than they would ever let me be? Or was it because I felt a failure and needed something to restore my confidence? I shrugged. 'I don't like seeing ordinary people pushed around, by them up there.'

She let out a bark. 'Claptrap. Do I detect a teensy-weensy bit of anti-government vitriol? Only I couldn't...'

'No,' I said, 'this has a political angle, I'm sure of it.'

'Bollocks.'

'All right, I need to get to the truth.'

She thought for a while and then said, 'Against my better judgment, I will try to help. Only because I have a soft spot for you, mind.'

'Thank you, Doreen.'

'But this is the last favor. Ever. Understand? All this digital surveillance malarkey is getting beyond my comprehension. Soon we won't be able to take a pee without it being recorded on a sim card embedded in the toilet seat, and sent on a blasted satellite link to Langley for analysis. The days of individuality have long since passed.'

'Thanks Doreen.' I held onto her hand a squeezed.

Her brief, sad smile looked genuine. 'I mean it, though. No more contact. They are watching me... I don't want to give them a reason to issue a termination letter.' Then she prized her hand away and looked at her watch. 'Hell fire! They'll want to know what I was doing in the missing ten minutes.' She got up. 'I'll do what I can, Jamie. Come and see me in Berkshire when I've bought the stud farm I fantasize about. We'll get drunk on Pimms and yarn about the good old times.'

I said of course I would, though I knew she'd not tell me when retirement happened. Besides, she was careful never to get drunk. And she hated horses. Why do people dream of living in the country when they get old? Makes no sense.

I went to the Guildhall and the Barbican libraries to look up everything on Niger in the 80's. There was nothing about a coup in the 80's (though they did have one in the 90's). Their economy seemed to be bumping along on mining, agriculture, forestry, and a little fishing - in the Niger River and in Lake Chad. Some exports of textiles, furniture, chemicals, and cement. There were sandy plateaus and desert in the north; mountains in the center; and savannah in the south. Plenty about the makeup of the population, their GDP, carbon footprint and all that. The internet resources were senselessly huge but there was nothing that helped. I was suffering information overload so I needed to put my mind in neutral.

I headed back across the ex-wobbly bridge and let the Tate Modern swallow me up. For some reason, the bizarre has the power to evaporate my worries. I was puzzling over a Tracy Emin, when I got a text from the Colonel: RYAN MISSING PRESUMED DEAD NORTHERN AFRICA OCT 1980. OFFICIALLY ON LEAVE. NOTHING ON ZINDER. FURNISH MORE DETAILS?

I walked to Trafalgar Square and on to the Foreign Office. I gave the receptionist an invented story about a personal delivery and got my ex on the phone. 'Hello Mary,' I said politely. 'You wanted to speak.'

'Horseguards Parade in ten minutes.' She slammed the phone down. My old irritation surged back. Mary was obviously intending to treat me like a servant after all this time. Nevertheless, in the interest of still attempting to prove I wasn't the ogre in the relationship, I headed down King Charles Street.

Tourists were crisscrossing Horseguards but nothing else was happening. I stood in the dead center and, at the end of the eighth minute, Mary appeared through the arch. She marched towards me like a horse-guards captain *sans* horse. I told myself to stay calm. Not to get into an argument. Not to floor her with a right hook.

At twenty meters she barked, 'What the hell are you up to?'

I replied, 'Hello Mary, how have you been?'

At ten meters she snarled: 'Cut the clever talk. I got accosted by a deeply unpleasant oik from the Security Service. Wanted "background" on you for some shitty operation he's running.'

'What did you tell him?'

At one meter: 'I told him to piss off and follow correct procedures.'

'Good for you.' Mary had always been a stickler for rules. For once, it had worked in my favor.

'I didn't do it for you, idiot. Some of those weirdoes in MI5 think everyone should roll onto their backs and go gaga as soon as they open their mouths. Come on. I want to know what you're up to.'

I had to be careful. Mary in high dudgeon was fearsome. And she was now quite senior in the FO. I said, 'I have a new job.'

'After being kicked out of the SIU.'

'How did you know?'

'Never mind. Stick to the point.'

'I run a detective agency called...'

Her laugh frightened a group of Chinese tourists who scampered away. She poked a finger in my chest. 'You are a complete idiot, Jamie Nelson. Grow up, get a sensible job, and drop this stupid "investigation".'

'Why?'

'Because I do not want the secret services crawling back and poking their noses into my life. Professional or private. Understand?'

'I hear what you say.'

'And drop the politician-speak!'

'Very well. Did this person who asked for information give a name?'

'Brown. He also thought I would want to know about your current bit on the side.'

My, my, he was working overtime. I said, 'Don't let's go there. And she isn't my 'bit on the side'.'

'As you wish. Brown also insisted on telling me about the death of a certain Tatyana Olizarenko. An FSB secret service agent. Tell me you didn't really have an affair with her.'

I wouldn't answer. She had no need to get so worked up.

'Well?'

'You seem to have forgotten that we divorced, Mary. Nothing I do can hurt you now.'

She exploded. 'You pea-brained little shit! You fornicated with a Russian secret agent! Have you any idea how that compromises me? That's you all over. Selfish little prick. For once in your life, Jamie Nelson try thinking of others rather than giving into the urges of your smelly loins?'

I laughed. I shouldn't have done, I know. But really, my loins have never smelt of anything stronger than Wrights soap. And that had been an impulse buy in Superdrug.

'This is not a laughing matter, you twat. Tell me everything that happened.'

'No, Mary. Watch my lips: we-are-no-longer-married. Tatyana was well after we split.'

She closed her eyes and then said, 'All right. Listen. Brown threatened me. He said he could make things difficult if I didn't co-operate.'

I felt sorry for her. Odd that, after our years of conflict. I put my hand on her upper arm but she shook it away. 'Look, Mary, if Brown comes back, just tell him everything you know about me. But I'm pretty sure he won't use official channels, because I think he's running a renegade operation.'

'What do you mean?'

'The less I say is better for you.'

She considered that. 'Are you being totally honest with me?'

'Cross my heart and hope to die.'

'I got the impression Brown wants to bring you down. Why?'

I shrugged. 'He sent a thug down to my detective agency to hire me. Turned out all he wanted my help for was to abduct an old guy. I decided not to play ball so, when I tried to get the old fella out the way, Brown took offence.'

She softened, looked around to make sure no one was near. Then she leant closer to whisper, 'Be careful. That Brown - or whatever his real name is - worried me. I will stay out of this as much as I can, but my career comes first. Understand? I will not endanger it over you. Comprendez?'

I said, 'Message received loud and clear.'

With that, she turned and strode towards the archway that led her back to her safe and well-regulated Civil Service world. She looked well but she hadn't noticeably softened.


I met Chloe in the café on the first floor of Trafalgar Square Waterstones bookstore. The speakers were playing a cool jazz number led by a breathy saxophone. Not Coltrane, but someone almost as good. Chloe seemed jumpy. I said, 'Heavy day?'

She nodded.

'Find anything?'

She shrugged. 'A long list of current MPs and peers who served in the army in the eighties. I was whittling it down to those who had served in Special Forces when I became aware of people watching me.'

'People?'

'They knew I shouldn't be there. They kept whispering.'

'Whispering?'

'Don't keep repeating what I say!'

'Sorry.'

'A security person eventually asked for my ID. When I couldn't produce it she wanted to know who I worked for and what information I was looking up.'

'What did you tell her?'

'I said it was confidential.'

'Well done. What did you get?'

'Um, well. Not a lot. She said she was entitled to confiscate my notes, so I had to hand over my whittled down list. Then she escorted me out. After that I made sure I wasn't followed.'

'Well done.'

She unfolded five A4 pages of scribbled names.

'All those?' We didn't have the time to follow up every one.

'Sorry,' she said.

I smiled, 'You did OK. Better to fight another day etc, etc.'

'Actually it's, "He that fights and runs away, May live to fight another day."'

'Quite.' An email arrived on my phone from the dear professor:

*The Captain told us to stay silent. We marched in the dark for many kilometers and the terrain grew more desolate. When we stopped, the Captain told us we were close to the border and would cross just before dawn. He said if we were careless, the border guards would shoot us. Something about this Captain I did not trust. He told lies as easily as he told the truth. But he had a violent temper so no one dared question him. One of the locals whispered to me that he knew there were no border guards, and that we were already deep in Niger. Then we continued our march north and, as the sun rose, we arrived at a newly-built road running straight as a ruler from west to east across the desert. We marched east on it and, after several hours, we saw buildings on the horizon. The captain said it was a town called Zinder. He detailed us into twos and threes and told us to enter town at ten-minute intervals. Once there, we had to go to a house on the corner of the main square with a red lorry parked at the front of it. Zinder was small - just mud houses and dust roads. The main square had been decorated with flags and flowers, because there was to be a ceremony that morning to officially open the new road to Niamey.*

'Is that all?' said Chloe.

'It confirms they went to Zinder. And that the unit was there for a ceremony to open the road. That should give us an exact date.'

Chloe's eyes widened, 'You don't suppose they were there to assassinate someone at the ceremony?'

I shrugged. There was no evidence yet. Thought it might explain why the British government was nervous about Fraser's desire to tell all.

'But why Niger? Isn't it just desert?'

I filled her with what I had learnt. 'Now, I'm bushed. Let's get something to eat.'

'But what about finding Mr Fraser?'

I sighed. 'Next time I see Brown I'll ask him.'

## 9

When I got back to the flat in Chertsey, I found a note on the kitchen table. Not propped against a ketchup bottle. Not placed neatly. But stabbed to the breadboard with a carving knife. It read, "Don't play silly buggers, Nelson. Cross me again, and the girl will suffer." Melodramatic, but probably Brown's normal style, stripped of the urbane veneer. I was whacked out but I had to put the brakes on him somehow. I didn't want to bother Doreen, so I thought I'd see if Evan Evans, the Welsh lapdog would lead me to him.

I entered the Crown through the back door. There was no receptionist, so I went across the lounge to peek into the bar. Bingo. Evan Evans was immersed in a fat paperback. It looked as if he had been in the same chair for a considerable time. I bought a couple of pints of ale at the counter and took them over. He jumped when I sat down. 'Evening Evan. Bought you a drink.'

'Where the hell have you been?'

'Here, there and everywhere. Who sang that? Sixties song, wasn't it?'

'I'm not in the mood to play games. Brown said...'

'I need to meet him.'

'What?'

I said slowly, 'I would like to meet Mr Brown face to face. Person to person. In the flesh. Now, if possible.'

'Uh, well, I don't know about that. He travels around a lot and...'

'He was here earlier.'

'Yes but...'

'You do, of course, have his mobile number.'

'Yes, but...' He dried up.

'What?'

'He's off-duty.'

'And I though Zombies never sleep. Where does he live? I'll pop over and say how-do.'

'You can't do that! Look, all I'm supposed to do is sit here, eat and drink my meagre expense allowance and report when you come in, who you speak to, where you go after that. Except you haven't been here. I don't mind telling you I'm fed up to the back teeth with all this. I never thought I'd say it, but I wish I'd never listened to him. Full of it he was. With his, "It'll look great on your CV," and "I can tell you're a born agent." Since I've been on his "team", I've never seen anyone except Brown and the car driver. There's not been a single word of encouragement. I know why he's doing this.'

'Oh?'

'He more or less admitted that this is an unofficial operation. As far as I'm concerned, He can't pull any strings to get me into the Service proper. Bastard. So my only hope is that, if I keep my nose clean, do what he says, there might still be a slim chance that he'll recommend me to MI5. So, no hard feelings, but I'm not giving you Brown's number.'

At the end of his speech, he downed the pint in ten great gulps and then slowly set the glass down. He wiped his lips with the back of one hand and burped. I went to the bar and bought him another pint – of the stronger brew. He knocked off half and then frowned at me over the glass. 'Why are you doing this?'

'Buying you a beer?'

'No. All this business with...' he looked over his shoulder to see if anyone was listening, '...Fraser.'

I shrugged, 'I set up a detective agency that no one wanted. Then this job came on that paid, which gave me the use of a flat.'

'Brown said...'

'Brown set me up. He appeared to have hired me to nanny an old man. Then he implicated me in Fraser's abduction. Because I was ex-Service, he expected me to comply. But I decided not to play ball.'

'Why?'

'I didn't like the way they were treating the old boy. I tried to stop the abduction but Brown took Fraser anyway. Now he has it in for me.'

'You sure that's all it is?'

'Well not quite. I've been trying to find out what's behind it all. It all seems very... murky, though. I think there is a cover-up going on.'

'Around Fraser's abduction?'

'About the reason he had to be abducted.'

Evans nodded and then drank the rest of his second pint in silence. I tore a blank page out of my notebook and placed it in front of him with a pen. I said, 'Fraser is old and sick. As far as I can see, the only person he's a threat to is someone high-up in government. All I want to do is find out. If it's all legitimate, I'll walk away. Go back to my failing agency in Kent. I need Browns address, though. All I ask is that you write it down on this piece of paper. Then you can honestly say you never told me.'

'What makes you think I know it?'

'Evans, I know we don't get on, but I also know you're not stupid. Even you wouldn't get involved without researching Brown. Look, I'm knackered. I need to go back to the flat for a decent night's kip. I promise I will never let Brown know you gave me the address. I promise I will go nowhere and speak to no one until the morning cock crows thrice. And, for what it's worth, here's my parting advice to you. Return to the SIU, accept their offer of promotion, and forget Brown. He won't get you into MI5. Now I'm going to buy you a last drink.' When I returned with it, he had written something on the paper I had given him. I thanked him, picked it up and left.

Next morning, despite my intention of haring off to confront Brown, I had to change my plan because I got a text from Doreen asking me to meet her at eleven. That meant Jubilee Market in Covent Garden. When I arrived, the stallholders were having a thin time. In the serendipitous way of tourists, they had bypassed the area that morning, so the walkways were empty. Music throbbed but no money changed hands. Bored traders read books, or Manga comics, or filed their nails. I saw

Doreen up in the coffee bar. It was a good place to watch people though, for my liking, too visible. Maybe she assumed no one would bother looking there for someone from MI6 Facilities.

'You are deep in the mire, my boy,' she said and pushed a mug of black coffee towards me. 'After this morning, I'm off the case.'

'Why?'

'Because there is a distinct whiff of High Priest about this. One desperate to cover something nasty up. I value my future, and my pension, too much.'

'Who is it?'

She wiped a hand over her face. She looked years older than when I had seen her in the pub. 'No idea. I tried, dear boy, but I failed. Though it's at least someone on the JISC.'

'At least?'

She shrugged. 'My best guess. I am a mere mortal in Security, so my clearance won't get the right answers. Though I did find some severed archive trails and reference to some slush fund allocated to Brown. And he has clearance to run a closed operation. Though, according to what I can see, he has only one MI5 Field Operative on his team - Adam Khan, and he's only a probationer. The others you described are unlisted.'

'Is that allowed these days?'

'Not really. Though if there is sufficient justification...'

'Anything about the Niger operation?'

'I found a file reference, but...'

'Let me guess: it was empty?'

She nodded.

'When was it removed?'

'Two months ago, yesterday.'

Before I had been sacked. And a fortnight before I'd submitted my arms dealing report. So perhaps the case had started when Fraser contacted his MP the second time. 'Which department removed it?'

'As the Americans say, "Protocols were violated". No tag was left.'

So, whoever erased the file, didn't want to be traced. Nevertheless, they would have needed senior clearance, and expertise. 'Did you find out where Fraser is?'

She handed me a slip of paper. It was an address in Rye, East Sussex. She said, 'Two days ago, one of my colleagues was told to send Albanian magazines and a bottle of Raki there. Of course, it may not have been him and, if it was, there's no guarantee he will still be there. Maximum risk, minimum stay; random circuit of underused safe houses. You know the rigmarole.'

Nevertheless, it was something. Even if he had moved on, I might be able to pick up something. It puzzled me, though, why they were bothering to give Fraser magazines and booze. Unless they were part of the carrot. What if I charged in, yelling Human Rights and Violation of the Geneva Convention, only to have Fraser tell me to sod off? Perhaps I needed to concentrate on finding out who wanted the cover up. And why. I also had to keep the pressure on Dunning to deliver the translation... assuming it wasn't total fiction. I became aware that Doreen was speaking. 'Sorry?'

'I said, parting is such sweet sorrow.'

'Uh?'

'Concentrate, Jamie. I'm trying to say goodbye.' She stood and held out her hand. We shook, and she held on to my hand longer than was strictly necessary. 'Be careful, my sweet. Wolves are apt to kill when they are cornered.' She started to leave.

'Doreen.   Does the name Constantin mean anything to you?'

She paused and looked back, 'Not offhand.   I meant what I said, Jamie. I'm backing out.'

'But you will do the passport?'

'It's in hand. But it might get stopped.'

I blew her a kiss.   'Good luck with the retirement.'

She gave me a V sign and then tottered down the stairs. I watched her weave slowly round the bright stalls doing a good impression of being an idle shopper.   She examined handbags, picked up a model of a red London Transport bus but didn't buy it, went back the way she had come, tried on a Chinese silk scarf in front of a mirror, and then disappeared.   Her current job may have been in Facilities, but she hadn't forgotten her fieldcraft. So, now I was on my own.   Apart from the added complication of me potentially falling in love with Chloe. Despite my feelings for her, I had to get her away from any trouble.   That meant distancing myself from her - without alienating her.   Maybe, after all this, we could pick up again. I decided a day in Canterbury would help me focus. I rang Dunning, but his secretary said he was tied up all day. So I thought I might as well check out the safe house in Rye.

To get there by train would have involved three changes, so I went back to Chertsey and used the replacement hire car.   For once, the M25 was clear and, as there were no holdups on the M2, I decided to visit Canterbury after all.

The visitors' car park at the university was full, so I braved the student one and then walked the short distance to Dunning's block. It was towards the end of the afternoon and young people were hanging around. Presumably waiting for the restaurant to serve hot food. In the language block, everything was as it had been. Dry, academic heat. Faint whiff of BO mixed with cleaning fluid and the atmosphere was heavy with ennui. For all I knew, the same students were still plugged in to their cubicles. It was when I entered Dunning's corridor that I heard the scream. A woman's scream. It ended abruptly and then Dunning flew of his office and smashed into the opposite wall. Someone in a grey hoody followed. He hauled Dunning up and pushed him in front of him towards a far exit. It didn't look like a rag stunt. Dunning looked back and saw me. His face was contorted with fear. I sprinted down the corridor and glanced into his office. The desk drawers were on the floor, metal filers hung open, papers were scattered everywhere, furniture was upended, and Dunning's secretary was on her knees with blood oozing through her hands from a head wound. I went in and helped her to a chair. 'What happened?'

'I heard something. A man was going through everything. He was pointing a gun at poor Dr Dunning.'

There was a long surface cut on her scalp. She'd need a couple of stitches and be checked for concussion. I bunched some tissues and got her to hold them against the wound. Then I looked into her eyes. The pupils were wide but each eye appeared the same size. I said, 'Phone the police.'

'It's not University procedure.'

'Sod procedure. Phone them. Tell them an armed man has abducted Dunning. Thirties, athletic, white, wearing white trainers, blue jeans and a grey hoody. *Then* phone university security.' She nodded, though whether she understood, I couldn't tell. I dashed back into the corridor but Dunning and hoody had gone. I sprinted after them. At the top of a stairway, students were fussing round a girl who was slumped against the wall. Her nose was gushing blood that had already soaked the front of her white jumper. 'Pinch the top of your nose. You, get her some tissues. You, call the police.' The more who rang, the quicker they'd come. I leapt down the stairs three at a time. In front of the exit door to the road, another student crouched over a puddle of sick, and held his stomach. I wrenched open the door and ran out.

The two figures were heading towards the visitors car park. I shouted Dunning's name but this time the hooded man made sure the professor didn't turn around. I ran harder and wished I had kept myself fitter, because I could feel my heart thumping dangerously hard. Ahead of Dunning, I saw the tousle-headed student who had come for a tutorial when I was first there. He was watching what was happening and, in his lazy manner, changed course to block the pair. 'Get out the way!' I yelled. The lad hesitated, and the hoody hauled Dunning on, into the car park. I took a short cut across the grass toward them. I heard the shriek of an over-revved engine behind me and turned to see a grey Renault Espace heading for me. I dived out the way, hit the tarmac hard, and rolled.

The car roared on and its tires squealed as it slewed in front of Dunning. I scrabbled up and ran towards the Renault. The side door slid open and Chisel leant out to grab Dunning. The hoody pushed Dunning inside, and then leapt in. They had trouble shutting the door because one of Dunning's legs was hanging out but the driver didn't stop. There was no way I could catch them on foot, so I ran for my hire car. The driver of the Renault was hitting the horn like crazy and scattering students. I started my engine, bumped over the concrete curb, careered over the grass, and weaved between the trees. A gardener shouted and shook his rake at me but I put my foot down, skidded onto the entrance road, and hared after the grey car. By the time I reached the junction with the main road, the Renault had disappeared. He could have gone one of three ways. I chose left and broke the speed limit going down the hill into the city. At the bottom, I had to slow at the roundabout but I could see no Renault. A police car was heading towards the Uni. I would have to go back and sort things out or the police would start looking for me. I hoped the professor wouldn't do anything stupid.

Dunning's secretary was still holding the bloody pad to her forehead. 'They got away,' I said, and gave her a clean wad.

'But Dr Dunning has a meeting with the Vice Chancellor in half an hour.'

Was that concussion? Or devotion to duty? I said, 'Did you know Dr Dunning was working on an Albanian project for me?'

'I... don't know anything about that.'

'Did he have a... procedure? If anything like this happened?'

'What do you mean?'

I tried to keep my edginess in check. 'Did he ever say something like, "If anything suspicious happens to me, look in such and such a place"?'

She shook her head until she remembered it hurt.

149

'Has he posted anything to me? Jamie Nelson?'

'No.'

'How about Mr Apollinaris?'

'Oh yes.'

'What?'

'I put a packet in the mail collection this morning. He insisted it had to go First Class though normal procedure is...' The phone rang before she could finish and she picked it up, efficient secretary that she was. She gave the person a concise resume of what had happened but when she put down the handset, she blubbed. I went over and put my arm round her. She gripped me with a startling fierceness and wouldn't let go. 'What was the address?' I asked gently. 'Where you sent the Apollinaris letter?'

She snuffled into my chest, 'A Surrey hotel. Chertsey. I can't remember...'

I patted her back. After a while, I eased her away and said, 'Is there a medical facility on campus?'

She shook her head.

'Did you phone the police?'

She nodded once.

'Tell them you'd been hurt?'

She nodded.

Then they'd send a paramedic. I led her to her office and sat her in the chair. 'Do you drink tea?'

She nodded.

Sweet tea for shock, my mother always used to say. It would fill the time before the police turned up.

She said, 'Doctor Dunning will be all right, won't he?'

'Oh yes.' He would, providing he didn't try to be a hero.

She said, 'He's so... so kind. And so... honest.' Then the blubbing resumed so I had to give her another cuddle.

They had taken Dunning because of me, of course. Or, rather, because of the tape I had given him. Brown was very good at his job to have connected us. I now had the added responsibility for his release. Hopefully, he would just tell Chisel everything. They would pat him on the head, say it had all been a big mistake, and tell him to forget it happened. National Security and all that. On the other hand, if they judged he knew too much, they might decide to make him vanish, too. Because even if Hoody had found the tape, Brown wouldn't know how much Dunning had translated for me. I allowed myself a grim smile; Brown would be apoplectic. Unfortunately that meant Chloe was in the firing line. I knew I ought to get back to protect her but I still needed to check out the safe house in Rye. While I was still holding Dunning's secretary, I studied the South East England regional road map pinned to the wall. If I took the road via Ashford to Rye, I could do a quick look-see, then shoot back up the A21 and along the M25 to Surrey. Shouldn't take much longer than the direct route.

Paramedics patched the secretary up and then Kent Police had their turn. They were thorough. I stayed with her while they questioned her and grew increasingly irritated that no one from the campus had come to find out what was happening. The police left to get other statements but told me to stay put because they wanted more from me. I got the secretary to call a colleague she trusted. When the girl arrived, they went off to the Gulbenkian. Then I used the secretary's phone to ring Chloe's mobile. It was a risk using the public network but I had to warn her. Her phone switched to the message service so I didn't say anything, in case GCHQ had it flagged. Next, I rang the hospital switchboard and persuaded them to put me through to Chloe's phone in the staff hostel. No reply. I asked them to keep trying because it was life and death. Then I asked them to try Ursula. She answered immediately and I started to explain who I was.

'Stop right there mister. You're not using me as a go-between.'

'Ursula, listen. Chloe's in danger. I need you to...'

'Danger? From what?'

'Listen!'

'Don't use that tone with me.'

I managed to control myself. 'Look, I'm sorry. I can't give you any details, Ursula, but I have reason to believe someone is on their way to harm Chloe.'

'You are making no sense.'

'I can't say much over the phone because... someone might be listening. If you really are her friend, please find her. Tell her what I've said, and tell her to go to the room the Russian used. Understand?'

'You're winding me up.'

'No Ursula, I'm deadly serious. Just say that: "the room the Russian used". She'll understand.'

After a pause, she said, 'I knew you were trouble the first time I saw you. And I knew you were not a doctor.' She slammed the phone down. I tried to get back to her but the switchboard said the number was permanently busy.

The police were eventually satisfied with my statement. My story was that Dunning and I were old friends. I had been in the area and had decided to drop by. No, I hadn't made an appointment. His secretary had apparently confirmed she had seen me before and that Dr Dunning had gone to have coffee with me. She hadn't mentioned the Albanian tape or the package for Mr Apollinaris so I didn't. I told the sergeant I didn't know who the assailant had been, though I did give a detailed description of him and Chisel and the get-away car. I told them about the curly-headed student and that he might be able to give more info.

When the police released me, I went to the hire car and checked my phone. Nothing from Chloe. I rang the Ship Hotel but they said no one had asked for room 12. Thankfully, I still had one valid credit card so I made a reservation for that room in Chloe's name to give her a bolt hole. I asked them to leave a message for her to ring me as soon as she checked in. 'Of course, Mr Apollinaris.'

I managed to keep up a good speed to Rye. I was pretty sure, even if Fraser had been there, they would have moved him on after Chisel reported what had happened at the university.

Ordinarily, Rye would have fascinated me. It had cobbled streets winding up the hill from a medieval entry gate; it had a castle, an ancient church, smugglers' inns, and quaint tearooms. The address Doreen had given me was a quiet cul-de-sac that ended in a stunning view across Romney Marsh. The red-tiled Georgian town houses looked far too refined to experience dodgy goings on, but of course that was why someone had chosen it as a safe house. Number 31 was towards the end. As far as I could tell, there was no back way, so I had to tackle it from the front. The windows were shut and all the venetian blinds were closed. A charity collector's plastic bag hung out of the letterbox. There was a puddle on the flagstone path that led to the front steps but there were no footprints around it. I went up the steps and rang the doorbell. It shrilled inside. No one came. I pushed open the letterbox and looked inside. Empty hall. All doors shut. Quiet as a grave.

'Can I help you?'

I bumped my head on the door knocker. The voice had come from behind. I stood and turned, knitting together a cover story. A plump woman. Each arm dangling a full shopping bag.

I said, 'I was hoping to visit my friend.'

'They've gone.'

'Oh?'

'This afternoon. All of a rush. I don't know what it is with that house. No one stays long. If I was the owner - though no one round here knows who it is - I'd change the agent.'

'Who is the agent?'

'Doughty, Jones, and Voller. You thinking of renting it?'

'I wouldn't mind.' If she was a nosey neighbor, she might have seen Fraser. I said, 'Perhaps you know my friend. He's about seventy, little beard, hooked nose, scar here...'

'He didn't have a beard when I saw him, but the rest fits.'

'How did he look? He's been rather ill lately.'

'He didn't come outside much. Had a lot of staff... at least that's what I assumed they were. But I thought he looked fit enough. Seventy you say? He was well dressed - in a foreign gentleman sort of way, if you know what I mean.'

It didn't sound like the Fraser I had met. Perhaps they were treating him better than I'd imagined.

She said hopefully, 'Important is he?'

'I suppose so.'

'Celebrity? Has he been on the telly?'

'Can you describe any of the carers?'

'Well the one that called this morning, in the big car, looked like a wrestler if you ask me. He strutted. I said to my Arthur, that man ought to go on a diet. The other ladies and gentlemen... well they was always changing. Never the same two days running. Famous is he, your friend?'

'Not really famous, no.'

'Only we get film stars here. Richard Burton, Michael Caine, Johnny Depp...'

'He's quite important to the government. All a bit hush-hush I'm afraid. Best if you said nothing about it, other than to your husband of course.'

'Well, there's a turn up for the books and no mistake. A Mr Smiley in Rye? You in that line of business yourself?'

'Good heavens, no. Just dropped by for a cup of tea. What time did he leave? I might be able to catch them up.'

'Let's see, I was just off to the shops. That'd be... an hour and a half ago.'

I thanked her and walked away. When I found a payphone, I got the house agent's number from directory enquiries. When I rang the London number a frosty female with an upper class accent answered but became distant when I told her which property I was interested in. She said that, regretfully, it was on a very long let with no expectation of becoming vacant. And no, she couldn't possibly divulge the name of the landlord. Of course, if cared to leave my contact details... I hung up, then drove into Hastings and bought another pay-as-you-go phone, in case Dunning had been traced through me. I was eating into my advance, but it was better to be safe. I rang Ursula again but there was no reply.

In Surrey, having endured a crawl on the M25 due the rush hour traffic and a jack-knifed Hungarian articulated truck at junction five, I went to the Ship. Chloe still hadn't arrived, so I said I'd take the room. It was stuffy and no message had been slipped under the door. I opened the window, made myself a coffee, took a pee, and freshened up. I left a note for Chloe, then I went out.

I retrieved the car, drove to the hospital, and paid for a bay in the front car park. I worked my way through the maze of corridors to the rear of the campus. Out in the fresh air, I rounded the outside of the Princess wing, ambled towards the little car park behind and pretended to be waiting for someone. I examined my watch and surveyed the parked cars as if I was seeing if my lift had arrived. The blue Volvo was parked beyond the security office. It pointed towards the blocks of the staff hostel beyond the car park. I went over, opened the passenger door, and got in.

'Hey!' Adam span round and looked frightened until he saw me. 'What do you want?'

'Why are you here?'

'What does it look like?'

'What are your instructions?'

'I don't have to tell you.'

I reached over, grabbed him round the neck, and pushed my face up to his. 'I'm not playing, Adam. What's going to happen to Chloe?' I felt his hand going for something, so I took one hand from his throat and gripped his wrist. Hard. It was a torch. He dropped it into the foot well and then rubbed his throat.

He grumbled, 'There was no call to do that.'

I took a deep breath and cancelled the slap round the face. I needed co-operation. I'm rubbish at reconciliation but I had to try. 'Sorry Adam. Nervy. Is Chloe in there, or were you waiting for me?'

'I'm on surveillance. You know the score: log everything. Photograph everything. Get bored witless. Ache in every joint. Be bursting for the toilet only two hours into the shift but knowing you can't leave your post.'

'Is she in there?'

Adam shrugged. I balled my fist and he said quickly, 'I've been here four hours. I haven't seen her.'

I considered asking him where Fraser had been moved to, but that would give too much away. Anyway, the more Adam knew, the more trouble he would be in. I patted him on the arm. 'OK. Sorry'

'You're very protective of her. You getting the hots?'

I laughed. 'I feel responsible.'

'Perhaps it would be best if you kept clear of her.'

I nodded.

After a while Adam said, 'Brown thinks you are more than a private investigator.'

I tried to look surprised. 'But that's all I am.'

'He says he knew you before. When you were in the Service.'

'Well, we must have met. But he didn't make a big impression on me because I can't remember where it was.' It was annoyed I still couldn't remember. Perhaps it dated from way back when I had been a junior desk officer in MI5. There, I had spoken to more people than anyone could possibly remember.

'If it's any consolation, he doesn't trust me, either,' said Adam. 'Says I'm over-encumbered by ethics.'

'He's a poser, but be careful of him,' I said.

'I'll try. You should take the hire car back, collect your stuff from the flat and return to deepest, darkest Kent.'

I nodded. 'It would be the sensible thing to do.' Though it was impossible, now Chloe and Dunning were involved. After a pause, I said, 'Can you do me a favor Adam?'

'Depends...'

'The guy I first saw you with... who used the strong-arm stuff on me at the hospital?'

'Toby.'

'He really doesn't look like a Toby.'

'Operational name. I've no idea what his real one is, or where he comes from. Frankly, I feel uncomfortable working with him. But I have to do as I'm told.'

'He's recently abducted a friend of mine. Doctor Frank Dunning, from the University of Kent. My fault, because I asked him to do a bit of research for me. He's an academic and not up to rough stuff.'

'I haven't heard anything about that.'

'Don't put yourself in the firing line, but do you think you could find out where they're holding him?'

Adam pursed his lips, then nodded. 'I'll try.'

'By the way,' I said, 'I have reason to believe that Brown's only giving you access to the outer shell of his operation.'

Adam frowned. 'How do you know?'

I tapped the side of my nose. 'Be a pal and keep me out of your log.'

He grinned. 'Wouldn't exactly increase my promotion prospects if I said you dropped by for a chat.'

I got out, thanked him, and then walked away. I went round the corner, counted up to five, and then looked back at the Volvo. Adam was on his phone. Of course, he may have been ordering a takeaway.

I found the canteen and rang Ursula on the new phone. 'Hi, it's me again.'

'Who?'

'The man at the party who wasn't a doctor.'

'What do you want?'

'Your flat is being watched from the car park.'

'Don't be ridiculous.'

'Take a look. The blue Volvo, near the white Cardiac Cathertisation unit.'

I heard her go. When she came back to the phone she said, 'What the hell are you up to?'

'I'm in your staff restaurant. Come over and I'll tell you all I know. But I can only stay here for fifteen minutes.' Any longer and GCHQ would alert Brown. And I didn't want Chisel/Toby joining our tea party.

They called it Cafe Delight but maybe I wasn't seeing it at its best. The empty, rectangular tables had their chairs tucked neatly underneath. The place had a curious smell of overheated food, coffee, and peaches. In a drinks dispenser, the bearings of a fan growled. On the furthest table from the servery, a single man ate methodically. It seemed to embarrass him that, in the relative silence, his knife clicked on the plate. Above him a large notice in black lettering said, "Be a Helping Hand & Return Your Tray". At the till, a Chinese guy was reading a paperback. Steam seeped around the stainless steel lids on the hot food counter.

A female in an overcoat, not Ursula, came in and stood deciding what to eat. A baggy-eyed server appeared wearily from the kitchen and put her hands on her hips as she waited for the woman's order. I watched, because there was nothing else to do. Food was doled onto a plate, the customer slid her tray along the metal shelf to the cashier, who put a bookmark in his paperback and then swiped the woman's cashcard. The till peeped and the change tray clattered open. The woman took her food to the corner away from the methodically eating man. She put her tray down, took off her overcoat to reveal green operating-theatre gear. She seemed almost too tired to eat. I looked at my watch. Twelve minutes since I'd phoned. Time to go. As I headed for the door, Ursula appeared and strode towards me. She managed to look beautifully confident at the same time as being incredibly haughty. 'Well?' she said when she got close enough.

I pulled out two chairs where we met, and we sat. I said, 'Can I get you anything?'

She shook her head. 'The Volvo man proves nothing. He could be waiting for someone visiting a ward.'

'With a zoom lens on his camera?'

The people in the restaurant were paying no attention to us. Nevertheless, I leaned closer to her and said, 'Do you know where Chloe is?'

She closed her eyes, then nodded.

'Where?'

'I can't tell you.'

'Oh for Christ's sake!'

She opened her eyes and looked at me. 'She needs protecting. Men have hurt her in the past. I don't know enough about you.'

'You can trust me.'

'So you say.'

'Ok, Ok. Look, I appreciate that you care deeply for her.' Ursula's pupils widened slightly. Which probably meant I was spot on. I continued, 'She's caught up in something nasty and I admit it was mostly my fault.' Ursula lifted her hand to hit me but restrained herself. 'It is all over a patient I brought to Chloe's outpatient clinic. He has been abducted and now I'm trying to find out where he's been taken. I didn't want Chloe involved but she insisted on coming along because she was anxious over his wellbeing.'

'You're not police.'

'No. I'm a private investigator. He was taken from my car.'

'Who by?'

'The security services.'

'Hospital security?'

'No. MI5.'

She screwed up her face in disbelief. 'You're not telling me the man in the blue Volvo is a spy?'

'He's just a lowly Security Service officer. Forget him, he's just doing his job. Listen, the reason the patient, an old man, was abducted was because he had threatened to talk about something bad from way back. Something the government wants kept quiet.' No reaction. 'And Mr Fraser needs regular medication.'

'I find it hard to believe any of this,' she said. 'All I know is that Chloe was suspended because of you.' Ursula stood. I grabbed her arm but she yanked it away.

'Ursula, please, hear me out.' She didn't leave, so I ploughed on. 'They took Fraser's medical notes and erased all his files on the hospital database. I have a contact in MI6 who suggested this isn't a wholly official operation. Which means the person running it probably had no right to abduct the patient. Or mess with the records.'

She sat. 'So you are mounting a one-man campaign to put everything right?'

'I'm trying.'

'Then you're more of an idiot than I thought.'

I ignored that. 'A colleague of mine was abducted this afternoon just because he was working with me on the case. I must find Chloe before they do – or she will disappear.'

That got her attention. 'Who was abducted?'

'Doctor Frank Dunning at the University of Kent. He's a doctor of languages.'

'MI5 took someone from a university? You're kidding me!'

'No. But I don't think MI5 knows all this is going on. Anyway, my main priority is to get Chloe to safety. Forgive me, Ursula, by being "safe" I don't mean keeping her in your flat.' It had been a hunch, but I saw I was right. Maybe they were more of an item than I'd realized. 'Besides,' I went on, 'you can't stay with her 24/7. At some time you will have to go on duty. Then they'll get her.'

'But why do they want her?'

'Leverage. To get at me. I've prodded a hornet's nest. Or the queen hornet. I've been told to stop... or else.'

'Then for God's sake why don't you stop?' She shouted so loud even the Chinese man looked up from his book.

I said quietly, 'My mother always told me to stand up for what is right.' Well, not strictly true. Had mother been able to stand up to my bullying father, and had she possessed more in the way of communication skills, she might have said that. For once, Ursula said nothing. The two customers finished their food simultaneously. They met as they slid their plates on a stacker containing a visual record of that evening's dining. They didn't look at each other. They left, isolated in their separate worlds. If Ursula wouldn't help, I suppose I could con a nurse to let me into the flats. Or order a pizza, then bribe the delivery boy to let me take it in.

Eventually, Ursula spoke. 'What do you want from me?'

I reached over the table and put my hands over hers. She snatched them away and her eyes blazed.

I said, 'It was my way of saying thank you.'

'Don't ever touch me again.'

'Sorry.' I didn't need another enemy. 'Is there any other way out of your flats?'

'The fire exit,' she said, 'round the back. It goes to the turning circle, but it's alarmed.'

'Is it out of sight of the Volvo?'

Ursula nodded.

'Do you have a car?'

She nodded again.

'What is it?'

'A grey Mazda Demio. Parked in the staff car park.'

'Go back to your flat. If I don't ring your landline within fifteen minutes, go to your car and drive it to the turning circle. Collect Chloe from the fire exit, then make her lay down in the foot well at the back of your car. Take her to the Ship Hotel, Weybridge. Do you know where that is?'

She nodded again.

'Ask for the key to Room 12. It's paid for, in the name of Mr Apollinaris. The hotel staff are expecting Chloe. Stay with her. I'll come when I can. I'll make sure you're not tailed.'

There was a sudden influx of people to the cafe. They were excited and wanted to talk rather than order food. I heard someone say "fire". 'Come on,' I said, 'something's up.'

.

# 10

As I pushed my way through the crowd in the canteen entrance, I heard people talking about The Fire. I asked someone where it was.

'Block J.'

Ursula gripped my arm. 'That's ours.'

Out in the fresh air I heard an alarm wailing up the hill and, beyond the roof of the Princess wing, white smoke billowed. I pulled Ursula into a run. The fire could have been due to faulty wiring, or a burning toaster, but it might also be an attempt to flush Chloe out. The top of the site was pandemonium. People in pajamas and others wrapped in heat blankets were streaming away from the staff hostels, some obviously suffering from the smoke. Security staff struggled to keep order, and Fire Marshalls yelled as they tried to do roll calls. The blue Volvo had gone. 'Come on,' I said to Ursula, 'we have to go in.'

'No way.'

'Can you see Chloe out here?'

She looked. 'No.'

'Then she might still be inside. Did you tell her to stay put - whatever happened?'

She didn't answer and when I looked over my shoulder, Ursula was backing away. I called, 'What's your room number?'

A pause. 'Fifteen. First floor.'

'Wait here in case Chloe comes out.' I ran to the front door of J block but a Fire Marshall barred my way. 'You can't go in there.'

'My friend's inside.'

'What name?

I told him and, as he ran his finger down a list, I pushed him out the way and wrenched open the entrance door. He shouted at me as I went in, but the screaming fire alarms drowned his voice. White smoke sausages oozed down the stair well. I ran up the steps, yelling Chloe's name. No answer. On the first floor landing, the smoke was thick. A redhead emerged from the whiteness, coughing and holding a towel to her face. I guided her to the stairs and she staggered down. I ran along the corridor but the further I went, the smoke became thicker and it stang my nose and throat. I entered an open flat, wetted my handkerchief at the sink, and held it over my nose and mouth. Then I returned to the corridor. Number fifteen was at the far end. The door was wide open and the smoke seemed thicker from there. I shouted, 'Chloe!' Nothing. I was coughing now, and my eyes were streaming but I had to check it out. Each room I searched was empty. Then I realized the smoke was coming from the bedroom at the rear. The curious thing was I couldn't hear a fire, nor was there a red pulse from flames. But as Chloe might be unconscious in there I stumbled in and was puzzled to see smoke streaming out of a broken window.

My brain said "smoke canister". I felt around with my foot and something metal clanged against the wall. A smoke bomb. Down in the turning circle there was a whoop from a fire engine and blue flashes stabbed the smoke. I grabbed the canister, and threw it out the broken window. As the smoke in the flat began to thin, I did another recce of the rooms. No Chloe. Nor any evidence she had ever been there. There were no upturned chairs, half-drunk mugs, or scattered clothes that might indicate an abduction. I didn't know the number of her own flat, so I couldn't check that, so I ran back down the stairs and out the rear fire escape to check if she was there.

The fire crew were bent over the smoke canister. On the other side of the turning circle, I saw an ambulance crew member slam the back doors of their vehicle and sprint to the front. The two-tones went on and they sped off, towards the hospital. I ran after it, expecting to see it to turn left at the roundabout and race down to A&E. It didn't. It turned right, past the Cowley unit. That was the exit from the hospital site onto the Longcross Road. A few people were milling about on the turning circle watching the fire engine. I ran back and asked a black guy with a dreadlocks, 'Did you see who they put in the ambulance?'

'No.'

An Irish nurse said, 'I did.'

'Who?'

'Blonde. Nurse, I think.'

'Chloe? Chloe Hall?'

He shrugged. 'Looked in a bad way, whoever it was.'

Shit. 'Anyone with her?'

'A man helped her in.'

'Can you describe him?'

The nurse shook her head. 'There was a lot of confusion. People running around. Are you the police?'

'I'm Chloe's friend. The ambulance didn't take her to A&E. It left the hospital that way.' I pointed. 'Why?'

The nurse screwed up her face as she thought. 'Might be taking her to Ashford. They are part of the Emergency Evacuation Plan.'

'You said she was in a bad way. From smoke inhalation or an injury?'

The nurse shrugged.

'Describe the crew.'

'Look. There was a lot going on, OK? How do you expect me to...?'

I lost my temper and yelled, 'I'm not playing games. Who were the crew?'

'A tall man, I think. Yes. Thin. White.' Which may have been Chisel. It could equally have been Brown, or a million other people. I closed my eyes and told myself to calm down. I had only assumed it was Chloe in the ambulance. The smoke canister had been meant to panic, not to hurt. Though it could have been a cover for an abduction it may just have been a warning. To persuade Chloe to distance herself from me.

'You all right, mate?'

I opened my eyes. The black guy had moved between me and the nurse. He looked concerned. 'You better get yourself checked out.'

'Sorry,' I said to the man and the nurse. 'Shock. I'll be fine, thanks.' I had to find out who had been in the ambulance and where it had gone. I ran round the building to find Ursula. She hadn't seen Chloe. I told her about the smoke bomb and what the witness had said about the ambulance.

She said, 'If our A&E is full they have to take emergencies to Ashford or Frimley Green. The dispatcher would know.'

'Can you ring him... or her?'

'I don't know who to...' She saw my anger. 'OK I'll try. Do you have a mobile?'

I gave it to her and then felt my frustration rising as she rang one, two, three different people.

She gave me back the phone. 'The dispatcher hasn't sent any ambulances here yet. All their units are incoming with cases.'

So it had to be an abduction. 'How long had Chloe been in your flat?'

'I asked her round when you phoned.'

'How did she seem?'

'Frightened.'

I realized the next question might earn me a Grace Jones left hook. 'Was she in your bedroom?'

Ursula nodded.

'Did she go to the window?'

Ursula took a deep breath, and closed her eyes. I tensed myself for the attack but it never came. She shook her head, and then opened her eyes. They were wet. 'I made her tea. I wanted to calm her. I hoped that...' A tear ran down each cheek. She wiped them off with her hands. 'I suggested she have a lie down. She may have got up to look out the window when I left, I don't know.'

Adam had said he had been out the front and, in the four hours of his shift, he hadn't seen Chloe.

169

Assuming he was telling the truth. 'Did anyone knock your door? Ring the phone?'

'The phone rang soon after you called. I told Chloe we shouldn't answer it. We decided we would go out for a meal later. I told her you were being stupid.'

Of course, the canister might have been vandalism. Someone with a grudge against the NHS. Or had it been directed against Ursula? I wrote my new number on a page from my notebook and tore it out. 'Ring me on that as soon as you hear from Chloe. Ring Ashford and all the other local A&Es – find out what admissions they've taken from here.'

'It's my fault. I should have got her to safety.'

I patted her on the arm. This time she didn't flinch. 'You did all you could in the circumstances. After all, why should you trust an idiot like me who pretends to be a doctor?'

She managed half a smile.

'Check the other hospitals, Ok?'

She nodded.

'Thanks. I have some groundwork to do myself. I'll let you know if I find her.'

She nodded again, then turned and walked away. She was sobbing. I felt a heel.

I parked in a quiet residential street in West Byfleet, walked under the train tracks and took a taxi to the Ship Hotel in Weybridge. No one followed. I went up to room 12. There was a folded slip of paper on the carpet just inside the door. It was a till receipt for a cappuccino at *The Brasserie on the Quadrant*, Weybridge. I rang hotel reception but they had no message for Mr Apollinaris. Only three people knew of my association with the Ship: Chloe, Ursula, and Salnikov. I searched the receipt for the time it was printed... eight thirty one pm. I looked at my watch: nine sixteen pm. Luckily the hotel receptionist knew where the Brasserie was.

It was trying very hard to be up-market. Perhaps it was succeeding, though I'm no judge of such things. It was all dark wood, tiny wall lights illuminating expensive-looking art works, candles flicking on white linen tablecloths – that sort of thing. I saw all that from the other side of the green because the place had huge picture windows. I walked up both sides of the street but there was no Volvo, no Renault, and no one sitting in any car trying to be invisible. I went round the corner to the Queens Head pub and ordered a half of London Pride. No one followed me in. When I left half the drink to go to the toilet, no one batted an eyelid.

I went back to the Quadrant. Nothing had changed. Traffic passed. No one loitered; none of the walkers looked familiar. I crossed the green to the restaurant and pretended to look at the menu in the window. Inside, there were a dozen or so diners but no one I recognized. However, there were two diners in the rear I couldn't see because they were in shadow. To get a visual, I would have to go in. I opened the door. A buzz of polite conversation, and discreet music. I used to have a CD called *Music to Make Love To* that must have come from the same studio. Here it was probably an album called *Music to Chomp Expensive Food By*. A waiter blocked my entrance and said in what I thought a sneering way, 'Have you a booking, sir?'

I hate that. They know full well you haven't but they want to put you in your place. 'No,' I said and reminded myself of my promise to keep my anger in check.

He sucked in his breath and shook his head. 'We are very busy tonight, sir.'

I did a quick count. There were five spare tables. 'I'll have that one.' I pointed at an empty table towards the rear, dodged round the waiter and marched to it.

The waiter grabbed my arm, 'I regret, sir, all the tables are reserved for diners coming later this evening.'

Then, on the shadowy back table, I saw Salnikov. With a young redhead. She turned round to see what was happening. A redhead who looked remarkably like Chloe.

The waiter said, 'I must ask you to leave, sir, or...'

'It's ok, I've just seen my friends.'

The waiter wasn't falling for that. 'If you do not leave, sir, I shall ask my manager to call the police.'

Much to the alarm of the diners, I sprinted down the restaurant and pulled a chair round to face Salnikov's table. 'May I join the party? Or is it exclusive?'

The waiter grabbed my collar and started to haul me upright.

'Leave him, Max,' said my ex-boss. 'I know him. Bring him a black coffee. I smell alcohol on his breath and I suspect he will be driving later.'

I looked at Chloe and realized she had been the redhead I had guided out of the hostel. What an idiot I had been! I said, a little grumpily, 'Red doesn't suit you.'

She laughed. 'But effective, don't you think?'

'So,' I said, after the waiter plonked a microscopic cup of coffee in front of me, 'what's going on?' I was annoyed and suspicious.

Salnikov chuckled, 'When an attractive young lady asks me out to supper, how could I refuse?'

They were enjoying themselves. To bring them down to earth, I told them about Dunning, about Adam keeping the flats under surveillance, and the unaccounted-for ambulance that had taken a blonde away.

Chloe took my hand in hers. I wondered what it meant. Nothing probably. She said, 'I intended to go to the Ship but I worried that someone else might know about it. So instead, I went to Mr Salnikov's house. I thought he would know what to do.'

Anger bubbled up, 'Oh right! So he walked you down to a place that has huge windows where all the world and his wife...'

Salnikov interrupted. 'Calm down, Jamie. There was no one on surveillance and the staff here humor my strange, foreign peccadilloes over secrecy. I have sent my wife and children away and I will soon follow them. I planned my exit a long time ago - when I realized your government might withdraw from its obligations. As for the restaurant windows, I can see everything, yet I know I cannot be seen. I saw you do your reconnaissance, for instance. You have lost few of your old skills. Though you showed yourself in the open too much.'

If Salnikov was about to go into hiding, I had to get answers from him now. I said, 'Dunning was translating bits of Fraser's memoirs for me. Turns out the old man was a mercenary recruited by the British for a covert military operation in Niger in the early eighties. They saw action at a town called Zinder - possibly to put down a coup. Something bad must have happened there but Dunning hadn't translated that bit before he was taken. Whatever happened must be the reason someone in the government is worried about Fraser spilling the beans. So MI5 had me sacked so they could then use me to abduct Fraser. Now they're putting pressure on me to back away.'

'Theories,' said Salnikov, and looked away to spear something on his plate.

I ignored his taunt and said, 'Why would the British organize a covert operation in Niger?'

Salnikov shrugged. 'As you know, I was still in Moscow then.'

'Exactly. You must have heard something. The KGB kept tabs on everything.'

'You, like the old MI6, overestimate our efficiency.'

'Come on, Sergey, what were the Brits up to?'

The waiter came with a menu to ask if I wished to order some food. I hadn't eaten, so I picked the first thing that came into my vision. 'I'll have the chop, please. But boiled potatoes instead of chips.'

'We do not serve boiled potato, sir. Perhaps I might suggest Creamed Crushed Charlottes or perhaps Dauphinoise?' He had decided I was trailer trash and needed to be shown I didn't belong. 'Dauphinoise is potato combined with...'

'Charlotte will be fine.'

When the man had gone, Salnikov said, 'Don't take it out on him. He is good at his job.' He paused. 'The British were interested in Niger because of the uranium.'

Chloe said, 'Niger had uranium?'

'Oh yes,' said Salnikov looking at his watch, 'The ore is at Arlit... in the high ground to the north of the country. Also at Akouta. Of course, it has to be refined to produce uranium.'

I said, 'Were the Soviets involved?'

'The Red Army was desperate for weapons-grade material. They were even interested in the trickle they could smuggle out of Niger.'

'So the British went in to stop the smuggling?'

Salnikov shook his head. 'Our generals hatched up a crazy plan to invade Niger but, in the end, the Politburo vetoed it because it would have upset the French. Secretary-General Brezhnev needed France as an ally in case the Americans tried to force NATO to get tough on Russia. The French were suitably anti-American at the time.'

'So you didn't get involved?'

Salnikov pursed his lips and rocked his head slightly. 'Brezhnev persuaded the Army not to invade, as long as the KGB came up with a plan to increase the flow of Uranium ore from Niger. Even Soviet politics were a matter of compromise, you see.'

Chloe said, 'So were the British after the uranium? I thought there were international regulations.'

'No my dear, the British were not *after* it. Their mission in Niger was to prevent us - the USSR - getting uranium. One of our KGB sections were tasked to design a more... viable smuggling operation. All went well until Blunt was exposed as KGB agent. MI6 wanted revenge. Also, President Carter wanted to score a point after we replaced the Afghan leader with one more favorable to USSR. So the US suspended economic and cultural exchanges, and refused to ratify SALT II. But Carter wanted to hit us harder. Our advice to the Secretary-General...'

'KGB advice?'

'Yes. Andropov suggested to Brezhnev that we should suspend the Niger project until, how do you say, the dust had settled. The Americans had lost the war in Vietnam. They had lost their Iranian ally. If we gave them too much provocation, it was thought they might launch First Strike.'

'What happened?'

Salnikov sighed. 'Andropov was overruled. The US put Cruise missiles in Britain, and Cruise and Pershing IIs in West Germany. They escalated their production of ICBMs. The Politburo went crazy and demanded USSR regain its weapons parity with US. The original problem returned: we could not increase production because we did not have enough raw uranium. As usual, Brezhnev dithered. In the end, he told Andropov that the Moscow Olympics would be perfect cover for a shopping trip to Niger. The world would be looking at Russia and all the athletes, rather than keeping an eye on a small, dusty African state.'

'But the Moscow Olympics were held in the summer.'

Salnikov nodded. 'Yes. The Polish problem had flared up you see. When - despite our best efforts - Solidarity started to become more effective in Poland, the Politburo told Brezhnev that Russia must become an iron fist again. They suspected, rightly as it turned out, that if we lost Poland, every one of our satellite states would topple like dominoes. The Politburo gave Brezhnev an ultimatum. Increase flow of uranium from Niger, or else.'

'Or else what?' said Chloe.

Salnikov shrugged. 'Or he would be removed from office. So, our glorious leader touched forelock, kept the nomenklatura happy, and ordered Andropov to launch the Niger Operation by September 1980.'

'But Britain found out about it.'

Salnikov sighed. 'MI6 was desperate to prove its reliability. Mrs. Thatcher had told C that as she could no longer rely on the integrity of the secret services, she intended to cut their power and budget. As if that wasn't enough insult, Muskie issued guidance to the CIA not to trust the Brits any more.'

'Who,' said Chloe, 'was Muskie?'

'President Carter's Secretary of State,' said Salnikov. 'MI6 aimed to humiliate the Soviets to prove that Muskie - and the Iron Lady - were wrong. And get revenge on Blunt and his friends. From our point of view...'

'The KGB point of view?' I asked.

'Yes... from our point of view it was irritating. Our planning was sound. We had diverted many roubles from the agricultural budget to bribe Niger politicians and their cronies. It should have been... what do the Americans say, a walk in the park?'

He made it sound like a game of strategy, rather than a deadly component of the Cold War. We fell silent when the waiter brought my food. Then I said, 'What was the plan?'

'Simple, as the best plans are. We discovered that the Niger foreign minister harbored an old grievance with his President. So we suggested that, if ever he was motivated to mount a coup, we would aid him. In return, we had his agreement that when he was President, he would allow the uranium ore to be smuggled to us across the border.'

'How would you have smuggled it?' asked Chloe, who seemed to be getting rather too interested.

'Two routes, interchangeable. North from Seguedine into Libya, or east from Ngugmi, across Lake Chad into Cameroon. The local people had been smuggling goods for generations. We would merely guarantee them a steady income - and a way to hit back at their colonial overlords.'

'France.'

Salnikov nodded, 'Though of course we had taken steps to distance Russia from all this.

'The KGB organized it all?'

'Da. At least, the plan was. The military did the practical work.'

'Why them.'

Salnikov shrugged. 'Perhaps we, too, were not trusted by our leaders.'

'How did the British find out?'

'Back then, Britain paid well for information. And, of course, the quality of life was deteriorating in Russia.' He looked sad, and I wondered if it had been him who had leaked the Niger plot to MI6. 'After Carrington was briefed, he rang the hotline to demand an explanation. Of course, the Kremlin denied there was any such plan.'

Chloe said, 'Carrington was...?'

'Your Foreign Secretary. I met him once. A gentleman.'

I said, 'But I assume MI6 didn't believe Moscow.'

'Well, let us say, they trusted their source. Moreover, the SAS were still preening their plumage after storming the Iranian Embassy, so said they would sort it. Actually, I believe that was what they said: "We will sort it".' He shook his head. 'You had no embassy in Niger, and with not wanting to tread on the toes of the French, MI6 convinced the Prime Minister it would be best if the Intelligence Service organized things rather than leaving it all to the regular army. C promised there would be sufficient safeguards in place so that Britain would never be implicated – whatever happened. The aim was to foil the coup and encourage a counter-coup. If things went wrong, they would blame the mercenaries.'

'Let me get this straight,' I said. 'MI6 recruited mercenaries, trained them, and used them as a fighting unit, led by British Army officers, to go into Niger to scupper a Soviet-led coup?'

Salnikov grinned. 'I believe you say, "That is it in a nut shell". Although, technically, it was a Soviet *backed* coup. We had no military personnel on the ground.'

I still didn't understand why so much fuss was being made about it now. OK, it may have been a British incursion into French colonial territory, but surely that was ancient history. I was missing something somewhere. I said, 'Did something go wrong?'

Salnikov looked at his watch again and patted his lips with his napkin. 'I believe I have told you enough to explain why your Mr. Fraser was involved.'

'Oh come on!'

He rose. 'I regret I can say no more. I shall pay for your meals, but now it is time for me to go. Please do not follow me, Jamie. Also, please do not try to locate me for, if you do, it will put my family in danger. Do I have your agreement?'

I nodded. He held out his hand and I shook it. It was a very weak handclasp. Salnikov used to have an iron grip. He got up and bent over to kiss Chloe on each cheek. 'My dear, do not let this hot-head lead you into more danger. He means well, but has tendency to be obsessive.' With that, he walked to the front desk, paid and then left. I watched to see if anyone got up to follow him but no one did. The waiter enquired whether we wanted to see the Sweet Menu. We said no.

I didn't think the diplomats and spin-doctors would have much of a problem smoothing over such an old skirmish if it surfaced – even one that had been on French territory. No, something else had happened that implicated someone on Chloe's long list. Perhaps a way forward was to find out who ordered my sacking. I fished out the piece of paper Salnikov had given me earlier. Now that I knew more of the story, Doreen might be able to unearth something on this Constantine. Then I remembered that Dunning's secretary had posted a package to me. Trouble was, that meant going to the Crown at Chertsey and engaging with Evan Evans. Though I couldn't take Chloe. I looked up at her.

'Welcome back,' she said. 'Are you going to let me in on your private brainstorming?'

'Sorry. Um, first we need to find somewhere safe to stay tonight. The Ship's as good as any…'

She shook her head. 'I didn't come away with anything.'

Considering the circumstances, I was surprised she needed anything. Nevertheless, listed what she referred to as essential needs for an overnighter. So I said, ok, we'd go to the twenty-four hour superstore at Brooklands.

'But that doesn't mean we… we…' She blushed. 'I don't think we should… '

Hit the sack together?

'…you know. That, uh, togetherness thing. Until we get to know each other better.'

So she was thinking about sex. Or, she had correctly assumed I wanted to make love to her. A setback, but at there was a hint of progress. I didn't want to push away the girl who wanted to get to know me better but I also couldn't afford to let the trail go cold. A British compromise was called for. I said, 'There's an easy chair in the room at the Ship. I'll sleep there.'

She looked relieved. 'You must think me a prig.'

Which sounded delightfully private girls' school talk. For all I knew, that's where she had been schooled. I said, 'No, you're right, we shouldn't make things more complicated than they are.' Remembering Ursula's concern, I told Chloe she needed to text her friend to say that she was safe, but not to say where she was. Then she was to switch off her phone and not use it again.

## 11

Next morning I went to the Crown and entered via the back door.  Evan Evans was in the lounge, finishing his paperback.  On a table next to him, a half-eaten croissant and a cup of coffee.  By his crumpled look, he had been there a while.  I went outside and used my clean mobile to call the receptionist.  I told her if there was a Mr. Evans in her lounge, would she please tell him to go, immediately, to Chertsey station to meet a Mr. Nelson.

'You are Mr. Nelson?' said the receptionist.

'No, my name is Brown.'

I watched from the corridor as a different girl approached the weasel.  She bent and held out a folded note to him.  He stared down her cleavage for a long time before he took the note.  Bounder.  Should be drummed out of the scouts.  Having read the note, he jumped up, knocked the table so hard the coffee cup fell to the floor and smashed on the marble tiles. Like an eager puppy, he scampered out the front door of the hotel, leaving his croissant, his book, and the mess. I counted to ten, and then went to help the receptionist pick up the jagged porcelain. 'That's all right, sir. I'll get maintenance to finish off.'

I asked her if there were any messages for Mr. Apollinaris.

'Oh yes. May I see some ID?'

At her desk, I showed her the relevant credit card.

She handed me a puffy mailing envelope.

I said, 'I couldn't help noticing a ginger-haired man in the lounge earlier. Was it David Eccles?'

'No sir. A Mr. Evans.'

'Oh Evans, of course. He cornered me the other day. Is he staying here?'

'Yes, sir. Shall I tell him you were asking after him?'

'No please don't.' I winked. 'I'd rather not meet him again. I'm afraid he rather fancies himself as a ladies' man. Insists on telling long, graphic stories about his conquests. To be honest...' I leaned a little closer and made a supreme effort not to gaze at the magnificent upper slopes of her breasts, '...he's a bit of a pest, if you know what I mean. Not to be trusted.'

She nodded. 'Wandering eyes. We get a lot of that sort here.'

To have suggested to her that her push-up bra and unbuttoned sheer white blouse sent come-on signals to every lonely man who walked through the door, would have exceeded my brief.

I didn't open the package until I was back in the Ship. To get there took an hour of evasive work, but at the end of that, I was certain no one had followed me. Chloe had eaten the All Day Healthy Breakfast Selection from room service. She'd had a shower, changed into her new Tesco outfit, and she had made it look terrific. 'Any bother?' I asked.

She shook her head. The blond hair moved seductively and sparkled in the lights. I took a deep breath. It was going to be monumentally difficult to concentrate on the matter in hand but it had to be done. I opened the package carefully. There was a single sheet of typing on headed University paper, a clipped bundle of ten or so handwritten pages, and the cassette tape.

First, the cover letter:

Dear Mr Nelson (or if you prefer, Apollinaris),
I enclose the extent of my translation of your tape. Regrettably, I can spend no further time on this project. Indeed, I have decided the contents are inappropriate to be dealt with by this University. I trust your organization will remunerate me, for what I estimate to be eight hours of work, via the usual channels.
    Yours,
    Dr. F. S. Dunning (Cantab), FRST, AILT

I skimmed through the other pages dense with spidery handwriting. Dunning had already given me the headlines of the early episodes. However, towards the end of his translation was a new episode. I read it out to Chloe.

*'7 October 1980. A big ceremony in Zinder. We were told that President Kountché was to arrive at eleven thirty local time on his private jet. He would*

*land on the new road, 5km from Zinder. Then he would get into a waiting limousine and be driven - in convoy - into town. A rally had been organized in the main square, to celebrate the opening of the road from the capital. At noon, the president was to give a speech. The Captain told us he had received intelligence of a Russian-organized coup during the ceremony. No one knew who the fighters would be or where they would come from. Our mission was to suppress the coup... by any means. We took up positions around the main square. Of course, we Europeans attracted attention, but our Nigerians did not. Zinder is a small market town. The highest place was a minaret over the mosque and a square tower - like you have on English churches. Eleven thirty passed and the crowd began to get noisy. I look hard but I see no one who is armed. Most of the people are poorly dressed and unhappy. They had probably been ordered there, to give a show of support. That often happened in Albania during Communist era: the people had to show visiting dignitaries how much we supported government. Then, on my radio, I get call from the Captain.*

*[FRASER INCREASINGLY ADOPTS A FIRST PERSON NARRATIVE. IT IS NOT AN ERROR IN MY TRANSLATION - D.]*

*He says he sees a sniper, high in the square tower and he orders me to take him out. I creep round back streets and get into the building. The stairs are dusty and dangerous so I go slowly, testing each step as we had been trained in Albania. At the top is single room. Four unglazed openings look north, south, east, west. A man in camouflage is kneeling at east side, looking down on square. He had an...*

*[I CANNOT UNDERSTAND THE FOLLOWING SENTENCES. HE SOUNDS VERY AGITATED AND*

*UNCLEAR BUT I ASSUME HE IS REFERRING TO A TYPE OF WEAPON - D.]*

*I hear cheering and, over the man's shoulder, I see shiny white Mercedes saloons of the presidential motorcade sweep into square.  A small colorful flag flutters from the bonnet of the second vehicle and the sniper aims for the rear of that car.  Using the noise from the crowd, I creep closer to the man.  The cars stop in the middle of the square.  The front doors of the presidential car open.  Bodyguards tumble out of that and the other Mercedes, and they crowd round the presidential car.  One opens the rear door and the president starts to get out.  I see the sniper's finger begin to squeeze the trigger.  I grab him from behind and break his neck.  But I cannot stop his finger pulling the trigger.  By some intervention of the gods, the bullet hits another sniper, on the roof of a building on the other side of the square.  That soldier tumbles over the parapet and lands, with his rifle, in the dusty street below.  The bodyguards hear the shot and see the man falling.  They start running towards my tower but then jeeps full of armed men roar into the square and start firing over the crowd.  They had not been part of our unit.  Bullets sing everywhere.  People scream, throw themselves to the ground, or run.  Our forces open fire on the rebels and there is a terrible slaughter.  Terrible.  Neither side cares who they shoot.  Wounded civilians cry out as they die but no one pays attention.  I see all this from the tower.  I know I should go down, but I am frozen in shock.  I have never seen such brutality.  Our Captain is in the thick of the action, shooting and cutting throats.  He urges our men on with yells and threats.  Blood soaks into the dry mud of the square and spatters the white walls.  The president is finally bundled into his car and, in a rush to get away, it bounces over bodies.*

*After the president leaves, the killing goes on. Our side is the stronger, though you cannot say we had victory – it was a massacre. What I had seen made me sick. Even I, a soldier of many years. I watched the Captain begin to collect our unit together, so I stumbled down the stairs of the tower. But instead of going to him, instinct told me to run into the scrub. I crept further away from the town and hid until night. For many hours I heard single shots of gunfire. I felt a coward but I was also desperate to live. I suspected the gunshots were the captain, killing witnesses. I used the stars to guide me back the way we had come. Eventually, I returned to Babura. I decided not to contact anyone, and made my way to Lagos. I stayed in Nigeria for many months. Then...'*

'Then what?' asked Chloe.

'That's it.' I supposed it was progress of sorts, though not a lot.

'This Captain,' said Chloe, 'is he the one from the British Army?'

'I assume so.'

'If we find him, he can tell us what really happened.'

'If he wants to talk about it. Fraser says he was bad.' Finding the captain would be difficult anyway. If MI5 records had been scrubbed, then so would every other database. Only two ways forward presented themselves: one, find out who had given the order to get rid of me from SIU and two, lean on Doreen Allard to dig deeper into the archives. I decided the best first step was to pay the SIU offices a late night call, to see if I could unearth anything. If I drew a blank there, I'd call on Doreen's flat. That meant I had a free day. I said, 'Fancy a trip out?'

Chloe laughed, 'Where to?'

'The sun's shining. I found a decent pub by the Thames the other day. Let's go for a walk and then eat.'

After a great day in the fresh air, Chloe complained that she didn't want to be "locked up" again in the Ship. Though, eventually, she agreed with my reasoning. I caught the nine p.m. train to London Waterloo, walked along the Southbank path, crossed Blackfriars Bridge, and got to the SIU offices in Temple Avenue at a quarter to eleven. I stood opposite the building, under a tree branch that reached over the wall from Temple Gardens. The only lights in SIU were in the security office just inside the street entrance, and in the Duty Office on the top floor. I could see the shining dome of Ron the security man, watching a TV program.

On the hour, every hour, his instruction was to do a patrol of the whole building. He always started in the basement and finished at the top where the Duty Officer signed off his sheet. It took him fifteen minutes - longer if the Duty Officer was in a chatty mood – shorter if there was a panic on. I couldn't rely on chance, though. At five to eleven, I rang the SIU number. Someone I vaguely knew from the Global Business department answered it. 'Oh hi,' I said, using my best Scottish accent (not that it would have fooled anyone north of the border), 'Foreign Office here. We've got a bit of a flap in Belize. Could you see if you have anything relevant on a chap called Mkusa? M-K-U-S-A, first name Absalom, last known in Luanda. Call me back on the usual number, as soon as. Thanks.'

I rang off before he could ask the Scotsman's name. It would keep him busy (because I had made the name up) and stop him wandering. At eleven, security Ron stood, stretched, put on his jacket, and left the fishtank to start his patrol. I watched him go down the steps to the basement. I waited, and he reappeared in reception to do his check of the ground floor. When he started to climb the main staircase to the first floor, I ran across the road and leapt up the white steps to the front door. I prayed they hadn't changed the entry code and punched the numbers into the door panel.

There was a buzz and the door unlocked. I went in, then I closed the door so it didn't bang. I passed through the automatic glass doors and stood listening in the Victorian entrance hall. Church-like, I'd always thought: square, encaustic floor tiles in a checker-board pattern of red, white, and black; Portland Stone pillars; mahogany wood paneling; and brass handrails. It had once been the chambers for a defunct law firm who had believed too much in their own grandeur. I took off my shoes, and left them facing towards the automatic doors. I ran across the entrance lobby and down the stairs to the basement.

I headed for the third door along; the file store. I went in, closed the door, and switched on the light. I booted up a terminal and, while it sorted itself out, I pulled out my personnel file from one of the metal filers used as the HR archive. My severance letter was there with my acceptance signature. I looked behind it. There was a copy of an email to Salnikov from someone called Anderson at the FCO:

"As mentioned at our recent meeting, we suspect that you have a leak. We now have intelligence that the likely source is your head of Dissidents and Political Trends, James Nelson.

Worst-case scenario is that he has been compromised by a foreign security service unknown.  Hopefully, he is merely disloyal and, therefore, expendable.  I am sure you join with me in wishing SIU output to be of continuing value to the executive.  To avoid possible embarrassment to the government you must <u>not</u> confront him about this.  I have been cleared to authorize you to terminate his services <u>forthwith</u> under Emergency Regulations Act Section 5, Measures to deal with Suspected Insurgents/Agents.  However, UNDER NO CIRCUMSTANCES must you tell him this, or allude to the real reason he has to go.  I trust - with your background - you can fabricate a convincing story.  You are permitted to allude to the displeasure of the government at his recent reports and presentations.

You are to give him one month's salary in cash <u>in lieu of notice</u> and we will enhance his Civil Service pension.  However for this to happen, he <u>must leave forthwith and agree not to talk to anyone about the reasons he has left SIU</u>.  I hardly need remind you that, if you do not comply with these requirements, we shall take swift and decisive action against you, and the SIU.  Inform me <u>immediately</u> that Nelson has been dispatched.  You are to delete this email after reading.  <u>DO NOT</u> print it."

Obviously, Sergey had ignored the last instruction.  He had even been careful to file it where it could be found.  The email was dated twenty-four hours before he had called me into his office.  Sergey had otherwise heeded the threats because he had never mentioned the email to me or the real reason he was sacking me.  Clever of the FCO, because I could have scotched the accusations. So why was the Foreign and Commonwealth Office involved?  I looked further back in the file.  There was an earlier letter, this time from The Office of 10 Downing Street:

'The Prime Minister wishes me to inform you that the tone, and the timing, of the recent report on munitions trading emanating from your Agency was unhelpful in the extreme, and potentially damaging to UK exports. We have reviewed previous reports from your "J. Nelson" and conclude there is a worrying trend. Nelson's reports increasingly employ an overheated style bordering on the tabloid. We also take exception to his obvious political bias which, it seems to us, is far to the left of our position.

The Prime Minister wishes me to remind you that the Strategic Intelligence Unit was set up, albeit under a previous administration, to make "Detached, Considered, and Thorough assessments of trends to **assist** the government of the day in its decision-making". The Prime Minister wonders whether, in the current economic climate, the government can continue to justify the funding of your agency. It seems especially likely to being cut if it uses taxpayer's money to produce material that is patently critical of government.

I trust you appreciate the gravity of the situation and will take the necessary urgent steps. The Prime Minister would be interested to learn of what action you propose."

Presumably, the "action" had been the dressing down Sergey gave me in front of my section. I looked further back. Nothing between the letter from No. 10 and my annual appraisement, three months previous. Then, Sergey had congratulated me on my work and recommended I get a bonus.

To be fair, that had been a week before I had submitted the arms-dealing report.

I checked my watch. Five minutes until security Ron finished his rounds. I put the papers back and turned to the terminal which was now ready for my password. I keyed in "George Fraser" but it said there were no matching records. I tried Zinder and Kountché. Still nothing. I tried Niger and Uranium and it came back with four hundred and twelve postings. I limited the search to 1980. That reduced it to three.

One was an entry dated 3.3.1980 from the Commercial Secretary at our embassy in Abidjan, Cote d'Ivoire, noting that the Niger Minister of Mines and Industry had recently met the Russian Atomic Energy Commissariat in Angola. A later communication from the Station Officer at Abidjan suggested that money from the UK Ministry of Overseas Development had been misappropriated by Niger in violation of the Memorandum of Understanding. The final note from Abidjan to the FO said:

'12. Mar.1980  Tks fr yr brf on Op$^n$ NOVERCAL – Can add no further pertinent information re Niger or beyond. Sgst covert invtgn on site.'

At least it confirmed something had been going on in Niger, and that an operation Novercal existed. I wanted to put in the name Sergey had given me, Constantin, but I had run out of time. I shut down the terminal, switched off the light, ran up to the landing, and listened. I heard an electro-mechanical clunk from the lift and then the whirr as the cage started its downward journey with Ron. He was obviously keen to get back to his TV. I ran across the lobby, slipped into my shoes, went through the automatic doors, and turned the lock to open the street doors. Out in the cold night, I pulled the doors shut as the lift doors began to open. I squatted so that I was hidden by the lower wooden panels of the outside door. I did up my shoes, and then backed down the steps. I crossed the road to where I had started, and looked back at the SIU offices. Ron had his hands behind his head, back to watching his TV program. The light still burned in the Duty Office. Of course, I would be on the CCTV hard-drive but if there were no incidents that night, no one would bother to review them.

In Fleet Street, I hailed a cruising cab and I was at St Pancras International within fifteen minutes. At twenty to midnight, I was outside Doreen's Art Deco block of flats. They must have had huge service bills because every crevice was floodlit. I found the right entrance and pressed Doreen's buzzer. It took a while for her to answer.

'What?'

'Your favorite nephew.'

'I told you to stay away.'

'Something's come up. I just need...'

'Don't tell the bloody world about it.' The door release clunked.

She wore a long, pink, candlewick dressing gown and had curlers in her hair. 'Sorry,' I said.

'You will be,' she snapped, 'if this isn't life-threatening.'

I told her about Dunning, and brought her up to speed with what I had found. 'So if I've upset someone at the Foreign Office,' I said, 'the person behind all this must be the Foreign Secretary.'

'Doesn't follow. The culprit would put plenty of barriers between him - or her - and any investigation.'

'Then can you find out who this Anderson is? And what about that name Sergey gave me? Constantin?'

She sighed. 'I told you, I had to back away.'

'I'm desperate for a lead... anything.'

'Are you sure you're not putting too much reliance on the Albanian's story?'

'No. I've since established that Novercal was an MI6 operation. I know the government had me kicked me out. I know I was recruited to be part of an MI5 abduction of Fraser. I know Brown is using a slush fund to pay for sub-contractors – and I know there is a cover up. Isn't that enough?'

'Novercal might have been the code name for a development funding assessment. Or a visit by some obscure writer for the British Council... anything.'

'Except that it was live in April 1980... exactly when the mercenaries were being recruited. Doreen, please, if you only do one more thing, look up Novercal for me.'

'It's probably been weeded out.'

'But you'll look?'

'If I do, will you push off and let me get some beauty sleep?'

'You're perfect as you are,' I teased.

She threw a cushion at me. 'If you'd been thirty years older, I would have taken that as a compliment. Now off you go. And, Jamie...'

'Yes?'

'No more pestering, there's a duck. The new management are bastards and I'd like to carry on living here a bit longer. Savvy?'

'Message received. Any news on the passport?'

She shook her head. I gave her a nephew's kiss on the cheek and left.


I just caught the last train from Waterloo to Weybridge. When I got to the Ship, Chloe was in bed. Looked as if she had been in dreamland a long time by the sleepy way she mumbled, 'Where have you been?'

'My train was delayed at Surbiton by a convention of badgers on the line.'

She yawned and said, 'Oh dear.' She looked incredibly beddable. Nevertheless, if we were going to have a proper relationship, I wanted it to start right and be for the long haul. No fumbled one-nighters we might regret afterwards.

She sat up and said, 'What did you find out?'

I went over and stroked her hair. It was wonderfully soft. I kissed the top of her head. Warm. Freshly laundered. 'Tell you in the morning.'

She yawned so wide I could have counted her tooth fillings but I didn't think it polite. Then she sank back onto the pillows. 'All right. Night night.'

'Sleep tight.'

'Mind the bugs...' But she was asleep before she could finish the rhyme. I pulled the duvet covers up to her shoulders, switched off the light and, for a while, I sat in the chair musing. When her breathing became regular, I left the room.

Downstairs, everything had been closed down. I heard tinny music so I followed the sound. I found the night porter, sitting in a cubicle with his feet on an untidy desk, drinking from a can of cider. 'Sir?' His training made him put the drink in an open drawer, and his feet on the floor in one smooth movement. 'Problem?'

'Could you do me a favor?'

He licked his lips, sensing a tip. 'Depends what it is.'

I took out a wad of ten-pound notes and peeled off two. 'Had a bit of a row with the girlfriend in room 12, so I need to bed down somewhere. Then, could you wake me before you go off duty? When is that?'

'Six am.'

'Wake me at five thirty.' I gave him the money. He kept his hand flat for more. I gave him another two tenners. 'In the morning, when I've gone, tell room service to send up a full English breakfast to her room at eight.'

'That'll cost you extra.'

I patted his shoulder, 'Nice try, but Room Service is billable.'

In Chertsey, Adam was on dawn patrol. For someone whose ancestors had probably come from India, he looked grey. He was trying to keep awake by revolving his shoulders and marching on the spot. 'Morning,' I said.

He jumped and banged his head against the door he was sheltering by. 'Shit!'

I put my finger to my lips and pulled out a pad and pen. I had seen the transparent curly cord emerging from his collar and connecting to his earpiece.

I wrote: WHERE IS DUNNING?

He shook his head, and then looked both ways down the empty street as if he expected Brown to stroll down the center of it, like the gunslinger in

*High Noon.* I wrote: HE'S AN ACADEMIC - HE CAN'T HANDLE THIS.

Adam shrugged.

I wrote: IT WAS MY FAULT. I HAVE TO GET THE GUY OUT. HE ONLY GAVE ME A HISTORY LESSON.

Adam looked at me quizzically. I knew, then, I had a chance. I wrote: SOMEONE IN THE GOVERNMENT IS DOING A COVER-UP. IF I DON'T GET DUNNING OUT, BROWN MIGHT HARM HIM.

Adam grabbed my pen and wrote: HOW DO I KNOW THAT'S TRUE?

I replied: DO YOU WANT TO TRUST BROWN, OR YOUR OWN INSTINCTS?

He thought about it. I heard a high frequency screech as someone gabbled into Adam's earpiece. He looked for the gunslinger but the street was still empty. Then he raised his sleeve to his lips and said, 'No. Banged my elbow. All clear here.' Then he wrote an address on the pad and walked away.

## 12

The address proved not to be a street, but a
mooring on the Basingstoke Canal at New Haw, in
Surrey. Old canal narrowboats lined one side of the
tranquil water from the humpback bridge to a far
bend. The barges had been converted to
houseboats with varying degrees of finesse.
Unfortunately, the only public right of way was the
towpath on the opposite side of the canal. If I
walked along there, looking across the canal for the
boat I needed, I would be far too visible. My only
other option was to use the service path that ran
alongside the houseboat moorings. For the first
twenty meters or so, tall fences divided the path
from the back gardens of some houses on the left.
That made the path narrow and I wouldn't be able
to avoid the bouncer if he was lurking about. I
couldn't waste time, though, so I pushed through
the gate marked Private - Houseboat Owners Only.

My initial approach would be hidden from most of the boats because of the curve of the canal. Not that I had formed any plan.

I squeezed past a row of garbage bins and then came to the first boat, *Onedin*. It had recognizably been a canal barge, and had a red hull and a sloping blue superstructure. The next, *Kontiki*, looked like a floating summerhouse. An extremely long and posh one. I passed four other boats before I detected any life form: a Doberman shot out on deck, barking with bared fangs. 'Oi, you!' A grizzled, middle-aged man wearing a red New York baseball cap, a white string vest, and pink shorts appeared at the top of his gangplank and pointed a finger at me. 'This is private property. Get lost.'

I looked for the name of his boat. *Vantanaa.* Thankfully, not the name Adam had given me. I said, 'I was told there was a boat for sale along here.'

'Then you was told wrong.' His finger swiveled to point the way I had come. 'Hoppit.'

I fished out my notebook and peered to confirm the name. 'The, uh, *Britannia.*' Which had to be a heavy-handed MI5 joke.

'Oh that one. It's near the end,' he said tossing his head right. 'But it ain't for sale. New people just moved in.'

I wondered whether to push my luck and take a look anyway but the man said, 'So now you know, sod off. Shut the gate behind you. My dog's due for a run.'

I have nothing specifically against Dobermans, but any breed trained by that owner would hardly be waggy-tailed and companionable.

A quarter of an hour later, I risked walking down the public towpath. It was like going along a narrow, green canyon. Both sides of the canal were lined with mature oak trees and their branches almost met in the middle. Sun sparkled through the leaves which rustled in the autumn wind. Shadows danced on the bare earth of the towpath and, had I brought my camera, the light would have been perfect for a photo. Except I wasn't there to be creative.

The *Britannia* was where the man had said. Next to last, painted black and white, with pretend Tudor beams on its superstructure. All the windows were shut and, thankfully, the venetian blinds closed. On the forrard end - the one facing the humpback bridge - there was a small triangular deck. At the stern, a square deck with a metal table and chairs. A small rowboat was tethered to the rudder post of the houseboat.

I walked along the towpath past the last barge and continued a hundred meters or so to the wooden lock gates. I wondered if that would be my way to cross the canal and avoid the Doberman. Unfortunately, there was no path on the other side, and the thick tangle of brambles would make any approach too noisy. As I sat on the wooden arm of the lock gate trying to figure things out, an erect woman, wearing a sheepskin gillet, approached from further down the canal. She hauled behind her a tiny dog in a red tartan jacket.

'Lovely day?' She barked it, in a tone that demanded to know why the hell I was sitting there on a cool September morning.

'Yes it is,' I said, friendly-like. 'Um. Where does the path go, that way?'

She frowned as she looked back to where she had come from, as if surprised anyone would be such an imbecile not to know. 'The Wey Navigation of course. You go over a footbridge. It's not far. Though...' she looked at my footwear, 'the mud will ruin those shoes. Why do you want to know?' Maybe Surrey people are inherently jumpy when strangers ask questions. I said I was after some fresh air before a difficult meeting. She screwed her lips sideways and then walked off towards the bridge without another word. She either disliked business people or she thought I was lying.

Every time her pooch dug its heels in to do a sniff or a pee (which seemed to be unnaturally frequently) she turned and glared at me. And at the dog. The fifth time of doing so, she took out her mobile and keyed in a number. I got up and walked towards her. It would be inconvenient to have a Police Community Support Officer arrive and quiz me why I was making a nuisance of myself.

The woman seemed mollified, cancelled her call, and dragged the pooch towards the humpback bridge. When I reached its arch, reflected sunlight shimmered magically on the underside curve of its red bricks. The towpath continued under the bridge to the dirt car park the other side. The woman hauled her dog into the boot of a shining estate car and started to wipe its paws. When she saw me, she reacted as if I was stalking her. She slammed the tailgate of the car, scurried to the driving seat and drove off so fast she scattered dust and gravel. I got into my car for another think. I would have to spring the professor in the dark. And I needed a driver waiting, with the engine running. The only person I could ask was Chloe.

I returned to the Ship to collect Chloe and we walked to a pub near the weir at Weybridge for lunch. Then we went for a long walk by the Thames. It should have been idyllic. Other couples ambled hand in hand. Pairs of swans sculled by. Ducks quacked, boats puttered, anglers angled. I told Chloe what I intended to do and asked if she could drive. I expected her to be scornful but she said OK. Just that. I hugged her. 'It shouldn't be a problem,' I said. 'They won't know I know they're there. And where you'll park, will be out of sight of the boat and the access path.'

'When do we do it?' she said.

'Dusk. Tonight.'

She linked her arm with mine. 'Then we have time for a bit more walking. Come on.' Personally, I would have preferred to return to the hotel but there you go.

The light was fading when we got to the little car park by the canal bridge. I had mulled over the options all afternoon, but I couldn't come up with anything foolproof. My ace was surprise. To use it to the full, I had decided to approach the barge across the canal. I had seen no boats on the towpath side, so that meant I had to swim. I had a packed a change of clothes, a waterproof torch, a black plastic sack to put the wet stuff in, and a towel. I was dreading wading into the murky, rat-peed canal but, as our fieldwork tutor used to say, "You ain't here for a picnic ladies and gentlemen, you're here to achieve the bloody objective."

I turned to Chloe. 'When I go, position the car to face the exit; switch off the lights and the engine, but keep the radio on. Nosey people will assume you're having a crisis and will leave you alone. I'll flash the torch three times when I come from under the arch with the professor. Start the engine, push open the front passenger door, and then drag him in. I'll shut the door behind him. Don't bother with his seatbelt. As soon as I dive in the back, switch on the lights and drive. I'll change on the way. Any questions?'

'Drive where?' Now we were there, she sounded worried. I hoped I could rely on her. I put my hand on her arm. 'Sure you're up for this?'

'Yes.' She didn't sound over-confident. 'Where do I drive?'

'Turn right out of here.'

'How long will you be gone?'

'If I'm longer than fifteen minutes, call the police. Tell them everything.' I got out. There was nothing to be gained by hanging around. As I reached the bridge, I heard Chloe turn the car. So far, so good. I made an effort to steady my breathing and slow my heartbeat.

It was black under the bridge. I stopped and listened to the disconnected burr of cars as they passed over the top. On the canal, nothing was happening. No ducks and no night fishermen. Thankfully, it was too late for dog walkers. A stiff breeze made the surface of the canal choppy. When the little waves hit the bank, they made rhythmical lapping sounds. A very cold sound. I started my walk up the towpath. Lights were on in several of the houseboats. Most had curtains pulled. Further down the canal, a coot shrieked. To my right, on an embankment beyond the trees, a long train slid by like an illuminated snake. The wind fidgeted the leaves and hissed in the grass. When the clouds drifted away from the moon, I could see the towpath clearly.  I tried jogging to loosen my muscles and calm my nerves.

A long time ago, I had run every day... pounding the road until the poisons left my body, and I felt the euphoria that comes from perfect pacing and syncopated breathing.  Then I got lazy.

It didn't take long to reach the *Britannia*.  There was a light in every window but all the blinds were closed.  I could see shadows of people at a window forrard but nowhere else.  The decks were empty.  I couldn't see anyone guarding the service path but the houseboat hid most of my view.  I prepared myself for the shock of canal water and then edged over the bank.  My trainers slid in the mud but I kept going.  The freezing water gripped my calves and crept up my thighs.  I gasped as the icy shock hit my groin and stomach.  But there was no backing out.  I leaned forward, slid my top half into the water, and swam silently across the canal.

I touched the stern of *Britannia* and pulled myself round towards the bank.  The rowboat was still tied to the rear of the houseboat and also to a small landing stage.  I undid the rope tied to the landing stage - in case I could use the boat to ferry the professor.  I used the remaining rope to haul myself up the stern of the houseboat.  Then I put both my hands on the bulwark and bobbed my head up and down.  No one on the rear deck.  Door to the houseboat closed.  I slid over the stern rail and stood on the deck.  Water dripped from me.  I crossed to the door and put an ear to the glass.  I heard a faint sound... voices and music.  I twisted the handle and it turned.  I pushed the door and it opened.  The music was from a TV, because now I could hear a compere whipping up an already hysterical audience.  I pressed the door wide enough to see in. A tiny, empty lounge. Beyond, a narrow corridor ran along the left side of the boat. There were four closed doors along the corridor but the door at the far end was open. I smelled food but could see no one. I picked up a cushion from the lounge and put it on the floor against the outer doorjamb to stop the door closing. Next step: find Dunning without alerting the crew.

I tried the first door along the corridor. It was dark inside. I flicked on my torch and saw two empty bunk beds. The crew's, probably. I went up the corridor to the next door. From forrard came the tinny deluge of television laughter and I heard the click and fizz of a can being opened. Then I heard two male voices, though I couldn't hear what they said because of the TV. I opened the door of the second room and shone the light in. Another bedroom but this one was occupied. By the professor. He was tied to a chair. He was also blindfolded, and had adhesive tape over his mouth. I went in, shut the door behind me, and padded over to him. I whispered close to his ear, 'Frank, it's me, James Nelson. Understand?'

He nodded.

'I'm going to take off your gag and blindfold, but don't speak and don't make any noise. OK?'

He nodded again. He was as good as his word. Then I untied the ropes that bound him and stood him up. He must have been sitting for a while, because he stumbled and I had to grab him before he fell. We careered across the floor like drunk dancers and knocked into something. An object thumped to the floor and rolled. I pushed the professor back into the chair. I hissed, 'Put your arms behind you.' I replaced his blindfold and the gag before hiding behind the door. I began to think that I had over-reacted when light flooded in, and a large silhouette spread across the carpet. Someone up the corridor called, 'So?'

The man picked up an alarm clock from the floor and set it back on a shelf. 'Nothing. Boat must have rocked.' It was the bouncer.

'You're jumpy.' That was Chisel. 'Come on, man, I'm on a roll here. You're about to lose serious money.'

The bouncer stood where he was for a while, listening. I could hear the air going into him; I could smell beer fumes. Then he grunted and left. I went back to Dunning, took off his blindfold and gag again and then led him to the door. I opened it and peered out. No one there. Up front, Chisel laughed.

I pulled the professor into the corridor and pointed aft. He walked off as if he was strolling to the Gulbenkian café. I grabbed him and put a finger to my lips. He tried his best to be quiet but it didn't bode well. I considered whether to use the service path but suspected the Doberman would bark and, anyway, there could be a guard. The safest option was to pop the professor in the dinghy. I pulled the houseboat's rear door open, tossed the cushion onto a chair, and then pushed Dunning out. I shut the door quietly, then grabbed one of the chairs and angled its back under the handle. It wouldn't stop the bouncer long but it any delay might be useful. Somewhere out on the canal, a duck guffawed at a filthy duck-joke. The clouds parted and the moon shot silver down the canal. The wooden lock gates clamped a dark barrier across and I wondered whether to head there through the undergrowth. Then I could get Dunning to walk across the wooden gates. I pushed the professor across the rear deck towards the gangplank - until I saw the brief red glow of someone pulling on a cigarette on the service path. I whispered the information to Dunning and told him we would have to swim across the canal.

He whispered back, 'Not possible.'

'Why not?'

'I can't swim.'

I made an effort not to swear. I told him my Plan B. About using the dinghy and, credit where credit's due, he clambered almost quietly over the stern and dropped into the rowboat. He nearly sank it in the progress, but there you go, you can't have everything. I went over the stern of the narrowboat, using the rope that held the dinghy. Then I lowered myself hand over hand until I was in the water. It seemed to have got colder. I cut the rope, held the end that was attached to the front of the dinghy in my teeth, and then swam on my back towards the opposite shore - pulling the dinghy along.

The professor sat bolt upright as if he was out for a Sunday afternoon jaunt on the river. Luckily, there was no activity on the *Britannia.* My head rammed into vegetation on the far bank. I yanked the rope and let the dinghy nudge into the bank. Dunning stayed sitting there like a ninny. I rose from the shallows, dripping mud and water like a beast from the marsh in one of those 1960s Hammer Horror films. I whispered to Dunning that he needed to get out. He stood. Then, instead of carefully stepping off, he jumped to the bank. I suppose he had wanted to keep his feet dry. If so, he succeeded, because he landed in the middle of the towpath. Unfortunately, the physics of equal and opposite forces came into play with the result that the empty dinghy sailed back across the water towards the *Britannia*. I lunged for the rope but it slithered away into the water.

I considered diving for it but there was a good chance I'd miss it and we needed to be running for the car before the dinghy hit the houseboat. I squelched onto the towpath and pushed Dunning towards the bridge. 'Run.' The professor only managed a shambling trot. 'Faster!'

I didn't hear the dinghy bump the *Britannia* but I did hear the resultant shouting. Then I heard a crash as the chair at the back door shattered. More shouting. Powerful torch beams shone up the canal towards the lock. Then the lights worked back along the undergrowth of the left bank to where the gangplank rested. It wouldn't be long before they figured out where else we could be. I pushed Dunning to go faster but he stumbled and fell into a puddle. I yanked him up, dragged him back into a run, and then I looked behind.

They had spotted the dinghy floating in midstream. Then they trained their torches on the towpath. We were still twenty paces from the bridge. 'Faster!' Ten paces away, the torchlight found us. A gun fired and I heard the bullet whizz by and thud into the brickwork. We pounded under the bridge with our footsteps echoing. Another gunshot, and ducks cried out in alarm, but we were out of sight now. I hauled Dunning into the car park. Chloe had both doors open and she started the engine.

'I heard shooting,' she said.

I crammed Dunning into the front seat, slammed the door after him, leapt in the rear and yelled, 'Drive!'

'Was it a gun?'

'Just drive!'

As she accelerated, I yanked my door shut and started to pull off my wet clothes.  Chloe was winking left – which would take us past the service path.  'No, right!  Turn right!'

She braked because a lorry was coming around the corner from West Byfleet.

'Just put your foot down and go,' I yelled.

She accelerated too fast, and made the rear wheels spin on the gravel.  When she realized, she eased off the pedal, the tires gripped, and we leapt forward.  The car bounced over the pavement and there was a blare of a horn and flashing from headlights.  We missed the Tesco delivery truck by centimeters and rocketed towards West Byfleet.

'Take the next right... here!'

Chloe misjudged the turn and we mounted the curb and scraped along a hedge before she righted.  A hubcap came off and span away.  'What's the speed limit?' she shouted.

'Never mind.'

She pushed forty.  Headlights were approaching in the middle of the road, forced there by the cars that were parked both sides.  Chloe slowed and began to pull into a gap on the left.  I said, 'No.  Keep going.  He'll get out the way.'

'But what if he doesn't?'

'Do it!'

She put her foot down and the full-beam headlights of the approaching vehicle lit our car like daylight.  The oncoming driver was thumping the horn.  At the last moment, the car veered out the way and I heard a crash.  Chloe increased her speed and we squealed round a bend.

'Brake hard, take the next right.  Ninety degree turn.'  Dead ahead was West Byfleet station.  Late commuters were streaming towards us across the green. 'Slow to thirty. Follow the road to the right, then left and turn up the first road on the left.'

A little way up that road, I got her to stop and turn off the lights. I was pretty sure we had put enough turns between the bouncer and us so I could concentrate on getting changed. We also had to hide the professor because it would be dangerous to let him go back to Canterbury. I decided the Ship would be best, so I told Chloe how to get to Weybridge, avoiding the canal.

We smuggled Dunning into room 12, then I went down to see if Doreen had sent anything.

'Oh yes, Mr Apollinaris. A message came in ten minutes ago.'

It was in a hotel envelope, unsealed, so anyone could have read it. I hoped whoever had sent the message, knew what they were doing. I took it up to the room and opened the envelope.

*Dearest Nephew,*
*That old drug, Novercal, was it? Well Priscilla, a friend in another branch, remembers something about it. You can't get it in the UK now – almost as if it never existed. You mentioned someone called Mr. Anderson in connection with it. Well, I ran that name past my friend too - she has a brain like a computer - but she hasn't heard of him. Nor Brother Constantin. Anyway, she did remember the drug company once had a rep's team leader called Mr. Phillips. Apparently, he left in the 1980s and moved abroad. Someone said they had bumped into him last year in Brussels, of all places. In the Place d'Espagne, sitting at a bar. Priscilla said he has been seen there several times recently. She thinks the name of the establishment had something to do with mussels.*

*Anyway, there's a rumor that Phillips is running some sort of freelance operation in Belgium - unconnected with the old firm or anyone in it. I understand the firm sent a rep out to question him – to make sure he wasn't treading on our toes – you know the sort of thing. Anyway, Phillips got awfully prickly about it. But swore he was doing nothing to hurt our business. Perhaps, if you dangled the right enticement, he might come up with something useful about Novercal. Be wary, though. Priscilla says he used to have a reputation for coloring the truth to suit his own pocket, if you know what I mean. At the moment he is calling himself Oswald Mandleson - though he may have changed it again by the time you see him. Good luck. I'm sending your present by Special Delivery to the other place.*

*Happy Birthday, from your loving aunt.*

*PS  Forgive the method of delivery. Done at the library on the way to my bridge cruise. Be away for at least a month, so don't contact me here. Blasted answering machine is acting up too, so don't leave any messages.*

Bless her. I gave the sheet to Chloe. When she had read it, she wrinkled her brow. 'What the hell does all that mean?'

'Doreen says the database has no listing of anyone in the FCO called Anderson... the person who supposedly demanded that I be sacked. Probably someone in the Service. Nor can she find anyone called Constantin - the supposed "lead" Sergey gave me. However, she confirms there *was* an operation Novercal, though all the files have been erased. The Case Officer for the operation had the cover name of Philips. He left the Service in the 80s but was logged last year as being operational in

Brussels for unknown employers, calling himself Oswald Mandleson. So that means we need to pop over to Belgium, find this mussel bar, ask Mandleson the names of the army personnel in Niger in 1980 and Bob's your uncle, Fanny's your aunt as they used to say in London. Oh, at the end, she says I mustn't contact her for a month because she thinks she is being monitored.'

'You got all that from the gobbledygook?'

'I've had plenty of practice.'

'Anyway I can't go with you,' said Chloe.

'Why not?'

'My passport's out of date.'

'Hopefully, we might have a solution to that. I hope the special delivery is a new one for you... in a different name. That means we'll have to stay here tonight. Might as well order a cozy meal for two from room service, and then snuggle down with a movie.'

The toilet flushed and Dunning said, 'What about me?'

I had forgotten about him. He was standing by the bathroom door, looking dirty and confused. He probably hadn't experienced so much trauma since he'd passed his school exams. 'Sorry Frank. We'll order a meal for three.'

'No, I mean, what about me when you go to Belgium?'

I would have preferred that he'd not heard any of that, but what was done was done. I said, 'I'll pay for this room for two more days. Eat in the bar or restaurant here and charge it to the room. But don't leave the hotel, OK? Phone the university in the morning and tell them you are safe. Say the criminals who took you made a mistake. They released you in... in Portsmouth, and you've decided to stay there in a hotel to get over the shock. Tell them you want to be left alone for a couple of days, and then you'll be back.'

'Impossible. I can't leave my students that long.'

'Frank. Listen to me. You've seen what these people can do. They weren't firing blanks at us tonight.' I wondered if he had a partner to tell, though he had no ring on any of his fingers. I said, 'Do you need to phone someone special now? To reassure them?'

He frowned. 'What do you mean?'

'Wife?'

He shook his head.

'Partner? Lover?'

'How dare you!'

I felt sorry for the dry old stick. I'd used him. Now I was treating him as if he was an annoyance. Who was I to judge his lifestyle? For all I knew, a billion single people in the world were in love with their jobs. I said, 'Sorry. Look, tomorrow morning, when we've gone, would you please do something for me.'

'What?'

'Phone your secretary. Tell her you are OK. Will you do that?'

'If you think it is necessary.'

'I do. Then, when you get back, for God's sake take the poor girl out to dinner.'

'That would be most improper,' said Dunning, though I saw him blush as he turned away.

'She's in love with you, Frank. Probably has been for years. Do something about it before it's too late. For both of you. If you're worried about your reputation, get a job somewhere else. Or get her transferred. After you've proposed to her.'

213

He turned back to protest but no coherent instructions reached his voicebox so his mouth just opened and closed rhythmically, like a bony fish. I took his hand and shook it. 'And thank you, Frank, for all you have done. It's been really important. One day I'll tell you how much you contributed. Though I'm afraid we might never be able to make it public.'

'To be honest,' he said, finding his voice at last, 'I very much hope that nothing does come out. And that you continue to stay out of my life.'

Funny how some people never let you say thank you.

'And another thing,' he ploughed on, 'I will not lie to my colleagues about my whereabouts.'

I sighed. 'OK Frank, have it your way. But be careful. The people who abducted you might try again if you show up too soon.' He frowned at that, so maybe the message had finally sunk in. 'Now you need a wash, and I need a shower, to get rid of the au de Basingstoke Canal. Tell Chloe what you want to eat and she will order it from room service. I'll have the posh ham, egg, and chips. Then we'll work out the sleeping arrangements.'

13

The Special Delivery had indeed been Chloe's passport. A Republic of Ireland one for Erin McGowan. Nice name. There was also a sheet of paper printed with a series of numbers, plus a rubber-banded wad of Euro notes. No covering letter. I assumed the figures weren't a coded message (because I had no key), so I hoped they were a telephone number to ring if I got into trouble. I decided to avoid airports because of the crowds and the security checks. Hiring a car and using the ferry to get to France was an option but I decided it would take too long to get to Brussels – time when someone might get to Mandleson before we did. So I opted for the Eurostar and managed to get us standard class tickets for the 15.36 to Brussels that afternoon.

In Prêt a Manger on the St Pancras concourse, Chloe and I worked on her new identity. She would have made a decent spy.  We passed through x-ray and passport control without a hitch.  The holding area was crowded because two trains were late arriving due to loss of power in the tunnel.  I needed to get us away from the patrols and the gaze of security cameras and found a table tucked away in the café between platforms seven and eight.

Around us, people going on holiday were knocking back alcohol as if prohibition was about to come in.  Or maybe they were just nervous about the trouble in the Channel Tunnel.  There were plenty of business types, too, hunched over electronic gizmos or yelling into their phones (why do people do that?).  The coffee was reasonable.  I ached to have one of the golden-glazed croissants but I knew I would feel guilty at taking in unnecessary calories.  It didn't take long to locate the plain-clothed security agents.  They had long-abandoned the pretense of being passengers.  I blame sloppy team leadership.  It happens when you do the same boring job for ever.  I turned my chair round so my back faced them but I also made sure I had a good view, using the mirror to the right of the servery.

We had a smooth journey on Eurostar.  Of course, Brussels was its usual chaotic self.  It has a completely different feel than Paris.  Still a bit raffish.  A crazy Arab drove his taxi from the Midi station like a bat out of hell to our dowdy hotel, the Richmond, on Rue St Pierre.  When we had freshened up, I walked Chloe to the Grand Place because she hadn't been to the city before and it was a convenient point to start our search for Mandleson.

She was gratifyingly impressed.  I've always thought the place is magnificent, in a clunky northern way.  An amalgamation of no-nonsense Flemish, showy French baroque, with a dash of Spanish pizzazz.  The sun shone on the gold leaf, the guild flags, and the canopies of red and gold that stretched over the café tables around the square. Before we got down to business I decided it wouldn't hurt to squeeze in a beer, so I took Chloe upstairs at the brasserie called La Chaloupe d'Or. The heavy old furniture looked faintly Bavarian, and it was busy with local families, old ladies, and pairs of earnest girls.  The tourists stayed downstairs or hugged the expensive, windy tables outside.  The Chaloupe felt comfortable - what I imagined the continent used to be before the European Union tried to make it conform.  The top-class waiters were in the uniform of their guild: white shirts, black waistcoat, black trousers, and spotless white aprons that reached almost to the floor.  They did panache but without the Parisian snarl.  Through the big windows, we gazed down on the square.  In the center, the weekly flower market forced the walking tours into doing a one-way, slow-motion conga.  The furled umbrellas held up by the tour guides were like exclamation marks punctuating the endless trails of tourists.  The only difference was the color of the umbrellas: red, blue, white, red again.

As Chloe worked though her Tarte du Jour I watched the stress of the past few days fall off her.

'Welcome to Brussels,' I said, as she eventually laid her fork down and dabbed her lips.

She grinned.  'I could get to like this.'

'Unfortunately, we have to go to work.  And find this elusive Mandleson.'

We took a narrow alley that led from the square, past the Tintin shop, to Rue du Marché-aux-Herbes. The place we wanted was in the Place d'Espagne. There were about ten café's and bars around the square, but the Bar Moule was the center of three on the left. It looked scruffy, perhaps to deter tourists. It had been a tad too successful in that it was empty inside. A few unscrubbed clients lurked on its pavement tables. Just the sort of place an ex-agent on limited means would hang out.

We sat outside and ordered coffee. Surprisingly, it was a hundred times better than anything I had tasted in London. I asked the waiter if he knew of an Englishman called Mandleson. The man rasped his two-day beard with his fingertips and made a face when he remembered. 'Oui, I know him. Who are you?'

I gave the man a five-euro note in reply. After he had tucked it in his jeans pocket he said, 'He comes most days. When he get drunk, he shout at people. Makes a scene, uh? Sometimes he "forgets" to pay. And he never tips. Never!'

'Know where he lives?'

'Je regrette mais....' He spread his hands wide and lifted his shoulders.

I thanked him, we finished our coffees, and I paid and left a tip. To make the point that some Brits can.

'Now what?' said Chloe.

'We find somewhere to watch and wait.'

On the opposite side of the Place d'Espagne, was a modern building called the Royale Café. From its windows I had a good view of the Moule. My onion soup came in a bowl big enough to bath a baby. The place was brisk, contemporary, and used by professionals rather than tourists. I finished the soup and Chloe stopped pushing the omelet round her plate. 'Don't you like it?'

She shook her head. 'I don't feel that hungry.'

I ordered gauze beer but it proved too sour for my taste. The café gradually cleared of home-going clients. Staff squirted the tables and scraped the chairs. Europop jangled on a radio station. I saw the Moule waiter talk to a bloated gent, and then he pointed to the Royale. The gent got up quickly and started to leave. The waiter grabbed him and demanded money. The gent scooped some coins from his pocket and threw them on the table. Then he walked briskly northeast.

'I think we have our target,' I said. 'Walking to the right... blue raincoat and a shuffle? See him?'

Chloe nodded and collected her things. The Royale Café staff were relieved we were going and quickly locked the door behind us. Mandleson - if it was him - was well in front but failed to check whether he was being followed. He did no road crossing, no use of alleys, no sudden changes of direction. Almost as if he had ditched all his fieldcraft and was acting like an old rabbit, limping for its burrow. Either that, or we were following the wrong man.

He had turned left into the Rue de la Montagne and was now steaming up the Boulevard De Berlaimont. He passed the ivory pile of St Michael's Cathedral without a glance, and continued along the Boulevard Pacheco to the petite ring. He crossed the frantic double boulevard, went through the manicured Jardin Botanique without slowing, and then turned left in Rue de la Limite.

'If this is going to be a marathon,' said Chloe, 'I'll need a wee.'

'Not until he goes to ground.' It was beginning to concern me that he had exhibited no signs of once being an agent. Perhaps the waiter had heard the name wrong and we were following some poor Brussels banker who thought the Revenue Police had caught up with him.

Chloe said, 'Are you always this pushy?'

'Only when necessary.' We were entering a more run-down area. Immigrant workers hung about on street corners and stared at us. The few women wore burkas. Shops sold exotic vegetables that had labels in Turkish and Arabic. The person who might - or might not - be Mandleson was beginning to slow.

'How much further?' panted Chloe.

'Not far.'

She pulled me to a stop. 'Jamie, this is a seriously dodgy area.'

I watched Mandleson. Still walking. I couldn't give up now. I said, 'Go back to the hotel if you like.' I felt sick as soon as I'd said it because I saw hurt show on her face. She let go my arm. It had been stupid to bring her along. I never learned. 'Sorry. Look, if this is Mandleson...'

'If?' she exploded. 'You've dragged me all this way for an "if"?'

I checked him again. He had slowed almost to a stop. He turned, so I grabbed Chloe and kissed her. She struggled and pushed me away. Some Turkish men smoking on the steps of a tenement laughed and jeered.

'What the hell was that for?' she said, wiping her mouth with the back of her hand. A rather worrying sign.

'I didn't want him to see you.' She frowned, looked over my shoulder. 'Well, he's gone.'

I looked. An empty street. Damn. 'Right, here's what we do. You stay on this side. Carry on walking, but not too fast. Don't look where he went. Keep walking on until you hear me whistle.'

'And if you don't whistle, I end up in some ghetto and get raped?'

'Chloe, concentrate. I shall be on the other side of the street. I'll cross where he disappeared and we'll meet as if by chance. It'll give me time to study the buildings.'

'There's a lot of "I" in this.'

'Sorry.' I wanted to tell her it was me who'd got a B+ in field-craft training but I knew it would have come out all wrong so, instead, I bared my soul. 'I was usually marked down as a poor team-worker. I'm afraid when I get into an operation, I get a bit of tunnel-vision. Sorry. Look, I'll make it up by buying supper. OK?'

She nodded, though her eyes were glistening rather too much for it to have been the wind. That I even noticed, was worrying. The more I thought about her, the less efficient I would be. And that would put us both in danger. I said, 'Let's go.'

She walked away as instructed. The Turks went into a fresh barrage of taunts and laughter at our apparent split. I ignored them, crossed the road, and stayed a little back from Chloe. All I could see on her side of the street were tenements, each with steps out the front. It would take too long to knock on every door and ask for Mandleson. Besides, I didn't know any Turkish. Or Arabic come to that.

A bit further on, there was a crummy bar with no name, then more tenements, and a dark-fronted shop on the corner. I was sure Mandleson hadn't gone that far, so I guessed he had gone into the bar. If he was a soak, he'd need a wet after his forced walk.  It wasn't the sort of establishment I would have been keen to enter, even without Chloe. However, we weren't sightseeing.  I whistled, and Chloe stopped.  I crossed the road, and went to her. My body language suggested we hadn't seen each other for a long time.  I muttered, 'He probably went into the bar.  I'll kiss you on the cheek and we'll go inside.  Keep your eyes open.  Watch everyone. Concentrate on anyone paying particular attention to us.  Ignore those who just glance.  Don't leave my side, and tell me if you think anyone moves to cut off our escape.'

She squeaked.

I patted her bottom.  'Everything will be fine. This is boring Brussels, right?  EU HQ.  What could go wrong here?'  A lot, but I didn't want her to freak out.

I went in first.   Middle-eastern music was playing.  My nose twitched at the sweet smoke of grass, then the rancid tang of stale beer hit the back of my throat.  The bar was small and square.  And too dark for my liking.  They may have been doing their bit to reduce global warming, but more likely hoped the gloom would prevent any nosy police *agent* from recognizing faces.   Most of the customers were Turkish or from that general neck of the woods.  The barman was Belgian.  He had a square, belligerent face and a grey, drooping moustache.  He frowned at us but said nothing.  I clocked Mandleson sitting with his back to the rear wall, at a table on his own.  He was staring at some clear liquid in a small glass that he gripped with both hands.  The barman lent over the counter and beckoned me close.  'Go back to the center.  This area is not... suitable for... tourists.'

I thanked him but said we were there to meet someone. He frowned and said, 'You are officials?'

Everyone in the bar stopped what they were doing so they could listen to my answer.

I shook my head. 'We do not represent any organization or any government.'

All around us there were whispered translations. Then the bar noise resumed.

'By law,' said the barman, 'I am entitled to ask for your identification.'

'Only if we look as if we might be underage, or likely to cause disruption. Look, we arrived from England today. I am a private investigator and we wish to ask a British national some questions that might help us with a problem in the UK. Nothing, I promise, to do with you or anyone else here.' I suppose, when your main customer-base has a high proportion of illegal immigrants, you would want to protect them. Otherwise, you'd go out of business.

The barman grunted and wiped the counter with a cloth that was happy homeland to a million amoebae. 'Then, what can I get you to drink?'

It was his gatekeeper's fee. Fair enough. Even though I didn't want a drink, I ordered a beer. This time it was not from a designer bottle, but squirted from an anonymous tap into a smeared glass. He pushed the cloudy liquid towards me, daring me to object. 'What does she want?' Chloe shook her head and the man shrugged his shoulders. He asked for double the price they had charged in Grand Place but, as it would get me access to Mandleson, it was worth every cent.

We walked my beer to the back of the bar room and pulled chairs to Mandleson's table. He never took his eyes off his tumbler. I said quietly, 'Mr. Mandleson I believe. Or should I call you Phillips?'

He looked up but didn't seem to like what he saw. 'Please don't tell me you're from the Service.'

'We're not.'

He relaxed slightly.

'I'm a freelance private investigator,' I said. 'I'm not after you, but you may have information that could help my client.'

He sneered. 'A private dick? Who's your client?'

'An old guy the government cheated out of a pension. When I dug into his ancient history, your name cropped up. I have a contact in MI6 who did a bit of research for me. That's why I'm here. Can I get you another drink?' He didn't reply, so I turned and signaled to the barman to bring a drink over for Mandleson. The bar was now hoping for some drama. After a delayed reaction, the barman poured vodka into a tumbler and then slouched over. He banged the glass on the table and then held out his hand for money. I gave him another double fee and he walked off, muttering. The customers, disappointed that nothing exciting was about to happen, went back to their jawing.

Mandleson downed his first drink, then pointed at Chloe. 'Who's she?'

'A friend. We're on holiday.'

'What's in it for me?'

'I'll pay for information received.'

He thought about it and then said, 'Five hundred Euros minimum. Price goes up depending on sensitivity of the material.'

I nodded.

He licked his lips. 'What do you want to know?'

We had reached the threshold. I could pussyfoot around or lay my cards on the table. Mandleson didn't look like the kind of man who did much pussyfooting so I said, 'Tell me about operation Novercal.'

He nearly choked on his second Vodka and proved that even a bloodshot drunk could go white. 'How do you know about that?'

'I told you.'

'Who's this "old guy" you're working for?'

'Mercenary you recruited in Morocco – at the Hotel Toubkal. Goes by the name of Fraser now, though you probably knew him as Gjergj Frasheri. Albanian, now naturalized British. He thought he was due an army pension but someone in government blocked it. Fraser threatened to talk about Novercal so MI5 put him in close containment. I need something from you to unblock the system and get Fraser released.'

Mandleson stood and in doing so knocked his chair over. The bar hushed. Had there been a piano player in the corner he would have stopped in mid bar, just like they did in the old Wild West saloons. But there was no piano and Mandleson didn't reach for a Colt 45. He just stood there, swaying. A few people laughed, as if they were used to his ways. When he spoke, his voice was hoarse. 'The Service pays me to keep quiet.'

'But you wouldn't be against earning a little extra?' If he told me to get lost, it had been a wasted journey.

He thought for a while, cleared his throat, and then said, 'Why should I take the risk?' It was the right thing for him to say yet he didn't tell us to get out. Nor did he move. Apart from his swaying.

I said, 'I'll give you a hundred Euros cash for all the names of the British army personnel involved in operation Novercal. And another hundred for the name of your controller.'

He laughed but it carried on too long and ended in a hiccup. Then he licked his lips. Perhaps working out how many shots of liquor the offered money would buy. 'You got the cash on you?'

I shook my head, 'I'm not that stupid.'

He looked disappointed. 'Can't do business here, anyway. Meet me tonight at the Atomium. Bring the money and I'll tell you what I know.'

'You can tell me now what Novercal was about.'

He sat, closed his eyes, and then groaned. 'It's a bloody albatross round my neck. You know that poem? Ancient Mariner? Haunts me.' He sighed. 'All right. It's ancient history anyway. The Niger foreign minister did a deal with the Soviets.'

'And?'

'He was hatching a coup and got the Reds to supply arms and military support. The deal was, once he became President, he would let smugglers deliver uranium ore to Soviet trucks waiting across the border.'

'More.'

'The Ruskies needed it for their enrichment program. Couldn't get it on the open market. Not flavor of the month.'

'I know all that.'

'OK! Novercal was our op. to scupper everything. If the military take-over failed, no ore would go to the Soviets. Status quo meant Niger would carry on selling ore to the West.'

'Why did Britain get involved? Niger was French.'

'America wanted to isolate the Soviets but the CIA didn't trust the Frenchies. Bastard CIA didn't trust us, either. But they spoke our language, sort of, and they could pull more strings in London. Novercal started well. A nice, simple exercise but, halfway through the planning, the politicos got cold feet so we had to put in extra firewalls, fail-safes and then recruit mercenaries through an agency. The more crap you do, the more crap hits the fan if it goes wrong.'

'I know about Schulenburg.'

'Uh?'

'I know you hired the mercenaries through Schulenburg's agency.'

'Who told you that?'

'Fraser.' Well, sort-of.

'He wasn't the only one.'

'Then what?'

'We set it all up, ready to go. Then some MoD twat insisted the military had to lead it on the ground. In case, "Things got out of hand". Basically, they didn't trust us, the Americans or the French. I'd had a string of successful operations as long as your arm but the bastards sidelined me like I was the village idiot.'

I waved the barman over with another drink. He had it ready. I gave him another note and then I waited until he left. 'So tell me what happened in Zinder.'

'You have enough. Bring the money tonight.'

'I want one name now.'

'Not until I see money.'

I counted out fifty Euros but kept my hand on the top of the notes. 'Tell me what happened in Zinder and tell me one name.'

He took a deep breath. 'OK. We had two separate operations. One unit went to Zinder to defuse the coup, the other – with the overall commander – went to Niamey, the capital, to protect the government. The Niamey unit had to identify any coup members there, arrest them, and hand them over to the Chief of Police. Concurrent with the Zinder operation. The commander did his job there to the letter. No one was killed. Well, not until they got into the police cells, but that wasn't our problem. The mercenaries were disbanded; the commander returned to the UK; got mentioned in secret dispatches and all that shit.' Mandleson closed his eyes and held his head in his hands. The rest of the bar had become bored and had turned their collective back on us.

I said quietly, 'What was his name? The commander?'

Mandleson said equally quietly, 'Major Montgomery Rhodes. Army through and through. Sandhurst, Queen and Commonwealth, honor and service and all that bullshit.'

Chloe chipped in, 'Not the Monty Rhodes in government?'

Mandleson looked at her as if he had forgotten she was there. He sighed and nodded. 'Minister of Education. Had the world been a fairer place, Rhodes should have been Prime Minister. But he's too honest for the politicos.'

I said, 'Who was in charge of the Zinder operation?'

'That, you'll find out tonight. I want a hundred Euros for the rest of the Zinder story and two hundred Euros for the name of the officer. Bring used cash in medium denominations. The people I have to deal with now are suspicious of high-end notes. Agreed?'

'Agreed.'

'Meet me in the Atomium Park, Heysel, at eleven tonight. Be alone.'

'OK.'

'Now push off.'

Well, it was something. I didn't want to make him angry. Besides, I didn't have any more cash on me. I shooed Chloe out in front of me, and we walked briskly up the street. I used a couple of shop windows to check whether anyone was following us. There was. A stocky, white, older man in a black porkpie hat and a beige, three-quarter length raincoat, black trousers and shoes. Clean-shaven, medium build, maybe five ten. I had never seen him before, but he was apparently very interested in us.

.

## 14

I pulled Chloe to a stop in front of a grocery shop selling exotic produce and told her about our tail. When she started to look, I blocked her.

She said, 'The police?'

'I don't think so,' I said. 'Security service agent probably'.

'Whose?'

I shrugged. The Belgians would know about Mandleson, so they might keep a watching brief. There again, London may have requested someone local to keep an eye on him in case I made contact.

Chloe said, 'So what do we do?'

'The textbooks call it, "Eluding hostile pedestrian surveillance." For now, we continue walking towards the city center. Act as if you are angry at me for whatever happened in the bar.'

'How?'

'Use your imagination. They say, "The best subterfuge is one you are most comfortable with. Appropriate something near the truth." '

'Is that another quote from the textbook, or are you making it up?'

I chuckled. 'Section 3A. I think. Or was it 13B? That's why I only got a B+.' I linked my arm with hers. 'Up ahead, see where the road goes up a slope?'

'Yes.'

'At the top, is the petite ring – the inner ring road we crossed? There are two slip roads, one to the left, and one to the right. Straight on is the underpass that leads in to the city center. Go that way and meet me upstairs at the Grand Place café we were at earlier. The Chaloupe d'Or. Say, in an hour?'

'How do I find the Grand Place?'

'There are plenty of tourist signposts. Or ask someone. The natives are friendly. Use French.'

'What are you going to do?'

'The man following is probably more interested in me, so...'

'Not that you're a sexist with an incredibly overinflated ego...'

'Brown might have sent my file photo to the British embassy here, and possibly others. I'm the thorn in his side, not you. There's only one person tailing me as far as I can see, so he'll have to stick with the prime target. Me.' We came to the last shop and I guided Chloe to look in the window. There was a steel grill over the glass, but the display case in the doorway gave me a perfect view of the street behind me. The tail bent to retie his shoelaces. After all, we all sing by the same hymn sheet. No one else stopped, altered course or looked at us. That didn't mean there wasn't a team. A relay of three, perhaps, leapfrogging if compromised. Nevertheless, the lack of other pedestrians suggested that our man was on his own.

The boulevard was solid with cars, trucks, and coaches. There were no free taxis in sight and I didn't intend to wait for one. I would have to extemporize. I said to Chloe, 'Off you go, then. Meet you in an hour.' I gave her a peck on the cheek, she slapped me round the face and marched off. I hadn't been expecting the slap, but then I had told her to improvise. I turned right, and walked swiftly down Avenue Victoria Regina towards the high-rises. At Place Rogier I turned right, and checked that I still had the tail. Yes. He was just coming into the square. No one else followed. I headed for the Sheraton Hotel and, inside, I asked a receptionist where I could make an outside call. He pointed to a cubicle between the lifts and the bar.

I got to the booth as my tail entered the lobby. He sat there on one of the overstuffed couches, checked his watch, shook open a newspaper and pretended to read. I pretended to finish my phone call and went into the bar. It was a dark, clubby place. Leather armchairs, dark panels, low wooden tables, and a shiny grand piano. There were only a few people in. At a round table, a New Yorker was sitting opposite a tired, elderly couple and was rattling through a travel itinerary. 'Now at Detroit, you have to change. Do not let your baggage go with the herd. They push them about like sheep there. Make yourself known on the plane before it gets there...' I ordered a Kriek beer and the barman poured it as if it was nitro-glycerine. It was the closest thing I had tasted to alcoholic Tizer. I picked up a *Herald Tribune* from a pile at the end of the bar and took it to a table well away from the travel agent, but in view of my tail.

Eventually, the elderly couple tottered out. The travel guy ordered a scotch on the rocks and washed his face with his hands. A couple of US army guys, hair a uniform grizzle, came in and ordered baseball to be put on the TV screen. I looked at my watch, made a face, and then returned to the bar. The tail hadn't moved. I paid for a white wine spritzer and asked the barman to make it, while I used the washroom. I said it was for a young lady who was going to join me shortly: dark, bobbed hair, great figure, good tipper. The barman nodded in a tired, "I've seen everything a hundred times over" sort of way. I went towards the toilets but as soon as I was out of sight of the tail, I ran to an unmarked service door. Beyond it was a white painted breezeblock corridor. I kept walking until I found a fire exit. Outside, I ran to the Nord station and caught a train back to Central. I joined Chloe before she had finished her cappuccino.

I tried not to grin. I was chuffed to find I still had the knack, though slightly worried I had enjoyed it so much. This wasn't a game.

'Now what?' said Chloe.

I had to lay my hands on some extra money – or at least enough to bluff the names out of Mandleson. I still had some of the money Auntie had sent, and there was a small amount in the Apollinaris' account, though I had to pay the hotel and we also had to get home. The only other option was to try some of my other credit cards at an ATM and hope they weren't all blocked. Of course that would alert Brown to where I was, but there would be a delay before the information filtered through to him. Obviously, I couldn't take Chloe to the meet so she would have to stay in the hotel room. Even that would make her vulnerable. I had to hope she wouldn't get bored and go sightseeing. At the Atomium I needed to squeeze the maximum information out of Mandleson - and be alert in case he double-crossed me. "To read the Vibes," the old instructor used to tell us, "you need to clear your mind of distractions". God, how out of date it all seemed now. We had signed up to a cozy, government-funded information circus that meshed - with varying degrees of efficiency - with other government-funded circuses, friend and foe. A worldwide, integrated network of rule-following nosey-parkers. It had probably all changed by now. Most of my instructors were dead or living quietly on the coast, drawing their index-linked Civil Service pensions. In the training schools, there would be no more references to "vibes" or complicated words such as "subterfuge". It would all be high tec; digital analysis; psychometric tests; immersive simulations; and doctorates available on the law of covert operations.

One of the advantages of being on the outside was that I could make up my own rules. The disadvantage was that I didn't have a handy controller in London. Nor did I have any technology to speak of. Or any back up, to ride in to rescue me with the cavalry. There was still a slim chance that Mandleson would play it straight of course. A very slim chance. My experience of human nature suggested that he would try to maximize his investment and sell me to the highest bidder. My tail, for one. Brown would be low down his shopping list. Even Mandleson would be reluctant to help the organization that had hung him out to dry. The tail had looked faintly Slavonic so maybe the GRU or FSB had an interest. Russians have very long memories. Perhaps the new tsar wanted to keep the lid on Novercal. Well, if Mandleson did show up, I would find out. I assumed he would pack a weapon. I didn't own a gun and, anyway, the old man was bound to frisk me to make sure I wasn't tooled up or wired. I needed to lay off the booze, too, so I could think straight. Maybe down two strong coffees for clarity and to heighten my reactions, followed by a chocolate bar for energy.

'James?'

'Uh?' Was she already trying to tidy me up?

'I said, now what?'

'We get something to eat, and then go back to the hotel.'

'Then to the Atomium?'

'I go on my own.'

She glared at me and I leant over to kiss her to defuse the situation but she avoided me. 'You think I'll be in the way. A nuisance.'

I sighed. I really should have left her in England. Or dropped her off in Lille so she could do a few days shopping. I said, 'It's not that. I don't want to put you in danger.'

Night alters places. Changes people, too, I guess. Twelve hours earlier, tour groups would have been milling around the Atomium, snapping away at the shiny steel balls. They would be buying souvenirs to show the folks back home how cultured they were. Knick-knacks that, before the first anniversary of their trip, would be gathering dust in some forgotten corner. Before the second anniversary, they would be sent to the nearest thrift shop. At least the gravel walkways around the Atomium were empty. No shrieks from kids on the fairground rides. No roar from traffic circling the park. No old people resting their bones in the autumn sun; no toddler-pushing mums; no park gardeners, dogs, or police. The food stalls no longer exhaled sweet breaths of waffles; there was no cigarette smoke; no coffee smells. It looked as if I was the only person there. White lasers gripped the monster spheres above me and made the structure look like an alien space ship. I shook my head and squeezed my eyes tight. Perhaps that second coffee had been a mistake.

As my eyesight adjusted to the dark, I looked again at the shadowy areas beneath the trees to see if there was anyone lurking in the shadows. At least there were no parked cars or walkers. To the south, the city seemed to hum. Sporadically, vehicles heading to or from the center hurtled down one side of the park. The only thing that stopped them was the set of traffic lights at the south end of the park. A tram whirred as it slowed, sighed, and then stopped. From its interior, a few pale faces looked out. They wouldn't have seen much in the dark. The traffic lights changed, the tram clanged, and then started with a whine as it trundled downtown. The park had temporarily lost its purpose. I suppose that was why Mandleson had chosen it. Because he had too.

I should have packed something warmer, because the cold north wind needled into my top. I looked at my watch. Ten to eleven. I had been stupid to agree to meet here because there were too many hiding places and it was too isolated. I walked to the central promenade where at least I would be able to see anyone approaching. The neat flowerbeds flanking the wide pathway looked grey under the sodium lamps. The wind rhythmically twanged a rope against a flagpole. Still, if Mandleson felt safe in the park, he might give me what I wanted.

A drunk staggered past and yelled abuse at me. At least I assumed it was abuse from the method of delivery, though I didn't understand a word. I checked my watch. Nearly eleven. A police car, blue light pulsing, came yah-yahing from the city center, passed along the east of the park and disappeared off towards Heysel. In the following silence, I walked slowly towards the Atomium. I remembered a scene from an old movie where a sniper in the observation platform of one of the balls, was waiting to shoot the hero. It wasn't a very comforting thought. I sat on a bench. The cold was eating into me now and I shivered. Somewhere a bell tolled eleven. It began to look as if Mandleson wasn't going to show. A uniformed man approached from the direction of the Atomium. The police officer asked me in French what was I was doing. I replied in English that I couldn't sleep, so I thought fresh air might help.

'Return to your hotel, monsieur. It is not safe to be alone here at night.'

I saw no ordinary danger but thanked him anyway.

'What is the name of your hotel?' he said.

I lied that it was the Ibis. There were bound to be several.

'The receptionist will tell you where it is safe if you wish to take… night exercise.' He made it sound like a euphemism for being desperate for the services of a prostitute.

I thanked him and he walked off. When he reached the end of the park, he turned round and stared at me. I got up and followed him and then he walked away. If Mandleson had watched the little episode, he would assume he was walking into a trap and wouldn't show. I sighed. That meant another visit to the Turkish bar.

A tram squealed round the bend from Laeken and then slowed to a stop. I wondered if I had time to sprint over to catch it but I was still a hundred meters away when it started off again. It hummed away towards the city to leave a single man standing on the pavement. Mandleson. He stood there with his hands in the pockets of an anorak. I waited. Eventually, he headed towards me across the road. He stumbled as if he was unwell – or drunk. Perhaps both. In the cold night, his breath puffed out in quick, white clouds.

'Have you got the money?' he called when he was thirty meters away.

I didn't say anything.

The old man continued to walk towards me and repeated his question.

'Yes,' I said, 'I have the money.'

When Mandleson was ten paces away, he stopped, looked left and right, coughed, and then said, 'Show me.'

'What?'

'Show me the money.'

I suppose, in the circumstances, it was a reasonable request. I had told him before that I didn't have enough. I fished into my pocket, pulled out a wad of notes, and waved them in the air. 'So now give me the names.'

Mandleson looked to my left at the closed Waffle stand and I thought I heard a faint sound of feet on gravel. My phone rang and I checked it. Chloe.

'Are you all right?' she said.

'Yes.'

'Reception just phoned me.'

'And?'

'Two men are asking questions about us.'

Perhaps the tail had been working in a team after all. One being obvious, leaving the others in deep cover. I had been an idiot to imagine I was still sharp after all these years.

'What shall I do?' said Chloe.

She sounded frightened. If I told her to get out, she would be picked up. 'Sit tight. Lock the door and barricade it. Take the phone off the hook. Turn the TV up loud. Do not let anyone in, for any reason. I'm coming back now. I'll phone your mobile when I'm in the hotel. OK?'

'OK. Don't be long.' She cut the call.

'Problem?' said Mandleson.

As I put my phone away, I turned my head slightly and out of the corner of my vision I saw a dark shape move between the Waffle stall and me. 'Nothing I can't handle. Now, Mandleson. The names?'

He came closer and held out his hand for the money.

'No money until you tell me who was in Zinder.'

He licked his lips, and then nodded. 'The captain was called...'

The someone I had sensed near the waffle stand started to run towards me. I looked round to see a thickset man in a leather jacket pulling a cosh out of his pocket. I ran past Mandleson towards the road because I knew if I stayed to fight, I would get hurt, and where would that leave Chloe? 'Sod you, Mandleson.' Now I could see another person running from the shrubbery on my left. I veered right, charged across the flowerbed, with Mandleson screaming, 'Get the money from him!'

I careered into the road, which was a crazy thing to have done because it put me in the path of an oncoming car. The driver hit the brakes and caused a lot of tire screeching and smoke. Mercifully, the car stopped before it killed me. I wrenched open the passenger door and tumbled in. 'Drive on,' I said. 'Those men are trying to kill me.'

The blonde-haired woman looked at me, looked at the men who were closing fast, put the car in gear, and accelerated. She shot through the red light at the crossroads but, half a kilometer down the road, she pulled over to the side. She said, 'Get out.'

'Look, I'm sorry I did that, but could you just give me a lift into town? My girlfriend phoned to say...'

She reached into her handbag and pulled out a small silver handgun, which she rammed against my temple. 'I do not wish to know, monsieur. Get out. Immediately. I will use this. I have done so before very effectively. Now get out.'

I wasn't sure I could grab the gun before she pulled the trigger, so I got out. She roared away. I looked back. The two thugs were running towards me. I sprinted towards the city center and thought I would easily outpace the thugs but, when I checked over my shoulder, they were still coming. My phone rang. 'What?'

'Someone's at the door,' yelled Chloe. 'They say they are the police.'

'Don't answer it! Run a shower. Pack our bags. I'll be there as soon as I can.'

After a pause she said, 'Are you running?'

'Yes.'

'Are you in trouble?'

'Me? No. No trouble at all.'

## 15

The few taxis heading into town were occupied. A mixed blessing: no easy way for me to escape; though also no way my pursuers could hail one to get to me. Unfortunately, that meant I had to keep running. I had two problems with that: I knew I didn't have much stamina for sprinting and, even if I got to Brussels North station, they would mug me while I waited for a train to arrive. Then I heard the joyful sound of a tram's warning clang behind me. I couldn't see any stops ahead so I ran harder, keeping the silver tracks to my right. I began to detect the rumble of the tram wheels and the hum of the electric motor so I knew it was closing on me. When I rounded a bend, I saw the tram stop. I ran like the time I won first prize in the 400 meters at junior inter-sports day. (To be totally honest, it was the only time I won anything at school - much to the disappointment of the teachers and, of course, my parents.)

I flapped my hand at the approaching tram in what I hoped meant "Stop". It didn't seem to have worked because it began to overtake me. Then I heard its brakes squeal. The doors thudded open right by the tram stop and I tumbled in. 'Thank you. Merci. Danke.'

I didn't have a ticket but the driver waved me away. He closed the doors and set the tram in motion. I walked down to the rear and looked out the back window. The two men had stopped. One kicked the other as he bent over with a stitch. Then they tried flagging down cars but every one avoided the pair. Behind the men, I could see the blue flashing lights of an approaching police car. Presumably, the blonde with the gun had rung in to complain about disreputables in the area. I allowed myself a smile and sat. The carriage was nearly empty and after the run the electric heat made me sweat so I took off my jacket and jumper.

'Dangers despised, grow great.'

I looked at the speaker. A whiskery old man, with rheumy eyes. He spoke good English with a Flemish accent and Yoda phrasing. 'Sorry?' I said.

'I paraphrased Edmund Burke. I do not think he would mind.'

'Right.' I sighed. Just what I needed; a know-all, ready to bore the socks off me.

'I observed the men who were chasing you. Mugging? Or a drug deal that went wrong?' He chuckled and shook his head.

'Neither,' I said, hoping he would shut up.

'I am relieved. Thankfully, our country is relatively safe. Though anywhere can harbor a threat, if you court danger.'

'Is that another quotation?' Brown liked to show off his learning, too. 'I didn't do that well in English Literature.'

'Then you should be ashamed of yourself. When the English have given the world so much: Marlowe, Shakespeare, Aykbourne... No, young man, that was merely an old man's observation. Your pursuers appeared spectacularly determined for their bulk. As if you had badly upset one of their number. Yet I perceive you are slightly less worried about them, than in reaching somewhere.'

I frowned at him. Was he a mind reader?

He chuckled again. 'Forgive me. You frequently look at your watch and keep checking where we are. You need to meet someone? Someone also in danger? A lady, perhaps?'

This was getting bizarre. I needed to ignore the odd man and concentrate on finding the quickest way back to Chloe. Unfortunately he changed seats to sit closer to me. He smelt musty. A sort of old book mustiness as if he routinely dried his clothes in his book-lined, dusty rooms. 'If you wish,' he said, 'I can help you. I live in the city. Always have.'

It occurred to me that he might be one of the team who were tailing me. Then I told myself I was being paranoid. I said, 'I need to get to the Theatre National.' I didn't, but I had noticed signs pointing to it near the Richmond Hotel.

He thought for a moment. 'It is relatively close. I will tell you when to get off. When you do, you must walk down Rue Nueve. Then take the third right, cross two roads, and at the third crossroad, look right and you will see the theatre at the end of the road.'

'Thank you...' A lonely old gay, perhaps, out on the prowl. '...Professor.'

He laughed so loud the tram driver frowned at us in his mirror. 'No, no. Merely an overworked psychotherapist. Over the years, I have absorbed so many of my patients' terrors that I find it difficult to sleep. Therefore, I am condemned to ride the tramways until exhaustion overwhelms me. Insomnia can be very tiring.' He chuckled at his joke and he fished in his coat pocket. He produced a pack of dog-eared business cards, held by an elastic band. He teased one out and proffered it to me. His name was Jan de Maas. 'If you are in need of help, give me a call. Anytime between 7am and 3am. Now, your stop is approaching. I wish you God Speed.'

Someone would be watching the hotel of course, and they would have our IDs, so I needed to be vigilant. When crossed the Boulevard Adolphe Max, I could see the side of the Hotel Richmond in Rue St Pierre. I couldn't see anything untoward but, to be sure, I went round the block and approached it from the left. Opposite the hotel I could see a crowded bar. If I had been in charge of the team watching the Richmond, I'd have put one pair of eyes in there and another along the street. If the budget allowed, someone in reception too. Sure enough, inside the bar, one table back from the window, I saw the east European who had followed me to the Sheraton. He wasn't interested in his food - only the view through the window. I looked for others in the street but could see no-one idling. At the back of the hotel, two roads merged. I'd scouted the area before we had checked in, and I knew that, with a bit of a climb, I could get into the hotel via its service area. But to get there I had to avoid the watcher in the café so that meant doing another wide circuit to approach the hotel from the rear. Running would have attracted too much attention so I did a power-walk, which proved more of a strain on my muscles than my earlier dash.

When I got close to the back entrance of the hotel, I stepped into the shadows to check for movement. Further up the dimly lit road, a cat sat in the middle of the carriageway. Near the far junction, a couple were enthusiastically necking. I waited until they came up for air. I didn't recognize either of them. After a while, they wandered off, still entwined. The cat finished washing, then wandered off. When there were no pedestrians and no moving vehicles, I ran across the road towards the service yard. I hopped on the bonnet of a parked car, clambered onto its roof and, from there, leapt onto the top of the wall that surrounded the Richmond's back yard. I did a brief high-wire act along the wall, then dropped down onto an oil tank, and so to the ground. Thankfully, there was no guard dog. Or an employee having a crafty smoke. I unbolted the gate ready for a quick exit with Chloe.

The back door of the hotel was open so I squeezed into the light. An untidy corridor led between linen store, office, laundry room, and washroom. All were empty. That meant the night man was at the front desk. I went further along the corridor to check. He was sitting behind the desk, watching a small TV under the counter. His back was towards me but there was no way I would get up the stairs without him seeing me. Thankfully, no one else was hanging about the small lobby. I backtracked to the yard and phoned Chloe. 'I'm in the hotel yard. I need you to call reception and talk to him while I get up the stairs.'

'Now?'

'Yes. Everything packed?'

'Yes.'

'Good girl. Phone now. Turn off your room lights and I'll tap the door – three short, three long.'

After I got to the room and tapped, I heard her pull something heavy from the door. Good upper body strength from nursing. When the door opened, she looked frightened. I eased into the room and she gripped me so hard I thought she was going to crack my ribs. She was shaking. I pushed myself far enough away so I could draw breath to speak. 'Anyone else come?'

'No.'

'See anyone watching from across the street?'

'I didn't look.'

'OK. We need to move quickly.' She did an odd kind of squeak. Stress probably. 'Have you packed everything?'

'Yes.'

'Right. We'll go downstairs and tell the man we have to leave by the back door because we need to avoid someone. Guests probably do that often in a place like this. Understand?'

'Yes.'

'We go across the yard, through the gate, into the road. Then we turn left and run.'

'You think the front is being watched?' Her voice cracked with tension.

'Sitting in the bar opposite is the guy who was tailing us earlier today. I didn't see anyone else, though I assume there are more. It's a bigger operation than I expected.'

'You mean you're out of your depth.'

'I didn't say that. Come on. Plan A.'

'You didn't tell me what Plan B is.'

246

'There isn't one.' She hit me. It wasn't a play hit. And she didn't laugh at the joke. Actually, it wasn't a joke. I really didn't have a Plan B.

We closed the door and tiptoed down the stairs until I could see the lobby. Unfortunately there were two men down there, talking to the receptionist. One, I didn't recognize. The other, I did. The tenacious Mr Brown. I pushed Chloe back to the landing and whispered, 'Fire escape.' We ran silently on the landing carpet to the far end of the corridor. We had scouted the route earlier but the notice on the fire door had warned that it was alarmed. Unless the receptionist connected the alarm with Brown's enquiries, we might still have an advantage. Briefly.

I slammed the door bar on the fire escape and cold air rushed in at the same time as a distant buzzer sounded. I pushed Chloe out onto the metal landing and pointed to the gate. There was shouting in reception. 'Quick!' I hissed to Chloe. I pushed the fire door shut as Chloe clumped down the metal steps. I followed less noisily and we ran across the yard and through the gate. I pulled that shut behind us. No one grabbed us, no one shouted. I pulled Chloe into a fast walk away from the hotel. Any second, I expected Brown to shout, "The game's up, Nelson". But we reached the Boulevard Adolphe Max without being followed. We crossed it and then I pulled Chloe into one of the narrow alleys that led east. We turned right, then left, and somehow ended up by the Cartoon Museum. At that hour, the area wasn't the most happening place in the capital. The wind buffeted dark, empty streets lined with dingy old warehouses. Our breathing slowed. No one appeared. Across the next boulevard, I saw the lights of the Radisson, so we headed there.  The bar was still busy but I managed to find a secluded table and ordered a snack.

When we had checked in at the Richmond, the receptionist hadn't bothered to ask for our passports, so we had made up new names.  That left us free to use our false passports to exit Belgium.  Trouble was, if we used one of the regular border crossings, the police would be doing a visual scan of everyone who went through.  There was no point now going to see Mandleson.  It was time to ask aunty for advice.  I used the lobby phone, in case my mobile compromised her.  I heard the call being re-routed, then she answered immediately.

'Yes?'

I said, 'I'm afraid we'll have to cut our holiday short.  Too many wasps.  Any chance of a lift home?'

After a pause she said, 'See the sights?'

'The one we came for.  Though we were forced to leave rather quickly, so we couldn't do it complete justice.'

'Pity.  I suggest you try 'T Waterhaus in Ostend.  Wasps hate the seaside.  Knock on the back door - the one that faces the church - and say Brenda sent you.  No further contact, please.'  She cut the connection.

'Eat up,' I said to Chloe.  'We're off to catch a train.'


It was after one a.m. when we got to Ostend and, by then, the station was nine-tenths dark.  The empty marble floors shone, and every sound echoed.  Ours had been the last train in, and the staff were urging us to leave so they could get to their beds.  We mingled with the revelers who streamed onto the windy plaza in front of the station.  Wind tinged the rigging of boats in the marina on the other side of the open space. There was a salty, fishy smell on the air. Beyond the wharf was the main road. On the far side, a line of narrow Flemish buildings with stepped gables. Most of them seemed to be cafés and restaurants. Beer signs illuminated their facades: Jupiler, Maes, Primus, Leffe. Beyond the buildings floated the twin, floodlit steeples of a big church. A police car swept silently along the road, its blue light flashing. The revelers began to split up. I grabbed the arm of one of them, 'Do you know where 'T Waterhaus is?'

He pointed right. 'The other side of this road. At the end. However, it will be closed. Come with us, we have good bottles to share at home.'

'Thank you, but a friend is waiting for us.'

Everyone in that particular group insisted on shaking hands with us before they moved away. Then they began singing. Extremely loudly and totally out of key.

'We'll follow them as far as that sailing ship,' I said to Chloe. 'I need to find out if we are being followed.' That meant walking in the opposite direction to the bar but I was pretty sure no one was following us. All the passengers must have left the station because the staff had switched off the remaining lights.

The sailing ship was called the *Mercator*. Wind whistled in the stays and yardarms. We crossed the main road but I still wasn't confident enough to go directly to the bar, so I led Chloe down Aarshetagineestraat and took the second right when I saw the big church. The traffic was sporadic. A few drunks weaved home. I saw the side of 'T Waterhaus. It was a two story white building with a tiled roof. The windows were dark. There were no cars out the back, or parked along the side. An empty bus roared along the main road, dragging a splash of yellow light. I could detect no one hanging about, so we walked to the rear of the building and knocked on the door. It had a small square of armored glass as if it was a speakeasy. A light went on inside, a chain rattled and then the door opened. A tired, saggy-faced man of about forty looked out. 'Ja?'

'Brenda sent us.'

'In. Quick.'

As soon as we were in, he locked the door and turned out the light.

'Follow, please.'

We stayed close to the man as he led us through the kitchen to the café. Chairs stood on the tables. A light on the bar said, "Hougaerdse Das – Hij is terug!" Through the big windows that enclosed the pavement tables, I could see the traffic on the main road and, in the distance, the chunky front of the dark station. He opened another door, waited for us to go past him, then he closed the door and switched on a light. A corridor. Greasy, scored walls. No windows. He said, 'I was told to expect you.'

He was on edge. A part-time agent, probably, who had not been activated in years. Goodness knows what strings Doreen had to pull.

He said, 'You need to get to England.'

I nodded. 'As soon as possible.'

'And avoid the authorities.'

I realized these were not questions but statements. I said yes anyway.

He cleared his throat. 'You have done something... illegal in my country?'

I shook my head. 'We came from England yesterday to Brussels. I wanted some information from a British subject who lives there.'

He said nothing. I went on, 'The information is not about anyone, or anything connected with your country. We have done nothing wrong, and the Belgian police do not want us. However, some British nationals are upset that we have been asking questions. They are a threat to us. Brenda promised she would... organize a quiet way for us to leave.'

The man said, 'You have passports?'

'Yes.'

Finally, he nodded. He had received his absolution. He said, 'It will cost you two hundred fifty Euros.'

I peeled notes off the roll I hadn't given to Mandleson and handed them over. He riffled through and nodded again. He did a lot of nodding. 'Very well,' he said. 'I arrange passage for you with fisherman.' He looked at the bags we were carrying. 'You cannot take luggage.'

'Why not?'

'Your cover story will be that you hired the boat to do fishing, for maquereau. Eh? Mack-er-al? However, in the channel, the boat will get engine problem. The captain will get close to English shore to... to enable repairs. As you swim ashore, the boat engine will be fixed, and my friend will return to Oostende.'

I didn't like the sound of the middle bit. I said, 'I can't swim very well.'

He looked incredulous, 'You cannot swim?'

Maybe all Belgian children are required to do a hundred lengths before they leave school. My PE teacher hadn't cared what I got up to at the swimming pool - as long as I didn't damage anything, run, or make a noise. Snogging broke none of the rules, so I chose that rather than getting wet. Things had worked fine until I kissed the hard man's current squeeze. When I recovered from the beating, I discovered that everyone else had become proficient swimmers. The PE teacher told me - not for the first time - I was useless, and he banned me from future swimming trips. So I never did learn to swim. Nevertheless, I learnt the lesson that it was always best to find out whether the girl I fancied had a current boyfriend. Admittedly, it wasn't a whole lot of use in the current situation.

Eventually, the Belgian said, 'I will arrange.'

I thanked him.

'Rest here,' he said, 'in spare bedroom. The boat will leave before dawn. I will bring you clothes suitable for fishing.'

We followed him up two flights of narrow stairs. The walls were streaked with grime and with scrapes from years of luggage. There was no pile left on the carpet. In places, there was no carpet on the carpet. On the landing, he opened a flimsy wooden door and ushered us in. The room smelt of old sweat and cigarette smoke. He switched on the light. No shade to the bulb. No windows. An old brass bedstead against one wall, pre-war. On it, a pink candlewick bedspread dotted with cigarette burns. A heavy, dark wood wardrobe in the corner. A gnawed pine table next to the other side of the bed with a pink porcelain jug sitting in a basin decorated with pastel roses. A wooden chair with arms. The light bulb swung in the draught from the open skylight and rhythmically stretched the shadows in the room. I heard a ship hoot. The place was sufficient for our needs but I hoped the

Ostend Tourist Office hadn't given it any stars. He said, 'You have eaten?'

'Not a lot.' I realized I was hungry. A steak and chips would go down well with some grilled tomatoes and a dob of Dijon mustard.

'There is some hutsepot left. I will get it.' He went.

Chloe asked what the hell hutsepot was. I shrugged. It was new to me.

We didn't sit. The man returned with a wooden tray on which sat the end of a loaf, two spoons, and one steaming bowl. 'I will be back in one hour, maybe two. Eat, then rest. Do not leave this room.'

He closed the door and locked it. We listened to his feet clump down the stairs. The street door opened and then closed. We burst out laughing and held onto each other to stop ourselves falling over. There was nothing particularly funny about the situation- it was just a tension release. Still, it got me close to Chloe. Her hair smelt of daisies on a summer day. I could feel her breasts pushing against my chest. Then she levered herself away to see why I had gone quiet. I kissed her and, once she got over the shock, she kissed back. I wanted her so much. I'd not felt like this about a woman since... well, since Tatyana.

Still kissing Chloe, I maneuvered her towards the bed. The edge of the mattress hit the back of her legs and she sat heavily on the bed. A spring went 'boing' and she burst out laughing again. I bent down to kiss her but she put a hand on my chest and pushed me away. 'Not now. Not here.'

To say I felt disappointed would be an understatement. I took a deep breath and told myself to be adult about it. After all, she hadn't said no. Just "not here". So maybe she wasn't totally against having sex. Progress. Of a sort. I told myself I had to be patient. To be an officer and a gentleman. Chloe, meanwhile, lay back on the bed, closed her eyes, and said something I didn't catch. 'Pardon?'

'Thank you.'

For being a wimp? For not perpetrating Date Rape? The more I looked at her, the more I wanted to rip off her clothes. I forced myself to think of something serene. No use. Then I tried reciting the twelve times table in my head. Still no good (mainly because I wasn't that good at it at school). My mind kept flipping to an erotic fantasy of making love to the beautiful woman spread out on the pink candlewick bedspread.

With her eyes still closed she said, 'So what is this hutsepot?'

I went to the tray, pushed a spoon around the brown liquid, and then tried one of the lumps. Then another. It was very good. 'Mixed meat stew. It's good.'

We ate in silence - me standing, Chloe sitting on the edge of the bed. Then she edged back on the bed, propped herself up on the greasy pillows, and closed her eyes. I slumped in the chair and mulled over all that Mandleson had said. Which was a waste of time because no eureka moment arrived.

I woke with a start. A church bell was tolling. I looked at my watch; it was two in the morning. I had been asleep for an hour. My neck was stiff from laying awkwardly in the chair. On the bed, Chloe was curled up, asleep. I heard footsteps on the stairs. The door was unlocked and the café man said, 'It is I.' I laughed, because it was a line from an old corny British sitcom. Chloe sat up and rubbed her eyes as the man came into the room. He dumped a fishy-smelling rucksack on the bed and pulled out some foul-looking over-clothes. 'Put these on.' He dropped a black plastic sack on the floor. 'Put into the sack everything you cannot fit into the rucksack. Leave an address and I will send your articles on.'

Really? And penguins take holidays in the Sahara desert.

'Be ready to leave at five a.m.' He went. And locked the door again.

I felt exhausted, though I doubted I would get back to sleep. Perhaps the old psychoanalyst was still riding the Brussels trams, also wanting to sleep. Chloe and I changed into the fishy clothes and sorted out what we needed to put in the rucksack. The remainder of our clothes we put in the black sack. Then Chloe shuffled to the far edge of the bed and patted the empty space she had vacated. 'Come here and rest,' she said, in a nursey sort of way that meant she would tolerate no funny business.

When the man returned at five, he had to wake us. We used the toilet in the café, then followed him in our noisy, fishy clothes. He handed me two mineral water bottles and a foil-wrapped package. 'For your journey.'

I thanked him and put the food in the rucksack.

'Follow me. It would be best if you do not talk. If anyone asks, I will tell them you are just two stupid English tourists who want to go on an early fishing trip.'

'For mackerel.'

'Exactly. The reason for the early start, is because of the tide, and also the long distance to the best fishing area.'

'Where will we be dropped?'
'That is up to the captain.'

The morning was cold but, because we walked fast, we gradually warmed up. The man led us round the back of the station to a commercial dock. We went under a new bridge, over which growled a few articulated trucks, and then we passed a memorial to *HMS Vindictive*. After that, the dock narrowed. The few rusting trawlers tied up to the side had names like *Jean* or *John*. We stopped by one of the smaller boats. It looked unloved, though I noticed that grime and flaking paint disguised powerful outboard motors. We boarded and shook hands with the captain, a grizzled, weather-beaten man the upper side of sixty. He pointed to the rucksack and then at the locker in the cabin. I stashed it there and wondered how long it would be before he snuck a look. We shook hands with the man from the café and he climbed back up to the dockside. The captain started the engines and cast off. The café man neither waved goodbye nor looked.

It occurred to me, rather late, that we had been taken for a ride. In mid-channel, we could be robbed and then dumped overboard to feed the famous mackerel. If our bodies ever turned up, there would be no ID. Perhaps Auntie had decided I was too much of a threat to her pension. No, I was being stupid. Due to sleep deprivation.

Dawn turned everything into a shade of grey and there was a damp, cold wind blowing in from the North Sea. The boat thrummed slowly up the dock. No other boats moved. No people were about. A couple of bored gulls flew over with no particular mission. A call crackled on the radio and the captain answered briefly. We passed the train station, passed floating landing stages advertising Zee Excursies, passed the entrances to the freight terminals and headed into the channel that led to the open sea. When we got to the end of the moles, the captain waved and, up on the dockside I saw an official wave back. Then the captain gunned the engine and we surged towards the ocean. The bow came up and a white wake spread behind us.

On our left was the deserted beach and promenade. Lights shone in some of the apartments. Waiters at the promenade cafés were already bringing out tables and chairs. Soon they would prepare breakfasts. My saliva began to run so I looked over the other side of the boat. Grey sea. Grey sky. Nothing else. The captain changed course, away from the shore. Bye, bye Ostend. The swell increased and waves slapped at the hull. We began to lurch up and down and I was glad, after all, we hadn't eaten any breakfast. I felt a grip on my arm and turned to look at Chloe.

'I didn't tell you did I?'

'What?'

'I'm not a good sailor.'

She looked like death warmed up. 'That makes two of us,' I said, and put my arm around her. As soon as it got there, she puked. Thankfully, the wind took most of it overboard to feed the fishes. I gave her a tissue and she slumped over the rail and retched again. It was going to be a memorable voyage. I looked behind to check how far we had gone and saw a boat following us. By the size of the bow wave, it was a very fast boat. It was uniform grey like the sea and sky but the reason it stood out was because there was a blue light flashing on the roof of the cabin. I heard a snatch of tannoy but the

257

words were indecipherable.  I lurched across and pointed it out to the skipper.

He growled, 'Merde!'  Then he cut the engine and we wallowed on the heavy swell to let the launch catch us up.

# 16

The uniformed personnel on the Belgian Navy boat appeared jumpy, which was a bad sign. They threw a line over and then two of them hopped aboard. A perma-tanned beach god and an Asian girl whose ponytail stuck out the rear of her Navy baseball cap. It was clear that she was in charge. Our captain handed her a document in a smeared, laminated sleeve. She nodded, then turned to me. 'Avez-vous une piéce d'identité?'

'Voici mon passeport.' I didn't look at Chloe in case the officials misinterpreted the signal. We were doing nothing wrong. Well, apart from using fake passports and being on the run.

When Chloe handed hers over, the girl scanned each of them with a handheld reader. There is no escape these days. She kept hold of the passports and said in English, with a slight US twang, 'Thank you. What is your business out here?'

'Fishing. For Mackerel.'

She raised her eyebrow. 'Here?'

'No, no, further out. The skipper knows where they shoal.'

She repeated the word "skipper" with an upward inflection at the end.

I said, 'Capitaine.'

She nodded. I was tempted to ask her what the weather forecast was in mid-channel but decided it might make her suspicious. Proper fishermen would have known. I willed Chloe to stay quiet. The officer's radio squawked with a response about our papers. She signed off and stashed the equipment on a spare clip on her uniform belt. The one on the opposite side to her gun holster. Before she handed back our passports, she stared at us. Waiting for us to flinch or break down in tears and admit to smuggling? We disappointed her. Eventually she gave us our little red booklets and said, 'I hope you catch many fishes.'

I thanked her and resisted the urge to correct her grammar. Or to help her up onto the gunwale. She skipped back to her boat. Perma-tan followed. No one spoke. Our capitaine threw their line back. The blue light on the launch ceased its flashing. Their engine roared, they peeled off, and then curved round to head back to port. The skipper took his time putting the papers back in the locker. Then, when he saw how far the launch had got, he spat into the sea. 'They thought they caught me with illegals.' He laughed. 'In daylight? They are as idiotic as they act.'

By which, I assumed his main night-time occupation was not fishing. He turned his back on us and powered up the boat. As we got further out, there was more swell and the hull banged rhythmically into the waves. The continual juddering had given me a headache and the cold spray had soaked through my top. Chloe looked a little less ill though she wanted to be left alone. I remembered the food the café man had given us. As I reached into the rucksack, I felt bile rise up inside me and I rushed to the side and puked up the hutsepot. Chloe joined me and vented the rest of hers. Behind us, the skipper laughed. I was glad someone was enjoying the ride.

After two and a half hours of agony, in which we dodged ferries, cruise ships, and assorted freighters, we saw the coast of England. It was a beautiful sight - even though it looked flat and featureless and serious rain was falling. The radio rattled. 'Fishing boat Renard. Fishing boat Renard. This is Dover Coastguard. Please state your business and destination, over.'

The skipper turned down the radio volume and faced away from us to answer. He didn't bother to share what he'd said but, as he swung the wheel towards England, I didn't much care. As we got closer in, I could see we were heading for the low-lying coast between the end of the Hastings cliffs and the beginning of the Folkestone ones. The only harbor along that stretch was Rye.

As we approached the buoys that mark the channel, he eased back the throttle. To the right were the long, undulating dunes called Camber Sands. The beach was deserted. 'I will not tie up in the harbor,' the skipper said. 'Get your bag. Be ready to jump.'

The tide was rushing out. As we entered the narrow harbor channel, we passed between grey, pillow-like lumps of mud hugging the steep sides.

Gulls squabbled over exposed crustaceans. A dog was walking its owner along the top of the harbor cut. As we got closer to a desolate-looking group of buildings on the left, the skipper turned and said, 'Ready?' We nodded and he slewed the boat to bump against a ladder that was suspended vertically from the end of a wooden walkway. 'Go!'

I pushed Chloe up then, as I got my feet on the ladder, the skipper revved the engine and did a U-turn in the harbor before powering back to sea. He failed to observe the 5knots speed limit on the way back.

I thought no one had seen us but, when I got to the top of the ladder, there was a man standing at the landward end of the walkway. He had a full beard, wore a navy roll-neck sweater, navy trousers and, on his head a white peaked cap. He was the spitting image of Captain Haddock from Hergés Adventures of TinTin. I expected him to say, "Blistering barnacles". Disappointingly, all he said was, 'Welcome to Rye.' Not that there was any welcome in his voice. He held out a hand as large as a shovel for our passports. He didn't move from the end of the walkway, so he effectively barred our entry into England. Not that we could go back, because our boat was already clear of the harbor and heading at full speed back to Belgium. 'Unusual mode of transport, wouldn't you say?' He was a Scotsman.

I shrugged.

'The coastguard gave me a call. They've been tracking you. They thought I should check you out.'

'The mackerel weren't biting.'

'Oh mackerel was it?' He clearly didn't believe me. 'No luggage?'

'Just this.' I held up the fishy rucksack.

'Mind if I take a wee look?'

I handed it over and he rooted through the contents.

He said, 'You travel light.'

I shrugged.

'I'm authorized to search you. For drugs or firearms or whatever. You have the right to refuse. If you do, I will take you to the police station to be processed. This time of the morning they'll not be best pleased.'

'Go ahead,' I said, 'we've nothing to hide.' To help, I pulled out what was in my trouser pockets and then pulled the pockets inside out. Handkerchief, comb, notebook and pen, phone, Euros, wallet. He watched but touched nothing.

'And where would home be in the UK, Mr...' He looked again at my passport, 'Mr. Apollinaris?'

I told him an address in Notting Hill I had memorized when I was in MI5. I hoped it was still an accommodation address and hadn't become the HQ of a terrorist cell on the watch list.

He harrumphed. Then he said, 'First bus leaves here for the station in thirty minutes. While you wait for it, knock on the side door of the pub. Tell them I sent you and say they should take you inside and brew you a mug of tea. You look as if you need something. The sickness, was it?'

I nodded.

'Not used to sea fishing, then?'

I shook my head. 'It was a trial run.'

'Hmmm.' He returned our passports and then stood aside so we could get off the wooden boardway. We walked off but he stayed where he was, watching the fishing boat Renard get smaller. When we were halfway to the pub, Chloe said, 'Do you think he believed you?'

263

'No.  While we're in the pub, he'll check us out on the Home Office database and then contact the Belgian authorities to get info on our skipper.'

'What shall we do?'

'Carry on walking towards the pub.  Make out we're ringing the doorbell.  Then, when Captain Haddock isn't looking, we hotfoot it into town.'

'Town?  All I can see is this set for a particularly gloomy Charles Dickens movie.'

It was an apt description.  The damp clapboard buildings, the shingle banks spattered with sea cabbage that was fretting in the wind, the discarded nets, decrepit boats, ancient lobster pots, and the rutted, single-track road that terminated in front of the only pub.  It wouldn't exactly qualify for an award of outstanding natural beauty, though it had a satisfying bleakness about it.  'Rye town is inland,' I said.  'Not far.'  Actually, it was at least two miles but I didn't want her to start a campaign to go by bus.  'Come on.'

After we had passed a sprawling factory, I saw the squat church spire on the hump that is Rye old town.  I showed Chloe.

She said, 'That's miles away.'

'Optical illusion.  Come on.'  We walked faster along the empty, pot-holed road that was bounded on one side by pebble banks, and on the other by marsh.  Fifteen minutes later, a tiny, battered bus came from the direction of Rye, heading for the Harbor.  There were no passengers.  I speeded up. Even if our passports checked out, I couldn't be sure how much more digging the Scotsman would do. There had been plenty of time for the Home Office to alert Brown.

When we reached the outskirts of Rye proper, I heard the wail of a siren. I pulled Chloe into the car park of a hotel next to the river. On the road that ran along the opposite bank, I saw a police car weaving through the traffic, heading for the bridge over the river. 'Inside. Quick.' We went into the hotel reception. Muzak twanged lazily from ceiling speakers but there was no one behind reception and no sound of anyone in the hotel. I went back to the front door to watch for the police car. It didn't appear. The siren receded. It must have gone west, on the Winchelsea road.

'What's up?' said Chloe.

'Bit jumpy. Sorry.' I was glad I had been cautious, though. The Rye Harbour bus came back and, following it, a van painted in the green and yellow chequerboard of HM Revenue and Customs. I showed Chloe.

'He could be going off duty.'

'True. Or he could be going to the train station to pick us up and take us to the police. It might be best if we stay in town tonight.'

'And give them more time to find us? That's not logical.'

'If Brown has flagged us up as a problem, they'll try the obvious first: bus companies, train station CCTV, taxi firms - that sort of thing. They'll assume we tried to get back to London so they'll put someone at Charing Cross, Victoria, and Ashford International. When they find nothing they might get round to phoning hotels and B&Bs here, but I doubt they have the resources. Nor would the Sussex police have the budget to do a door-to-door search. When they draw a blank, they'll assume we got away. Tomorrow, when the heat's off we'll get the train to London.'

'If you say so.'

'We need to find a B&B or small hotel and use false names. I've enough Euros to pay for a room.'

'Room?' she said.

'Uh?'

'We need to have two single rooms. Because aren't they looking for a couple?'

She had a point, though the implication was that she didn't want to spend the night with me. So much for thinking chemistry was building between us. I shrugged, 'OK we'll get singles.'

She laughed. 'Don't sound so upset.'

'Upset, me? Do you know how much you snore?' If I let her know how eager I was to bed her, she might never let it happen. On the other hand, if I played things too casually, she would think I wasn't interested. Hell, why is romancing so difficult? Why couldn't I go all macho and just bed her?

She leaned across and gave me a sisterly peck on the cheek. 'No need to rush things, Jamie.'

She was entitled to her opinion.

The view from my bedroom would rank low in the world's most picturesque B&B vistas, but the place was cheap and quiet and the bored owner was more interested in her morning TV program than us. There was no computer login. She didn't even bother with a paper registration. Just cash up front and no questions asked. Perfect. We each had a good wash in our Shared Private Facilities (there being no showers, and the only en-suite was apparently taken by one of her "regular gentlemen" – whatever they were). Then we ate the bread and cheese the Ostend café owner had given us. After that, we went out to buy clothes from a charity shop, had a coffee and a snack in the local bakers called Jempson's, and then returned to the B&B.

Chloe said she wanted to catch up on lost sleep so she went into her room and I heard her lock the door. After ten minutes in my room, I went out and locked my door. The B&B owner was still glued to her TV. My plan was to see if there was any activity at the safe house. Not for any great strategic necessity, but because any activity was better than sitting in the room and dwelling on what might have been.

The safe house still looked empty. A little further down the street a priest was sweeping the front yard of his small Italianate church. Sweeping and watching me. 'Good morning,' he called. 'Are you lost?'

I went over and shook his hand. He seemed surprised that anyone should want to do that. He said, 'I am Father Liam. Can I help you in any way?'

'That house, with the blue venetian blinds. Is anyone there at present?'

'Why would you be asking?'

'I was told a friend was living there. But it looks empty.'

'And what would this friend look like?'

'Old, bald, beard, thin. His name is Fraser. George Fraser.' The priest's face showed either cluelessness or a mask of discretion so I provided more detail. 'Sixty five? Maybe seventy? Frail. Originally from Albania. Scar on his face...here.' I sketched the line of it on my own face. That did it. The priest glanced left and right, then pulled me into the porch. He ushered me into the church and closed the door. A recording of sacred music floated amongst the incense. The nave appeared bigger than the narrow frontage. The priest looked me up and down. 'Would you mind telling me who you are?'

I couldn't lie in a church. Perhaps that was why he had brought me inside. I said, 'A private investigator. I have an office in Tonbridge, Kent. I was hired to keep an eye on Mr Fraser.'

'Why?'

'He annoyed someone.'

'You said "was"?'

I didn't intend telling him the whole story. I only wanted to know whether they were using the house or not. But Father Liam lifted his chin to prompt me. I said, 'I was giving him a lift to hospital when he was taken from me by... a government agency. And I think he is being kept in confinement against his will. I decided to find him but the trail went cold at the house opposite.'

The priest said, 'Who had he annoyed?'

'A politician. Though, as far as I can tell, Fraser has done nothing illegal.'

The Father said, 'I can't get involved in political matters. The Roman Catholic church has enough problems without...'

'It's not really political.'

'I think you need to tell me more.'

I got the impression the priest knew something, so I said, 'When Fraser didn't receive the army pension he expected, he complained to his MP. When that didn't work, he threatened to expose something he knew about a military action years ago.'

'Would that be during the Troubles?'

He meant in Northern Ireland. 'No. Africa. 1980s.'

The priest licked his lips. 'So who is paying you to carry on your investigation?'

This was beginning to feel like an inquisition. 'No one now.'

'Explain.'

The priest definitely knew something so I said, 'He has no friends or relatives so I feel responsible for him. And he needs medication. As to the money, I'm using up the retainer my client paid me.'

'Who was your client?'

'A member of the government agency that abducted Fraser.'

The priest closed his eyes briefly. I wondered if he was praying, or was annoyed that he had spoken to me. Then he turned and walked off down the aisle. He said, 'I'm afraid I cannot get involved.'

I followed him. 'You don't have to. All I want to know is whether the house over the road is in use. I know Fraser was there, not long ago.'

The priest turned back and said, 'Are you of the faith?'

I assumed he meant the Roman Catholic version, so I shook my head.

'But you know that what a priest is told in the confessional must remain a secret.'

My heart started thumping. So Father Liam had spoken to the Eagle. I said, 'When did he come in?'

The priest paused and then said, 'A few days ago. He was as you described him, though without a beard. Two big men came with him. At the time, I assumed they were his personal staff. We have a few East European millionaires in the area and they are never without minders. It makes you curious why they need them. May I ask your name?'

I considered using my alias but, in the end, I told him my real one. The one Fraser knew.

'Wait here,' he said and swirled out.

To tell the truth, I don't feel totally comfortable in churches. Something about them gives me the jitters. This church was no different. Oh, it was light. The pictures were bright. The statues tasteful and the architecture modern. Nevertheless, there was an indefinable something that put me on edge. I heard a rustle and turned to see the priest returning.

'That is our patron saint,' he said, pointing to the picture I had been standing in front of. 'St Anthony of Padua.'

I said, 'We're a long way from Italy.'

'Ah, well, many of us end up a long way from home.'

Was he referring to himself? Or to Fraser?

'Your Mr Fraser told me that if a young man called Jamie Nelson came asking after him, I was to give him this.' He held out a folded piece of paper. I started to open it but Father Liam put his hand over mine to stop me. It was a soft, white, cold hand. He needed to put an extra jumper under his surplice or he would get rheumatism in his old age.

He said, 'Don't open it here. I almost shredded it, but I could see the man was troubled. I prayed about what I should do but got no guidance so I thought I'd wait to see what happened. Perhaps you are my answer to the prayer. But please leave now. We have to be so careful, these days, not to upset anyone.'

I nodded, bottled up my impatience, and stuffed the paper in my pocket. I wondered if I ought to give him something for his trouble. Churches are always in need of money. But would he consider it tainted money? In the end I just said, 'Thank you Father.' And shook his pale, limp hand again.

He said, 'May God bless you my son. And may He keep you safe from danger.'

No one had said that to me before. Well not with the sincerity Father Liam packed into the words. It gave me an instant lump in my throat and a desire to exit sharpish. The priest didn't stop me.

Outside, Watchbell Street was empty. I turned left and walked down the cobbles to stand on the old gun platform at the end of the street. Below me was the town quay. A couple of old boats were lying on the mud and didn't look as if they would be going anywhere fast, even when the tide came back in. Out on Romney Marsh, a cluster of white wind turbines circulated lazily. The Dungeness nuclear power station sat like a boil on the horizon. I opened the paper Father Liam had given me. In biro, Fraser had written in badly formed capitals:

STOP FOLLOWING ME NELSON. IF I KEEP QUIET, THEY GIVE ME DOUBLE ARMY PENSION. SO I STAY WITH THEM UNTIL AFTER ELECTION. THEY TREAT ME GOOD. UNDERSTAND? GO AWAY. THANK YOU.

The note was signed *Gjergj Frashëri.* His lettering was shaky, but the signature looked flowing enough to be genuine. Not that it was evidence that Fraser composed the note. The message had been written in the blank panel next to an empty crossword puzzle grid. On the reverse, was an article from a magazine that could have been in Albanian. Perhaps the magazine supplied by Doreen's colleague - ripped out while the guards were elsewhere, and then slipped to Father Liam during confession. Of course, it might still be a clever ruse of Brown's. However, on reflection, I decided the note gave too much away. Fraser said he was being kept out of circulation *until after the election.* I'm not an enthusiastic parliamentarian, but I was sure the government still had two more years to run. So what election did he mean?

Back at the B&B, I knocked on Chloe's door. Inside, I could hear the unmistakable urgency of a TV news station. The door opened a crack until she saw it was me. Then she opened the door wide and said, 'Where the hell have you been?' Had she changed her mind about sex? I started to explain where I had gone but she pulled me into her room. Excellent. Things were definitely looking up.

'Jamie, listen to this...' She pointed to the TV. All I saw were suits giving a press conference.

'So?'

She went over to the screen and jabbed her finger at the central person of three men in the shot: a square-jowelled, overweight man who was sweating under the lights. He was considerably older than the other two men.

'So?'

'Wake up, Jamie! That's Montgomery Rhodes. Ex-Major Rhodes of Special Forces? He's giving a press conference about tomorrow's conference of education providers.'

'Oh.'

'In the Guildhall. In the City of London.'

'Right. So?'

She looked puzzled. 'I thought you'd be excited. We need to go and see him.'

'I've found out that Fraser was in Rye.'

'How do you know?'

'He gave a priest this note for me.' I handed it over.

After she had read it she said, 'Don't tell me you're going to back off?'

I shrugged. If Fraser really was sorted, my "rescue" mission was over. I didn't want to be responsible for him losing double his pension. I switched my attention to the TV. Rhodes was trying to be authoritative, but was failing miserably. 'The Government intends,' he said, 'to support education providers by, uh, by pursuing illiteracy, to... I mean we intend to pursue *initiatives* that will eradicate illiteracy. Yes. Eradicate. Root and branch. Root and branch. Lessons have been learnt from past... past inadequacies and we hope to propose a concerted, robust agenda of improvements.'

A reporter asked if it meant the government would have to raise taxes to pay for them. Rhodes glanced at his watch, then at his neighbor on the left, and then at the man on his right. Neither volunteered a reply. Eventually he said, 'Our long term fiscal strategy has built-in... safeguards that will... that will...' The slim young man in a sharp suit on his right, no doubt hungry to occupy the minister's position, leant over to whisper in his superior's ear. The minister nodded. 'The funds,' Rhodes repeated, 'were ring-fenced and are available without any need for a tax rise.' With that, he lurched up and left.

The head and shoulders of the broadcaster's Senior Political Editor came on screen to wind up the piece by saying that a Downing Street Source had indicated that though Rhodes was going to open the conference and stay for the morning session, but then he was going leave negotiations to his team. 'I understand,' continued the reporter, 'that Mr Rhodes intends to concentrate on preparing his bid in the forthcoming elections to be the party leader.' Was that the election Fraser had referred to? The commentator continued, 'The result of the second leadership ballot - effectively for the job of Prime Minister - has pitted Rhodes in a head to head with Deputy Foreign Secretary Watkin Whiles. A fight, you might say, between chalk and granite. Back to you in the studio, Alison.' The newscaster then switched her look to sad as she talked about an earthquake in Japan.

'See,' said Chloe, 'you can't drop it now.'

I wasn't convinced. Maybe it wasn't just about Fraser now. It was more about dishonest politicos trying to pull strings. I was definitely against that, but if I made too much noise, Fraser would lose out.

'You are going to drop it. After all I've been through!'

The only thing that might make me continue, was to stop a politician who had been associated with an atrocity becoming the next Prime Minister. Mandleson had insisted Rhodes was blameless. But could I trust anything he said? If so, why had all the records about the mission been removed?

'Jamie!'

'Uh?'

'Are you going to drop it?'

'No. Well, not quite.'

'What the hell is that supposed to mean?'

I was beginning to worry that she was displaying what you might call an Aunt Agatha side to her character. I said, 'I'll not do anything that might mess up Fraser's pension. But I will go up to London and ask Rhodes point blank what happened in Niger. He might tell me why the government still wants it hidden.' Privately, I doubted it.

I could also try tapping the CIA for information. Quinn Shelby owed me a favor from way back -

though I would have to call him from a public box in London. Just in case our friends in GCHQ were taking a special interest in the Rye landlines.

# 17

I stood under the glass porch of a City of London office building, to shelter from the monsoon rain. From there, I had a good view of the Guildhall. A succession of cars and taxis turned in from Gresham Street to the square, and then did a circuit before queuing at a red, white, and blue canopy. Greeters emerged, holding up white golfing umbrellas to meet the delegates and then escort them in. The rain had done a good job of shining up the old building. Though it now seemed a bit out of place and time, being hemmed in by the glass and concrete slabs of the modern City. Security was as tight as a duck's sphincter, so there was no way I could get to speak to Rhodes outside. That meant I would have to blag my way in.

'Your invitation, sir?'

The security man knew I didn't belong. On his face, I saw the effect of his brain working as it tried to work out what level of threat I posed to the delegates.

I said, 'I don't have an invitation.'

'Then, obviously, I can't let you in. Sir.'

This second 'sir' was a warning. I said quickly, 'I'm with the caterers.'

'Then go round the back.' He turned away to deal with far more important members of the human species.

I said, 'Where, "round the back"?'

The guard pointed, none too helpfully, and snarled, 'Now piss off.'

Such is the attitude these days towards humble casual workers who are trying to earn an honest crust - even though it's on the minimum wage.


"Round the back" turned out to be a service entrance where a bony guy with deep-set eyes was dragging on a roll-up. 'You from the agency?' he said, before I introduced myself.

I nodded.

'About bloody time. You need to see Mr McPherson, sharpish.'

He waved his cancer stick towards the open door. I didn't need telling twice. The corridor was frantic with catering staff. I walked away from a man who was yelling orders. Then someone shouted, 'Oi, you!'

I turned, expecting to see a security man, but it was a sweating suit, waving a sheaf of papers at me. 'What are you doing?'

'Just arrived.'

'Then go to the Gresham Lounge. Put cloths on the tables and set out a hundred and fifty cups and saucers. Have coffee brewed, and an urn of water boiling ready for their 10.30 break. Biscuits, sugar, tea, milk are all under the tables in boxes. Stay to serve the delegates. Understand?'

'Yes.'

He peered at me. 'What's your name?'

'Walter Smith.' I wondered where the hell that had come from.

He scanned one of his sheets, 'You're not down here.'

'From the Agency? Just arrived?'

He was about to say something but out of his walkie-talkie squawked a panicky female voice. The man yelled at her that it had been her responsibility to organize the water bottles. While she flustered a reply, he flapped me away with his papers, so I walked. Until he shouted, 'Not that way, idiot!'

I looked back and he was pointing in the opposite direction. As I passed him he said, 'Get yourself a badge from security. And don't barge into any room - there might be a side meeting. Ask someone the way to the Gresham Lounge. Now go. Go, go, go!'

The Gresham Lounge was a long room with two bare tables set up at the end, on which were plastic bags of folded white linen. There were also plastic crates of crockery, boxes of supplies, an industrial-sized coffee filter, a hot water urn, and big plastic cubes of water. I considered leaving and looking for Rhodes until I realized that, being a politician, he would eventually turn up for coffee and networking. With a drink in his hand, he might not get into a panic when I buttonholed him. I set to work on the catering supplies. After twenty minutes, the harassed suit with the papers poked his nose in to check my progress. He didn't notice I had failed to get a security pass card. Nor did he offer me any praise.

I finished minutes before the first delegates drifted in. I was proud of what I had achieved. The spoons in the saucers all shone and faced the same way. I'd set up coffee on one side, tea and cold drinks on the other. Someone had delivered two trays of little pastries and posh biscuits, which I had tested in the interests of quality control. It showed me that, if the detecting lark didn't work out, there were other things I could do. Less well paid, but potentially safer.

The delegates burst in with a gale of conversation. They were all seasoned event-goers so they helped themselves to drinks and eats. A German delegate asked me for Fruits of the Forest infusions. While I was searching in a box of herbal teas I saw Rhodes bumble in, surrounded by a sycophantic posse. He looked as uncomfortable as he had been on the TV. Blood pressure troubles, if his florid cheeks were anything to go by. I looked after the German delegate and refilled the coffee machine while keeping an eye on Rhodes. He remained in the center of a shifting force-field of delegates. Somewhere, a bell rang to summon the delegates back to business. If I left it much longer, Rhodes would hightail. I went over and put pressure on his elbow. He span round, frightened.

'May I take your empty cup, Mr Rhodes?'

He relaxed a tad, and handed it over.

I said, 'Someone would like a private word with you, sir. In the corridor.'

He didn't ask who, nor did he excuse himself. Just marched towards the door. I put the cup on the floor by the wall and followed him. In the corridor, delegates passed in twos and threes, chatting amiably. They were in a good mood because they knew that after their next session it would be the free lunch. Rhodes looked for the person who wanted him and then turned back to me. 'Who wanted me?'

'I do.'

'You?' He squinted at me. Shortsighted, too. At his age, he needed to look after himself better. 'I'm not giving interviews. Go through the Press Office like all the rest.'

'I'm not a reporter.' That puzzled him.

'Then who the hell are you?'

'Private investigator. An old man has disappeared and, during the investigation, your name came up.'

'Mine?' he squeaked. Rhodes looked over his shoulder, left then right, and pulled me back into the Gresham Lounge. By now, it was almost empty. 'What's your name?'

I told him my real one. It meant nothing to him.

'Who do you work for?'

'Myself.'

'No, I mean, who is paying you to find this man?'

'An MI5 agent.'

'A what! Who?'

'I only know him as Mr Brown.'

'I'm sorry; you must approach my department. Using the proper channels.' He made a move to follow the last of the delegates but I held on to his arm.

I said, 'Does the name George Fraser mean anything to you?'

He shook his head. Unconvincingly, because I could see by his eyes that he knew something.

'Or Gjergi Frasheri, to give him his Albanian name?'

'I know absolutely nothing about him. Now I must return to the conference. Kindly remove your hand.'

I didn't. 'I'd like to hear from you about Operation Novercal. Niger in 1980. I understand you led it.'

This time, his face drained of color. Chameleons do it faster, but Rhodes did it more completely. He stared at me and breathed hard through his open mouth but said nothing. He was sorting through memories. Not liking them. Assessing their importance. Worrying about the impact on his career; on the party; on the country. And the scandal! Oh the scandal. Then he furrowed his brow as he thought what defense to use; wishing someone from his team was there to bail him out. He cleared his throat. 'I have no recollection of any such operation.'

I kept the pressure up. 'Oh come on! I know that George Fraser was a mercenary hired by MI6 for the operation, though it's true he wasn't in your unit. I know your operation in Niamey went well and that you were decorated. What I need to know is who led the operation in in Zinder and what happened there.'

'You're making this up.'

'No. Fraser tried to get an army pension. The Ministry of Defence refused, so he threatened to go public about the operation. For that, MI5 had him abducted. Someone intends to keep him quiet until after the leadership election. You are in it, so doesn't that kinda point the finger at you as the guilty party?'

Rhodes filibustered. 'The British Army does not operate with mercenaries. Besides, the government would not condone abduction of someone just to...

to... Really, Mr... Mr...' He had already forgotten my name. 'Your allegations are entirely groundless and... and, frankly, malicious.' The response was automatic and half-hearted. He looked at his watch, 'Now I must go. I shall report you to Conference Security for... for...'

'Impersonating a catering employee?'

'Yes. Yes!' He wrenched his arm from my grip and ran to the door.

I called out, 'I spoke to Mandleson. Or, rather, Phillips.'

Rhodes stopped at the door but didn't turn round. He said, 'Who might that be?'

'You know who I mean. The MI6 case officer who set up Novercal and who you probably reported to.'

Still facing the door, Rhodes said, 'What did Phillips tell you?'

In the circumstances it was an admission of sorts, but it didn't get me any further forward. I said, 'First, tell me the name of the London Control for Novercal when it was operational.'

Before Rhodes could answer, a suit burst through the door. 'Oh there you are, sir. The conference is waiting to resume.'

'I'll be there in a minute.'

'But sir...'

'I said I'll be there in a minute!' The woman looked puzzled but went out the door and glared at me through the glass panel. Then she did some frantic talking on her radio. Rhodes turned to face me. 'What did Phillips tell you?'

'He confirmed everything I've just told you. What was the name of your captain in Zinder?'

'So he didn't tell you everything.'

'Our conversation was interrupted. What was the name of your captain?'

No reply.

'For god's sake, Rhodes, Fraser is ill. He needs regular medication. They've promised him double his pension if he keeps quiet but do you want to be responsible for his death?' No response. I tried another approach. 'If you have not been involved in the abduction and cover-up, do you feel comfortable about it? If it comes out, won't you be tainted by association? I'm told you are a good man. An honest man. I mean you no harm but what will all this do to your reputation? Your career? Your chance of becoming Prime Minister?'

He flushed and hissed, 'I know nothing about any... abduction... or cover-up. Or Brown, for that matter. I swear. Anyway, it was all a long time ago.'

'Maybe. But it has a big impact on things that are happening now. So if you're not orchestrating this, who is?'

Rhodes frowned. Then he looked horrified. 'No! It can't be... '

I was about to ask him what he meant, when the door burst inward and two security guards ran in. One thrust himself between Rhodes and me, while the other dragged the minister into the corridor and hustled him off to the conference. The security man I was left with pushed me face to the wall and pinned me there using a considerable force on my sternum. He said, 'Where's your passcard?'

I pretended to feel for it. 'I must have put it down when I...'

'You're coming with me.' He twisted my arm up my back until it hurt. I mean really hurt, and then frog-marched me into the corridor.

'Hang on,' I said, 'I'm supposed to clear the coffee cups.'

'Shut it.' He pushed me along a service corridor until we came to a door marked Security Control. 'Wait here.' He knocked, and then went in. He didn't close the door but I legged down the corridor and was out of sight before you could say Risk Analysis. The Fire Escape route skirted the kitchens and emerged into a delivery yard. Seconds later, I was in Basinghall Street. I dodged across two streams of black cabs, ran down an alleyway, and headed for Moorgate tube station. There, I trotted down the steps into the dry, warm air only slightly out of breath though wishing I had taken a pee.

When I got to the café, Chloe was facing several empty cups bearing the unappealing brown scum that remains from cappuccinos. The place was relatively empty, in that lull between elevensies and lunch. 'Well?' she said.

'Rhodes sort of confirmed he was involved in Niger.'

'Sort of?'

'He wouldn't say much. He said he isn't involved with the abduction but I think he knows who is behind it.'

'Who?'

'He wouldn't tell. How did you get on?'

'I met up with an old friend. Rory Tremaine. He used to work for Reuters until he joined BBC News.'

'Well bully for him.' I felt the green knife of jealousy dig in. I had forgotten how nasty it was.

Chloe said, 'Don't look so arch. Rory has good contacts. He says he'll look into the backgrounds of the people on my list.'

'What the hell did you tell him?'

'Don't be so snappy. I told him nothing.'

'Oh, so he drops everything because you ask him to do a private job for you? Come on.'

Chloe's eyes closed briefly. Perhaps, once, Rory Tremaine had been more to her than just an "old friend". I reminded myself she was allowed to have relationships and that I had no right to act peeved because she had given me no clear indication yet that she wanted a relationship with me. She said, 'I thought you'd be pleased. Aren't I allowed to use my brain?'

I apologized. Like I said, I've never been a great team player. 'When will he get back to you?'

'He's on the late shift, so he agreed to meet us this afternoon. Near where he lives.'

'Where?'

'Shepherds Bush. His access to the news channels could be useful, when we break the story.'

The bit about "when we break the story" worried me. Did she mean me and Chloe, or Chloe and Tremaine? 'But can he be trusted?'

'Of course he can!'

She said it very quickly and very defiantly. She trusted him, yet they had split up? Was this Rory the "man trouble" Ursula had referred to? One part of me wanted to know. The chauvinist bit didn't. As that was the side screaming in my head to stay focused I said, 'OK. Let's go meet your friend.'

'Hi,' he boomed, 'you must be James. Great to meet you. I'll get the drinks.' I accepted the offered handshake from the famous Rory Tremaine, Special Correspondent, and he nearly snapped my metacarpals. I wondered what was most important to him: journalism or keeping his male-model looks. His wavy hair had subtle blonde highlights; he had a carefully trimmed three-day beard; he had puppy eyes that shone from a ridiculously handsome face; and he had a body that must have suffered long and punishing workouts in the gym. I hated him on sight. We were standing awkwardly in a long, narrow, Maltese café on the north side of Shepherds Bush Green. 'Shall we sit?' said the Special Correspondent, and he shooed us to a table. 'Chloe hasn't told me much about you. You in the media, too?'

I shook my head. Chloe kicked me under the table. I said, 'No Rory. I'm a Private Investigator.'

'How fascinating! What are you investigating?'

'Gathering evidence to get an old man a better pension.'

'Really?' Rory's eyes glazed immediately. It was not the sort of story he was interested in. Not the scoop that would propel him to being Chief Correspondent, or even the news anchor. He turned to Chloe, 'You still Mocha no cream, Flopsy?'

Chloe nodded, blushed, and avoided my look. Flopsy, indeed!

'And for you, uh...?'

'Jamie.'

'Right, Jamie. What can I get you?'

'Just a black coffee. Please.' I had to work hard to get out that "please". Just to show him even plebs did Polite.

Rory went to the counter. Chloe whispered, 'Be nice. Don't you want the information?'

I wanted to say I wasn't remotely interested in doing business with someone who thought he was god's gift to women. But I knew it would sound childish. OK, it was childish. I also had a strong paternal urge to warn her against this smooth-talking lizard. In the end, I kept quiet because it was the type of café where, if you said anything, the next three tables and the owner would chip in with their opinions. Rory returned to the table, flourishing a plate of odd-looking savories. 'Dig in,' he said as he turned a chair the wrong way round and sat on it. Prig.

An uncomfortable silence followed. A girl came with the drinks, and Rory made a big show of stroking her bottom. If I had attempted anything like that in public, I would have been arrested for sexual harassment.

'So,' said Chloe, brushing crumbs from her chest in what I thought an unnecessarily suggestive manner, 'how's life been with you Rory?'

His eyes lit up. She had handed him his favorite subject: Rory Special Correspondent Tremaine. For the next ten minutes, he gave us a résumé of every story he had worked on since Christmas. Including the big names he had interviewed; where he had flown to at incredibly short notice; and which hell-hole of a five star hotel he had been cooped up in until he got his story. A yawn was forcing its way out of me and I knew I couldn't suppress it much longer. I also knew that if Chloe kicked me under the table any more, I would get a serious bruise on my shin. I pasted on a renewed look of semi-interest and drifted away from the monologue.

Out the front window, taxis, busses, cars, and cyclists roared round the green. Everyone was on the move - except for one man who was leaning against a tree, staring straight at the café. It took me a moment to place him. Then I remembered the Slavonic tail from Brussels. I excused myself and went to the toilet. I thought there might be a way for us to leave out the back. There wasn't. Even the food preparation area had no outer door. The place was a fire trap. Ought to be shut down. I returned to the table. The tail was in the same place. Chloe was telling the Special Correspondent about her nursing. Thankfully, she didn't mention her suspension. After that, there was another uncomfortable silence. I couldn't stand any more pussyfooting around so I said, 'What did you find out, Rory?'

The bastard made a show of not understanding what I meant. He made it plain I was the gooseberry, upsetting a cozy meeting between two ex-lovers.

'The list of MPs Chloe gave you?' I prompted.

'Oh yeah.' He pulled a folded paper from the rear pocket of his designer jeans. He gave it to Chloe who, to her credit, slid it unopened to me. She wouldn't look at me. There were only six names: Rhodes, Harding, McNulty, Whiles, Barnes, Parry-Smith. I said, 'Tell me about them.'

He said, 'I gather you already know about Rhodes.'

I nodded. I wondered if Chloe had also told him I had failed to get anything from him.

Tremaine went on, 'Apart from Rhodes, who was a major, the others were army captains at the time you are interested in. Harding was medical corps. Mc Nulty was based in Hong Kong as an interpreter. Whiles was in the SAS. Barnes infantry. Parry-Smith a pen pusher.'

The prime candidate had to be the SAS man. 'What can you tell me about Whiles?'

'Watkin Whiles. Born Vasile Orsova in Bucharest, Romania in 1955. Parents escaped to Turkey after the Hungarian uprising. Came to Britain. Changed their names to fit in. Watkin was bright enough to get into Oxford – my college, actually.'

'You're implying that makes him totally respectable?'

I received another kick on my shin.

I took a deep breath. 'Sorry. Go on.'

'He read political history. Entered SAS as graduate recruit in 1976. Captain in 1979. Good record.'

Despite my intense dislike of Tremaine, I was impressed.

'Curious, though,' he went on.

'Why?'

'He left the army soon after, on medical grounds. December 1981.'

'What was the reason?'

Rory shrugged. 'Nothing recorded. You know who he is now, of course.'

'No.'

'Deputy Foreign Minister. In a contest, with Rhodes, for the leadership of the party.'

Bells pealed, and choirs sang Alleluia. So, were the two ex-comrades slugging it out for the big prize? That meant they both had a motive to keep their old embarrassment under wraps. I said, 'Tell me more about Mr Whiles.'

Rory pulled out his smartphone and rattled off facts about the man. His directorships in industry, his career as MP for Edgely, his steady progress from backbench to ministerial office. He had a wife and three daughters; a large detached house in Henley; another house in Warwickshire; and an apartment in the city. The facts dried up and Rory stopped stroking his technology. 'Now I need to ask you a question,' he said. 'Why are you interested in him specifically?'

The veneer of charm dissipated. This was Rory the journalist, sniffing out a lead. I suspected that, despite his air of confidence, he was still the underdog. Desperate for the Big Story that get him live on air. Though it might eventually work in my favor, I had to put him off the scent. 'No, not specifically interested in him. Tell me about Barnes.'

Rory frowned but tossed out fact after exhaustive fact. Then, when I questioned him about Parry-Smith's career, he became bored. Eventually I said, 'Well, I think Parry-Smith is our man. Admin type... had access to service records and all that. Could have misfiled them. Yes it's Parry-Smith I need to speak to.'

'Not Whiles?'

'Whiles? Oh no, not a chance. I suppose he could have been my man's captain at one time, but what would an SAS man be doing messing with pension records?'

Rory couldn't hide his disappointment. 'I thought... That is to say...'

I'm afraid I enjoyed watching his discomfort. He had put himself out for an old flame, hoping to score twice, but everything was crumbling. He had probably even drafted his "Breaking News" bulletin in his head, implicating Whiles in a plot. No one spoke. I sneaked a look out the front window. The shadow was still in the same place. Tremaine stood suddenly, and thrust out his hand for me to shake. This time, there was no power. No need to impress. 'Well, uh, Jerry... if there's any other way I can help...' He let the sentence die to show he didn't mean it. Our audience with the demigod had come to an end. He kissed Chloe on both cheeks, readjusted his hair, and then left. The girl came over to clear the table. She said, 'He works for the BBC, you know.' Maybe she was also on his old flame list.

I turned to watch the tail. He didn't follow Rory but continued to stare into the café. 'I think it would be a good idea,' I said to Chloe, 'if you went into hiding for a few days.'

'Why?'

I told her about the man outside. 'It's me he's after. Remember in Brussels?'

She looked at the man. 'You sure it's not to do with Rory?'

'He didn't even glance at him.'

'No I meant you. You want me out the way, so I can't get involved with Rory again. Because you are jealous. You are, aren't you? It was all over your face.'

I shook my head. 'I just think it's best if you stay away from any... nasty business. Can't you stay with your parents?'

'My mother is dead and my father married someone who hates me. So, no.'

'Brothers or sisters?'

She paused, 'I haven't spoken to my sister in years.'

'Aunts? Uncles?'

'Look, honestly, Rory doesn't mean anything to me anymore.'

I didn't believe her but, with a shock, I realized I didn't care that much after all. I said, 'The watcher on the green wants us to see him. Perhaps he needs to escalate things. I can cope with what might happen, but it's not fair to expose you.' For a while after that, neither of us spoke. An odd feeling of sadness washed over me. As if we both knew we had come to the end of the road. I didn't want to say anything or make any move in case it hastened our parting.

Chloe flung her hair back and took a deep breath. 'I have an aunt.'

'Great.' I hoped she lived in Reykjavik. Or Australia. A world away from Tremaine.

'She lives in Belsize Park.'

Bugger. A lazy pigeon could fly there in ten minutes.

'She might let me stay a few days.'

I nodded. Better than Shepherds Bush, anyway.

She said, 'Are you carrying on with this?'

I nodded.

'What do you want to happen?'

I didn't know whether she meant about us, or the investigation. So I didn't say anything.

She said, 'Rory could have helped more, but you put him off. With your ridiculous act.'

'Chloe, Rory Tremaine is only interested in himself and what he can get out of life - on his terms.'

'And that doesn't apply to you?'

Ouch. She got up, briefly stroked her hand down my cheek, and then walked out the café without looking back. After a while, the serving girl who Tremaine had caressed came over and placed in front of me an espresso and a proper pastry. I said, 'I didn't order...'

'Is on the house,' she said. 'Next time, I overcharge that Tremaine bastard, to get the money back.'

I thanked her and smiled. Sometimes kindness comes from the most unexpected places. When I looked out the window, my smile waned. The tail was still there. Still staring at me.

## 18

'So what is it this time?'

Quinn Shelby stood, ramrod straight, on the deck of the *Golden Hinde* with his feet spread wide and his hands on his hips.  His heroic stance in the prow of the old wooden ship made him look like a buccaneer.  Or at least an actor from one of those old Hollywood swashbucklers.  Not that Hollywood used black leads then.  As usual, Shelby was impeccably dressed in high-end Regent Street clothes.  We hadn't met for a year or so and I thought he looked unhealthily thin.

'And why the heck here?' he said.

'I didn't think your CIA buddies would be interested in British Elizabethan history.'

'You're dead right there.'  The cool Bostonian sniffed.  'Have you an odor?'

'It's probably the river.'

'Then they need to fix it. No way to attract tourist revenue. So let me guess, Mr Nelson, you're in trouble? Again.'

'Not really.'

'Oh? Then how come the FSB is tailing you like you top their hit list?'

'FSB?'

'Vyacheslav Kirichenko. Ring any bells?'

'No.'

He laughed. An easy laugh, full of confidence and style. 'You have a singular ability, my friend, to ruffle people's feathers. Even when out of the service.'

I liked Quinn, even though he was career CIA. From the *Golden Hinde* shop, a gaggle of sub-teens emerged, led by an actor dressed in Elizabethan doublet and hose. They were heading for the ship so I said, 'Let's move.' We threaded our way through knots of tourists trying to find something cheap to get excited about. We passed the old Clink prison, all jazzed up as a horror attraction, and then followed the path round to the Anchor pub. As we walked, we talked on old times, in the shorthand that friends use. Our business wasn't right for inside the pub, so I led Quinn to the riverside walkway by the wall.

Across the Thames, the refuse department was loading containers of rubbish into a barge that squatted on the low-tide beach. Behind that, the city of a million deals got on with its business, oblivious that people had to clear up after them.

Quinn said, 'Is the FSB on your tail because of Tatyana Olizarenko?'

I shrugged. 'I assumed that was all over.'

He said, 'Care to tell me your version of what happened?'

'Look, I didn't ask you here for...'

He put his hand on my arm to stop me. 'Let me put it this way, Jamie, I have to know. Because I don't intend upsetting the FSB any more than necessary. And certainly not over some romantic interlude conducted by an ex-British Secret Service agent.'

He had a point. So I told him the story. That I had met Tatyana in the autumn, in the Sherlock Holmes pub. She was blond and blue-eyed though not exactly beautiful. More vulnerable girl-next-door. She said she was in London to look for work but I knew, from our first conversation, that she was FSB. She was probably waiting for a parliamentarian to get so pissed he would exchange secrets for sex. The day we had met, though, there was only me and a walking tour of Australians in the pub. I was reading a book and making my second pint of Doctor Watson last. My arms-dealing report, which had taken me seven months of hard slog to put together, had just been rubbished, and I was wondering what way to jump. Tatyana was a good listener. Of course, that was what she had been trained to do. I told her I used to be an agent, and that made us equal somehow. Anyway, we got something to eat, went to a movie, and then ended up in her hotel room. We swapped phone numbers and promised to text each other, though I didn't expect her to. She said she didn't think she was up to being a field agent. I didn't think it was ethical to encourage her so we agreed to make our professions off limits.

Later that week Sergey called me into his office and told me I was a complete idiot. It wasn't, as I had expected, a dressing down for the arms report, but for spending the night with a Russian agent.

Goodness knows how he found out. According to him, she had since been casting around for information on Sergei Salnikov and the SIU. I reassured him that our meeting was a coincidence and that we had never mentioned him or the SIU. Irritating, though.

Anyway, Tatyana texted me so we did go on another date. After that, we were hardly apart. A few weeks later an MI5 agent stopped me in the Strand late one night and ordered me to drop Tatyana. Said I was "muddying the waters".

When I next met Tatyana, she was distant and upset but wouldn't tell me why. Said she had realized we were not good for each other and, besides, she had met someone else. More likely she had received a telling off from Moscow. Thereafter, she wouldn't reply to my texts or my phone calls. I tried to get information from contacts in MI5 and MI6 about her, but everything had gone quieter than quiet. I never got to speak to her again.

After a pause, Quinn said, 'You're breaking my heart, you know that? You should write love stories for a living.'

I punched him on the arm.

He said, 'Do you want to know what happened to her?'

I turned to face him. 'You know?'

'A little.' Somewhere across the Thames, a church bell tolled the hour.

'Well?'

'There was an order to terminate her.'

'What? Who?' A chill came over me.

'She was abseiling down the outside of Parliament House one night - as you do - when her ropes failed. Didn't you see the Standard? "Mystery Catwoman Falls to Death"?'

I nodded. 'You sure it was Tatyana? I was told she was murdered, and the police were desperate to put me in the frame.'

'She died from falling from a government building. Was it murder or was it an accident... who can say? Anyway a member of the public witnessed it, so your police had to get involved. The Met's statement said it was assumed she had been trying to gain entry when her equipment malfunctioned.'

'Had it?'

'Not the way we heard it.'

'Which was what?'

'Someone cut the ropes. Did the police interview you?'

'Yes, but I was nowhere near.'

Quinn shrugged. 'Well, nothing was stolen; there were no suspects; no leads; and no admission from the Russian Embassy that she had been working for them, so the police passed on condolences to the next of kin who turned up from Russia and then they shelved the case. MI5 kept shtum. But something was up because, ever since, the FSB has been poking about. They had high hopes for her, apparently, and didn't take kindly to someone wasting their asset. Perhaps they just want revenge, though they still don't have anyone as their target.'

'You think that's why this Kirichenko is on my tail?'

Quinn shrugged, 'I guess. Way I heard it, someone whispered your name to the Ruskies.'

At least Tatyana hadn't used me. 'Who?'

'Wasn't us. Essentially, it's a UK domestic issue.'

'You mean it was our Security Service?'

'Who knows?'

Not Sergey. Brown? To get me out of his hair? To get his own revenge?

Quinn went on, 'The FSB handed it to Vyacheslav Kirichenko. He's nearing the end of his contract but he's still good, and as sore as hell about Tatyana's death.'

'Why?'

'Mainly because she was his niece.'

Shit. I said, 'I had nothing to do with her death.'

'Make sure you tell Kirichenko before he kills you. He's still lethal.' Quinn looked at his Patek Phillipe watch and then shot up his brows. 'Now what was it you crave from Uncle Sam?'

I filled him in on the Fraser job and what I knew about Novercal. 'As someone has erased the UK files,' I said, 'can you look in your archives? I need concrete evidence before I confront Whiles.'

'Long time ago, Jamie. Paper files will have been shredded. And with the cutbacks...'

'I know the CIA and their record-keeping, Quinn. There'll be a summary, at least.'

He shrugged. 'Maybe in Langley. But you're no longer in the firm, Jamie. I can't give you anything that might rebound.'

'I'll make sure no one finds out where I got it from. There's something else.' I told him about Mandleson/ Phillips. 'Can you find out who he's working for?'

'You don't want much.' He looked at his watch again. 'Look, I have to go.'

I said, 'Has there been any Service chatter about me?'

'I have to go, Jamie.'

'Quinn, I'm on my own here!'

He considered his reply. 'Your name was mentioned in connection with some flap they had in the Cabinet Office. Don't know what it was about, but a request was sent to Special Branch to keep an eye on you. You're sure not flavor of the month, buddy. By the way, a word of advice. Your new squeeze, the nurse? People are busily trying to dig up all they can about her. Be careful. I know what it's like to lose someone you love.' With that, he walked away towards the Globe. I headed the opposite way. On the *Golden Hinde*, the actor was telling the children that Sir Francis Drake had claimed San Francisco for Elizabeth the First. I was sorry Quinn had missed that bit.

When I rang Doreen, it worried me that she answered immediately. 'Yes?'

Of course it may have been absolutely kosher. Because I was using a new phone who's number wasn't stored on her directory. I said, 'Your loving nephew.'

'You know what I told you,' she said.

Her voice sounded odd. Tense. I said, 'Something's happened.'

There was a long pause. 'Yes?'

I realized during that pause I couldn't hear any background noise. Usually, Doreen's department is frantic and you can hear phones trilling, people chattering, footsteps passing - that sort of thing. And her flat echoes and there is a pronounced tick from the cuckoo clock. But where she answered this call, there was nothing. Anechoically dead. I noticed, too, she didn't prompt me, beyond that "yes?", almost as if she was letting me listen and then work things out. If they had dragged her into operations, someone would be busy tracing the call to find out my location. 'OK, forget it,' I said. 'I'm sorry I...'

'Wait!'

I waited. Still no background noise. Nor any whispered instructions. They'd already had enough time to get on to the telecom provider. Soon they would know the aerial I was using. Then they'd do a triangulation and in thirty seconds they would know where I was.

She said, 'I'm tied up here. I'll send someone to you.'

Tied up? She never said that. Never involved anyone else. Brown must have got to her. I had to play out the scene, or they'd know I had rumbled the situation. I said, 'Have you heard anything about an FSB agent called Kirichenko operating in London?'

'No.'

'Could you have a look? But do nothing that would get you into trouble.'

A pause. This time I did hear someone whisper an instruction. Then she said, 'When do you want it?'

'As soon as.'

'I'll send someone to meet you. Where?'

Because Doreen had always insisted on setting the place and time, it told me she was not in control. I had to engineer a smokescreen.

I positioned myself dead center of the wobbly bridge, sorry, the Millennium Bridge. The one that spans the Thames between St Paul's and the Tate Modern. Along with scores of tourists, I leaned on the rail, gazing at the view of the river and the bridges. It was my third change of location in twenty minutes. I had identified two possible agents other than Kirichenko. From my position on the bridge, I could see all three.

The agent who turned up supposedly to deliver Doreen's post was a knockout. Italian parents, I should guess; a rangy, toothy girl in her mid-twenties. She had enormous designer sunglasses perched in her black hair, she sashayed in her red dress as if she was on a catwalk, and she held up a copy of the *Times Literary Supplement* so I would know Doreen had sent her. I watched the crush in front of the Globe Theatre part to let her through. Many eyes followed her. A helicopter droned over the top of me but didn't stop. It weaved left and right as it followed the river towards Greenwich. The Service wouldn't have had time or budget to throw that much resource at me, but I needed to stay alert. The sassy agent in the red dress headed straight for the ramp at the Tate end of the wobbly bridge. When she got there, she turned $360^0$ to show herself, then moved half way up the ramp and stood there. Everything precisely as I had instructed Doreen. The student I had given a £20 note to, went up to red dress. He also carried a *TLS* – one I had bought. He hardly had time to say what ho, lovely weather for the time of year, before the two agents (who did not include Kirichenko), grabbed the student and bundled him off across the front of the Tate Modern to a waiting vehicle. The girl threw her TLS in a rubbish bin and followed them. Kirichenko waited until the quartet had disappeared, and then he walked towards me. He didn't acknowledge me but stood a few meters away and stared at London Bridge.

I could see him out the corner of my vision. His grey suit matched his grey face and grey hair. I said in my best Russian, 'Zdrahstvooite.'

After a pause he said, still looking straight ahead, 'I wonder... Mr. Nelson, would you care to tell me what is going on?' His English was impressive but, even in these times of equal opportunity, the BBC would never have let him read the news. To anyone else, he looked like a businessman nearing retirement, wondering whether life would be worth living after the office. I said, 'How do you mean, Mr. Kirichenko?'

'Ah, so you know who I am.'

I shrugged, 'It is a small community.'

'Why are your ex-Security Service colleagues pursuing you?'

I wondered what to say. It was annoying having him bug me but it would be stupid to make an enemy of him. I didn't want to mention Zinder, in case Moscow Centre made mischief out of it. He didn't seem to be in the MI5 loop, so maybe Quinn was right, and he was only after information about Tatyana. 'Buy me a drink,' I said, 'and I might tell you.'

'Very well,' he said at last. 'But I also am being followed – by an extremely clumsy American agent. I need to shake him off without it seeming too obvious. You understand?'

'Perfectly.'

'He has a red and black baseball cap. With a white and black striped long-sleeved t-shirt, faded blue denim jeans, and designer trainers. About twenty-three, I should think. Why are the CIA sending High School recruits on field operations?'

'Budget cuts?'

'Or perhaps I really am getting old. Meet me in the Cheshire Cheese in fifteen minutes.' He said that as he passed behind me. He walked briskly across the bridge towards St Pauls. I stayed where I was. Less than thirty seconds later, his clumsy shadow trotted past, muttering into his sleeve microphone.

I had used the Cheshire Cheese ("Rebuilt 1667") a few times when I worked at SIU. Not lunchtimes because of the tourist crush, or the early evening because of the drowners of sorrows. Outside those times, the pub settled into its dust. The only entertainment was the creaking of its floorboards. It was a cozy, atmospheric place that may even have comforted Charles Dickens. Certainly Doctor Johnson, who had lived in the next lane. I ordered a pint of Sam Smith's Yorkshire Bitter and took it to a far table in view of the bar, the stairs, and the toilets. Kirichenko came in from the street but didn't look around. He bought a vodka and took it upstairs. I waited five minutes. No one followed him in, so I went up the sighing wooden staircase. He was waiting in a cubicle.

'So, Mr. Nelson. What can you tell me?'

'You didn't buy me a drink.'

'You were early and I saw you already had one.' Then he laughed. 'I notice you are not too, uh, rusty... in your field craft.'

There we were, two operatives from the same profession. Except we were potential enemies, whose military still possessed enough nuclear warheads to cinder the planet. I said, 'I'm truly sorry about what happened to Tatyana. I had nothing to do with it.'

He pursed his lips. 'Not what I was told.'

'Who by?'

He waved his hand impatiently. 'You do not deny you were involved with her. Romantically?'

I told him everything about our time together. I said that, improbable as it sounded, we had fallen in love. I told him I had only just found how she was killed.

'Who told you?'

'An American.'

'Ah, your Mr. Quinn. You have been friends a long while, I think. But why turn to the CIA? And why is MI5 after you?'

'Vyacheslav, you have to believe me, I had nothing to do with Tatyana's death.'

He finished his drink and set the glass down carefully on the wooden table. 'Then why did MI5 suggest you killed her?'

'Who? Who in MI5?'

He shrugged and stood.

I grabbed hold of him. 'Hang on, I told you what I know, at least you could...'

He held up both of his hands. 'Patience, Mr. Nelson. I am merely going to buy another round. Same again? Never let it be said that the FSB does not keep its promises.'

He went downstairs to get the drinks. Nearby, a phone rang and a girl took a restaurant booking for the evening. When she went downstairs, I nipped to the phone and keyed in Chloe's number. It switched to messaging. I told her not to contact any of my phone numbers and that I would let her have a new one when I got it. I told her to lay low and I would try to contact her that evening. I was back in my chair before Kirichenko came up the stairs. He dropped two bags of Salt and Vinegar crisps on the table. 'Why do the British make the best crisps in the world? What is your secret?'

'Excellent spuds. Cheers.'

He chuckled. 'Spuds?'

'Potatoes. Bottoms up.'

He chuckled. 'Bottoms up, indeed.' He had brought us both pints of bitter as well as vodka chasers. I hoped we weren't in for a long session, because I knew I could never beat a Russian. That meant I needed to get the information sooner rather than later. 'Who said I killed Tatyana?'

He shrugged. 'They used a long-dormant method to post the accusation. So it is someone who has been in the Service a long while.'

'In London?'

He nodded.

'What did it say?'

'That you picked Tatyana up, and then killed her. Because she would not comply with your sexual perversions. At first I was outraged, then puzzled. Until then, your intelligence services had insisted it was a matter for your domestic police. When our ambassador made formal request to them for a progress report, he was told, "The police are making ongoing enquiries, following a fatal accident sustained during an attempted robbery".'

I said, 'Did the method used to contact you, tell you where it came from?'

'An indication. Yet those people deny everything.' He paused. 'Do you know who killed my niece?'

It could have been Brown. To frame me, then let the Russians eliminate me. Though it sounded over-complicated. Too open to flaws. And besides, Brown might be a bastard, but I had no evidence he was a psychopath. I said, 'When did you get the note?'

'Five days ago.'

Which certainly put Brown in the frame. I said, 'Can I ask you something?'

He spread his hands wide, 'Within reason.'

'Were you in the KGB in the eighties?'

He nodded.

'Were the Soviets planning a coup in Niger?'

He looked up to the ceiling, apparently searching his memory. Eventually he looked back at me. 'I was not involved, but I heard talk. You know, that section included your ex-boss, the traitor Salnikov. Where is he, by the way?'

'MI5 told him to disappear.'

'How extremely convenient.'

What did that mean? I said, 'What part did Salnikov play in the Niger operation?'

'An active one.'

'You mean, he was there?'

Kirichenko nodded.

'Doing what?'

Kirichenko shrugged. 'Maybe he had tired of his desk job. Maybe he was desperate to be hero. He was a strategy expert but perhaps he did not trust the people on the ground. Or perhaps he intended to defect to the French. Who knows? Long time ago. Drink up. Your round.'

'What happened in Zinder?'

'It is a long time ago. Drink!'

'I need to know.'

'It failed. The British bungled a covert operation to defuse the coup. Many people killed. When Salnikov returned to Russia, he was blamed. They demoted him and then sent him to a freezing border post in Karelia. You know the rest.'

Sergey had walked fifty miles through the forests into Finland and had given himself up to a bemused police officer in Kontiomäki.

Kirichenko said, 'Tell me truthfully Jamie Nelson, did you love Tatyana?'

'I did. But I think Moscow told her to end our relationship. So we obeyed. I didn't see her again.' The uncle sobbed, then wiped the tears away with his hands. 'Spaseeba. She was good girl.' He sighed deeply. 'I feel responsible. She so wanted to follow her Uncle Vyacheslav's profession. Secretly, I was proud... I have no children, you see. She was almost like a daughter. I should have told her no.' Kirichenko shook his head. 'God, Nelson, ours is a shitty business, do you not agree?' Then he knocked back his vodka in one go.

I said, 'How did you know I was in Brussels?'

'Tip off. Same method. The note said the person who had been involved with Tatyana was going to visit Mandleson. You showed up, so I followed. I was an idiot to fall for your trick in the Sheraton. Are you going to buy me another drink?'

'In a minute. Later, I saw you watching the Richmond Hotel.'

'I wasn't following you then. When I told my control I had lost you, they instructed me to find out why MI5 agents had turned up in Brussels. I followed them to the Richmond. Whoever they were after, they failed.'

'It was me. I got out the back.'

Kirichenko laughed and stumbled off for more drink. I would soon have to find an excuse to leave, or the old Russian would get maudlin.

When he returned, he said, 'That Mandleson. He knew everything that happened in Niger. He was operation control working direct to London Control.'

'Who was London Control?'

He thought for a moment then said, 'The working name was Black, but I do not know his real one.'

'Hang on, you said Mandleson "knew".'

'Did you not hear?  Yesterday morning, Belgian police found him face down in Parc d' Egmont.  Near the Palais de Justice.  Two bullets in the heart, one in head.  Short range.  The police say it was a drunken feud with the immigrants he lived with.  I doubt it.  Only professionals are so accurate.  No it is all connected somehow.'  Kirichenko downed his beer and his vodka, stood and held out his hand.  We shook.

I said, 'Is there any evidence about the Zinder thing?'

He wobbled his head from side to side and pursed his lips.  'Who knows?  Many sensitive archives from soviet era were burned.  And I do not think the British authorities would be keen to let their people know what happened.  They are quietly eliminating files all the time.  Now, I must go.  Russia still pays me to work for them.  But for how long, who knows?'  He headed for the stairs.

'Vyacheslav.'

He paused and turned.

I said, 'Where is Tatyana now?'

'In the morgue of St Thomas' hospital.  Someone has blocked the exit visa.'

Brown, possibly, holding onto the strings in case he needed to pull one.

Kirichenko said, 'You have an idea, don't you, who did it?'

I almost told him about Brown but decided it would be a step too far.  Official Secrets Act and all that.  'I have no evidence yet.  Sorry.'

He nodded.  'If you find out for sure, you will let me know?'  He looked at me with sad eyes.

It was the least I could do.  Besides, I owed it to Tatyana.  'If I find out.'

'Thank you.'   Then he walked down the stairs and was gone.

19

Quinn reached into his inside jacket pocket, brought out folded sheets of paper, placed them on the table, unfolded them, smoothed them flat, and then swiveled the pack round for me to read. Quinn had always been fastidious. The whole process lasted no more than ten seconds but it felt like an hour. We were alone, downstairs in Bella Italia, just off Covent Garden. Loud voices and laughter floated down from a group of tourists on the ground floor. Quinn said, 'I'm taking a hell of a risk, letting you see this.'

'I appreciate that. Thank you.'

He pushed the paper closer to me. It was headed "Top Secret", addressed to Director of African Affairs, Langley, and was dated 12th April 1980. Underneath, in large capitals, was: "MI6 BRIEFING FYEO CIA: SUBJECT - NOVERCAL". It had originated in MI6 Requirement and Production and was copied to C, Heads of Department, JIC, and the Foreign Secretary. I looked up. 'Plenty of people knew about it.'

Quinn shrugged and continued toying with his rigatoni. The document went on:

### 1. BACKGROUND
Secretary of State Edmund S. Muskie indicated that, following Senate decision not to ratify SALT II, your executive intends to increase political pressure on the USSR specifically in response to their invasion of Afghanistan. You also wish to inflict economic damage on the Soviets, principally to curtail their expansionist aims. The Secretary of State further indicated to us that the likely response of Brezhnev to any US initiative would be to authorize increased nuclear warhead production - in line with recent demands from the Soviet Army. This will, we agreed, lead to an escalation in tension, and could be a direct threat to the West. For the record, you specifically requested us to:

  (a)  be on the utmost alert and

  (b)  inform the CIA of any soviet initiative

  (c)  instigate actions concomitant with the need to:

    (i) intensify pressure on the USSR, and

    (ii) diminish the threat of military action by the Soviet Union.

### 2. NIGER
We would like to inform you that, on 3 March 1980, our Station Officer at Abidjan, Cote d'Ivoire advised us that the Niger Minister of

Mines and Industry had recently met the head of the Russian Atomic Energy Commissariat, in secret, in Angola. In the opinion of Commercial Secretary D.F.G Farr at our Abidjan embassy, the meeting suggested an overture by the Soviets to establish a new source of uranium ore (possibly to be covertly routed via Angola). Currently, a consortium of Niger Government departments funds the mines together with the French Atomic Energy Authority. We have intelligence that some local private backers are lobbying for an amended arrangement for mining operations that would effectively lead to privatization. Such a scheme would have to be authorized by the FAEA and monitored by them. For the record, we remain highly suspicious of the proposal and consider that deregulation could lead to hidden abuses of IAEA codes of practice in Niger.

3. INVESTIGATION
   3.1 Grounds for Intervention
   Concurrent with the above, we have established that aid money supplied to Niger by HMG's Ministry of Overseas Development, has been misappropriated. The Memorandum of Understanding with the Niger administration specifically stated that the money must solely be used for education and health improvement. We have evidence that a significant proportion of the money was diverted to fund armament acquisition - mainly purchased from the USSR and PRC. This,

we believe, gives us legitimate grounds to take an active interest. Accepting, of course, that Niger is a Francophone country.

### 3.2 Niger administration

CX from Intelligence Branch (together with digests from GCHQ, and Memos for Information from CIA Langley) indicate a growing split within the Niger Supreme Council. Chief Minister Senyi Kountché does not approve of the Minister for Mines' championing of the privatization scheme. Reliable sources suggest that Kountché wishes to retreat from the associations the previous administration had forged with the USSR. This may be because he does not want to jeopardize western aid, including the upcoming (and potentially significant) Joint Development Loan from France and the US.

### 3.3 Possible Coup

We have recorded several conversations (both substantiated and unsubstantiated) that suggest to us a faction (or factions) unknown is plotting a coup against Kountché. After wide but discrete consultation, we believe this might occur this coming autumn (possibly on Republic Day?). Unfortunately, we have been unable to determine who will lead the coup and what form it would take. Nevertheless one logical conclusion is that it would be a joint initiative led by the Minister for the Economy, Abdou Amadou (who has been heavily critical of

Kountché), and the Minister of Mines. Nevertheless, we do have concrete evidence that the overthrow will be covertly backed by the soviets. However, as far as we can ascertain, Moscow will not allow Soviet Army personnel to engage in direct military action. Their intention is to supply logistics and training plus the necessary hardware. Essentially their resources are finite in this endeavor, as Afghanistan is currently stretching them more than they had expected. Andropov has cautioned Brezhnev that it would be unwise to open a new hostile front.

## 4. THE UK RESPONSE

We have reason to believe that French President Barré will not agree to any official intervention in Niger by the UK (or any other sovereign nation) – whatever the provocation. It is doubtful that France would send a force of its own to deal with any coup in Niger as she continues to be highly exercised over the Algerian issue. However, we have been given <u>private</u> assurances that the French would register only a token complaint <u>as long as we inform them of our action immediately after the event</u>. They stressed that there must be no overt British or American involvement, and <u>no future reference to the operation</u>. Her Britannic Majesties' Government has recently ratified a concordance with France that, in essence, confirms our strong wish to maintain the status quo throughout the British and French territories in Africa.

5. OUR PROPOSAL

The main thrust of any proposed mission must be to prevent - or, if circumstances dictate, put down - any uprising. We remain convinced that if we successfully thwart the coup, then no deal to supply uranium to the Soviets –either covertly or overtly - can take place. Hence, the Soviets will not be able to escalate their nuclear capability. In addition there is another advantageous outcome if the coup is thwarted. President Kountché is bound to look more favorably on British (and, of course, US) contractors – providing, of course, that he remains in power. It would be expedient if we both (the UK and US) remind him, via our separate diplomatic channels, that our desire is to support his regime (though cognizant of the accepted diplomatic conventions of engaging with a member of the Francophone community). We intend to stress that this support will be terminated if he opens any new diplomatic initiative with the Soviet Union.

6. AUTHORITY

Our Prime Minister believes this presents an ideal opportunity to support Secretary of State Muskie in a practical manner. Informal contact with President Carter has taken place. He indicated that he would not stand in our way, though he does not wish to be formally briefed. Similarly, our Prime Minister is not to be updated with developments. C has therefore taken full responsibility to mount a specifically-targeted, covert operation to neutralize the planned coup in Niger using a small, expendable force recruited by intermediaries. No official recognition will be given to the operation by Foreign and Commonwealth Office or the Ministry of Defense. In the event of the mission being compromised (and at the successful conclusion of the said operation) we have put in place measures to eliminate all traces of the unit, to ensure no information leaks. Her Britannic Majesties' Government, the Executive, and the Intelligence Service will, in all situations, strenuously deny any direct involvement. If comment becomes necessary, the line we intend to take is that we were told of a local uprising but passed the information to Paris, as we decided it was up to France to intervene. Obviously, no rescue will be attempted if personnel become isolated as a result of hostile action. However we will authorize a S.A.D exercise to account for any displaced personnel.

## 7. CONCLUSION

The operation as described in paragraphs 5. and 6. above is now live and London Control has been allocated. Currently, we are obtaining further corroborative CX and building the team. I am asked to strenuously remind you that this must be a <u>solely British covert operation</u>. This memo is for information, for your eyes only, to prevent any misunderstandings. In line with your President's wish that the US is not to be directly involved in the operation, we will send no further communication to you on this subject – until we inform you of the outcome. No reply is necessary to this or future communications on this topic. I would respectfully ask that, in line with our wish for secrecy, you destroy this copy forthwith.

(signed)

*Frank Brandon*
*Requirement and Production*


*Henry Pusey*
*Undersecretary, Intelligence Co-operation, Foreign and Commonwealth Office*


I sat back and let out my pent-up breath. 'Wow.'

Quinn pushed his plate away. 'One more thing. The name of your old boss popped up in a file summary of Novercal.'

'Which boss?'

'Sergey Salnikov.'

'Oh?'

'Seems when he was in the KGB, he spent time in Angola, then Niger, around the time the coup was put down. He defected to you Brits soon after. Seems to me it was more than coincidence.'

'Meaning?'

'Meaning that Niger might have been a smokescreen to cover his defection.'

'He didn't defect until weeks later, in Finland.'

Quinn shrugged. 'So, he prepared the ground in Niger. Talked with one of the Brits leading the action in Niamey or Zinder?'

So where did all that get me? MI6 had masterminded the plan with government agreement. The Eagle had escaped the Search And

Destroy cleanup (presumably carried out by the British Army captain). With everything quiet after the operation, and with the excitement of Salnikov's defection, no one had bothered to track down Fraser. And so things had rested until the old boy had made a stink and threatened to tell all.

'You sure poked a hornet's nest here, Jamie.'

I said, 'Mandleson has been terminated.'

Quinn raised his eyebrows. 'I suppose Kirichenko told you that in the Cheshire Cheese?' He laughed at my surprise. 'You're rusty boy. Left a trail a mile wide. Don't be fooled by the obvious next time.'

Meaning, the youth in the baseball cap wasn't the only agent on Kirichenko's tail. I said, 'Did you find out who Mandleson worked for?'

'Low-level freelancing for beer money. Some for the French... some for us... occasionally for the Turks. Curious thing, though...'

'What?'

'He got a monthly bank transfer from your government.'

'He would: his index-linked Civil Service pension.'

'No, on top of that.'

'Where did it come from?'

'Couldn't find out.'

I sighed. 'This is getting complicated.'

'Complicated and potentially lethal.' Quinn picked up the Top Secret papers, tapped them into a precise shape, re-folded them, and then pushed them back into in his inside pocket. 'Well, that's all I can do for you, Jamie.'

'Do you know someone in MI5 called Brown?'

'No.'

'How about Black in MI6?  He was London Controller for Novercal.'

'You could go through the whole damn color spectrum, Jamie, but I know nothing more.'  Quinn waved the waitress over.  'Meal's on me, Jamie.  Call it a farewell supper.'

'How so?'

Quinn waited until the girl had given him change and had returned to the bar.  'Been recalled to Langley.  Can't say I'm looking forward to it.'

'Do they know about me?'

Quinn laughed.  'Langley?  They are as ignorant of your life post-Agency as they are about this investigation of yours.  I suggest you keep it that way.'

'What about the person who followed me to the Cheshire Cheese?'

'She was working for me.  An intern.  Good at her job but I made sure she's not plugged in to the system.'

I was sorry Quinn was leaving.  He had been a good mate and I would miss our drinking sessions.  However, being a man, I never said anything soppy and so just shook his hand as if we were parting after a routine meeting.

'I guess it would be best if I leave first,' he said.  'Have yourself another coffee?'

I nodded and watched his legs disappear up the curve of the narrow stairs.  I heard him say goodbye to the staff up there.  I asked the waitress for an espresso.  It was an agreeable place to hang around.  The ochre walls looked ancient and, well, Italian.  There were some old Italian adverts, old sepia photos of Venice and Rome and, from the speakers, came a sad Italian song.  But it wasn't Italy, it was London, and time I moved things on.

319

It was dark when I reached the Brown's address. The house was located in a quiet, tree-lined street on the east side of Croydon. Detached, with at least four bedrooms, a drive wide enough for a game of hockey, and a low- maintenance border surrounding a lawn that had such pronounced mower stripes, I could see them in the streetlight. Two cars sat on the drive. A Porsche and a Ford Galaxy. In the house, all the windows were uncurtained and every room was lit. Obviously the Browns had no money worries, nor were they concerned about their carbon footprint. I could see a woman, who I assumed was Brown's wife, in the front room. She and her daughter were watching television. Not a discrete piece of black equipment, but a stonking great plasma screen that dominated one wall. From the two-bay garage came boisterous rock music. The son and his mates, presumably, rehearsing for a gig. No sign of Brown, but then he could be in the kitchen washing up, or in his home office, keeping in touch. Anyway, I knew I wouldn't solve anything by lurking in the shrubbery, so I walked up the drive and rang the bell. It ding-donged merrily in the hall. It was a bell that hadn't come from the neighborhood DIY store, that's for sure. Through the frosted glass panel of the red plastic door, I saw the wife approach. She opened the door as far as the security chain permitted. 'Yes?'

'Sorry to trouble you at this hour but...'

'We don't speak to doorstep callers; and we already give to charity via the payroll.'

'No I'm not...'

'And we are not interested in hearing about salvation. Good night.' She began closing the door but I pushed my hand against it until the chain twanged. 'I'm here to see your husband.' It crossed my mind that this might be the wrong house after all. She and the children seemed far too young for Brown.

She said, 'Who are you?' Her frightened look had changed to irritation. 'Tell me it's not about That Woman.'

'I'm involved with a case he's working on at the moment. The Fraser thing?'

She obviously knew nothing about it. She said, 'Show me your ID.'

I shook my head. 'Not the sort of thing we carry around in my branch of the Service.'

She sighed. She seemed fed up with her husband's shenanigans. 'Well he's not here.'

I said, 'May I ask where he...'

'He *said* he was going to the pub.'

'Which one?'

She paused then said, 'The Chequers. On the Addiscombe Road. If he is there - which frankly I doubt very much - tell him from me I can't take much more. He has to choose between that woman and me. He told me he would sort everything out. Well, obviously he hasn't.' She slammed the door shut and, when she got back to the lounge, she yanked the curtains closed. Whoops. What was that line about a woman being scorned?

The Chequers was a typical redbrick suburban drinking establishment for the middle classes. All claret carpets, brown leather chairs, and shining brass. There were art deco Parisian adverts on the walls; a vast rack of wine bottles behind a locked grill; a coffee table loaded with *Country Life*, *MotorSport*, and *Golf Illustrated*. It said, alcoholic drinks are consumed here, but please look at the signs: we do not welcome plebeians. To prove the point, there were no real ale pumps on the bar. Just a few obscure lagers, presented on thin, ostentatiously curving pressure taps. The customers - predominately men - were drinking wine or shorts. A few people glanced at me but their brayed conversations never faltered. I was judged not to be a troublemaker. Equally, I was not someone they needed to know.

It took four minutes, fifty seconds (I timed it) for the bartender to peel himself away from a discussion about short dealing in electronic companies and head towards me. He put on a look of pained tolerance. 'Can I help you, sir?' He meant, "I think you have strayed into the wrong place." He was dressed in a crisp white shirt, pretend old school tie, and black trousers. Perhaps he moonlighted at the Conservative Club. I didn't ask him for Brown, because in the mirror behind the bar I had just seen my man drinking alone, in a far corner of the pub. I forced myself to say, 'Small apple juice please. No ice.'

'No ice, sir?' He implied I had made a serious error of style. He made a meal of obtaining a fancy glass, over-shaking the juice bottle, and made a feint at going to the ice bucket, just to see if I reacted. I didn't. I carried my overpriced fruit juice to Brown's table and sidled onto the bench opposite him. He had a small glass of amber liquid in front of him. He frowned at my intrusion but it was a while before he placed me. Clearly, he'd had more than one whiskey. He didn't like what he remembered. 'What the hell are you doing here, Nelson?'

'Your wife told me to pass on a message.'

'My wife?'

'Attractive young brunette who lives in your house. Mother of your son and daughter?'

'Cut the clever talk. What's the message? And how come she gave it to you?'

'She said that she can't take much more of this. Said you was supposed to have sorted things out with That Woman. Her emphasis, not mine. The implication seemed to be, "or else".'

'The stupid bitch thinks I enjoy all this.'

'Don't you?' I realized I sounded like one of those Service shrinks they wheel in at debriefs.

'I wouldn't tell you, Nelson, if you were the last person on earth. You still haven't told me why you're here.'

'I need some answers.'

'You won't get them from me. Now get lost. I'm busy.' He slugged down his drink, got up, and lurched for the toilet. 'God,' he said as he went, 'you've got a nerve, calling at my home.' His jacket was bunched up in the corner of his seat and his phone was on the table. When the toilet door shut I grabbed the mobile and accessed the in and out trays. Empty. The directory was also blank. I put the phone back and checked his coat pockets. Similarly empty. Brown came out the toilet, went to the bar, and then returned with another double whiskey. He said, 'Are you still here?'

'Tell me what happened in Zinder.'

He swung a punch at me but it was miles off and he only succeeded in knocking the table lamp over and slopping his drink. I went to the bar and got a cloth and another whiskey. Brown didn't even say thank you. People seem to have lost the art of being polite. After he sank both drinks, he said, 'Anyway, who told you where I live? Oh, of course, your asshole woman from facilities.'

So, Doreen had been reeled in. I hoped she would be all right. I said, 'Don't know what you mean.'

'Exactly. You don't know anything, Nelson, beyond rumors and guesses.'

''Fraid you're wrong there. I recently saw a copy of the brief on Novercal that MI6 sent to the CIA. I know Rhodes and Whiles were there. I know Mandleson was case officer with the code name Philips. I know that Mandleson has recently been terminated in Brussels. Was it you, by the way?'

'No.'

I went on, 'I also know that when Salnikov was in the KGB he was working on the coup and, you might remember, he defected to the Brits soon after. Maybe the two things are tied up. Maybe not. Anyway, all I need from you are two trifling things. One: the name of the sergeant who was under Whiles in Zinder. Two: the name of the London Control who went under the code name Black.'

Brown said, 'Never heard of Novercal. Never heard of Black. Now get lost.'

I said, 'Come on, the reason you had to make George Fraser vanish was to keep the lid on Novercal. You were frightened he would talk about it and mess up Rhodes' or Whiles' chance of becoming Prime Minister.'

'Guesswork.' Nevertheless, I saw a frown. 'How did you...?' Then he shut his mouth with a snap.

I went on, 'Let me guess some more: Fraser isn't in purdah because the government is afraid of upsetting the French. Or worried about people knowing that our Army hired mercenaries. Or even the Russian angle. Someone is running scared because they don't want the public knowing how you put down the uprising.'

'Who said I was there?'

That really had been a guess, but seemingly a lucky one. Perhaps the nameless sergeant in Zinder had been the Mr. Brown sitting in front of me. It might fit if he had been a young recruit.

Brown shut his eyes. When he opened them, he reached for his phone and keyed a number. The call was answered immediately. Brown said, 'Nelson's here... yes Nelson! I'm at the Chequers... in the Addiscombe Road. Make it quick.' He threw the cellphone on the table and it slid across and landed my side with a thud on the carpet.

I picked it up and placed it in front of him. 'Special Branch?'

'You'll find out.'

I had to get past his guard before his minders showed up. I said, 'Where did we meet before?'

'You don't remember?'

I shook my head. So we had met.

He said, 'We were on the same Service induction course.'

I thought back. There had been a lot of us on my intake, and we had been split into several groups. Brown certainly wasn't in mine.

He went on, 'You were a cocky sod, even then. You got a cheap laugh when you made fun of us "oldies".'

Then I remembered. There had been a group of mature recruits destined to be Investigation Officers. Ex-coppers, ex-army officers, ex-colonial policemen - that sort of thing. From the start, they had treated us like idiots. We responded by treating them like dinosaurs. Eventually, the instructors separated us. We never saw the dinosaurs again.

Brown continued, 'They should have weeded you out long before Induction. You never embraced what the Service stood for, did you? Thought you knew better than the system. So you crashed around, wrecking people's lives.'

'Whose life have I wrecked?'

'Melissa's. She's pregnant.'

That stunned me. OK, I know Evan Evans had already told me, but he had done so to score a point. Brown wasn't point-scoring, he was livid. In fact, he seemed close to tears. 'You used her, you bastard. Then you dumped her.'

'Now hang on, Brown, I didn't make her pregnant. We split up ages ago.'

He leaned over, gripped my front, and dragged me out of my seat. 'But you knew she was vulnerable. You knew she needed protecting. You knew she was... unstable.'

I pushed him away and wondered how he knew all that. Then I realized, she was Brown's other woman. Perhaps he'd had the hots for her but she had chosen me over him. I remembered that someone had said, after our fling, that Melissa was going out with a spook. It must have been Brown. No wonder there was marital tension and alcohol abuse. And no wonder he knew so much about me. Perhaps he was the stabilizing influence Melissa had yearned after. A father-figure. The rock to lean on. Trouble was, he had gone and complicated things by making her pregnant. I said, 'So it's yours?' He didn't acknowledge. Nor did he deny. He looked at his watch, and then popped a couple of Extra Strong Mints into his mouth. He was getting ready to meet the minders. And sobering up fast. Some people can do that.

He put on an unconvincing smile and said, 'Look, we don't have to fight. Let me get you another drink.'

I nodded, even though I hadn't touched my first one. I knew I wouldn't get any more information from him. As he headed for the bar, I left. When I got out the front, I met a highly pregnant young woman waddling up the path. I held open the door for her.

'No! Is that Jimmy! Wadderyoudoinghere?'

'Melissa?'

'You been with Charlie? How is he?'

I assumed she meant Brown. Charlie Brown. Ha, ha. Very Funny. 'Concerned, I'd say.'

She said, 'As well he might. I'm pregnant.'

'I can see. Congratulations.'

'I told him I'm going to keep the baby but he...'

'Look, Melissa, don't think me rude, but I do really have to dash. Life and Death and all that.'

'Oh.'

'Catch up some other time?'

'OK.' She didn't care about me; I was old history. She went in and I watched her through the window. She went straight over to Brown who was still leaning on the bar. She put her arms round him and hugged good ol' Charlie Brown. They stayed fixed in the same position until the barman hovered for payment. Now that particular loose end was tied up, I needed to make myself scarce.

I jogged down the road and, as I approached a corner, I saw silent, blue flashing lights in the distance. I nipped down a side road and walked away from the junction. I glanced back occasionally and then saw an unmarked saloon whizz past. The blue lights had been switched off. When I heard the car screech to a stop outside the pub, I ran.

It was late by the time I reached Salnikov's house. There was no surveillance out front. None of the windows were lit. Maybe they really had gone away. I went down the short alleyway at the right-hand side of the house but a locked gate barred the way. I jumped up and gripped the top to pull myself over but my fingers closed over something sharp. I let go and fell back to the path. In the light from the streetlamp, I saw blood seeping from neat, straight cuts along the fingers of my left hand. Razor wire. I wrapped a clean handkerchief round my hand to stop the bleeding and hoped I hadn't picked up any infection.

Either side of the gate was a short section of wooden paneling. The left side was attached to the wall of Salnikov's house, and the other side to the neighbor's brick wall. I had to assume the razor wire went the whole width. I dragged two full terracotta pots from the front garden, down the alley and placed one on top of the other in front of the right-hand fence panel. I got on top of them and peered over the fence. The razor wire did, indeed, go the whole length. Near the ground, a green LED blinked. Maybe attached to a micro switch on the gate, and connected to the intruder alarm. Or possibly, it was an infrared beam. Either way, I didn't want to use it to announce my presence.

I remembered there was a coconut Welcome mat on the porch, so I went back to get it and draped it over the right-hand fence. Then I leapt from the top of the terracotta pot tower so my chest landed on the mat. Then I cantilevered over. It wasn't a textbook entry. I crashed on top of a trash dumpster, nearly dislocated my shoulder, and then slid off to land heavily on my left hip. I lay still for a while and listened. No dogs. No shouts. No lights. The LED behind the fence continued its green blinking. I was in.

The side door to the house was locked and no light showed through the frosted glass, so I crept round the back of the house. I gave my eyes time to adjust, because there was less ambient light round there. A dark window and then a conservatory, also dark. However, when I peered through one of the conservatory windows, I saw a sliver of light under an inner door. Of course, it may have been a light on a timer to deter burglars. Or Salnikov could be holed up inside, having sent his family into hiding and then had called MI5's bluff by becoming a hermit in his own house. I checked out the conservatory doors. Good quality double-glazing and firmly locked. I'd not get in without waking up four sets of neighbors.

I explored the garden, but there was nothing of interest there. I wondered if I was way off target. What would Salnikov be able tell me that I didn't already know? I decided I might as well call it a night. Not that I could bed down at the Ship, or the Crown, because Doreen may have told them about the Apollinaris angle. And in any case, after my visit to Brown, they would have intensified security. Even the Welsh hopeful would be popping stay-awake pills, hoping I would show up in Chertsey.

Then a light came on in the kitchen – the window left of the conservatory. I waited, because it still could be a timer. It wasn't, because an arm pushed one side of the curtains closed. From behind the closed half, they reached over and pulled the other curtain to the middle. All I had seen was a red jumper. Sergey? Or someone minding the house?

Someone waiting for me. I needed to find out. The drain gurgled as water ran down from the sink. I went over and pushed my unbloody hand over the bottom of the pipe. I heard the water steadily fill the pipe. Eventually there was an exclamation in the kitchen, followed by rhythmical thumping as the person inside tried to unblock the sink.

After a pause, I heard a key turn in the side door. A wash of light swept into the side passage and diminished briefly as someone came out. They wore slippers or soft shoes. I was still bent down because, if I let the water escape too soon, the person would just go back in. I watched the shadow slide down the garden. When I judged they were about to appear round the corner of the house, I took my hand away from the pipe and stood. When the woman saw me, she swore and ran towards the kitchen door. I caught up as she stepped through the doorway so I followed, pushing her into the kitchen and, when I was in, slammed the door shut and locked it. She screamed and I reached out to put my dry hand over her mouth but I had forgotten the blood-soaked hankie so she did a lot more screaming. It was all very Hitchcock. She looked familiar. Then I remembered the photo my ex-boss had on his desk. 'Mrs Salnikov? Lisa?'

'Who are you?'

I put a finger to my lips. I was puzzled because I was sure Sergey had said he'd sent his wife and children away. There was a pad on the fridge door with a pencil dangling on a string. I tore a sheet from the pad and wrote: JAMIE NELSON. I USED TO WORK FOR YOUR HUSBAND. THEY HAVE PROBABLY PUT BUGS IN HERE.

She frowned but at least she didn't do any more screaming. She looked at my hand, unwrapped the

330

handkerchief, and pulled me over to the sink. She washed the wounds and applied some antiseptic that stung like hell. I was a big boy so I didn't yell. Then she dried the skin and put on three plasters. She did it quickly, efficiently, as if she was used to administrating First Aid. I suppose with two children you get plenty of practice. I ripped off another blank sheet. WHERE IS SERGEY?

She wrote: IN HIDING.

My turn: WHERE ARE YOUR CHILDREN?

AT SCHOOL.

Of course, they were boarders, courtesy of the British taxpayer in heartfelt thanks for Salnikov's contribution to Glasnost. I wrote: WHY ARE YOU HERE?

She replied: HE SAID YOU WOULD COME.

Who? Salnikov? Did that mean she had a message for me? Using the shopping pad would take forever so I grabbed the kettle, filled it, and then switched it on. When it was boiling noisily, I whispered in her ear, 'What is the message?'

She frowned. 'No message. He just said to expect you.'

Damn. So why was she here, then? And if Sergey had expected me, but hadn't told his wife about a message, did that mean he didn't trust her and had hidden something? I asked to see his office. She whispered, 'I must close the curtains upstairs first. Wait here.'

It was a reasonable request except, at that moment, I didn't trust anyone. There had been enough time for the Service to rent rooms in a house across the green as it was now probably against Human Rights law to force an agent to live in a car. She took her time. More than enough time to have signaled out the window. Or use the phone.

I went to the kitchen wall phone and carefully lifted the handset while putting my hand over the microphone. '...you sure?' It was a man's voice. Not Sergey. Not Brown. She replied in a whisper, 'Yes, it's definitely him.' The man said, 'Leave it with us.' The line went dead, and I replaced the receiver.

When she came in, her cheeks were flushed. I wrote: CAN I SEE SERGEY'S OFFICE NOW? She seemed a little confused but then beckoned me to follow her. I wondered how long I had. Minutes, if she had talked to the surveillance team. Longer, if it was a mobile response unit. Plenty of time if it was the unit that had gone to Brown's assistance in Croydon. No way of knowing, though. The office was upstairs, at the back of the house. I had been there once, helping Sergey finish a report. Lisa Salnikov snicked on the light, and then closed the curtains. She wasn't a very good agent, or she'd have remembered she was supposed to have already been upstairs to close them. But I suppose I shouldn't be too critical. She was a specialist. An agent that pretended to be a loving wife.

I went into the room but she hovered at the door to watch me. The boss's PC had disappeared. No laptop either. The desk was tidier than I remembered, courtesy of the cleaning party. I opened a couple of drawers but the files had disappeared. All that was left were pads of blank lined paper, a stapler, a new pack of highlighter pens. Then I saw the freebie magazine Chloe had delivered. It was propped behind an ornament on the mantle shelf of the blocked-off fireplace. On the top right hand corner of the magazine, someone had written in red felt-tip "Salnikov". We hadn't done that. I saw Lisa look at her watch. She was expecting the backup to arrive. I beckoned her over and whispered, 'Can you show me the lounge?'

She wanted to say no, but didn't want to upset me in case I did a runner. As she went out, I grabbed the magazine and shoved it up the front of my fleece. She led me downstairs and I made a show of leafing through a big picture book on the Cotswolds. I tutted, then held it up by the spine and shook it. When nothing fell out, I said, 'I don't understand. He said...'

As I returned the book to the coffee table, she said rather too eagerly, 'What did he say?'

'Not important.'

With desperation in her voice she said, 'Let me make you a drink!'

'No thanks. I'll be off.'

'No, stay, please. I... I never told you how much I liked you. Jamie. And now that Sergey has gone...'

'Sorry Mrs Salnikov. That won't work either. I'm off.'

She sat. Maybe, now the crunch had come, she realized she was better at being a wife than an agent. I went into the hall, unchained the door, went into the cold night air, and trotted down the path.

'Stop! There was something,' she called from the front door. 'Yes! I remember now! Come back and I'll tell you.'

I didn't hold it against her because she was fighting for her career. Or maybe, in an odd sort of way, Sergey. Sergey the provider. Sergey the father of her children. Scared old Sergey who, for all we knew, was still playing the double game he had been trained to do by the KGB all those years ago.

A few cars went up and down the road. If there were watchers, they would tell the mobile team which way I walked. So I didn't bother hiding. It had been a long day and I felt exhausted. I needed to find a quiet place to study Sergey's magazine and I remembered, when Chloe and I had been out for a walk by the Thames, there was a motel next to Chertsey Bridge. It wasn't far away, but the team wouldn't connect it with me. It was too far to walk though, so I trudged up the hill to the station in the hope a taxi was waiting for a late train. I was too tired to seek cover, even though the mobile team would do a rapid sweep of the local roads when they realized I'd left.

I got to Weybridge station without anyone grabbing me and there were three taxis waiting. An up train had just departed and a few people were drifting out of the station buildings. I didn't grab the first taxi but let a jolly elderly couple have it. I took the second. Old field-operative habit. I told the taxi driver to drop me on the Shepperton side of Chertsey Bridge, at the restaurant.

'It'll be closed by now, mate.'

'I work there. My night off.'

'Fair enough.' The taxi went down the hill past Sergey's house. All the lights were on and there was an unmarked white van outside. I looked out the rear window a couple of times as we zipped along the Addlestone by-pass but there were no vehicles following. My little ruse wouldn't out-fox a determined pro, but it would make them earn their money. Besides, I'd be long gone before they came calling. I checked my pockets for cash. Enough to pay the taxi, get a room and then some.

## 20

On the first pass I could see nothing obvious in Sergey's magazine. Certainly, nothing in the red pen he had used on the cover. There were no circled or underlined letters. I held each page slantways to the light but saw no indentations. Yet I was sure Sergey had drawn my attention to it. I ate one of the hotel's complimentary chocolates and put on the TV. I flicked through the channels but every one irritated me so I found Classic FM and turned the sound to a murmur before closing my eyes. Bad idea. I fell asleep, toppled off the chair, and thumped my head on the floor. I sprang up, my hands ready to deliver a killer karate chop, then felt embarrassed when I saw myself in the mirror. I looked a wreck. I went to the bathroom, washed my face, and did stretching exercises to push blood into my brain.

Back in the room, I opened the window and let the cold, damp air flood in. Somewhere a coot squawked. Then I went back to the magazine, separated the pages, and spread them along the carpet. I switched on all the lights, stood on the chair and looked down at a group of five in turn. There had to be a message somewhere but I was damned if I could see it.

I looked up at the abstract art print on the wall and let my eyes unfocus. I counted to ten and looked down. Then I saw something. A tiny black dot by the side of a letter. I got on my hands and knees. One dot could have been a printing error but, now I knew what I was looking for, I found more. Sometimes above letters, sometimes next to them. I reassembled the magazine and took it to the desk. There were no dots on the first three pages. Nor on any of the pages of adverts. And he had only marked articles rather than fillers.

I wrote down every page-worth of dotted letters on a separate sheet of toilet paper and numbered the sequence (oh, us ex-agents are so obsessive). My excitement soon dissipated. I ended up with sheets of letters that refused to fit into words, patterns, or even anagrams. I wondered if Sergey had teased me with gobbledygook. But why? To delay me? To give the spooks time to pick me up? Yet wifey had not been part of it and she had tried to delay me. Sergey must have used another level of cipher. I had a cup of coffee and, after working for two hours, I cracked it. Salnikov had used an anticlockwise points-of-the-compass logic. The first letter I had to use was north – a dot over the letter. The dot in the west, i.e. to the left of a letter – I had to ignore. The next dot was south, under the letter – that I also had to ignore. The next dot to the right,

I was to use. Every third page, I had to discount. Finally, at 2am, I had assembled the message:

WHILES DID DEAL WITH LOCAL WARLORD / ASSISTED TRIBAL MASSACRE / WARLORD SMUGGLED W TO CHAD THEN PAID HIS FEE INTO OFFSHORE BANK / ASK W ABOUT ABDOU AMADOU / AND WHY LONDON CONTROL LET HIM WANDER / FORGIVE ME AND GOOD LUCK / SERGEI ALEKSSEYEVICH SALNIKOV / WICKLOW 53

Bingo! Sergey had known, because the KGB must have made contact with the same warlord. Quinn had said Sergey had spent time in the area. Did he get out of Niger the same way as Whiles had? Perhaps they had met there. Did it even suggest Whiles was in the KGB? After all, he had been a young man in Romania. Communist Romania. More relevant: was Whiles currently working for the FSB? But it was all speculation. And Sergey could have made it all up.

If Sergey and Whiles had met, and Sergey knew what had happened in Zinder, he would have a hold over Whiles. Perhaps the deal had been that, if Sergey kept quiet, Whiles would broker Sergey's defection to the West. Whiles would get brownie points if the defector turned out to be useful. Though it would have meant he involved London Control. Black, in other words.

I needed to find Sergey and grill him. Except the only clue to his whereabouts was this "Wicklow53". Possibly. I didn't want to use my phone so I rang reception and, reluctantly, the night porter agreed to do a Google search. My room phone rang five minutes later. There was apparently a bar at 53

High Road, Wicklow on the east coast of Ireland. There was a café called Wicklow 1953 in Royal Greenwich. There was a blogsite of an Irish-American Senator in Wisconsin called "53 Wicklow Dreams". I didn't have enough money to get to Ireland - I barely had enough to buy breakfast at the hotel. So I decided to ring the Tourist Office for some more ideas. I looked at my watch. Two forty-five a.m. No one would be in any public office yet, so I put the lights out and was asleep before my head hit the pillow.

After what Quinn had said, I took extra care to make sure I had no tails when I got to London. I wasted hours doubling back, doing wide circuits, gazing in shop windows, jumping in cruising taxis, using the underground, walking through department stores and museums, pausing in café's with good views of the street. Not a sausage.

My feet were aching and I had the beginnings of an acid stomach but I got to leafy Tooting Bec as clean as the proverbial whistle. Sparrows cheeped, people smiled when they passed in the street, and the red Victorian mansions snoozed behind their green privet hedges. Chloe's aunt lived in a monstrosity that had been divided into three flats. I rang the aunt's entry buzzer. Someone barked, 'Who is it?'

'Jaime Nelson. To see Chloe.'

'Oh really?'

It didn't sound as if Chloe had shared any of my good points with the Aunt. 'Is she in?'

'She might be. Then again, she might not. Stay exactly where you are young man.'

I waited, basking in the afterglow of someone calling me "young". I was there long enough to decide that sparrows are very monotonous. If you are not a sparrow. A postman in shorts whistled up and shoved mail into the letter flaps. He said, 'Blinking cold for the time of year, ain't it mate?'

He left before I could suggest that he might feel warmer if he wore trousers. The door opened and a woman half my size, but twice as broad, stood there. Her arms were crossed beneath her rose-colored, jumpered bosom. 'So, you are the infamous Jamie Nelson.' She looked me up and down but did not like what she saw. 'I must say, you have a blooming cheek turning up here. What have you to say for yourself?'

'Er... can I come in?'

'No.'

'Ah. Well, is Chloe safe?'

'She is. Next?'

'Has anyone been acting suspiciously... odd callers, that sort of thing?'

'Not until you arrived.'

This was beginning to turn into a comedy sketch. 'Uh, look, I need her to... to do something for me.'

'Young man, I was matron in a boys' school, so I know every excuse under the sun. Out with it. Why are you here?'

I felt a blush heat my cheeks and immediately felt foolish and intimidated. 'I just want to see her. And ask her...' I steeled myself to say the words, '... ask her to contact Rory.' The effect on me of uttering his name wasn't pleasant. I hoped I wouldn't have to do it again.

'Would that be Rory Tremaine?'

'Yes.'

'The handsome reporter on the television?'

'I believe that is where he works.'

'Wait.' She slammed the door shut. The sparrows were still going full pelt. When the door opened again, it was Chloe.

'Hi,' I said.

'Hi.'

It was a bit of a bummer that she didn't seem the tiniest bit pleased to see me but I guess I had catapulted her into an awkward situation. I said, 'You OK?'

She nodded but looked sad. I took a step over the threshold and put my arms around her. She didn't push me away. However, my excitement soon dissipated when I realized I was not getting a responding cuddle.

'In!' commanded the Aunt from the hall. 'No hanky-panky on my step. What will the neighbors say?'

The front room was over-stuffed with a tired three-piece suite; photographs of boys' school cricket teams on the rosewood piano; glass domes of stuffed birds on a Victorian sideboard; an aspidistra on a pink china stand in the bow window; crochet work in various stages of completion; and, on one wall, a tapestry so huge, the bottom had been rolled up along the skirting.

'Sit,' barked the aunt.

I sat on the two-seater settee.

'Tea?'

'Yes. Please.' I half expected her to tell me to wash my hands first but she left after a warning glare. Chloe sat primly on the single chair nearby. Sporadically, a bush tapped the window. Simultaneously we blurted something out.

'What have you been doing?'

'I missed you.'

It had been me who said the bit about missing. It took a few moments for us to sort out what each other had said. I was gutted that she wasn't in the least bit keen to see me. Though I had to get down to business. I worked out the minimum I could tell her because I didn't want anyone putting more pressure on her. Besides, I didn't want her blurting it out to darling Rory before I was ready. She fiddled with her fingers and stared out the window at the waving bush.

I cleared my throat and told her that I'd had a message from Sergey. I would probably have got the same reaction had I told her I had memorized all of T S Eliot's *The Waste Land*. Backwards. The ensuing silence stretched until the Aunt bustled in with a tray of plates. Her next entrance was with a pile of ready-jammed scones. They looked very good scones indeed, though she slapped the back of my hand when I attempted to take more than one. She stood in front of Chloe and asked her if everything was all right. Chloe said that it was. I hoped that meant she would eventually talk to me. Then the aunt swiveled to stare at me and waited for me to confess to some crime such as scrumping apples from the headmaster's orchard. When I remained silent, she harrumphed and returned to the kitchen.

Chloe said, 'Do you really want me to contact Rory, or was that just a lie to get in here?'

I objected to her tone, but I let it pass. I said, 'Yes, I would like you to call him.' I almost added that I didn't trust him; that I hated the way her eyes had lit up when she had met him in the café; and that, in the long run, I would be a far better partner for her. I really believed I could be true and loving and would settle down with her, forever, in a cottage with red roses round the door and keep brown hens that would cluck in the yard and provide us with fresh eggs. But, of course, I said nothing like that. Couldn't, actually. Instead I said, 'I think Watkin Whiles is behind all this. I'm going after him, but I need Rory to do a story on...'

'He won't go public on anything unless he has verifiable proof. And that means at least two corroborating sources.'

'Sergey has all the proof he needs.'

'Where is he?'

'Well, right now, I'm not sure.'

She went, 'Hah!'

'Honestly, Chloe, if I knew I'd be there.' I sighed. I would have to tell her everything. Otherwise, I would get no co-operation. She listened without questioning, without emotion, without anything. At the end, she remained silent. 'There's one other thing,' I said. She looked at me this time. 'It's a bit embarrassing, but I'm kinda short of funds right now... and... uh...'

'You are asking me for money?'

'Until I get a job that pays. You'll get it back. With interest.'

She stood and went to look out the window. There were spatters of rain on the glass now. Without turning, she said, 'Have you no idea where Salnikov is?'

I told her what the hotel and the Tourist Office had come up with. I said I had a hunch Sergey would want to stay in London. Agents hate the countryside, especially Russian agents, and for him to go abroad would be too much hassle.

Eventually she said, 'What are you going to do about it?'

'Has your aunt a computer?'

Chloe pointed at a laptop on the piano.

'Could you boot it up and do a search for me?'

I didn't like the way Chloe closed her eyes briefly - as if an unwanted guest had outstayed his welcome. Nevertheless, she collected the laptop and brought it to the settee. She was wearing a different scent. Sophisticated. Expensive. Was it a present from Rory?

After she had booted the computer up, she said, 'What do you want me to put in?'

'Wicklow 53.'

Google came up with five thousand, one hundred and twenty six results. Travel guides of Wicklow, boats for sale in Wicklow, airfields near Wicklow. I told her to add the word café, and London. Up came the place in Greenwich Village, London. The picture showed a trendy shop, painted in earth colors. A retirement venture of an ex-hippy. The site listed wholefoods, massage and consultations as well as Fairtrade tea and coffee.

She said, 'Is that the sort of place your boss is in to?'

I shook my head. She narrowed the search to central London but nothing rang any bells. I said, 'Try Wicklow Road. Or Wicklow Street?'

She put that into maps and it offered a choice of four. Wicklow, Ireland, obviously. And three in England: Northampton, Liverpool and a short street near London's Kings Cross station. I decided that would be the most obvious place to start, even though it was a longshot. I asked her to show me what No. 53 looked like on Streetview. It was in the center of an undistinguished Victorian redbrick terrace - all of which had probably been divided into flats. I couldn't suppress a yawn.

'Are you all right?' asked Chloe.

'Tired. Sorry. Been busy.'

'Oh.'

I was well aware that if I did nothing viz a viz my rocky relationship with Chloe, it would soon end. So I put my arm round her and was going for a full-on kiss but, during the final approach, the aunt bustled in. She carried a tray, a cozied teapot, and rattling teacups. 'Not interrupting anything am I?' She knew she was.

We sprang apart and Chloe stood up with the computer.

'Jamie's leaving.'

The aunt frowned. 'Before tea?'

'He has to see a man near Kings Cross. Wicklow Street.'

The aunt pouted. 'We had a boy from Wicklow once. Bright lad. Died of pneumonia - because the games master insisted he stand in his wet kit throughout detention. Barbaric, some of those old teachers. Less likely now, thank goodness. Though sometimes, I can't help wondering if the pendulum's swung a little too far the other way. Know what I mean? No discipline. No respect. Now sit down and eat something before you leave, young man. You look peaky.'

At my council school, the teachers had found plenty of ways to keep the upper hand, even though they weren't allowed to make contact. I willed the aunt to vanish so I could tell Chloe what to say to Rory. 'Look, uh, Chloe's aunt, I really do need to speak to her in private. Please.'

The aunt gave me a look that was supposed to turn me into toast. When it failed, she said, 'You upset my niece terribly. You know that?'

Chloe said, 'Aunt!'

This Aunt, though, was not an aunt to be dictated to by nieces. 'She thought a lot of you, young man.'

Past tense?

'What you need to realize, is that Rory made her very happy before. Before her marriage, I mean. She was almost back on her feet from that awful tragedy when you crashed into her life. And what did you do? Got her suspended. Then took her on a wild goose chase to some foreign country where you put her in danger. In short, sir, you have undermined the stability she needed.'

I said, 'Hang on, I didn't intend...'

'Quiet while I'm speaking! Instead of caring for her, you were fixated by this... this... idealistic crusade. In my opinion, you are meddling with things best left alone. Don't you care who you hurt? That old professor, Dunning, for instance.'

'He's not much older than me, actually. And not really a...'

'Don't prevaricate! If you want to regain my niece's trust - though I have to tell you I have warned her never to do so again - you must drop this whole silly charade and try to act like a normal human being. Which, frankly, I doubt is possible.' With that, she stomped back to the kitchen where she proceeded to make an immense amount of noise as she loaded the dishwasher.

Chloe said, 'You didn't have to be rude to her.'

'I wasn't!'

'We didn't invite you here.'

'Look, hold on, Chloe. I'm sorry. Can we be a bit rational here and... ?'

'Rational? Since when were you rational?'

I closed my eyes. The situation was spiraling out of control. Even though I desperately wanted to stop Whiles becoming Prime Minister, had Chloe given me any hint she was willing to start over again with me, I was willing to drop everything. With the Fraser case, I mean. However, so far I had only seen negative signals and plummeting emotional temperature. It was one of those turning points that arrive at the worst possible moment. Did I really want her? Answer: yes, definitely. Did she appear to want me? No. Therefore, even if I only a slim chance of mending fences, I had to try. 'Look, I've been a bit of an idiot. I'm sorry.'

Chloe nodded, as if in agreement. She said, 'I think Aunt's going a bit gaga.'

From the kitchen, the aunt yelled, 'I heard that, young lady!'

Chloe laughed and I saw the person I had fallen in love with. I got up and went over to her with the intention of... well, I don't know actually; cuddle her or kiss her I suppose but she put up her hand out to fend me off. 'No Jamie. It's over. Really.'

I felt crushed. Defeated.

She said, 'I can't give you much money.' She pulled a few bills from her handbag.

I felt a heel taking the money but now I only had "the case" to think about. If I did manage to solve it, I would need to do some serious thinking about what I was going to do for the rest of my life.

'So,' she said, 'what is it you want me to tell Rory? If you find proof.'

'I'm not keen on you seeing...'

'Stop! Rory may be pompous at times but basically he's a good man.'

'Are you sure about that? Does he have your interest at heart? Do you trust him?'

'Stop it!' She cried and turned away to wipe her eyes with a tissue. I put my hand on her shoulder but she shook it off. She kept her back to me and said, very carefully, as if she thought I would mishear, 'Tell me what you want me to say to Rory. Then go.'

The final nail. I took a breath in and decided to act professionally. I had to believe in myself, even if no one else did. The aunt had made it sound cheesy, but I really did want to see good prevail and the bad punished. Perhaps, when all of this was over and Chloe had come to her senses over Rory, she might let me see her again. Elephants might fly sooner. I said, 'Tell Rory everything you know. So I can get the corroborating proof, I need Rory to find out the address for me of Whiles' apartment in the City. Can you text it to me?'

She nodded. Just that. She didn't say, "Be careful", or even "Good luck". I got a stupid lump in my throat and carried on standing there like a loon. Chloe walked past me and went to open the front door so wide I could hear the rain pattering. I sighed, called a goodbye to the Aunt (though got no reply) and left in as dignified a manner as I could muster. The door slammed before I reached the street. I was on my own again. Time to regroup or I would fail in every department.

Wicklow Street had seen better times and worse times, but being so close to the termini of St Pancras and Kings Cross developers were making it almost respectable again. The bell push box outside No 53 listed six flats. Two of the labels were blank. The others said: 'French Maid'; Mr&Mrs Smith; Lucy Love; and flat 53F said Alekseyevich. Bingo. I pushed his button. The phone crackled on but no one spoke. I said, 'Hello Wicklow 53. How about telling me about Amadou.'

The lock buzzed and I pushed against the door. It opened and the smell of boiled cabbage and cat wee hit me. I went in and shut the door. Down the end of an uncarpeted corridor a pale, thin girl leant against the wall in what she imagined was a provocative pose. She called, 'You want business?' She wasn't French and didn't wear a maid's outfit. Nor did she look like a Lucy. She was just a young, bewildered East European, enslaved into prostitution.

I shook my head, said 'Sorry' and started up the stairs. The girl stormed back into her flat, slammed the door, and turned up some rap music. Salnikov's flat was on the top floor. I wondered if he owned the whole place. Used Government money to buy real estate as a hedge against his uncertain future. If so, he had been wise, because with London property increasing in value, the place must have been worth a million. I knocked on his door. A polite knock. Not the knock of an impatient police officer. Not the knock of someone irritated as hell at being played like a fish by an ex-KGB officer only interested in saving his own hide. The handle turned and the door squeaked open.

'I hope you were not followed,' he said.

'No.'

The door opened wider. Salnikov stood there, pointing a gun at me. He used it to wave me in, then he scanned the landing, and looked down the stairwell. When he came back in, he bolted the door, shoved the gun in a holster under his left arm, and patted me all over to check for a wire. He said, 'How long did it take?'

'Sorry?'

'To crack my code. Did you do it yourself?'

'It took a long time, Sergey. Any chance of a coffee? I'm whacked out.'

He didn't move. 'Did you involve Lisa?'

I shook my head. 'She didn't see me take the magazine. She called someone while I was waiting. Who would that be?'

Salnikov took in a deep breath, and let it out slowly. I suppose he had known all along that his wife was in the pay of the Service. Knew they wouldn't have let a big prize like him hitch up with someone they couldn't control. Marriage was such a convenient way for the state to keep tabs on a loose cannon. He said, 'She played her part well. She was... is... a good mother to our children. Please, do not tell them about me.'

I shook my head.

'Though we knew the marriage was artificial, against the odds we grew to love each other. Does that make sense?'

I shrugged. I could not imagine a relationship where one partner has an external loyalty that was likely to end everything. Salnikov walked into the next room and I followed him. On a desk were three screens, each split four ways. They showed different views of the street; of the front door; of the rear of the property; and of each landing.

I said, 'You forgot the roof.'

'Uh?'

'Only joking. They'll find you eventually, you know.'

'I shall not give them time. What is it you want?'

'First,' I said, 'tell me why you sacked me.'

He walked to the kitchen and I heard a kettle being filled. He called out, 'You must have known your report would upset powerful people.'

I went to the sound of the kettle. 'Why didn't you back me up when the crunch came?'

Salnikov was looking up at the sky as if he worried that a helicopter would drop SAS troops onto the roof. 'Truth is a luxury I cannot afford, Jamie. They told me that if I did not do exactly as they wanted, they would take everything away. My career. My passport. My family. I accept it is not a normal family, but it is all I have. They threatened to tell my children I was a traitor.'

With such pressure, I would probably have done the same. Question was - what else did they order him to do? Lure me into a trap? I said, 'This Abdou Amadou... who was he?'

The kettle was taking its time. Salnikov doled instant coffee into two red Typhoo Tea mugs. 'He was the minister of mines and minerals in Niger.'

'And why should the Right Honorable Watkin Whiles be asked about him?'

'Amadou paid him to massacre the rebels in Zinder.'

'But I thought...'

'Amadou was being paid well by Soviets. I got involved because Moscow Centre suspected he was playing a double game. If he denied it, we would provide... what do the English say? Provide him rope to hang himself?'

I nodded.

'But Amadou was cleverer than we realized. Somehow, he already knew Soviet Union was not enthusiastic about the Niger solution. So he altered his plans. Oh, he still set up coup, for sure. And Red Army generals believed him. He also recruited Whiles – I do not know how – and promised him gold, plus percentage of future smuggling revenue.'

'Uranium?'

'No, everyday smuggling. It had become a way of life even though President Kontuché tried to stamp it out. Whiles was told to order his mercenaries to annihilate the supposed "rebels" - the tribe Amadou had paid to stage the coup. When the uprising was put down, Amadou declared it had been his hired army that had brought peace. He was hailed national hero. Kontuché discovered what really happened but, almost immediately, he resigned. He died so quickly afterwards it could have been poison. Then there was a quick election, which was probably rigged but no one really cared, because the people wanted national hero Amadou to become president. He rewarded himself well and let the contraband continue.

Even so, not a grain of uranium ore was ever passed to our trucks that waited patiently across the border. MI6 and CIA congratulated each other. Moscow Centre looked around for a scapegoat to blame.' Sergey beat his fist on the worktop. 'I told them putting trust in smugglers was too risky. Besides, the American Sirio satellite was logging everything that moved, and CIA had organized so many spy planes, it was like a scheduled service over Niger.'

I played my hunch. 'So Whiles was spirited across the border because Amadou was keen to get him out the way. Whiles met you; then he disappeared. Soon after, you defected. That was connected, wasn't it?'

The kettle clicked as it finished its boil. Salnikov poured steaming water into the mugs. He said, 'Things were changing fast. Brezhnev had decided to soften towards the Americans. He had admitted to them that USSR was supplying arms to Ethiopia. If CIA got a whisper we were also trying to smuggle uranium from Niger, the General Secretary would have been put in a... difficult position. I became an embarrassment. A danger to the Politburo.'

'But you got out before the KGB assassinated you?'

Salnikov nodded and sighed again, 'Many in the Party leadership wanted a return to Uncle Joe's ways. Stalin's ways. Ach! If only I had become a farmer. Or a writer. Do you like Turgenev? Do you not think he has knack of portraying the sadness of life?'

I didn't want to get into semantics so I said, 'When you met Whiles, did you do a deal with him for your defection?'

Salnikov handed me the mug. 'No milk, no sugar, I think?' He walked back to the room that had the screens, put his drink on a table, and sat in the swivel chair. London, within the view of his cameras, was going about its normal business. He said, 'It was too good an opportunity to miss. Whiles acted tough, but he was immature. It was obvious he was desperate to impress his British masters. Whiles is also a very self-seeking man, so I thought he might be a useful insurance. I told him I would let him to claim he had persuaded me to defect but I let him know I had all the details about his liaison with Amadou, and I would expose him if he turned against me.'

'Is that what he has done?'

Salnikov shrugged. 'Perhaps. But I am tired of all this. If I go quietly, they might leave my family alone. I shall be out of your country when Whiles becomes Prime Minister.'

'Help me stop him Sergey. After all, it's your country too.'

352

Salnikov took a sip of his drink. 'Is it? I am not so sure.'

'Meaning?'

He didn't reply.

I said, 'At least give me something. So I can nail him.'

'The old babushkas used to say, "It is difficult to put a pin in an eel."'

'How much did Amadou pay him? Where did it go?'

'You will have to ask him. I do not know.'

'Did Mandleson know?'

Salnikov shook his head. 'Mandleson set up Novercal. After the massacre, London Control switched him to another case. Lebanon, I think. Everything was left to the unit on the ground to clean up. Unusual, do you not think?'

'Who was behind that? Black?'

Salnikov shrugged.

'What about the Eagle? George Fraser?'

'Him? Just a hired gun, as they say in the American westerns.'

'If Fraser wasn't in on the massacre, why did MI5 need to abduct him?'

'Oh Fraser killed, for sure.'

'He said he just watched. From the tower, after he terminated a sniper who was going to kill Kontuché.'

Salnikov shrugged. 'People do not hire mercenaries for their honesty or tea-making skills. Have you not learnt, Jamie, things in this world are not always as they seem?'

Did that mean Sergey's version was no more reliable than Fraser's? Was he really Perfect Sergey? Put upon Sergey? Loyal Sergey, forced to defect to save his family?

A buzzer sounded and Salnikov span round to peer at the screens. A bald man was standing on the outside step. On the speaker, a female voice: "Yes?" The man said, "Algie. Quick." The door entry buzzer sounded. I watched the man enter and practically run to the door where I had seen the thin girl. He waited there and, when the door opened, he went in. The corridor returned to being empty. The street was bare. Salnikov turned away from the screens.

'A regular?' I asked.

Salnikov nodded. 'Every week. Always in hurry. He is office manager in recruitment agency the other side of British Library.'

Sergey was the big spider at the center of his little web. I was tempted to ask if he was comfortable accepting rent from sex workers but I decided I needed to keep focused. 'Was Brown involved? In the pay off?'

After a pause Salnikov said, 'Brown was Whiles' sergeant.'

'So he was in on it?'

'I cannot say. He was a reliable soldier - but not officer material. Good at following orders. Determined, but... conventional. Before Whiles disappeared, he told Brown to take charge of the Nigerians and lead them back home. After Brown got back to the UK, he was discharged from army and he joined the police in Hong Kong. He worked his way up and was recruited by MI5. You know that, of course.'

It annoyed me that I might have to adjust my opinion about Brown. 'So was it Whiles who wanted me sacked?'

Salnikov scratched his neck. 'He is on the board of a defense manufacturing company. I imagine he would resent any adverse publicity.'

'Why was Brown put on to me?'

He shrugged. 'Someone pulled strings to get him on board. They set you up, expecting you to play along, you being out of work and ex-Service. You British. Always playing The Game.'

There was another possibility. Brown had volunteered for the mission, to exact revenge for what I had supposedly done to Melissa. I said, 'If I'm to bring Whiles down, I need evidence.'

Salnikov spread his hands. 'There is none. Not even in Moscow archives. Everything controversial was burned. In case we upset the Americans, or the Europeans.'

'Then will you give me a signed statement about all this?'

Salnikov shook his head.

'Come on Sergey. It's in your interest to have Whiles discredited.'

'It is in my interest to disappear.' He swiveled his chair to look at the screens. Then he swore in Russian.

'What?'

He pointed at the top right of the middle screen. Two uniformed police officers were standing on the opposite side of the street. One was talking into his radio.

I said, 'It's probably nothing.'

'Normally, they never stop.'

'A crackdown on sex workers?'

'Or they are after you. Or me.'

We both watched the police. They paced slowly up the street, turned round, and walked back. Sergey said, 'You must leave by my emergency

355

route.  Now.  Opposite the prostitute's door on the ground floor is a cupboard.  Get into it and shut the door.  On the outside wall there is a small window.  Go out of that onto a shed roof.  Climb over the parapet of a wall, and you will drop down to the back yard of a betting shop on Britannia Street.  Knock on the door and they will let you in.'

'Sergey, I have to stop Whiles.'  I wrote my new number on one of his blank scribble pads.  'Call me if you find anything.  Anything.'

He tore the number off and stuffed it in his pocket.  We both watched the police take a call on their radio.  Then they began to amble across the road towards Sergey's front door.  'Go now,' he said.

'But...'

He got out his gun and pointed it at me.  'I said go.'

I left.

# 21

I wasted most of the day wandering around in the
British Library, St Pancras and Kings Cross and
drinking too much tea and coffee. By the time Chloe
texted me the evening rush hour was over. Whiles'
apartment was in the City of London so I walked
there to save money.

Knightrider Street was in a small crossway,
midway between St Paul's and the Thames. At the
eastern end of it, there was an old pub called The
Horns. Beyond that, a draughty piazza that led to
the Millennium Bridge. The pub was already
shuttered and dark. On the western end of the
short road, where it joined Godliman Street, there
were service entrances to the offices. Whiles' door
was left of the pub, which I guessed meant his flat
was above it. The windows were unlit. By the look
of the bricks, it had been around since Oliver Twist
was stealing handkerchiefs. I had expected there to

be an armed protection officer outside but there was no one in the street. Nor any car. There was a camera, though. On a motorized gimbal, coupled to infra-red lamps. It was across the road from the Horns and pointed directly at the pub and Whiles' door. I presumed it fed into Whiles' security system and, probably, the Met Police. On the trek from King's Cross, I tried to think of a sure-fire way to get Whiles to confess. I hadn't come up with anything. That left me with the direct approach: doorstep the weasel and hope for the best.

I was walking across the road to Whiles' door when a dark limousine started to turn in from Godliman Street. I dodged back in the shadows before the headlights caught me. The car stopped outside Whiles' door. He emerged, leaned on the car and said, "C'n go home now... won't need you any more". He was as drunk as a skunk. The car reversed down the street, then accelerated up Godliman Street towards St Paul's and was gone. Whiles belched and then peed against the pub wall. Charming. He pulled up his zip and staggered to the keypad next to the door. I seized the moment and padded across the road. Whiles pushed his door open, and was deactivating the alarms when I burst in and knocked him over. Someone shouted in the street, and I heard feet running, so I slammed the door and locked it.

'Get out,' said Whiles, as he got up. 'How dare you! Don't you know who I am? You'll get life for this.'

'I'm not a burglar, Mr. Whiles.'

'Then who the hell are you?'

I switched on the light. He peered at me, then almost gouged his eyes out trying to put on his spectacles. It made him look older. Statesmanlike.

He peered at me again. 'I know you. You're that... Nelson. You stupid bastard. Get out! You'll never work again. Anywhere.'

'Sticks and stones, Mr. Whiles. I just want some information.'

'You can forget all about Fraser.'

'Why?'

'Cos he's being looked after very comfortably. Ver' comfortably indeed. Doesn't need anyone to rescue him.'

'Things have moved on.'

'How so?'

Before I could explain, someone pounded on the door. Then Whiles' phone started ringing. He went for it but I clamped my hand round his wrist. 'Leave it,' I said.

Upstairs, another phone began to trill. Whiles didn't go for it but he said, 'What do you want?'

'A chat.'

'Then book an appointment with my secretary.'

I laughed. He was drunk and dealing with an intruder but he was a hard-wired smooth operator. I said, 'Shall we go up?' and pushed him up the stairs. At the top, there was a big security screen with a view of the street. Brown was standing in the middle of road, looking up at the flat and yelling into his phone.

Whiles nodded at the screen. 'Not long before you are arrested, Mr. Nelson. Until then, what is it you wish to "chat" about?'

'What did you do after you put down the coup in Niger?'

Whiles flinched. He had not been expecting that. Grown too complacent, maybe. Convinced that he had taken care of everything. He said, 'I don't know what you mean.'

'You did a deal with Abdou Amadou. You massacred the rebels; Amadou helped you get across the border, and then he sent your reward to an offshore bank account. Oh, and you did a deal with the KGB. What was that exactly?'

Whiles laughed. 'Who told you that pack of lies?'

'Different sources. They can't all be wrong.'

'Well they are. Come on, I want to know who's been slandering me.'

'It doesn't matter.'

'It will. When my legal team finish with you, Nelson, you'll have nothing. Nothing! Come on, who are your sources?'

It was beginning to go wrong. Whiles was meant to break down and confess under pressure, not threaten me. I said, 'You agree you were on a covert mission in Niger in August 1980.'

He shook his head, 'I refuse to interrogated, Mr. Nelson. I have highly placed friends. Nothing can hurt me.'

'So why did you make all this fuss about Fraser? Why get Brown to set me up? And why is he still on my tail?'

Whiles turned away. 'I need a drink.' He went to the kitchen diner and took down a half-empty whiskey bottle. He uncapped it and drank from the neck. Then he opened a drawer, pulled out a gun, and pointed it at me. He laughed again. 'The press will love this: "Future PM Corners Burglar in Flat." Alternatively, how about, "Whiles Stands up to Unemployed Thug"? Should help my campaign no end. Shows a certain Churchillian spirit, don't you think?'

'Not if you shoot me. Might show you lack judgment in a crisis. And do you hold a license for that?'

Whiles took another swig at the whiskey before throwing the bottle at me. It missed by a mile but smashed into the security screen. There was a bang and a fizzle. The gun continued to point at me. 'I'll say you tried to kill me.'

'Except I have no weapon and no motive. At least, not one you'd admit to.'

Whiles started to wander around, waving the gun. 'They told me you're a smart ass. Think you have all the answers. Want to be some lone vigilante fighting for the greater good. Well let me tell you, James Munroe Nelson...oh, yes, you see, I know all about you... you're just a... a shallow failure. You don't even have an office of your own. You're the sort of person who drags the country down. Ruining it for the majority of law-abiding citizens. Sponging, instead of doing an honest day's work. Expecting the community to... to support your ludicrous, selfish lifestyle.' He blinked and tried to recall the rest of the speech he had dragged up from somewhere in his past.

As his attention wandered, I leapt towards him, grabbed the hand holding the gun, and slammed it on the kitchen worktop. Whiles cried out in pain and pulled the trigger. There was a terrific bang, and a window shattered. I wrestled the gun from him and threw it across the flat. Then I steered Whiles to a chair and pushed him in it. Downstairs, the door banging resumed. Whiles vomited the contents of his stomach over his dinner jacket. I tossed him a towel and he dabbed at the mess. I got him a glass of water and he drank it down and handed back the empty glass for more. My mum was keen on me never kicking dogs when they were down. He said, 'You are finished, Nelson. You can't make anything public, because you have no evidence.'

'Really?'

'Really. All the records have been erased. You blab, I'll have you sectioned and locked in Broadmoor for the rest of your life. Say what you like there; no one will take a blind bit of notice.' He laughed. 'Admit it, man; you came here in desperation because you have nothing! By the way, the door you came in is the only way out. Eventually they will get in. I suggest you go out to meet them. That way, you at least stay alive.' As if on cue, I heard sirens approaching, and then several cars screeched to a stop outside. Blue lights flashed on the ceiling and a searchlight lit up the flat.

I said, 'Just for my peace of mind, then, did you order the massacre?'

Whiles stuck one finger up. 'Even cub reporters wear concealed recorders these days, Mr. Nelson. You'll not trick me that way. The past is dead and gone.'

'Zadie Smith said that, "What is past, is prologue".'

'How extremely interesting. I really should try to remember that. Now get out. I have a busy day tomorrow and I need some sleep.'

Then the alcohol finally won over his brain. His eyes went out of focus, he slumped, and puked again. After that he held his head and groaned. 'I was following orders, Nelson. Something you are incapable of.'

In the street, a tannoy blared. 'Armed police. We have the area surrounded. Come out with your hands on your head. Then lay face down on the ground with your arms and legs outstretched.'

Whiles looked at me, 'Do as they say, Nelson. If they break in, they might damage something valuable.'

'No, Mr. Whiles. I want you to ring Brown and tell him to call off the dogs. As you said, I can't make public accusations until I have proof. Tell the boys in blue that Brown made a mistake and this is a private meeting. It will harm your campaign if the police nose around - you being in the state you are. Leaks to the press and all that.'

Whiles stood and swayed. 'At last you are talking sense.'

I said, 'Tell Brown to come in on his own. The police may stay in the street until he has assessed the situation.'

Whiles hesitated but then did as I asked. I said, 'Unlock the door for Mr. Brown.'

He went to the control panel at the top of the stairs and pushed a button. The door buzzed. There was a pause before it opened. I stood behind Whiles and saw Brown in the doorway. The blazing searchlights put Brown in silhouette. He called, 'Are you all right, sir?'

'Perfectly safe, Brown. Do come up.'

'The police think...'

'On your own, Mr. Brown. Now. And close the door.'

Brown came up slowly. He looked old and tired. The aged retainer, tied to his former master. When he saw me he said, 'Oh it's you. What the hell are you up to now?'

'Mr. Nelson and I have reached an understanding, Brown. You will let him go.'

'But this is the perfect opportunity to...'

'Shut up Brown. Go back and tell the commander to disperse the troops.'

'But...'

'Don't keep saying "but"! When you return, make yourself useful and brew coffee while I take a shower.'

Brown glared at me.

Whiles said, 'Now would be an excellent time, Mr. Brown. Mustn't waste police time. We need them on our side if I am to make all those painful cuts in front line services.'

Brown hesitated, then turned and went down the stairs. I said, 'In Zinder, who did you take orders from?'

Whiles said, 'Enough, Nelson. Pull another stunt like this and you'll end up face down in a park - like that unfortunate man you visited in Brussels.'

I heard shouting outside, but then the searchlights and the blue flashing lights were extinguished. Doors slammed. Two cars left. Brown came slowly up the stairs. He said, 'They've gone. Now what?'

'First, escort Nelson from the premises. Then make me that coffee. My head is killing me.'

As I walked along the Victoria Embankment, I tried to sort things out. My mission to bring down Whiles hadn't changed but it seemed impossible without evidence. Whiles had said he was "following orders". From his military superiors? The KGB? Or his London Control - the nameless Black? Doreen reckoned a High Priest was involved in Fraser's disappearance. Did that mean a politician? Or a high-up career spook on our side? I was missing something vital. Though championing Fraser's case now seem to have been a pretty lame-brained idea. In my desperation to crack my first big case, I had put Chloe and Dunning in danger. Plus, I had lost

Sergey his job and had probably cut him off from his family. What an idiot. All I had to cling on to now was the determination to prevent Whiles becoming the next Prime Minister of Great Britain and Northern Ireland. That meant I had to uncover the dodgy High Priest.

'Dobry vyecher. You had an interesting evening.'

I had heard no footsteps but the voice behind me was very close. I whirled round to face Kirichenko. He came alongside me and we walked on. 'In my opinion,' he said, 'visiting Mr. Whiles showed desperation, no?'

'Have you been following me, Vyacheslav?'

'Recently. Though only to let you know that Tatyana's body has been released. Soon she will be on her way home.'

'Good.' I wondered if I should offer to go to the funeral. I said, 'Who ordered Whiles to massacre the "rebels"?'

'I do not know.'

'It wasn't really Amadou was it? So was it his London Control? Black?'

'Possibly. Whiles was under MI6 orders, not the military.'

'Did Rhodes know?'

'He too was under Black's control. However, I believe they isolated Rhodes. Too much of a risk. Too honorable. They needed him to persuade Kontuché the British were on his side.'

'Meaning Whiles was not.'

'Whiles was adaptable. He had needed to be from an early age.'

So perhaps Black was the Bad High Priest. 'Are you sure there's no evidence?'

'One possibility. Salnikov stole some files before he defected. Perhaps they included papers on

Zinder. Maybe he kept them as insurance. Against the British.'

But if Sergey had evidence, why hadn't he helped me? Besides, when the Service had started to put pressure on him, why hadn't he used it to keep them away? Perhaps he wanted me to thrash around and divert attention from him. Hadn't it been him who had put Brown into the story? I said, 'Where does he keep the stuff?'

'I do not know. However, he has been in contact with us. Perhaps, after all this time, he is homesick.'

'Would Russia allow him back?'

Kirichenko shrugged. 'The world has moved on. Russia is not Soviet Union. We are more capitalist than even your country, Jamie. Besides, there are very few ex- KGB left in FSB now. And we are all getting old. Why would anyone lose sleep over a defector who had nothing to tell?'

We walked on in silence. Then Kirichenko handed me a slip of paper on which was written a number. 'Telephone this tomorrow, at ten a.m. precisely. Prepare your questions well. Now, I can do no more. Will you come to Tatyana's funeral? But, no, you will be too busy.'

'I'll come.' I gave him one of my *Nelson Discreet Investigations* cards and pointed at my cousin's office number. 'Leave a message there: just the date, time and place and I shall come. Whatever happens.'

He examined the card. 'This is your business now?'

I shrugged my shoulders. 'I hoped it would be. I don't seem very good at detecting.'

'Do not be disheartened, Jamie. Starting a new business is, how you say, bloody murder. There is an old Russian saying, "When you jump on back of tiger, it is best not to get off".' He shook my hand. 'Da sveedanya.'

He crossed the Embankment, went into Temple Place and then disappeared up a side street towards the Aldwych. The phone number business was a bit odd, though hopefully it related to my need for evidence. Whatever, Kirichenko had given me renewed hope. Hope that I could still nail Whiles.

At exactly ten the next morning I rang the number Kirichenko had given me. Not knowing who it was, I had not been able to prepare. The phone was answered immediately. A muffled male voice said, 'Who is this?'

The speech pattern sounded familiar but I couldn't put a name to it. 'I was told to phone you.'

'Sorry, wrong number.' The line went dead.

Ten seconds later, my phone was rung by a withheld number. I answered it and Sergei Alekseyevich Salnikov said, 'How the hell did you get that number?'

I said, 'An acquaintance from your first company.'

He did some Russian swearing. I didn't request a translation. Eventually Sergey said, 'What is it you want?'

'A copy of the evidence you have on Whiles.'

'What evidence?'

'Our mutual friend said you kept something relevant from your old company.'

Silence. Then he said, 'What else did he say?'

'I'd rather not share it over the phone.'

'Why is he doing this?'

'I'll tell you when we meet.'

'I do not wish to meet.'

'I know where you live now.'

'No longer.'

'Sergey! You owe me!'

Silence. 'I have sympathy for you, but it is difficult. I am leaving.'

'When?'

'Soon.'

'Who is Black?'

Silence.

'Sergey!' I was beginning to lose patience. 'Give me some real help for a change.'

Eventually he said, 'Black is the same person as Constantin - the one who arranged my passage to Finland.'

'What is his real name?'

'I have said enough.'

'No, Sergey, all you've done is thrown me another scrap. It's time you came clean or else...'

'Or else what?'

I didn't know. I hadn't intended to threaten. I was going to apologize but Salnikov said, 'I shall be in touch.'

'Sergey, I need this if I'm to stop Whiles before the election.'

He cut the call. Ten seconds later the phone rang but it was Chloe. I answered, in as expressionless a way as possible with, 'Hi, how are you?'

She didn't bother with a reply. 'Dunning has contacted the BBC with his version of the story,' she said. 'Rory managed to get it but he needs proof from you before he goes on air. Have you got it?'

'Not quite.'

'Jamie!'

'I'm closer than I was.'

'That's not good enough. Rory's put his neck on the line for this. They've allocated him top slot in the ten o'clock news tonight.'

Well, bully for Rory. What about a bit of encouragement for the workers?

'Hello,' she said, 'are you still there?'

'I'll call back to you when I have something. I need to keep this phone free.'

'Make it quick. Rory says...'

'I said I'll get back to you!' I know, I know, I shouldn't have shouted.

I walked to St James' park and wandered around for a couple of hours, agonizing whether to ring Sergey again. High in the blustery sky a helicopter droned as it hovered. There were no riots that week, so they could be watching me. What the hell. All I was doing was enjoying the sunshine. And giving Sergey time to produce the goods. After all, he might have locked the stuff in a Finnish bank vault. The other possibility was that he was playing me for a sucker while he did a runner. Besides, even if there had once been evidence, he may have destroyed it long ago - in case it came back to bite him. And I knew my boss well enough to know that if I pushed too hard, he would go all contrary.

I was bursting for a pee so I called in at Waterstones café in Piccadilly. While I was there, my phone pinged with a text. All it said was, 'MEET AT THE PHOENIX ROEBELENII. REPLY TO THIS MESSAGE WHEN YOU GET TO WISLEY. S.'

## 22

Wisley, the Royal Horticultural Society's garden in northwest Surrey, is a pain to reach if you have no car. I paid off my taxi at the front entrance at three thirty, and texted Sergey that I had arrived. The person at the ticket booth wondered whether it was a little late in the day to do justice to the gardens. I said the purpose of my visit was to see the *phoenix roebelenii*.

She looked mildly impressed, got on her radio, and established it was located in the glasshouse. She ringed it on a map of the gardens but, before she slid it to me, she said that as I was so obviously interested in plants, why didn't I join the Society? She pointed out that, if I signed up, I would not only get my entrance fee back, I would be able to use a ten percent discount voucher in the gift shop. I thanked her but declined, grabbed the map and legged it up the slope into the gardens.

It was a glorious afternoon. The red brick of the old house glowed in the sunshine. Couples and young families ambled. A fountain splashed in an oblong lake speckled with water lily leaves and streaked with orange carp. I found a fingerpost that pointed to the glasshouse. I ran at first, but drew too much attention to myself, so I settled for an urgent walk.

The Bicentenary Glasshouse was a humongous construction that reared out of a semi-circular lake. It looked like the set for a science fiction movie. I scanned the dawdling crowds but couldn't see my boss. I weaved my way through a coach party of old folks listening to a green-jumpered RHS person lecturing them about the building, '...covers three thousand square meters, and has a maximum height of twelve meters. There are three distinct climate areas...' The entrance was blocked by a notice that said, due to congestion, entry would be timed. People were queuing diligently but I pushed past them. 'You there!' One of the coach party had assumed command. 'We are first! You're not allowed in yet.'

On the other side of the airlock, it was pleasantly warm and I could hear trickling water. I asked a gardener where the *roebelenii* was and he pointed towards a mass of green vegetation. When I looked puzzled he said, 'Palm tree, slender trunk, delicate glossy green leaves... by the waterfall.' I saw it. No Salnikov, though. Of course, he wouldn't have hung around all day, though he could be watching. I went over to the plant label and found out that it had come from Laos, that it was evergreen, had yellow flowers, blah blah blah. The heat was beginning to get at me so I peeled off my top layer. I wondered if Salnikov had hidden something behind the trunk. I felt in the dampness, but only got pricked for my trouble. Someone tapped my shoulder. Green shirt. 'Visitors must stay on the path, sir. And it is forbidden to take cuttings.'

'I wasn't.'

He looked over his shoulder and then back at me. 'Was you <u>particularly</u> interested in the *roebelenii*, sir?'

He said it in a curious way, as if it was a source of Class A drug. 'Uh, well,' I said, 'someone suggested I take a close look at it.'

'Foreign sounding gentleman?'

'Yes.'

'From Russia? Or somewhere thereabouts?'

'Yes.'

'He was here a little while ago. Said you might come. Asked me to give you something.' He fished in his back pocket and produced a folded piece of paper. I held out my hand for it. 'He said I should ask you for identification. Mysterious, but he seemed... vexed, sir. If you get my meaning. Could be our heat, I suppose. Some people find the atmosphere unsettling. Those not in the way of appreciating the conditions we need to replicate.'

I wondered what Sergey expected me to give as ID. I showed the man my credit card with the name Apollinaris. The man looked at it a long time and then pursed his lips. 'Greek name is that, sir?'

'Just give me the bloody paper!' I snatched it off the man and opened it. Three words: TEA AT FOUR. I looked at my watch: three fifty. 'Where are the tea rooms?'

The man turned his back and walked off without telling me. Presumably, because he had decided (a) I had no real interest in plants, (b) I had taken him away from his important plant work and (c) we were two silly men - obviously not members - who were engaged in a liaison, possibly of a dubious sexual nature.

Outside the glasshouse, there was a snack bar but there was no sign of Salnikov there. A post pointed across a lawn to the Conservatory Café and Dining Room. I got there at two minutes to four. It was busy with people grabbing a last drink before they were thrown out of the grounds. Toddlers had long since reached the end of their tethers and were screaming blue murder. Middle-aged plants people were in huddles over cups of RHS tea, RHS cake, and RHS plant identification books. Salnikov wasn't there. I went to the toilet and then queued for a pot of tea and took it to a window seat far away from the stroppy kids. I had a fizzing ball of frustration in my chest that threatened to explode into anger. I needed to do something positive, instead of hanging around a Surrey garden, dancing to Salnikov's tune. A table clearer came up and dropped a brown envelope in front of me. 'Man told me to give this to you.'

I said, 'Which man?'

She looked around and then pointed out the window. 'Him.'

On the outside path, Salnikov waved. He was on an electric golf buggy and shot off towards the exit. I contemplated running after him, but decided I first needed to see what was in the envelope. 'Thanks,' I said to the table-clearer.

She returned to her task and I opened the envelope. There were two pieces of paper inside. The first was a small square from a blue note block. Salnikov's characteristic scrawl said,

"I am booked on a flight this evening. I shall not return. I enclose my insurance letter. Do what you will with it.  Although please do not implicate me for the sake of my children.  S"

The second paper was flimsy and yellowing, typed in English using an antique manual typewriter.  It read:

THE OFFICE OF THE CENTRAL COMMITTEE
OF THE COMMUNIST PARTY OF THE UNION OF SOVIET SOCIALIST REPUBLICS
Nogin Square, Moscow.

October 15 1980

Let it be known.  The GENERAL SECRETARY and the POLITBURO authorize on this date a transfer of 7,000 roubles to the First People's Bank, Bucharest, Romania in the name of Vasile Orsova for services rendered by Watkin Whiles in Niger, Western Africa.

We also authorize transfer of 3,000 roubles to the Banque Lefarge, Paris, France in the name of Anderson Constantine, for services rendered by Oliver Franklin Knighton.
This signed memorandum gives authorization for withdrawal.

Leonid Ilyich Brezhnev, General Secretary

Alexei Nikolayevich Kosygin, Chairman of Council of Ministers

Three copies only of this English translation to:
    V Orsova, O F Knighton, Central Files

I stared at it for a long time.  Tremaine had said Whiles' birth name was Orsova and he came from Bucharest, so that nailed him.  But the other name?  Was he the High Priest?   Salnikov had said Constantin was Black's other operational name.  However, if Black was the Oliver Franklin Knighton, I had a bigger problem than I had expected.  Because he was the current Prime Minister of Great Britain and Northern Ireland.  It was time to contact Tremaine and show him the letter.  Surely, he would have enough to run the story now.

I booted up my phone but got a weird message from the service provider saying that my contract had expired.  I'd not had that before from any other Pay as You Go, so I assumed GCHQ was on to me.  I pushed the papers back into the envelope and asked the table-clearer if there were any public landline phones but she shook her head.

On the way to the exit, I passed the RHS library and, on the off chance, explained to them I needed to call someone urgently but my phone had just died.  They let me use their desk phone.  When I eventually reached BBC News, they said Rory was unavailable.  I left a message that I had the evidence he needed and would ring back.  Then I thanked the library staff and hurried out.  I needed to get back to London, make some photocopies, and then see Tremaine.

I reached the exit as a party of disabled folk were bunched up before the automatic glass doors of the gift shop.  I fumed at the way the self-important carers faffed about, marshalling wheelchairs and walkers and made things ten times worse.  As I inched closer the exit I saw, through the windows of the gift shop, a black car with blue flashing lights screech to a halt on the service road.  Three men and a woman tumbled out and ran to the ticket booths. I grabbed the handles of a wheelchair, walked purposefully with the lady into the shop, and navigated around the displays of garden-related knick-knacks.

'Wait a minute!' said the lady in the wheelchair. 'I want to buy a tea towel.' I backtracked to the till and asked a bag-packer if she could oblige. I nipped out the front door, threw my phone in a trash can and then hid amongst a group of American tourists. Sirens wailed from the direction of the A3. It could have been a pile-up on the dual carriageway, but it could also be the cavalry heading to Wisley. Sergey's parting gift? Whatever, I had to move fast. No busses served Wisley, nor was there a taxi rank. I had no car, and the gardens were in the middle of thousands of acres of heathland and marsh. I had three options: walk to the A3 and thumb a lift; steal a car from the car park; or head across country and hope I missed the bogs.

The Americans around me were asking each other where the hell their coach was. When one of the party saw it reversing out of the coach park they dashed for it, fearing they would be abandoned in the middle of this god-forsaken corner of England. I ran with them and we all piled into the coach. The driver called out a cheery, 'We all 'ere now?' Voices yelled, 'Sure' and 'Let's get the hell back to civilization.' So the driver shut the door and steered the coach towards the exit road. I squeezed in on the back seat. The people there were annoyed that I had changed my seat from the outward journey but, as the coach jolted over potholes, it bounced me into place. We turned onto the narrow lane that led towards the A3 and, through the front windscreen, I saw flashing blue lights approaching. Three police cars left rubber on the road as they turned into the Wisley Gardens drive. The Americans agreed that it was a damn fine thing they were leaving.

It wasn't until the coach was crawling through the town of Esher that the passengers got to ask me which State I came from. When they realized I was a stowaway Limey, they ratted on me to the tour leader. She offered me two options. One, I could stay where I was and she would call the police to meet the coach in London. Two, I could leave the coach immediately. I told her I'd get out. Luckily by then it was beyond the Sandown Racetrack, not far from Esher railway station.

When I reached London Waterloo, I got out the station quickly and searched for a public phone box. Not an easy task these days. Tremaine answered.

'Who is this?' He sounded edgy.

I said, 'I rang earlier about evidence?'

'Is it verifiable?'

'It's a genuine, original, document from the era.'

'Document?' He sounded disappointed. 'Anyone to do a piece to camera?'

He was already thinking how to compose his report. 'No,' I said.

'Will you let me interview you on camera?'

'No. I have people on my tail, and I need to get this over with quickly. Do you want it or not?'

'Of course.'

'Meet me where we met before. Understand?'

We had only met once, so it oughtn't to have caused him much mental anguish.

'Uh, remind me?'

How could Chloe fancy such a dimwit? 'On the north side of the green.'

'Difficult,' he said, 'I'm tied up at work.'

Why was it so hard to hand over a scoop? 'OK,' I said, 'Can you manage the box office of the Palladium Theatre?'

'I suppose so.'

'As soon as you can, then. I won't be able to hang around long.' I rang off. Cheltenham's algorithms had probably already locked onto my voice patterns.

The British Tourist Office in Lower Regent Street did some photocopies of Brezhnev's letter for a fee. Then I went via Savile Row and Maddox Street to reach the top end of Regent Street. In Great Marlborough Street, I found a doorway from where I could watch the Palladium Theatre. Homeward-bound workers were jostling on the pavements as they headed to the underground station. A black car stopped outside the theatre, a passenger climbed out the back, and then the car moved away. The passenger was Evan Evans and he stood on the pavement, looking bewildered. Then he skipped across Argyll Street, hid behind a public toilet cubicle, called in to base, and stared at the Palladium as if it might disappear if he blinked. I nipped round to Little Argyll Street where I could keep a better eye on the Welsh hopeful. Using my compromised phone I called Tremaine.

'Yes?' he said. He sounded as if he was walking and I could hear traffic noise in the background.

'Change of plan,' I said. 'Someone's waiting for us. Where are you?'

'Just crossing the road.'

I saw him jog across Oxford Street between two red double-decker busses. I said, 'Go back. West, up Oxford Street.'

The idiot ignored me and carried on walking. The he stood at the end of Argyll Street. 'What do you mean, west?' Evan Evans saw him and got out his phone.

I yelled, 'Just move Rory!' Belatedly, Tremaine headed west. Evans scurried after him. I said, 'You're being followed. Shortish, red headed, male. Don't look round! Buy a takeaway somewhere and then go back to your office.'

'But what about the...'

'Rory!

'Oh, yeah. But, look, I've already eaten. Can I just get some fruit?'

I groaned. 'Whatever. Just don't let on you know you're being followed. I'll contact you at work.'

'Make it quick, we're getting close to a deadline for the...'

'All right! Get your fruit. Speak to you later.' I ended the call before he let the cat out of the bag, and MI5 got a fix on me.

Being Rory Tremaine, he made it complicated. He walked to a deli and took his time choosing something. Evan Evans loved it. He tailed as if he was halfway through chapter three of the Distance Learning Guide for Secret Service Operatives. Personally, I would have failed him because he never checked once to see if he was being followed.

Tremaine eventually emerged onto Portland Place, crossed the road, and headed straight for New Broadcasting House. Evan Evans stuck to him like the proverbial to a blanket but I stayed on the opposite pavement. Evans got back on his phone when Rory went through the entrance doors. Then Evans leant against the iron railings of All Souls church, Langham Place to wait. Outside the front of the BBC, there was a group of silent protesters, waving placards and banners.  I managed to get between them and Evans and then I strode to the main entrance.

I told the receptionist I had an appointment with Rory Tremaine.

'Who?'

'A news reporter?'

'Oh.' I was glad he wasn't quite as famous as he - and Chloe - made out.  'What time is your appointment?'

'He said he'd see me as soon as I got here.'

'Wait over there and I'll arrange an escort.'

The receptionist was a long time phoning.  Any moment I expected Evan Evans to come in through the big glass doors, but he must have been told to stay where he was.  Eventually, Rory sashayed into reception, pushing back his immaculate hair.  He signed me in, and gave me an Official Visitor pass on a ribbon that went round my neck.  'Can't be too careful these days, James.  Follow me.'  The reinforced glass security doors buzzed open and he led the way to an interview room.  Inside it was windowless, soundproofed, and fitted with a prominent microphone and a video camera.

'This isn't on the record, Rory.'

'We need a record as evidence in case...'

'No.'

'We could get an actor to replace your...'

'No.'

He huffed like a thwarted teenager and then pointed to the seat beneath the camera.  'Well?'

I gave him a photocopy of Salnikov's insurance. He read it twice and then said, 'Is this genuine?'

'Yes.'

'You have the original?'

'Yes.'

'Wow! Where did it come from?'

I said, 'I can't divulge my source. Though you may say it was Russian.'

Rory said, 'Oh golly.' A grin spread across his face but, when it reached its broadest extent, it imploded. 'Hang on, though, this bottom bit. That's not our Prime Minister?'

'Probably.'

'Probably!' He stood and swore. 'I can't run with "probably"! The lawyers would never... is this all of it?'

'Isn't it enough?'

'We can't accuse Knighton of being... well... a KGB agent with just this.'

'It doesn't say he was an agent.'

He stabbed a finger at the paper, 'It says Oliver Franklin Knighton received money from the USSR for "services rendered". Even if he wasn't in the KGB, that's pretty damn explosive stuff. You sure you can't get something from your contact to back it up?'

'That's all there is. Contact is now unobtainable.'

He grabbed the wall phone and keyed a number.

I said, 'Be careful what you say.'

He frowned at me for daring to tell him his business and then he spoke into the handset. 'Hal, it's me, Rory... yes I do... yes it is. But we have a problem. No... no... the story's bigger than I thought. Can't say right now...no, too soon for tonight. Sorry... maybe tomorrow... right... right. OK. Ciao.' He put the phone down and slumped back in his chair. 'The producer wants me to go with him to see the lawyers.' He sighed. 'I know what they'll say.'

'What?'

'Shelve it.'

'Why?'

'If it is the PM, he will deny everything and slap a D notice on us. If it isn't the PM, he'll accuse the BBC of manufacturing a slur on political grounds, and get the DG to sack me.'

'So you're backing off.'

'I'm telling you the reality of the situation. The only way forward is to get supporting evidence. From an independent source.'

'How do you suggest I do that?' I was feeling pretty deflated and not a little peeved at his negativity.

'Isn't that your area of expertise? Private Investigator and so forth?'

At least someone thought I was worth my job title. Even if it was Rory Tremaine.

'Thing is,' he went on, 'this accusation - if it's true, and I'm not yet accepting it is - could bring down the government.' He leapt up as the enormity of the story hit him. 'My god! Knighton could have been working for the KGB for years. Organized top jobs for his cronies... Whiles... Rhodes... maybe they're all Russian agents!'

'Rhodes wasn't involved.'

'How do you know?'

'It was confirmed by my sources.'

Tremaine scrabbled for a pad and pen. 'So you have more than one! How do I contact them?'

'Nice try, Rory, but it's still no deal.'

'Oh come on!'

I could see by his face that he was desperate not to lose the biggest story of his career. 'Look,' he said, 'I've been given a twenty-four-hour delay. Isn't that time for you to get something extra? Eh? And you have to promise me you won't go to anyone else with this. Another... you know...'

'News channel?'

'Absolutely.' He licked his lips. 'After all this might be a clever forgery. You'll need to produce the original eventually.'

I nodded. He was right, Salnikov could have cooked it up. Rory held out his hand for me to shake. It was flabby and wet. The acting was over.

'No hard feelings?' he said. 'I mean, about Chloe?' He switched on the puppy-eyed look that I assumed Chloe went gooey over.

I shook my head, pretending it was all in the past. That I had conceded the best man had won the hand of the fair maiden. I said. 'Look after her.'

'Uh?' He frowned as he struggled to understand what I meant. Then he twigged, and nodded so vigorously, his hair flopped. 'Oh absolutely. Look after Chloe. Absolutely.' If they did get together, I gave the relationship three months max. It gave me no satisfaction knowing that he had no strong feelings for her. Chloe deserved better than either of us. I left, handed over my pass, and went out onto the street. Evan Evans had gone. I crossed the road at the lights and walked towards the Oxford Circus station. As I was heading for the steps, two men in dark clothes maneuvered in front of me. Behind, Brown said, 'A word, if you please, Mr. Nelson.'

## 23

Brown came round to face me and then ordered one of his helpers to search me. The man held up my wallet, my digital recorder, and my phone. Brown nodded and the man gave me back my stuff. Brown said, 'Follow me.'

I didn't have much choice. As he walked away from the station entrance, his men hustled me after him. A few people glance at us but they were thinking more about their journey home. Brown opened the rear door of a black limo that was parked in the bus lane and the heavies pushed me in. One clambered in either side of me. Brown oozed in next to the driver and said, 'Drive.' The car shot into the traffic so fast a bus screeched to a stop and blared its horn.

Brown turned to look at me. 'You have been very busy, Nelson. Applying for a job at the BBC were you? I presume, in the drama department. These days they have become rather choosy, so don't put your hopes up high.' He laughed.

When I didn't react, he switched on his serious face. 'What did you tell Tremaine in there?'

I said, 'The bastard stole my girlfriend. I was going to floor him.'

'Really?'

'Really.'

'Did you?'

'No.'

'Why not?'

'I decided that fighting over a girl was juvenile. Besides, Chloe would only have hated me more.' It sounded vaguely plausible.

Brown twisted back to face the windscreen. In the traffic mayhem in Regent Street, the car inched forward. Brown said, 'You're not very successful. With women, I mean.'

I didn't reply.

He swiveled round again, 'Melissa... Tatyana... Miss Chloe Hall.'

Determined not to be baited, I just shrugged, 'Maybe you're right.'

He looked surprised. Then he said, 'By the way, your Mr. Fraser... the one whose cause you championed? Because he couldn't get an army pension?'

'Well?'

'He was taken home yesterday. With a backdated, enhanced, active-service pension. Satisfied?'

I shrugged again.

Brown went on, 'Part of the deal he signed was a non-disclosure clause. If he talks to anyone about his military service - anyone - his army pension will disappear. With me so far?'

'Perfectly.'

'So I suggest you terminate your... "investigation". Return to Tonbridge and ask your cousin very nicely if you may keep a corner of his office.'

'He doesn't want me there.'

'You will discover he has changed his mind. He has been awarded a little-known government incentive to mentor new-start businesses. Yours, in other words. However, I shall not wish you well, Mr. Nelson. Frankly, I hope you burn in hell.' He turned away to watch the crowds on the pavement. As we were crawling round Piccadilly Circus and heading for Shaftesbury Avenue, I said, 'It's more than Fraser.'

Brown turned back to hiss, 'What did you say?'

'You know it's not about Fraser now.'

Brown colored and thrust his face towards me over the back of the seat. 'Listen carefully, Nelson. I know what you want to do. But the next session of parliament will tighten up on Private Investigators. You cause us any trouble - any - and you kiss goodbye to the new license. Understand? Go bury yourself in Kent. Find missing persons or whatever Private Investigators do. Forget about all this. And me. Or else.' He muttered something to the driver who switched on a two-tone horn. Cars and taxis in front pulled over for us and we roared through red lights by Leicester Square tube station and then left at Trafalgar Square to pull up outside the Charing Cross Hotel. The heavy on my left got out. The heavy on my right pushed me along the seat towards the open door. Commuters streamed past, heading for the station entrance.

Brown wound down his window and looked up at me. 'Think on, Nelson.' He glanced at his Rolex.

'Your train to Tonbridge leaves platform six in ten minutes. As an encouragement from the executive, you will find your bank account has been credited with... what shall we call it?... recompense for your wrongful dismissal? We will blame Salnikov now he is out of the way. My advice is to make the money last. Clients won't rush to consult you.' The heavies got back in the car, and then the limo sped away.

I considered dropping everything. Really, I did. I'd be a good boy, claim my reward and wait for the day they would let me become a bona fide, licensed gumshoe. Then, with a clean conscience, I could winkle out benefit cheats and obtain evidence of adultery until the cows came home. Trouble was, that prospect didn't fill me with excitement. As I entered Charing Cross station, I picked up a London Evening Standard. The headline said, "Rhodes Withdraws". Underneath, a smaller banner said, "Blames ill-health. Whiles to become the next PM." That decided me. I had to finish the job.

I bought a single train ticket to Tonbridge from the machine, and boarded the 18.10 train to Ramsgate on platform 6. As the carriages rattled across the Thames, I decided I would pay Fraser a visit. I didn't want to jeopardize his pension, but I thought he might be more co-forthcoming about Whiles now he had won. He might even be able to provide Tremaine's corroborating evidence. So I got off at the next station - Waterloo East. I got a shock when I marched along the walkway to Waterloo Mainline station. Adam Khan was waiting for me. He grinned, 'Going somewhere?'

I had to grudgingly admire Brown's intuition or whatever it was. Maybe he was better at his job than I gave him credit. I said, 'Hello Adam. I fancied something to eat before I went back to Tonbridge.

Look, I bought a ticket.' I waved my orange single to Tonbridge in his face. 'Why don't you join me? There's a decent place on the Waterloo upper concourse and apparently I've been given a sweetener so I can pay for us both.'

He shook his head, 'No way. Brown is more uptight than ever.'

'But we can walk and talk?' Adam fell alongside reluctantly and we headed towards the main terminus. I showed him the headline in the Standard. He shrugged. I said, 'Was Rhodes pushed?'

Adam said, 'Look, I know nothing about the details. OK? I'm not into politics. I just do my job. Mr. Brown says...' He stopped talking, but carried on walking.

I prompted, 'Mr. Brown says what?'

'That we should concentrate on the task before us, not bother with the "why" behind it.'

I sighed, 'That's because he always follows orders, Adam. Has done all his life. Is that what you want? Never questioning anything? Blindly following orders even though they go against your conscience?'

Adam remained silent until we reached the entrance to the restaurant. Below, Waterloo concourse was bedlam. The speakers blared delays: signaling problems at Wimbledon; a trackside fire at Clapham; a landslip at New Malden. 'Sure you won't come in, Adam?'

'I've learnt my lesson. He told me he's going to have me watched, so I'll stand out here, report to control, and follow you when you come out.'

I pretended to look at the menu in the window, though I already knew what I was going to order: Penne Arrabiata.

Adam said in a quiet voice, 'Brown is taking this very seriously.'

'Meaning?'

'He's acting on instructions from above. High above.'

'The PM?'

'I don't know. But he doesn't always follow blindly. He refused his last order. Caused an almighty stink. Everyone up and down the command chain jumped on him and told him not to rock the boat. But he stuck by his decision.'

'What did they want him to do?'

Adam didn't answer and walked away, to lean his back against the balustrade. From there he had a good view of the restaurant door.

Inside, it was feeding time at the zoo. I joined the ten deep queue for a seat and, as I shuffled towards the floor manager's desk, I read more in the newspaper about Rhodes. I learnt nothing new about him, or his decision, apart from the hint that he had a long-term health problem. He was now in a private clinic in Wakefield "close to where he lives". A spokesperson said that Rhodes was there for a complete rest. I had assumed his stress came from overwork. For all I knew he was an alcoholic, trying to hide from uncomfortable memories. The other possibility, of course, was that Whiles had told him to disappear – or else.

Eventually I was assigned a seat. The server apologized that there would be a twenty-minute wait for food but I told him I wasn't in a rush. I sipped a weak Red Label Peroni beer and ploughed through the rest of the Standard. A paragraph halfway down page seventeen nearly made me choke.

**"Soviet Defector Returns to Russia.**
At an impromptu press conference at Heathrow airport this afternoon Sergei Salnikov (68) said he had decided to leave Britain. He said he needed 'to put things straight before he died'. Salnikov defected to the UK in December 1980 towards the end of the Cold War. At the time, the government acknowledged the valuable contribution he had made to Perestroika. Salnikov refused to comment on his destination or what had prompted him to leave. He later boarded an Air France plane to Paris. Until recently he had been head of a government agency that was tasked with monitoring..."

Blah, blah - all the rest was archive stuff. The reporter puffed the piece out by suggesting the government might moving to normalize relations (i.e. trade) between Britain and Russia as a result of trade uncertainty with the European Union and competition from the Chinese. No mention of the family and no photo of Sergey. I wondered why he had made a deliberate scene. He could easily have slipped away and no one would have noticed. Unless he thought the publicity would give him some protection. I was pretty sure his wife wouldn't follow him. That meant he must have said goodbye to his kids. Life can be very cruel.

I phoned Quinn Shelby. I hadn't expected him to be around, but he answered immediately. He said, 'Can't speak. Ring you back.' I had nearly finished my pasta before he did.

'What now?' He sounded angry.

'I need all you have on the MI6 London Control called Black.'

'I told you before, there isn't...'

'He was also known as Constantin and...' I stopped because I realized GCHQ might be listening. But what the hell, the shit had to hit the fan sometime. 'He is now called Oliver James Knighton.'

'The Oliver Knighton? Who is currently...?'

I interrupted, 'Probably.'

'You're kidding me.'

'No.'

'Ring you back.'


I was settling the bill when Quinn phoned. He said, 'Constantin informed Langley in February 1981 he had landed Salnikov. Constantin arranged for Captain Whiles to reel him in via Finland. Soon after that, Whiles left the army and bought a riverside mansion in Henley-on-Thames. Go figure.'

'Anything specifically on Knighton?'

'Oliver James Knighton sent a note to Langley informing them that he was setting up an independent unit in London called the Strategic Intelligence Unit - with Salnikov in charge. Knighton left MI6 soon after. All rather cozy, but nothing incriminating. Look, I have to go.'

I thanked him and looked out the window. Adam was still there. At the deli counter, I bought a takeaway tarte au citron and an espresso, and walked them over to Agent Khan. He didn't refuse them. As he tucked in I said, 'No offence, Adam, but I have to disappear for a while.'

'Not possible,' he said, spraying pastry.

I said, 'Didn't you see that Jason Bourne film they set in Waterloo?'

'I did, and it was a total load of bollocks. They could never have coordinated such surveillance in time. And anyway...' he slugged back the espresso, 'how did Bourne know everything about the place when there was no suggestion he'd been here before?'

'Because,' I said, walking away, 'it was a movie. Story is more important than truth.' I ran down the escalator two steps at a time leaving Adam contacting his Control. Though Waterloo is a barn of a place and usually as busy as hell, actually there are very few exits. One tube station, one walkway to the Thames, the main entrance, one to the taxis, the walkway from Waterloo East, and the exit into Waterloo Road. Brown could have people at any or all of them. If Adam said he was being watched, they may already have someone in the Network Rail security control, and were currently screaming for CCTV angles on me. One of my ex-colleagues in MI5 used to say, "Never make things too complicated. Keep it simple." So I nipped out the taxi exit but instead of going right to join the queue, I opened the back of a white and orange Evening Standard transit and jumped in as it was pulling away.

'Oi,' yelled the driver, 'you can't ride in there!'

'Let me out at the bottom of the slope and this tenner's yours.' I waved the note in his vision.

'It ain't dodgy is it?'

'No, it came from an honest lady.' I poked the note through the wire grill and the driver took it. Then he said, 'Gis us another, and I'll drop you at my next stop: Queen Elizabeth Hall.'

'Perfect,' I said. I handed over another ten pounds, and tried to make myself comfortable amongst the parceled-up newspapers.

At Southbank I ran up the steps to the walkway that flanks the east side of Hungerford Railway Bridge. My plan was to get to the Embankment tube station on the other side of the river. I was half way across the bridge, when I heard a faint shout. It wasn't from behind.

'Over here!'

I looked through the wrought iron lattice of the bridge and saw, on the far side of the rail tracks, Adam on the other pedestrian bridge. He was running like an Olympian. I shouted, 'You're improving.'

'Don't patronize me. You won't get away.'

A blue South Eastern Railway train rattled between us, heading for the Charing Cross terminus. When the train had passed, I saw Adam on his radio. I looked behind me and saw two men sprinting from the direction of the Royal Festival Hall. Adam wouldn't get to me in time but the two runners might. A busker, playing steel drums, was ahead of me. I got out another tenner and said to him, 'Do us a favor.'

'Yes man?'

'See those guys running this way?'

He looked where I pointed and nodded.

'Is this enough for you to delay them?'

'You in trouble with the law? Only I'm not...'

'They aren't police.'

'OK.' He grabbed the note and I ran on. When I reached the top of the steps that led down to the Embankment, I saw another running man coming towards me from the passage at the side of Charing Cross station. I leapt down the steps four at a time and, at the bottom, I saw a black cab pull up and let someone out. But before I could get there, a woman beat me to it.

Over the roar from the Embankment traffic, I heard a faint commotion on the pedestrian bridge where the steel drum man had been playing. I glanced back at the steps I had come down, expecting to see the man from Charing Cross coming to grab me. Instead, he was on the bridge, fighting his way through the crowd towards the steel drummer. I decided I didn't have enough time to backtrack to the tube station because Adam would soon reach it from the Villiers Street entrance. The only sensible option was to cross the Embankment.

I risked death by dodging four lanes of fast-moving traffic and almost got to the other side when a courier cyclist ran into me and we both tumbled. He swore at me as he leapt back on his bike and sped off. My knee hurt, and was bleeding through my trousers but I limped down the ramp to the Embankment Pier, knowing that I would soon be hidden from the tube station. When I got to the floating landing stage, the cover over the ticket booth also shielded me from prying eyes on the bridge. 'Yes?' said the bored girl as she chewed gum and examined her nails.

'When's the next boat?'

'Which direction?'

'Any direction.'

She looked at me as if I was crazy, but she glanced sideways at a screen. 'One going eastwards in two minutes.'

'I'll have a single.'

'Return'd be cheaper than two singles. Cheaper still with an Oyster card. You got an Oyster card?'

'No. A single will be fine.'

She printed the ticket and I handed over most of my remaining cash. Then I hobbled down the gently swaying ramp to a waiting room packed with visitors, keyed up for their river trip into the heart of what the departure screen called "Cultural London". I pushed my way through the bodies until I could see Hungerford Bridge. The steel band man had resumed his playing. The three men who had been running were leaning over the rail, scanning the Embankment. The City Cruiser catamaran arrived and nudged the landing stage as it berthed.

A tannoy gave a dull, repetitive announcement, "Eastwards calling Bankside, London Bridge, Tower, Canary Wharf, and Greenwich." Gangplanks were lowered fore and aft. I went with the flow forrard and boarded. Inside the boat, it was cool and quiet after the roar of the traffic. The blue leather seats looked inviting but I walked to the stern as the public address went through its safety announcements.

I stood just inside the doors that led to the rear deck. There I had a decent view without being seen. The three men were now running down the steps towards the Embankment tube station. The engine of the clipper growled and I felt the catamaran leap away from the jetty. As we nosed into mid river, I saw Adam Khan standing on the rear steps of the tube station. The next time I saw him, he was running down the gangplank to the cruiser ticket office. The boy was getting good. I rang Rory. 'Give me the Prime Minister's appointments for today.'

'I need that evidence, Nelson.'

'You'll get it if you do as I ask.'

'I can't hold off the editor much longer. If I don't...'

'I said you'll get it! Now find out where the PM is. I need to speak to him.'

Tremaine yelled, 'You can't just walk in and...'

'Phone me back in five minutes or kiss goodbye to your big story.'

He went.

If Adam asked the ticket girl nicely, he would know I was on the boat. So I got off at the first stop before his control could organize a welcome committee. The Globe wasn't far enough away for my liking, but at least it was on the other side of the Thames, and there were plenty of back streets to get lost in. I was striding down Emerson Street when Rory rang. 'He's launching his autobiography at the British Museum in half an hour. Then he's back to Downing Street.'

I looked at my watch. I could just about walk to the Museum in time.

'One more thing,' said Tremaine.

'What? Make it quick.'

'On the wire there's a report of an old soldier being killed in Chertsey.'

I stopped walking. 'Go on.'

'Could it be your man? Originally from Albania and had served honorably in the British Army.'

'How did he die?'

'Hit by a train. No one knows why he was on the tracks, so they suspect suicide.'

It wasn't suicide. Had Brown refused the order to terminate Fraser? They had obviously found someone else to do the work. The bouncer or chisel, probably. I said, 'I'll get back to you.' Now I was even more determined to nail the gang.

When I ran into the open space in front of the British Museum, I saw the Oliver Knighton Roadshow to the right of the entrance. Knighton and his team were on top of the steps. The audience, at the bottom.  The plebs were equally divided between fans and protesters.  The latter were having most fun.  They were singing, heckling, blaring hooters, and blowing whistles.  The police were rather half-heartedly singling people out, and manhandling them away.  Knighton's voice boomed from speakers worthy of a rock concert.  He was droning on about Jobs for All, Protecting Hard Working Families, Freedom for LGBTs, More Development Aid for Africa, and Education for All.  The Prime Minister's groupies didn't seem to be enjoying the liberal tone of the speech.  Especially the bit about championing "Rights for the Common Man".  I wrote a quick note, gave it to a copper, and asked him if he would pass it to the PM's team.

He sniffed.  'And why would I do that?'

I said, 'I'm working for the BBC and I need to talk to Knighton's people urgently.'

'Tell me what it is.'

'No.'

He held up the note and was about to tear it in two.

I said, 'It's a matter of national importance.  Do you want to be blamed for not letting the message through?'

He hesitated, then took my note through the cordon of uniformed officers and bent to shout in the ear of a woman at the top of the museum steps wielding a tablet.  The copper pointed at me.  The woman spoke.  The copper beckoned me and I tried to walk forward but the police cordon wouldn't let me pass.  Tablet woman came down the steps to me.  'What is it?' she screeched over the PM's oratory.

'I need to speak with Knighton.'

'Impossible.'

'Then can you tell him I have information about Zinder.'

'Cinder?'

I spelt it out.

'What's that? It isn't in the book.' She held up a shiny new hardback with a photo of a statesman-like Knighton on the front in black and white.

I said, 'He'll know what you mean.'

'There are proper channels, you know.'

I said, 'Are you with the publisher or on the Prime Minister's staff?'

'The Event organizer.'

'Well, please would you pass the message on to one of the PM's staff? It's urgent.'

She huffed, but she went. I watched her shout to a pale young man hovering close to Knighton. I was jostled by ladies dressed in sensible coats and floral print dresses. They'd probably come up from Knighton's safe seat to support their local celebrity. Each waved Knighton's book: *I Made it Happen*.

I asked one of them if I could look through her copy. I skimmed the early contents: Baby boomer... Cambridge... recruited by Secret Intelligence Service... served country... joined leading defense manufacturer (i.e. arms producer). The book went into detail about how Knighton had entered politics and had clawed his way up. There was only a brief postscript about his directorship of Luegan Defense Industries. There was also scant information about Knighton's SIS days, and certainly nothing about Niger. I handed the book back.

'Isn't it simply wonderful?' she said, her eyes alive with excitement.

I nodded. No need to ruin her day out. Knighton finished his speech. The pale aide went along the top of the steps to whisper in his master's ear.

Knighton shook his head. The aide didn't bother to tell me the answer. People began to shout questions - about what famous people he'd met; what it was like to have lunch in the White House; and so on and so predictable. Knighton lapped it up. In a lull, I shouted, 'Were you in control of a covert operation in Africa in the eighties?' There was a momentary hush as people tried to work out what I had said and then they waited for Knighton's reply. Which never came. The protesters lost interest and got back to yelling their pet chants. Knighton's aides wrapped up the event and hustled him away into the main entrance of the British Museum. People began to disperse. The protesters went into group hugs and shoved props in rucksacks and handbags. Fans formed an orderly queue at the publisher's tent to buy one of the stacked hardbacks, "Signed copies at no extra charge!" I was just going to find where Knighton's car was parked when the events lady tapped me on the shoulder. 'Follow me,' she said.

She led me into the museum, and then to a storeroom behind the shop. I switched on my digital recorder before I opened the door. Knighton was in the store, plus a couple of wooden-faced minders. He said, 'Who are you working for?'

'Myself.'

'What was your question again?'

'Were you London Control for a SIS operation codenamed Novercal in 1980?'

He frowned, looked at each of his minders in turn, and then said, 'Never heard of it.'

'Oh come on, I have evidence.'

'What, exactly?'

I wasn't going to tell him "exactly". 'You don't deny you worked as a London Control in MI6 during the eighties?'

'It's in my book that I worked for Security. I didn't detail my work because of the Official Secrets Act. Where did you get your false information from?'

I said, 'You instructed Phillips to recruit mercenaries for Novercal.'

'I... look, who are you? What's your game?'

'My name is James Nelson.'

Knighton barked a relieved laugh. 'Oh now I understand. Well, Mr. Nelson, you won't get any satisfaction from accusing me. I know for a fact that all the documents were destroyed long ago. Deemed "Not in the interest of the nation". Costs money to hold onto archives, don't you know. Now, if you will kindly excuse me, I have some more important appointments to keep.' He started to leave.

I went close to him and whispered, 'I have evidence.'

'Where from?'

'Russia.'

Knighton froze and then told his minders to get out. They protested, until he yelled at them to go. When the door shut, he turned back to me. 'What evidence?' He was worried now and looked suddenly older. 'Come on Nelson! What evidence?'

'Brezhnev's authorization to pay you and Whiles for "services rendered".'

Knighton staggered and clutched at his chest. I thought he was having a heart attack. I didn't want that on my conscience, so I opened the door and told the minders their boss needed medical help.

One came in, and the other radioed for assistance. Knighton yelled, 'I don't want any help. Get out!'

They exited, reluctantly. Knighton's face was white and he was leaning on a stack of boxes. He said, 'What else do you know?'

'You organized Salnikov's defection, using code name Constantin.'

'He was desperate to come. Get to your point.'

'When you were operating as "Black", you sanctioned the massacre of African nationals who were staging a coup in Niger. You also authorized execution of the mercenaries Phillips had hired, to keep the operation quiet.'

'Don't believe everything Salnikov tells you. I assume that's where all this has come from.'

'I didn't get that from him.'

'Then who? Eh? Come on! There are no records.'

'Unfortunately, Langley disobeyed your orders.'

'What?' He screwed his eyes up, frowned, and shook his head. 'They said... it had... all gone.'

'They lied.'

'Bastards.' Knighton was quiet for a while, and then said, 'It was the Cold War, Nelson, dirty things happened. You're too young to appreciate that.'

'But you organized the Niger operation, didn't you Knighton?

He sighed. 'The superpowers were ready to blow each other up and the planet too.'

'But why order the massacre of innocent people. To me, that's a war crime.'

'Innocent? Amadou was intending to renege on his agreement with the Soviets. He was going to kill the Russian soldiers and blame it on the west. Had we stood by and let it happen, the Soviets would have gone ballistic. Literally.'

'So you contacted the KGB?'

'We thought it… expedient.'

'And you ordered the killing of the rebels.'

'Just them. After we ensured the Soviet troops were well away. Couldn't risk an international incident.'

'Is that why Brezhnev rewarded you?'

He shrugged.

'It wasn't a deal so that your company could eventually sell arms to Russia?'

'Don't be stupid.'

'But your company, Luegan Defense Industries does manufacture and export arms.'

'That is matter of public record.'

'Do you sell to Russia now?'

'I refuse to be bombarded with these ridiculous questions. Really, Nelson, you have gone too far.'

'Who was your contact in the KGB? Salnikov?'

Knighton appeared not to hear so I asked the question again.

'All right! Yes he was. He'd worked with us for a while. He'd wanted to defect earlier but I persuaded him to stay where he was. Too useful. Amadou put out a contract on Whiles because he had scuppered the coup. So I did a deal with Salnikov. If he got Whiles to safety, I'd arrange Salnikov's passage to the UK and provide him with a decent job.'

'How did he get Whiles out of Niger?'

'The smugglers took him over the border. Then he dressed in Red Army uniform. He stayed with the Soviet troops but slipped away when they were not looking. Then Whiles came back via Tripoli, as one of the press corps.'

'You had ordered Brown to liquidate the mercenaries?'

'He got squeamish. Damned if I know why I still tolerate him being around.'

'What part did Rhodes play?'

'I'm afraid Monty has always held that principles are more important than expediency.'

Somewhere a toilet flushed and water cascaded through the pipes at the back of the storeroom. Knighton said, 'So, Nelson, what now? Are you intending to blackmail me? Or do you just want your old job back? I hope you don't think you can make any of this public, because I'll just slap on a D notice. No editor will print it.'

'What I want, Mr. Knighton, is for you to resign.' The Prime Minister laughed. I went on, 'I also want you to cancel the contest for your successor on the grounds that Whiles is unfit to continue as an MP - you can work out why. Give the job to Rhodes.'

'He's in a clinic.'

'Where you told him to go?'

'Don't be ridiculous, Nelson.'

'If you don't do as I ask, I'll give the story to the BBC. They have a slot reserved in the six o'clock news.'

'And I will tell the Director General of the BBC that anything you say is fake news and will order him to scrap the story.'

'I shall also copy what I have to every Parliamentary Committee that has any power; to the Speaker; the Leader of the Opposition; and to your party headquarters. If that isn't enough, I'll copy it to the Press Association and Reuters.'

'You won't get anywhere. Reason? I have influence. You do not.'

'I know all about your background, Knighton.' He frowned. Closed his eyes. I thought I had him then. I was wrong.

'Look, Nelson, perhaps we got off to a bad start. Your manner of approach rather... threw me. Though I forgive you and even admire your zeal. But you are relatively young. You cannot appreciate how, in the Cold War, we had to work hard just to maintain the status quo. To stop evil forces in the world getting their own way. I am prepared to admit to you - but to no one else - that sometimes our methods back then may have been a little... unconventional. But we were at war. Anyway, it's ancient history. We have to fight a new threat now. A threat that demands our full arsenal of weapons. And it does not, frankly, need some lone crusaders messing things up.'

'Me, you mean?'

'Precisely. Now, I must get back to my Prime Ministerly duties. My aides will be fretting about slippages to my timetable.' He had recovered some of his swagger and made a move to the door, convinced he had smoothed his way out of the situation.

I said quietly, 'I know you ordered Fraser to be killed.'

He stopped. 'Ridiculous.'

'I know you have made Brown run a renegade unit to prevent Fraser's memories of Zinder coming to light.'

'Fiction.'

'I know you have a hold over Brown and Rhodes.'

'I am leaving, Nelson. I suggest you see a psychiatrist. You are delusional. I am the Prime Minister.'

He had his hand on the door handle. I said, 'I'm willing to do a deal with you.'

'You are in no position to offer anything, Nelson.' But he didn't turn the handle and waited to hear what I was going to say.'

'I will hold off contacting the news agencies for three days.'

'In return for what, Nelson?'

'In return for you resigning during those three days. You will also persuade Whiles to pull out of the leadership contest to 'concentrate on his business interests' or whatever is the current get-out phrase. And then you will confirm Rhodes as the next Prime Minister.'

'Is that all?'

'No. I want my ex-colleague Claire Hall reinstated in her nursing job, and I want you to approve Adam Khan's immediate offer of full-contract service.'

'You bastard.'

'Do these things, and none of the past gets raked up.'

'I don't trust you.'

'Oh dear... well, if that's the case...' I got out my phone and keyed Rory's number. I put it on the speaker so that the ring tone filled the storeroom. Knighton frowned, 'Who are you ringing?'

The phone the other end was answered with a 'Yes?'. I said, 'Is that Rory Tremaine, of BBC News?' He confirmed he was. I said, 'I have the Prime Minister here.'

Rory erupted. 'You idiot! I can't interview him like this! We need the lawyers on the line and...'

Knighton laughed.

'Rory, listen. Knighton has confirmed he organized the Niger operation using his code name Black. He colluded with the Soviets - via a double agent in the KGB - and the Politburo rewarded him for keeping them out of the picture. I have already given you a copy of the Kremlin's authorization to release money to Knighton. Under his code name Constantin, he organized Salnikov's defection and set up the SIU so that Salnikov had a cushy job, but it probably meant Knighton still had a hold on him. I wouldn't be surprised if his company, Luegan Defence Industries, currently sells arms to Russia – if not directly, then through an intermediary. You might look into that.

I have no idea whether Mr. Knighton still has links with the FSB, but it's a possibility. Possibly Knighton used his influence to get Whiles the deputy Foreign Secretary job so they could work together to build up their personal fortunes. However I suspect that Whiles is blackmailing Knighton about the past. Perhaps it was Whiles that persuaded Knighton to order Rhodes to a clinic, to make sure he became the next premier. I don't have evidence on any of that, but you might find someone who will talk. Now, I think Mr. Knighton is ready to make a statement to you about his future outside of politics.'

'I told you I can't....'

I handed the phone to Knighton but he knocked it away. As it skittered across the concrete floor Knighton shouted, 'No comment. You hear, BBC? No comment.' Then he leapt at me and the force of the attack slammed me against the door which made my head ban so hard against the door I saw stars. Then I became aware I couldn't breathe. Because Knighton had his hands round my neck and was pushing his thumbs against my Adams Apple to close off my windpipe. I kneed him in the groin and punched him but he hung on.

'Stupid, stupid, idiot,' he hissed.

Using my heel, I pounded the door and tried to push my fingers into Knighton's eye sockets. But I didn't have enough strength and I was beginning to black out. Then the door burst inwards and knocked us both onto the floor. I whooped in air and tried to get up but Knighton grabbed me from behind and tried to strangle me again.

'Sir! Mr Knighton, sir!'

I felt him freeze, still with his hands round my neck. I jabbed back with my elbows, twisted my body, punched him in the stomach and then moved out of his reach. The special branch men were standing in the room looking at Knighton then at each other. I couldn't speak because I was still sucking in air and my brain was too fuzzy to let me stand without holding on to something.

'Sir?' One of the special branch men came in to grip Knighton's arm.

'Get your filthy hands off me!'

'Your car is waiting, sir.' Then he hauled him out.

The other special branch man came over to me. 'You going to be all right, mate?'

I gasped, 'I think so.'

'Shall I call a first aider?'

'No. Thanks.'

'What was all that about anyway?'

'I gave him some uncomfortable news from the past.'

The man nodded vaguely. 'He can be a bit... well, you know... hostile... when he's cornered.' Then he turned, followed his colleague, and shut the door.

'Hello? Are you still there?' Rory's plaintive voice came from the mobile phone somewhere on the floor of the storeroom.

When I was able to stand, I retrieved the phone. 'Did you get all that Rory?'

'You idiot! I can't use any of that! You heard what he said, "No comment." You can't go around fighting Prime Ministers.'

'He tried to kill me. I was defending myself.'

'Grow up, Nelson.'

I sighed, 'OK. Listen, Rory, I know we don't get on, but try to put that to one side. Before I rang you, I put a few suggestions to him. If you nip over to party headquarters...'

'You killed my piece, you... you dickhead.'

'The story isn't dead. If you go over to party...'

'You promised me evidence! I put my neck on the line for this. I pleaded with the editor...'

'Listen, Rory. You need to go over to party headquarters and...'

'Shut up Nelson! Shut up! You've ruined me! She was right. You're nothing but an interfering... lame-brained... LOSER.' He screamed the last description of me and then cut the call. I wondered whether to ring him back and tell him to get the exclusive scoop on the Prime Minister's shock announcement of his resignation. But I didn't. He'd had his chance. I dictated the time and date into my recorder and then switched it off. My slim bit of insurance.

Then I remembered what he'd said: "she was right". I sat in the storeroom a long time thinking about that.

24

In the time I had been away the new owners of the Rose and Crown Hotel had done an upgrade. The cozy bar had gone, as had the fire and the cricketing memorabilia. The friendly Hungarian barman who had dreamed of setting up a café in Budapest was no longer wiping glasses. So I defected to the Humphrey Bean, further down the High Street. It was a large, anonymous place that had previously been the postal sorting office. There was cheap coffee that was passable, guest real ales, decent food, and had a big screen TV running silent but with subtitles. For two days, there had been nothing about Knighton or the affair at Zinder. I began to worry that I was, after all, a loser. Then, on the third morning, soon after I'd left my cousin's office, the Humphrey Bean TV came up with a red "Breaking News" banner. The ticker tape at the foot of the screen read:

"PRIME MINISTER RESIGNS OVER ILL HEALTH. DEPUTY FOREIGN SECRETARY WHILES ALSO RESIGNS TO CONCENTRATE ON BUSINESS INTERESTS. RHODES APPOINTED PM. OPPOSITION CALLS FOR VOTE OF NO CONFIDENCE."

I celebrated with a Full English Breakfast and to hell with the cholesterol. I had just mopped the plate clean, when my cousin rushed into the pub. Normally, nothing short of a fire – or another freebie "conference" in the sun - would have dislodged him from his financial advising. 'Jamie,' he said, 'you have to come back now.'

'Why?'

'There's someone in the office who wants to give you a job.'

'Does he look like a bouncer?'

'No. Nice chap. Says it's really important he speaks to you.'

'Describe him.'

'Youngish, slim, Asian. His name's, uh, now what was it? Adam. That's it. Adam Khan. Says he knows you.'

I groaned. 'Go back and tell him thanks, but no thanks. Tell him...' But it was too late. Adam Khan had entered the pub and was walking towards me with a Cheshire Cat grin plastered across his face.

'Hi Jamie,' he said, 'heard the news?'

I pointed at the screen, now showing a flurry of activity outside No10 Downing Street as Knighton emerged clutching a sheet of paper.

He nodded. 'You stirred things up right and proper.'

I said, 'Adam, I hope you won't take this personally, but I don't want any more work from MI5.'

410

He laughed. 'Things have moved on.' He picked up the menu. 'Do they do a vegetarian breakfast here?'

'Yes but Adam, I mean it when I say…'

'I'm in a totally new section now. And, goodness knows why, but they want you to be part of it. The salary is good. Some travel involved. Hotels paid for. Expenses… What is there not to like?'

My cousin coughed discretely. We both looked at him. 'You don't have any cases at the moment, Jamie, and this would get you out of the office.'

I said, 'Both of you, watch my lips: No.'

Adam sat and picked up the menu. 'At least let me order breakfast and then I'll tell you what it involves.'

**THE END**

*I hope you enjoyed this novel. Please leave a review on Amazon books. If you want to get in touch, go to* jamienelsonbooks@gmail.com *Thanks, and happy reading!*

*Sample chapter of the next Jaimie Nelson case follows....*

*Excerpt from the next Jamie Nelson case.*

## THE MISSING DIRECTOR

## TONY DALBY

### 1

The new landline rang on my mini-desk that was squeezed into a corner of my cousin's office. 'Nelson's Private Investigators, how may I help you?'

'Nelson? Is that you?'

I recognized the voice of my nemesis, Brown. Brown of the Secret Service. Brown who had a vast chip on his shoulder. Brown, who hated my guts. I said, forcing myself to be polite, 'Yes, it's me.'

'Against my better judgment, I need you for a job.'

He was still playing his role as the supercilious Civil Servant. I said, 'I may not want it.'

'You haven't got any work on, and your working relationship with your cousin is under strain.'

That's the trouble when you tangle with spies. They're always trying to pretend they are one step ahead of you. I should know; I was one once. 'I thought you hated working with me.'

He sighed, or sucked in his breath, I couldn't exactly tell. He chose not to comment. Instead he said frostily, 'As I understood it, you verbally agreed to work freelance for The Service. Do you want the job or not?'

He meant working freelance for their new Section of Lost Causes. Not their official name, but it fitted. It was a temporary bureau set up to deal with the mountain of mildly interesting cases that fell between the remits of MI5, MI6, the police, and the military. After the Niger case, Brown was persona non grata and had been given the ultimatum: leave or head up the new unit. I heard from a reliable source that he fought like hell not to. Anyway, this reluctant Brown was waiting for my answer. Either that, or he had ceased living and breathing – which fitted with my theory that he had a zombie somewhere in his ancestry. But Brown was right that sharing my cousin's tiny office was beginning to irritate both of us. So I said, 'What is it?' in as bland a way as I could.

'Can't talk on the phone. We will have to meet.' He made the meeting bit sound like a punishment. Which I suppose it was. For both of us. 'Do you know Somerset House in London?'

'Vaguely.'

'Be on the terrace overlooking the Thames at 3pm sharp this afternoon. Any later, and I'll give the job to someone more capable.'

The Southeastern Railway Company were having a

good day, so I was on an outside seat amongst the Kings College students at 2.30pm. I'd bought a black Americano and a pastry at the kiosk and was contemplating life. I hadn't been to Somerset House for years – since then it had turned itself into a sort of arty hub. Perhaps a little too arty for my taste, but the terrace was a calm oasis amidst the hubbub of London. The plane trees beyond the balustrade rustled their late spring greenery. The Thames was visible through their branches and I watched the tourist boats drifting back and forth.

'You are early,' said Brown as he approached me. He seemed even more annoyed by this, than having to meet me. 'I told you three, precisely.'

I looked at my watch. 'I make it five to three,' I said, not resisting a chance to wind him up. 'So, technically, you too are early.'

He harrumphed in a deliciously old-school Civil Servant-ish way. 'Look, Nelson, it wasn't my idea that you are part of this. But we have to work together and that's that. So please would you make an effort not to be as annoying as you usually are.'

'Whose idea was it that I be "part of this"?'

Brown waved his hand to say that it was unimportant. It might be to him but I was curious. However, I decided to leave it for another time. I would do their job, bank their money, and make the assignment spin out as long as I could. I had no commitments and, rather more important, no current income. 'Well,' he said, 'do you want the job or not?'

'You haven't told me what it is yet.'

He went to the next table and brought back a chair to sit on, despite protests from the students that it was someone's. 'It is a Missing Person case.'

'Don't the police and Salvation Army deal with those?'

'It isn't in the UK.'

'Oh?'

'Switzerland.'

I had never been there before and, if I played my cards right, I could use Brown's budget to see some of the country. 'All right,' I said.

Brown scowled as if he'd hoped I would refuse. There was probably a clause somewhere in the contract I hadn't signed that said if I turned down a job I'd be taken off the register. Brown pulled a brown envelope from his attaché case and laid it on the table. 'Inside there is a flight ticket to Zurich, a week's retainer in Sterling, plus a float in Swiss Francs for immediate expenses. You have been booked into a medium grade hotel in Zurich for a week. It can be extended if necessary.' He fished out an A4 sheet from the envelope and thrust it and a pen towards me. 'You need to sign here... and here... and here.' I did as I was told. He grabbed the pen from me as if he thought I would steal it. 'And this time, Nelson, no funny business. No riding off on your own crusade. Understand?'

I nodded, though only to move the meeting on. I said, 'You haven't told me anything about this missing person.'

'You will be given all the information you need once you are in Zurich.'

'Tell me the headlines.'

He turned his chair away from me to look towards Westminster. Big Ben tolled a lazy three. 'It's a scientist who had been working loosely with the United Nations. We had opened discussions about... an arrangement that would be beneficial to us both.'

'But?'

'It is difficult if there is no one to discuss things with.'

416

'Who is the "we"?'

'I beg your pardon?'

'You said "we had opened discussions". Who is "we"?'

'None of your concern.'

Firewalls. I didn't waste any more of my breath trying to find out more because I knew Brown was a master of obfuscation. So I tried a different tack. 'This scientist has gone missing in Switzerland?'

Brown nodded. 'The scientist was due to give a talk at the Zurich Film Festival before a documentary screening. However, both have been cancelled. And the scientist has vanished.' Brown looked at his watch. I wondered whether it was to check that Big Ben was right but it proved to be a sign that our interview was terminated. He stood. 'Your flight leaves tomorrow from Heathrow Terminal 4 at 09.25. I suggest you do not miss it because you need to meet our local agent at 3pm local time. The details are in the envelope.' He walked away, straight backed, head in the air. He looked for all the world like John Cleese's man from the ministry of silly walks. Minus the bowler hat.


So at 3pm local time I was in Zurich, standing near the fountain in the Lindenhof Gardens as I had been instructed, looking down on the Limmat River that runs through the center of Zurich. In truth, it wasn't much of a garden. Just a high flat plateau, mostly graveled and punctuated by trees that may or may not have been Lindens. On the plus side the area looked down at the Old Town on the other side of the river. I had always imagined Zurich to be a grey, anonymous city of modern office buildings, peopled by bland bankers. I was wrong. Even on the short tram journey from my hotel near the main railway station I saw that it was a vibrant town with many different buildings styles and sophisticated people walking the streets.

Anyway, I was early, so I sat on the stone seat next to the fountain and soaked up the atmosphere. The sun was shining and the air was cooler than in London, but wonderfully refreshing after the stuffiness of the plane and the train ride from the airport. Several clocks in the city chimed and then struck three. I heard footsteps heading towards me across the gravel. 'Good afternoon, Mr. Nelson. I hope you had a pleasant flight?'

A striking Italian girl came into view. I had seen her from a distance once before. When MI5 had tried to trap me outside the Tate Modern. 'Hello,' I said, wondering if I should have completed some secret code with "In spring the birds fly north" or something equally idiotic. But she didn't wait for anything and sat next to me on the bench and gazed ahead, over the low wall in front of us and at the roofs of the old town spreading higgledy-piggledy up the hill. She said, 'It is a delightful day.' I agreed that it was, and waited. Eventually she rooted in her brown Louie Vuitton bag and drew out a white envelope but held onto it. She said, 'My name is Valma. Valma Lazzerini. May I call you Jamie?'

'Of course.' We shook hands. It was a token shake. Her neatly-nailed hand was as limp and cold as a filleted hake. I would say she was mid-twenties, had long wavy black hair, and a longish face. Her upper teeth were perhaps a little prominent, but she had the most amazingly blue eyes I had seen in anyone. Overall, she looked exciting. Though I told myself she was well out of my league. Anyway, I needed to keep things professional, or Brown would haul me off the case before I had seen anything of Switzerland.

Valma said, 'The outlook from here is pleasant, do you not think?'

'Very pleasant.'

'Also, it is a good meeting place - when it is not raining or snowing.'

I waited, wondering if I should have asked her something. Eventually she stood and said, 'Now, we will walk.'

She led me to the low wall so we could look over as we walked out of eavesdropping range. The ground beyond fell away precipitously. Down on the river a blue and white police launch pushed its way against the current, followed by another open-backed craft crammed with what looked like divers in black wetsuits and breathing apparatus. Both boats slewed to a stop beneath a road bridge on the left. Then two divers slipped backwards into the river. The diving boat altered position and two more divers went overboard. I said, 'What's going on down there?'

'They wish to find a body. It is most inconvenient.'

'For the police or the body?'

She frowned at me as if she did not allow jokes. Perhaps she had graduated from the Brown Academy for Serious Secret Agents. She said, 'You were supposed to meet the person they are searching for.'

'The scientist?'

'No, the film director who has made a documentary about the missing scientist.'

'You think the film director is dead?'

'He is missing. We cannot presume he is dead. Although the authorities...' She nodded at the drama on the river to say that the authorities were convinced he was dead. She sighed. 'It is most inconvenient.'

If the director wasn't dead, it sounded to me that both he and the scientist wanted to stay well out of the reach of the British government. On the other hand, someone might want to prevent them speaking to the Brits and would kill to ensure it. Down on the bridge nearest the drama, a few people looked over at the activity in the river. The divers were still under water and the police launch was zipping about importantly. On the far bank of the river, a banner hung from a modern building announcing the Zurich Film Festival.

Valma said, 'I am required to remind you that you are still covered by the British Official Secrets Act.'

'OK.'

'Your relationship with us is as a private contractor with no official capacity and no connection with any department of the British government.'

I guessed where this was going.

'You will not be able to call on any official assistance if you are arrested or questioned by the Swiss authorities, or officials of any other nation. No one in the Foreign and Commonwealth Office of Great Britain and Northern Ireland will acknowledge your existence and will deny all links with you and your investigation. You are not to approach anyone in any of our Consular Offices. Are you clear about all this?'

'Perfectly. Now perhaps you could give me what information you have in that envelope.'

She pulled a face that said I was spoiling her script. I waited and walked beside her. We got to the end of the gardens and turned. Then she pulled out a sheet of paper but held onto it. 'The film director is... or was... named Kaspar Deiss. Born in Basel in 1997. He studied at the local university and then at the Contemporary Film School in Freiburg. That is in Germany.'

I was beginning to get tired of this drip feed. 'May I see his photo?'

She reluctantly handed over the paper. It showed the face of a miserable fifty-year old. Hair greying, worn long. Square face, deeply lined. He looked as if he hated the photographer – or maybe he was just acting for the camera. Being the big Auteur. I said, 'He doesn't look much like a film director.'

'Do you know what directors are supposed to look like?'

This wasn't going at all well. Maybe I needed to be a good boy and just accept the information she was willing to give and shut up. Beneath the photo were some biographical details and a list of all the films he had directed and his appearances at film festivals. I'd never heard of any of the movies. Not that it means a lot because, frankly, I'm not that discerning. I go to the movies to be entertained, not hit over the head by arty claptrap. 'Mister Deiss produced a forty minute documentary about the scientist and her work.'

'Her work? The missing scientist?'

'Yes. Do you not think women can be scientists?'

I groaned inside. I had definitely started badly with Miss Lazzarini. She extracted another sheet from the envelope. Why do secret agents always have to be so damn secretive?

She said, 'This is the scientist. Her name is April Wu.'

She handed over a sheet of facts below a photo of a black-haired smiling lady of about forty-five. Very un-scientist looking. I scanned the facts: born Shanghai; studied Nano-materials and Technology at Beijing Jiaotong University in Xizhiemen; emigrated to England with her parents; did a doctorate at Cambridge in applied micro engineering; joined a technology firm in Cambridge specializing in software design; went to Silicon Valley to work on developing occult data applications; and finally moved to Bern to work at Aar Industrial AG. I looked up. Valma was staring at me. I smiled and chose my next words carefully. 'Interesting lady.'

Valma nodded as if, for the first time, I had said something sensible. 'Despite the setback of the disappearances, Mr. Brown requires you to find her in the shortest time possible.' She handed over the final sheet from her envelope. It was a press release in English about the lecture Deiss and Doctor Wu had been scheduled to give to the Zurich film festival. 'I suggest your first move would be to go to the festival headquarters to find out if they have any information on Deiss or Wu.'

'You haven't then?' It seemed the most obvious thing to have done as soon as the lecture had been cancelled.

'We were told not to make any enquiries. That London would be sending someone who is an expert. So, over to you, Mister Expert.' She wrote a number in a little notebook and then tore off the page and handed it to me. 'You may contact me at this number. But please only do so if it is an urgent situation.'

I wondered what she considered urgent, but I didn't want to get into another prickly session with her. 'OK. Are there any other leads?'

'No. When you find her, you must get her to ring my number. Is that understood?'

'Perfectly.' We had reached the far end of the gardens. On the river, the divers were relocating further downstream. We turned and walked back to the fountain. I noticed for the second time that a young woman wheeling a buggy seemed to be keeping pace with us. Further back amongst the tree trunks there were two old men and a dog standing around doing nothing. I hoped it was just my paranoia and not the opposition already.

Valma said, 'It is very important that you get to the scientist before any other... organization does.'

'Anyone in particular?'

She thought about that. Either she didn't know, or didn't think I needed to know because she shook her head. She said, 'Your weekly fee will be paid into your UK bank account. A Swiss bank account has been opened in your name and your incidental expenses float will be forwarded to there. The card and details will be in an envelope held by your hotel receptionist. I suggest you switch you phone off now and only use it in emergency. You must give Mr. Brown a daily report by email and you must submit weekly details of your expenses to London. You should keep all receipts and submit them at the conclusion of the case to Human Resources in London in order for you to receive your Expense Compensation. The relevant contact details are on this envelope. She handed over the envelope she had been using. There were two anonymous email addresses written on the outside. I said, 'Can I take you out to dinner on expenses?'

'You are too frivolous, Mr. Nelson. This is a serious undertaking. I was told they were sending an expert, clearly they were wrong. Good bye.' She started to walk away.

'Does Mr. Brown take you out to dinner?'

She turned and glared at me, then strode away. I noticed that the girl with the buggy had perched nearby on the stone bench. The two old men and the dog were following Valma. Of course it could have been coincidence. There again, probably not.

*End of sample*
*The Missing Director* © *Tony Dalby 2018*

Printed in Great Britain
by Amazon